DANCE WITH WINGS

Amelia Carr

headline
review

First published in 2008 by Headline Review
An imprint of HEADLINE PUBLISHING GROUP

First published in paperback in 2009 by Headline Review
An imprint of HEADLINE PUBLISHING GROUP

5

ISBN 978 0 7553 4718 6 (paperback)

Typeset in Joanna MT by Palimpsest Book Production Limited,
Grangemouth, Stirlingshire

Printed and bound in Great Britain by
Clays Ltd, St Ives plc

Headline's policy is to use papers that are natural, renewable and
recyclable products and made from wood grown in
sustainable forests. The logging and manufacturing processes
are expected to conform to the environmental
regulations of the country of origin.

HEADLINE PUBLISHING GROUP
An Hachette Livre UK Company
338 Euston Road
LONDON NW1 3BH

www.headline.co.uk
www.hachettelivre.co.uk

To the brave men and women of the
Air Transport Auxiliary.

ACKNOWLEDGEMENTS

Where on earth to begin to thank all those who made this book possible?

Firstly, my gratitude goes to Jo Frank, a former editor of mine, who suggested I write a multi-generational saga, read the first chapters, gave me guidance and encouragement, and introduced me to Sheila Crowley at AP Watt, my wonderfully supportive agent. Secondly, to Marion Donaldson at Headline, an inspired – and very tactful – editor.

But DANCE WITH WINGS could not have been written without the help of numerous 'experts'.

Ann Wood Kelly was one of the American pilots who ferried aircraft for the RAF between 1942 and 1945. I found her name on a website, – thank heavens for the internet! – e-mailed her, and within hours received a reply giving me names of contacts in England. Sadly, Ann died in 2006 at the age of eighty-eight, but I would like to think she has been reading my book over my shoulder, and perhaps nudging me in the right direction.

One of the contact names Ann gave me was that of Richard Poad, a former BA captain who now runs the ATA museum in Maidenhead. He gave most generously of his time and expertise, and sent me home from the museum laden with wonderful books and a CD. If I have made any errors they are entirely my fault, not Richard's.

Along the way I have 'borrowed' some actual incidents and woven them into my fiction; I hope the real-life protagonists will forgive me and allow me a little artistic licence with their exploits.

Writing some sections from an American point of view gave me a few language problems; I called on my friend Sharon Haigh, then President of my Rotary Club, for assistance. Sharon hails from Ohio; she read the entire manuscript and corrected any errors in the Americanisation. She even phoned her sister, Nancy Hughes, in the States to check anything she was unsure about – she's lived in England for so long that she was no longer sure whether some expressions were English or American.

My heartfelt thanks also go to the team at Headline, who have worked tirelessly whilst at the same time making me feel special every inch of the way. And I must make special mention of Yvonne Holland, possibly the best copy editor I have ever had the pleasure of working with. Her thorough but sympathetic approach made my part in that very necessary process so easy.

My husband, Terry, and my daughters, Terri and Suzanne, have as always been more than supportive and my grandchildren, Tabitha, Barnaby, Daniel and Amelia Rose, have brought sunshine to my world even if at times they have distracted me from the task in hand!

And last but not least, a special thank you to my youngest granddaughter for allowing me to borrow her name!

Part One

The Present

SARAH

How much do you really know about your own family – about anyone, really? No matter how close we are to another person, there are always the secrets locked away that we know nothing about – the dreams and the fears, the passions and the resentments. The memories that are taken out and pored over only when we are quite alone, the dark thoughts that haunt us in the dead of night, the fears of inadequacies we never admit to out loud, the moments of despair for the future. We see only what others allow us to see, judge their actions and attitudes against our own experiences and values. And hug to ourselves secrets of our own.

Heaven knows, I've got enough of them – and I'm not noted for being the world's most discreet. When I was small I was known for a chatterbox. 'Little Big Mouth' my father used to call me – much to my chagrin – after a character in a comic I used to get from the newsagent's every Saturday morning, along with a chocolate bar or a packet of sweets. 'You are not to repeat this outside these four walls,' he would say, expressly to me, after my sister, Belinda, and I had been party to some discussion over Sunday lunch

3

between him and my mother. As if I would! Mostly it was boring stuff like could they afford to have a makeover in the kitchen, or who'd brought what in to the charity shop where my mother worked as a volunteer. I'd roll my eyes at Belinda, who was, of course, prim and perfect as ever, and give my father a hurt look. The financing of a kitchen was the last thing I'd be likely to chatter to my friends about, and I couldn't imagine they'd be interested in the state of the bag of clothes donated by Councillor Mrs Waite to the hospice shop either – jumpers with coffee stains and inadequately washed underwear, according to my mother. But there it was – I had a reputation for talking too much and not being able to keep secrets.

Perhaps that's why I became so good at it later . . .

My mother always was. So good that I never even knew there were secrets to be kept. People to be protected. A veneer of respectability to be maintained. Blame to be laid in private. In that dark world between sunset and dawn, when you lie sleepless and everything assumes a magnitude that daylight cuts down to size. Skeletons rattling in cupboards . . .

There are fewer of them these days, I suppose. There's no stigma attached to divorce or a child born out of wedlock. 'The wrong side of the blanket', they used to call it. How quaint is that? And yet still we have a certain light we want others to see us in. Still we care about what the truth would do to others – what sort of a world would it be if we didn't? Unpalatable truths revealed selfishly or thoughtlessly can destroy lives when uttered by grown-up Little Big Mouths.

But the flip side can be just as dangerous. Secrets kept with the best of intentions can cause trouble in the most insidious of ways that reverberate down the years. A family history can stretch out slimy tentacles into the next generation – and the next. There are things that if they were brought out into the open might lose their power, instead of thriving on the fear of discovery. If my family cupboard had been bare of skeletons some people would inevitably have been hurt. But for others, truth instead of half-truth, knowledge instead of suspicion, would have set them free.

I've always known there were things that were never spoken of. Tensions I didn't understand. Well, I've known since I was old enough to notice, anyway. That my mother rarely went home to Florida, which she'd left for England to marry my father when she was just nineteen. That she didn't often talk about her mother – my grandmother, Nancy – and never about her brother Ritchie. That she was always brittle and bad-tempered when I went for my annual holiday in the Sunshine State, first in the care of the airline cabin staff, and later alone. I used to wonder sometimes, try to piece things together from photographs and dates and snippets of information. But I never even came close. It's only now, in the last year, that I've unearthed the truth.

And discovered that I never really knew my family at all.

Florida, Summer 2006
If there is one thing I love, one thing that can ease me out of the straitjacket of stress that I've woven for myself, thread by thread, and call my life, it is flying. You could say, I suppose, that it's in my blood, and so it is.

My great-grandparents – Grandma Nancy's mother and father – were barnstormers who performed with the air circuses that were all the rage in the States in their day – her father a stunt pilot and her mother a wing-walker. According to Nancy, she was born in a barn somewhere in the Midwest, and she was roped in as an assistant to their act when she was only four years old – hidden behind a stack of bottles and charged with knocking them down at the precise moment her father flew over and pretended to shoot at them. She'd learned to fly even before she could drive a car; she'd gone to work for Grandpa Joe, who'd been a crop-duster and was trying to expand his business, married him, and together they'd built up Varna Aviation. Oh, and just for good measure, they'd both flown in the war – Grandpa Joe with the USAAF, Grandma Nancy with the Air Transport Auxiliary in England, ferrying planes from factories to airfields or from one operational station to another.

So, yes, it's in my blood, and there's nowhere I feel more at home than in the air. Especially in Florida. I learned to fly here in the summer that I was seventeen – a much longer holiday than usual – and by the time I went home I'd not only passed all the flight tests and written exams, I'd got in enough hours' solo to earn my Private Pilot's Licence.

My mother was not best pleased. 'They knew I didn't want you messing about in planes,' she said, very tight-lipped and disapproving. And: 'Don't think you're going to be able to keep it up over here. You've got college to think about, and in any case, it costs too darned much.'

She was right there; there was no way I could find ninety pounds an hour to hire a Cessna or a PA28, and no way she was going to help me out.

'That's how your uncle John got killed,' she'd said, as if I didn't already know it. 'I sure as heck don't want the same thing happening to you.'

John, her elder brother. Another of the flying Costellos. I didn't point out to her that the rest of them had survived into ripe old age. I knew better than to argue with my mother. But I did wonder why the bug that had bitten the rest of us had passed her by. As far as I know she's never flown, and never wanted to. There is a family story that when Grandpa Joe tried to get her into the left-hand seat for a lesson, she screamed and shouted and flounced away and walked the whole three miles home to show she meant what she said. She didn't want to learn to fly, and nothing and nobody was going to make her.

I can well believe it. My mother is the most stubborn woman I've ever met. But I can't understand how she could not want to fly. I shall never forget the excitement of walking round the plane with the wing level with my chest and the single propeller inches from my nose. Of clambering into the pilot's seat and listening to the Air Traffic Control clearing us for departure. Of the way the whole aircraft throbbed and vibrated as the engine power built, the surge forward as Grandpa Joe released the brake and we hurtled along the airstrip, gaining speed, the feeling of weightlessness when the wheels left the ground and the grass arced beneath us and the trees were a living, swaying mosaic pavement.

And most especially of the moment, ten days or so later, when I'd done enough halfway decent take-offs and landings – circuits and bumps, we called them – for Grandpa Joe to ask in that slow Florida drawl I remember so well: 'OK – do you wanna go round on your own then?' And I nodded, wordless for once, and he warned the ATC and got out of the plane, leaving me on my own. My first solo. My heart was pounding, pumping the blood through my veins as though it were a mini-tsunami, but at the same time I felt strangely calm and determined, and my hands were steady on the yoke. I knew I had to get this absolutely right. Once I took off nobody could help me. I'd have to fly a circuit and land, all by myself.

I did it. Not a perfect landing, but not bad. And my love affair with the skies entered a new dimension. I wasn't a virgin any more. I'd gone through the initiation ceremony.

Grandpa Joe was more relieved than he'd ever let on to have me back on terra firma. There was a sheen of sweat sparkling across his forehead and up into the broad bays where his hair receded, and when he yanked the door open and leaned in to ruffle my hair the palms of his hands were sticky-moist too.

'Well done, Sarah.' Matter-of-fact tone, rough edge beneath it. 'You're a real Costello now.'

I didn't point out that I wasn't a Costello at all, that my name was Sarah Lintern, and I was English, not American. In that moment I was alive and glowing with so much pride and exhilaration that I felt it was going to burst out of the top of my head, like Vesuvius erupting. And Grandpa Joe's praise was the icing on the cake.

It was always the same; I adored him, admired him, worshipped him almost. A word of praise from him was all I needed to spur me on.

'You fly like an angel, Sarah.'

I can hear him now as I bank over the expanse of emerald and sapphire that is the Everglades and set course to head back towards Varna.

'You fly like an angel, Sarah.'

There's a shadow to my right, just out of my line of vision, and it has the rangy shape of Grandpa Joe. I can almost feel him there in the co-pilot's seat, big hands relaxed on his knees, eyes sharp and watchful; I can smell the sweet pungent briar of his pipe which he taps out and tucks into his pocket before we take off. It's five years now since he died, as quietly and considerately as he lived – just fell asleep in his chair and didn't wake up –

but I still hear his voice when I'm flying. He's still there, offering me nuggets of his wisdom, chastising me sometimes as well as praising. Sitting on my shoulder, whispering into my ear. 'Always respect the skies, Sarah. If you mock them, girl, they'll have the last laugh.'

He was there when an unexpected thunderstorm caught up with me, sending torrents of rain cascading over the windscreen like a cataract, and the turbulence pitched and tossed me about like a broken butterfly. And the time when something overheated. I'd felt the radiance on my feet and smelled the burning stronger even than Grandpa Joe's tobacco, and I'd been forced to radio in an emergency, hurry back to the airfield to be chased down the runway by a fire engine. And that was in England, for goodness' sake! Grandpa Joe isn't fussy. Where I fly, he comes with me.

Just now, he's quiet, enjoying, just as I am, the freedom that comes with floating in a bubble of silence and calm over the mangroves, lush from the summer rain. There's the constant throb of the engine, of course, the occasional rattle of the doors and windows against their frames, the soft buffeting of the wind flowing over the wings. But they're comfortable sounds, integral almost to the peace, like the soft snuffles and snores of a person in a deep and restful sleep. Like me, I suspect, he's got his eyes peeled, keeping a sharp look out for anything else that might choose to share our air space; like me he doesn't want to return to reality. But we have to, Grandpa Joe. We can't stay skulking up here for ever.

I ease back on the power and lower the nose of the Cessna. There's an arrow-straight ribbon of silver road shimmering in the noonday heat, and ahead of me the first of the Ten Thousand Islands that are scattered like a handful of beads from a broken necklace in the sparkling blue of the Gulf of Mexico. I head for the bridge, a startlingly bright white arc that links Varna to the mainland, and drop down to a couple of thousand feet, scanning the still waters that cut a hoop-shaped harbour into the island in the hope of catching sight of a manatee. No luck today. The manatees are hiding.

There's an ache around my heart suddenly. Grandpa Joe used to point them out to me when I was little, dark humps that looked like slippery boulders. But this time the ache isn't for what's gone for ever. It's for what might never be.

I want to show the manatees to a child of my own. I want to hear the intake of breath that's a gasp of excitement, see a small face alight with wonder, eyes wide, mouth an open 'O'. Even up here, in a Cessna belonging to Grandma Nancy, I can't escape the longing that's growing day by day, week by week, month by month, into an obsession.

I'm thirty-six years old. If I don't have a child soon, it will be too late. Through my own stupid fault I've let the fertile years slip away. I've wasted them on a man I've finally accepted will never be mine, never be a father to my children, and the ones who might have been have all married other people, buried themselves beneath mortgages and piles of nappies and cosy domesticity. Ten years ago, my world hummed with spare men, even if they seemed no more ready to settle down than I was. Now there's just Fergus, and I'm not at all sure I want to spend the rest of my life with him, though he's forever trying to persuade me that I do. He's a good friend, but that's really all he is – and he wasn't even my friend first, but my sister's. Fiancé, actually. Even if I was in love with Fergus, which I know I'm not, I've had enough of Belinda's cast-offs to last me a lifetime.

But what choice do I have? Option One: marry Fergus, who I

know without doubt would be good to me – a generous, reliable husband, a terrific father. Option Two: I go for it as a single mother, but not with Fergus. It wouldn't be fair to him to use him like that. I'd have to find someone I'm less involved with if I'm planning that he should be an absentee father, or maybe even go for 'donor unknown'. Neither option really appeals to me. Each time I consider either of them seriously a little bit of me shrinks away, the way you shrink from picking up a slug that's crawled under the back door and feasted on the cat's food.

But both are preferable to the alternative. Which is to accept that I am not, ever, going to be a mother. To know what it's like to give birth, to have a small firm body nestling at my breast, to experience the rush of unconditional love, to feel small fingers curling round my own, to bury my face against soft hair that smells of springtime, and know that this little life, independent now, was once a part of me and will go on being a part of me for ever. I actually want to have sleepless nights and sticky bits of food thrown on the floor and piles of socks and T-shirts and underpants to wash. And I want to sing a little one to sleep, and make muddy footprints on the windowsill to make them believe Father Christmas came in that way, and be woken at dawn to have a stocking emptied all over my bed. And see the expression of wonder when for the first time my child sees a soap bubble, a newly hatched chick, a manatee . . .

There's no time for brooding now, though. I can see Varna Airfield, a scatter of white-painted buildings and workshops spaced along the edge of a wide expanse of green. I reduce height to just a thousand feet, reach for the handset, contact the ATC and ask permission to land. I recognise Gus Hadfield's voice. He's been doing air traffic control at Varna off and on for as long as I can remember.

With his customary disregard for the correct jargon, Gus greets me.

'That you, Sarah? Thought so. OK, honey, come on in.'

There's another Cessna in the blue and white livery of Varna Aviation parked on the grass apron in front of the office buildings. As I taxi towards it, Ritchie, my mother's brother, appears round the nose. A girl is following him like an eager puppy, a pupil about to take off for a lesson, I guess – maybe her first, or even a trial flight, since Ritchie is doing the preflight walk-round with her, checking the airworthiness of the Cessna. She is perhaps eighteen or nineteen. So young! Plenty of child-bearing years ahead of her.

Ritchie, clad in lightweight black trousers and a white shirt with captain's epaulettes, raises a hand to me in casual greeting. Most pilots out here choose to dress informally in jeans or shorts and T-shirt, but Grandma Nancy is a stickler for protocol. A pilot should look like a pilot and not a beach bum, she says. It gives people confidence. Though he's supposedly running the business these days he's long since realised that arguing with his mother is a waste of time and energy. He draws the line at wearing a tie, though.

I wave back, but Ritchie is no longer looking. He's giving the propeller a twirl and turning to say something to the girl, who is gazing at him with rapt attention and obvious admiration. I smile and shake my head. Funny how the girl pupils always flock to Ritchie, though he's old enough to be their father – grandfather, almost! But it has to be said he cuts quite a dashing figure, youthful still, for all that he is past his fiftieth birthday. He has the rakish air of a man with three failed marriages behind him, now determinedly single, and taking full advantage of the glamorous veneer that comes with his job. I very much hope that Ritchie does not take advantage of the girls he teaches to fly, but given his track record I'm not holding my breath.

Wife number three – Mary-Lyn – was a former pupil, though she never got her licence and, as far as I know, had never even gone solo. She'd really only been interested in flying when Ritchie was in the seat alongside her, telling her, no doubt, how well she was doing whilst handling all the tricky manoeuvres himself. The lessons petered to a trickle when she got an engagement ring on her finger – a rock that must have cost him a year's salary – and stopped altogether after he'd flown her down to the Little Chapel in Vegas and she'd become the third Mrs Richard Costello.

But at least that particular bit of history is unlikely to repeat itself. However besotted this new pupil might be, however flattered Ritchie is by her admiration, with three lots of alimony to pay, and the business – according to Grandma Nancy, at least – less than flourishing these days, there's no way he is going to be able to afford diamonds and white gold and romantic honeymoons in Mexico.

I park the plane, lock up and head for the stone-built block where Varna Aviation have offices.

There's an air of affluence about the foyer these days: wall-to-wall blue carpet, soft lighting, a drinks machine, a bank of computers. When I was a little girl, the HQ of Varna Aviation was just a tumbledown hut at the edge of the field. But the town decided to invest in spanking new facilities ten years or so back and Varna Aviation benefited from them. From a business point of view it's impressive but, from what Grandma Nancy has said, the high rent payable is contributing to Ritchie's problems in keeping the business afloat.

A young man in mechanic's overalls passes me in the doorway, clutching a sheaf of paperwork. We pass the time of day and I head in across the foyer, towards the mock-pine console where Monica Rivers is working on the computer.

Monica is plump, pretty and well-groomed – big blonde hair styled the way she's been doing it since the eighties, the miraculously unlined face large ladies often have, fingernails painted shocking pink from base to tip. She's an institution at Varna Aviation; I doubt it could function nowadays without her. She started on a part-time basis in the days when Grandpa Joe was still in charge – keeping the books, organising the diary and minding the reception desk. Her husband, an aero-mechanic and maintenance man, had died suddenly, leaving her with three young sons and only the most meagre of pensions, and Grandpa Joe had taken pity on her.

The gain was all his, though. Before long Monica was indispensable, and since her boys grew up and left home Varna Aviation is her life. She's at her desk every morning by nine and often still there at nine at night, seeing in the last pupil from an evening lesson. I have wondered if perhaps she has a soft spot for Ritchie that's kept her loyal all these years. I hope not – Ritchie really is bad news where women are concerned – and I tell myself she has too much good sense for that. But when did good sense ever win over the vagaries of the heart?

When she sees me she pushes the mouse away, clicks the computer into sleep mode and sits back in her comfortable swivel chair.

'You're back then, Sarah. Good flight?'

'Yes, great.'

'Want a coffee?'

'Love one. I'll get it when I've done my paperwork.'

'No, you're OK. I need the exercise.' Monica heaves herself up and heads for the coffee machine and I lean across the desk for the plane log and start filling it in.

Before I've quite finished she's back, setting one steaming paper mug down beside me and carrying the other round to her own side of the desk.

'So how long is it now before you go home?' she asks.

'Just a couple of days.' There's a slight sinking feeling in my stomach as I say it. The three weeks I've been here have flown – they always do. When I first arrive the days spread out ahead of me seem endless, then suddenly they're gone and I'm counting down the number of times I'll eat breakfast and dinner with Grandma Nancy, the number of times I can fly the Cessna out over the Everglades or down to the Keys before it's time to pack my bags.

Long enough, though, three weeks. You can't put your life on hold for ever, however much you might wish you could.

'You should think about moving out here permanently,' Monica says as if she's read my mind about not wanting to go home. 'Come and help Ritchie with the business. Flying has to beat . . . whatever it is you do in that office of yours . . .'

'Accounts. I'm an accountant.'

'Pretty pressured, huh?'

'You could say that.'

'And the weather here sure is a hell of a lot better than it is in England.'

'Believe it or not, I actually like the English seasons. And I can't just throw up a good job, sell my house, and move out here. I doubt the business could run to another salary and I'm not even sure if they'd want me here all the time.'

'Your grandmother would,' Monica says with certainty. 'She thinks

15

the world of you. And it's my opinion she's lonely. I don't think she's ever gotten over losing your grandfather. And your mother living in England too. And . . . her other loss . . .' She trails off, awkward suddenly, as if she has crossed an invisible barrier into forbidden territory and knows it. 'John,' she finishes without further explanation, yanks open a drawer in the desk and pulls out a carton of Krispy Kreme Doughnuts. 'You want one?'

I shake my head. 'No, thanks.'

'Well, I do.' Monica takes a bite, feathering her chin with icing sugar. 'My day would not be complete without a Krispy Kreme Doughnut.'

Easy to see why she's put on so much weight, I think. Aloud, I say: 'She has Ritchie.'

Monica snorts and another cloud of icing sugar fans out and settles like fine snow on the black keys of the computer keyboard. 'When he's home. Which is not often, if you ask me. And when he is . . .'

'I know.' I sigh. 'They don't really see eye to eye.'

'You can say that again!' The last morsel of doughnut disappears into Monica's mouth and she licks her fingers and her pearl-glossed lips. 'Two fine people, and they tear one another apart. Now if you were back here . . .'

I laugh, amused by her persistence. 'I shall not be here. Holidays, yes. To live, no.'

'You never know, you might just meet the man of your dreams. Now he'd persuade you to stay, I'll be bound.'

I laugh again, but it sounds hollow to my ears. Without knowing it, Monica is getting underneath my skin like a prickly thorn, scratching at tender nerves I don't want to admit are there, even to myself. I'm an independent career girl. I don't have dreams about

16

men. Not any more. The ache of yearning I get when I see a couple swinging a small child between them, each holding on to one small sticky hand, has nothing to do with illusions of romance.

Once I saw Mark and his wife, Claire, doing just that. Walking along the street with two-year-old Freddy, counting paving stones, then lifting him, his weight evenly spread between his arms, smiling down at him, laughing as he squealed with delight. Freddy was wearing a bright red jacket and red Wellington boots, and his face was rosy beneath the hood. Six-year-old Molly was holding her father's other hand, looking up to say something to him. They didn't see me, of course. I was just passing traffic. If Mark had looked in my direction he'd have recognised my car, but he didn't look. And to Claire I was a stranger, who, had she known it, knew an awful lot about her.

I knew in that moment that Mark would never leave her and the children, no matter how many times he'd promised me he would, and I knew too that I wouldn't want him to. I couldn't steal my happiness at the expense of those children. I'd never be able to live with myself if I had that on my conscience. I told myself that was it – over. It wasn't, of course; it wasn't that easy. Making up your mind to end an affair and doing it are two different things when you're in love. But it was the beginning of the end.

I don't want to fall in love again. I don't want to lose control over my life and my emotions. At least, my head doesn't want it. I'm not so sure about my heart. If I am serious about remaining uninvolved, why don't I do a deal with Fergus? Have his baby so that we can be the ones swinging a child over the paving stones between us . . . ?

'Monica,' I say, finishing my coffee, 'I do not imagine I am going

17

to be swept off my feet by some gorgeous hunk in the next forty-eight hours. And even if I was, I still have to go back to England.'

Monica eyes me shrewdly. I have the feeling she knows that underneath my flippancy lies hurt. That for all that outwardly I give every indication of being perfectly satisfied with a rewarding career and all the material things my fat salary, unshared, can buy me, there's a raw empty place. That my life isn't nearly as much under control as I like to pretend. She's known me too long.

'It'll happen,' she says, 'when you least expect it.'

I grin at her crookedly. 'I'm not holding my breath.'

'Me neither.'

I look at her, at the smartly turned-out woman who's been a widow for close on twenty years and who fills the empty spaces in her life by running the office at Varna Aviation and rewarding herself with Krispy Kreme Doughnuts, and wonder if she too is secretly waiting for something – or someone. If so, she's been waiting an awfully long time.

Varna is built on a grid of intersecting roads, laid out like the squares on a sheet of graph paper, tree-lined and dotted with shopping malls and pavement cafés. But the houses, rebelling against the uniformity, are all individual in design. Some are imitation Colonial, some sprawling one-storeys, some condos. Almost all have a pool hidden away in a shady back yard.

Grandma Nancy's house is on one of the identical avenues towards the centre of town – white-stuccoed behind a neatly trimmed lawn, spacious and pleasant without being in the least ostentatious. Varna Aviation never made Grandpa Joe the bucks to move into one of the ranch-style properties on the outskirts that hide away behind acres of shrubs and get peeked at by visitors riding the town tour bus, and I don't think they'd have wanted that anyway. I pull my rental car into the driveway and go into the house.

'Grandma – I'm back!'

'In here!' Grandma Nancy's voice from the living room. It's bright and vigorous, so that it's hard to believe its owner is well into her eighties.

Grandma Nancy is pretty amazing altogether for her age. She's still spry, though she struggles a bit with arthritis in her hands and knees. She's still fiercely independent – she insisted on continuing to fly until she was seventy-four years old, and was only prised out of the captain's seat by failing a medical on grounds of impaired hearing. And she looks good – a bone structure like hers more than compensates for the inevitable lines and wrinkles; her hair, snow white and wavy, looks as thick to me as ever it did, though she swears it's falling out by the handful – still enviably trim. But when I arrived two and a half weeks ago I thought she was somehow more frail than she had been last year. Nothing I could put my finger on, exactly, yet unavoidable, and it opened up a hollow some-where inside me. Grandma Nancy was growing old. *Was* old, for goodness' sake, by most people's standards. And I couldn't bear it.

She's sitting at the table now. There's a book, desk-diary size, open in front of her, a photograph wallet and a small square leather box at her elbow. She closes the book, looks up at me and smiles, that lovely smile that makes her eyes sparkle blue as the sea when the sun turns it sapphire at midday and lifts her cheeks up to those amazing cheekbones.

'Did you have a nice flight?'

'Great,' I say. 'You should have come with me.'

She stacks the photograph wallet and the leather box on top of the book, which I can see has a label stuck on to its cover, yellowing

19

now and curling back at one corner where the paste that holds it has dried out.

'Perhaps I will before you go home,' she says.

'You're sure you trust me?'

'I've flown with a lot worse pilots than you.' She meets my eyes directly, with a hint of mischief. 'Would you let me take the controls?'

I pretend to consider. 'I expect so. Just as long as you promise to fly straight and level only – none of your aerobatic stunts.'

'I think I'm a little past them,' Nancy says drily.

'I should hope so too! And you must promise not to tell Ritchie. I don't think he'd approve.'

Another wicked twinkle. 'As if I would! OK, it's a deal.' Then her face goes soft. 'You know I am so glad you take after me, Sarah. Your mother never had the slightest interest in flying. As you know, she avoids it whenever she can. I put it down to a bad fright she had when she was tiny. She was up at the airfield with us when a Cessna crashed on take-off – a young chap trying to show off, if I remember rightly. Climbed out too steep, stalled, and came down like a pancake. Ellen was hysterical. We thought she was too young to understand what had happened, let alone remember it. But no such luck. It put her off for life.'

'She doesn't remember it,' I say. I've heard the story before, and asked her about it. 'I think if she did, it wouldn't have had such a lasting effect on her. She'd be able to rationalise it as an adult, instead of still feeling it inside like a child, if you know what I mean.'

'Maybe.' Nancy isn't one to dabble with psychology. 'Anyway, I'm glad she didn't manage to inflict her fear on you. It's a good feeling that my granddaughter will still be playing in the clouds when I'm pushing up the daisies in the Home From Home Garden of Rest.'

A goose walks over my grave. 'Don't talk like that, Grandma. You'll see all of us out.'

'I sincerely hope not!' Her face becomes serious. 'Sarah, I want to talk to you.'

'Not about your dying.'

Grandma Nancy smiles faintly. 'No. Well, not exactly. But I am getting older, and it makes you think about things you want to do before it's too late. Something I want you to do for me when you go home to England. Someone I want you to try to find for me.' Her fingers, a little puffy from the arthritis, stray to the book and the items stacked on top of it, holding it all together as neatly as the stiffness of her joints allows. 'Let's have a drink.'

'I just had a coffee at the airfield with Monica,' I say.

'I'm not talking about coffee. I'm going to have a sherry. The sun is over the yardarm, as they used to say in England. Why don't you have one too?'

'I'd rather have a glass of wine.'

'Well, you know where it is.'

I pour her a sherry, fetch a bottle of Californian blush wine from the refrigerator in the kitchen where it's chilling, and pour a glassful for myself over a mound of ice cubes. The ice-making compartment is practically overflowing again, creaking and clanking as it deposits fresh supplies in the dispenser.

'We'll have it outside.' Grandma Nancy is in the doorway behind me, a diminutive figure in her straight-cut linen trousers and a printed silk shirt. The blue-covered book is tucked firmly beneath one arm and she's carrying the little box and the wallet of photographs. 'Could you bring my sherry for me? I don't want to drop it. A waste of good sherry – and my best crystal.'

I go to the living room to collect Nancy's sherry and follow her

21

outside. A table and chairs are set in the shade of a large floral umbrella; beyond the decking the obligatory pool shimmers azure blue in the bright sunshine. We sit down.

'So, what is it you want me to do?' I ask, sipping my wine.

For a moment Grandma Nancy is silent, as if she's not quite sure where to begin. Then she says: 'You know I was in England during the war.'

'Flying with the Air Transport Auxiliary. Yes, of course.'

But that is about all I do know. That she was approached by Jacqueline Cochran, one of the most acclaimed women pilots of her day, and asked to join the small select band of American women she was taking to England. That she was there for just over a year, delivering fighter planes for the RAF, and then she came home. The planes she talked about, and what fun she had flying them, but the reminiscences always stopped there. She's never talked about the people she knew or the relationships she must have formed and I have wondered if perhaps she was hugging to herself things that were too painful to share. Grandma Nancy can be an intensely private person. It's the same when it comes to John, her elder son. She adored him, yet she rarely if ever mentions him. She guards his memory within her heart.

Now I wait, curiosity burning bright, but saying nothing for fear of seeing the window close again, the shutters come down.

'We formed some very close friendships in those days,' Grandma Nancy says at last. 'Strange, really, how those people were your whole world and then . . . they're gone. The girls used to have reunions – the last I heard of was in Boston, and they wanted me to attend when the ATA Museum was opened back in the early eighties, but I chose not to go. Too far. Too many memories. Too damned busy! Now, though . . . there is someone I'd like to contact.

There's something I want to return to him – if he's still alive. If not, his family should have it.'

Him. I paddle my finger in the rim of condensation that has pooled on the table top beneath the bottom of my glass. This has taken me by surprise. As far as I was aware Grandma Nancy and Grandpa Joe had been together for ever. Certainly she'd been working for him before the war, and afterwards they'd been married for close on sixty years.

'Who is it, Grandma?'

There's the strangest expression on her face now; her eyes have gone very far away and she's half smiling. But it's a wistful smile.

She pulls the photograph wallet towards her, slides out a print and hands it to me. It's a bit grainy and indistinct, a bit faded. But I can see it is of a young man, tall, good-looking, wearing a leather flying jacket.

'That's him. That's Mac.'

I stare at the photograph and all kinds of questions are bubbling to the surface of my mind like the gassy effervescence of a glass of champagne. But for all my surprise, all my curiosity, it never for one moment occurs to me that I am looking not just at the picture of a young pilot who figured somewhere in Grandma Nancy's past, but the face of a man who shaped and changed all our lives. And whose long shadow is still affecting them today.

RITCHIE

For once in my life I'm feeling optimistic. The girl on the trial lesson – Jodie Polanski is the name on her booking form – has enjoyed herself. I've made sure of that. I let her take control for a while over the Everglades, and I've done enough bits of fancy flying myself to make her squeal the way she might riding one of the roller coasters up in Orlando. As we head back for Varna I take a quick sideways glance at her. She's pink with excitement, pearly little teeth chewing her lip in concentration, hands gripping the yoke for dear life, and I reckon I've done enough to persuade her to take a full course of lessons. Already I'm calculating how much that will mean in tuition fees. Say thirty hours' flying time before she gets her licence – more if I can string it out a bit before sending her solo – plus hire of the plane to make up her hours . . .

'You're a natural,' I say. 'You fly like a bird.'

She giggles. 'It's great! Really something.'

'So – you going to go for it? Couple of lessons a week – you could have your licence before Thanksgiving.'

She sighs heavily. 'I only wish I could! But this lesson was a birthday present from my boyfriend. There's no way I could afford it. I'm still in school.'

I reach up to adjust the trim wheel, let my arm brush lightly against hers.

'Persuade him to pay for you then. Tell him how great it will be for him to have his own private pilot when he's a rich businessman wanting to get from one place to another in a hurry.'

She laughs, shaking her head. 'I doubt he'll buy it. He's as flat broke as I am. This half-hour took all his earnings from working two weeks stacking shelves in the grocery store.'

'Shame.' Though inwardly I'm cursing, I keep my tone light. I sure as heck don't want to appear desperate for the custom and she might yet change her mind, persuade her old man to come up with the tuition fees. But I know I'm spitting in the wind. Setbacks follow me around. Nothing's ever come easy to me. Some folk reckon they were born under a lucky star. All I can say is it must have been a very dark night when I put in my first appearance on this goddamn planet.

As I fly a circuit round Varna Airfield I see there's another little problem waiting for me in the parking lot. I'd know that white Cabriolet anywhere. It belongs to Mary-Lyn, my third and most demanding ex-wife. Well, it's registered to her. I pay for it. What the hell does she want this time? Doesn't she know she's sucked me dry? But she won't have stopped by just to say 'Hi'. Not Mary-Lyn. She wants something from me all right. She always does.

Why the hell did I have to marry her? You'd have thought I'd have been old enough and wise enough to know better. With two failed marriages already behind me you'd think I'd learned my lesson. But no, I'd been as big a fool all over again. Leaped in with both feet, hoping that this time I'd got it right.

I'd hoped that twice before. I guess I could be excused the first time. Diane and I were an item since we were both fourteen. I wanted her so much it hurt, and the only way I could have her – really have her, and make sure no one else did – was to marry her. And maybe, if I'm honest, there was a bit of me that wanted to beat my brother, John, at something. I'd tried everything else – and failed. At least I'd beat him to the altar. It didn't work out the way I expected, though. Oh, yeah, it was great for a bit, and then we grew up and grew apart. We had not a single thing in common any more – not even sex. We were both relieved when we decided to call it a day.

Chrissie, wife number two, stifled me. She was the most possessive woman I have ever known. I couldn't go take a leak without asking her permission. She had this idea that being married meant being joined at the hip. That we had to do everything together, wear matching sweaters and pants, hold hands, finish each other's sentences. She was forever touching me, stroking me, my hand, my knee, my neck, even when we were in company. She opened my mail. She borrowed my cellphone. She accessed my computer. She never left me alone for a single damned second. It drove me insane. I started affairs with other women, hoping that when she found out she'd realise what a rat I was and blast me into the stratosphere, but she just clung on tighter. In the end I moved out with her threats of suicide hanging heavily over me. I was scared to death she would carry them out, but even more afraid of what I'd do to her myself if I stayed. Not so long afterwards she married a real estate agent from New England, who she met while he was on holiday in Florida. They have three children now, or so I hear, and I haven't seen her in more than ten years.

You'd think, then, that I'd have had the sense not to tie myself up with a woman again. But I'm a born sucker. I still have this damn fool notion that if I keep trying, one day I'll get it right. Be a bit more like John was. A bit less like myself. Even so, you'd think I'd have seen Mary-Lyn coming. Glamorous, twenty years younger than me, expensive tastes that run through fast cars to a fast lifestyle. And it wasn't for want of advice from family and friends to steer well clear.

Monica, for one, had tried to warn me.

'I know a gold-digger when I see one,' she told me bluntly. We'd stopped off at Vinny's Bar for a drink after a long day's work and we were sharing confidences along with a bottle of wine. 'She's just after your money.'

That had made me laugh. 'I don't have any money.'

'She doesn't know that,' Monica pointed out. 'She sees the boss of a flying outfit and thinks you must be a wealthy man. And the way you've been showering her with flowers and gifts, she thinks she's hit the jackpot.'

'It's my charm she's taken with, Monica,' I joked. 'You know I'm irresistible – come on, admit it!'

'If you say so.' Monica twisted her drink between her hands, her long fingernails clicking against the glass. The sound scraped on my nerves; maybe I knew she was a bit too close to the truth for comfort. 'I just don't want to see you hurt again, Ritchie.'

'It's OK – I'm a big boy, remember? I can take care of myself.'

'Have fun if you must. But for God's sake don't get married again.'

She sounded just like my mother, and I told her so. She seemed to take that as a compliment.

In spite of all their warnings – or maybe because of them – I did marry Mary-Lyn. And, just as they'd predicted, that marriage went the way of the first two. It's more than a year now since we separated and I moved in with my mother, telling myself she shouldn't be alone in the house at her age, knowing that the real reason was that I couldn't afford to live anywhere else. More than a year, but Mary-Lyn still looks to me to keep her in style. I make her a generous allowance, pay the mortgage on what was our marital home and the hire purchase payments on her car, along with the bills for their running and upkeep. She's ruining me and the business both, and she either doesn't realise it or doesn't give a damn.

I escort Jodie into the office to debrief her and apprise Monica that further bookings are a no-go with a slight shake of my head. The boyfriend is waiting for her, sitting in one of the bank of upholstered seats with an empty coffee mug and a pile of aviation magazines on the table in front of him. They leave, Jodie hanging on his arm and chattering excitedly about her flight, and I go out to the parking lot to see what Mary-Lyn wants from me this time.

She's leaning against the bonnet of the Cabriolet smoking a cigarette. She drops it onto the tarmac and stubs it out with the toe of her sandal as I approach. She's a big girl, tanned nut brown, and dressed in the Florida uniform of shorts and T-shirt. But the sun glints on gold at her throat and wrists and ankle, all jewellery I bought for her in the days when I wanted to impress her.

'Hi,' she greets me. 'Still pulling the bimbos, I see.'

I ignore the barb. 'What are you doing here?'

'Well, I sure as hell didn't come to watch the planes.' Mary-Lyn has perfected the one-line put-down over the years, just as she perfected the flattery that hooked me in the first place.

'So?'

'The air conditioning has died. Can you fix someone to repair it for me?'

Fix someone to repair it – and pay the bill.

'Can't it wait?' I ask, without much hope.

'In this heat? You must be joking! I'm nearly frying. I hardly slept last night.'

I sigh. 'OK, leave it with me.'

'You will call someone right away?'

'Sure.'

'Mind you do. I don't want us to fall out, hon.' She smiles sweetly, and I catch a glimpse of the girl I fell for, who all but disappeared when I had to put a stop to the way she was spending money I didn't have.

We had some good times, Mary-Lyn and me. I half wish we could start over, on a different footing.

She gets in her car, starts it, drives away in a cloud of dust. I get out a cigarette and light it.

Smoking is the last great taboo these days. Very anti-social. You can commit murder and someone will find an excuse for you. But smoke, and you're one of the untouchables. Hell, what do I care? If I want a cigarette on my own airstrip, I'll damned well have one. And I need one right now. Mary-Lyn's wound me up, as usual.

Where the devil am I going to get the money to fix her air conditioning? I can't draw any more on the business – the money just isn't there. If I stretch it any more the creditors will close in and we'll go bust. Hell, we're likely to go bust anyway. And though it's not my fault Varna Aviation just isn't paying for itself any more, I know I'll be the one to take the blame. My mother may not actually say it would never have happened if John were still alive, but she'll be thinking it. I'll see it in her eyes. And I'll snap and snarl

30

like a wounded lion, but inside I'll feel another bit of me shrivel and die. Ritchie the failure – Ritchie who can never get anything right.

Do you know what it's like to live the whole of your life in someone else's tall shadow? I'll tell you – it's purgatory. Especially if that someone is your brother.

When I was a little kid it was natural enough, I suppose. He was four years older than me; I hung around after him and he put up with me. It was natural that I wanted to be like him. To do the things he did, to have the things he had. I envied him his toys: the radio-controlled truck while I had to make do with one that worked by traction; the proper two-wheeled bicycle he raced around on while I trundled behind on my tricycle. I wished I could stay up late like he did on warm summer evenings. Many was the night I crept out of bed – the bottom bunk, of course; John had the top one – and watched enviously from the window while he bounced on the trampoline or climbed the tree. I just wished time would hurry by so that I could do the same and it never occurred to me that he'd be growing too and would always be one step – or several – ahead of me.

As I got older, though, I came to realise that no matter how much I grew I was never going to match up to John. I remember clearly the day it dawned on me. Sports day at grade school. John was good at sport – John was good at everything he tried, dammit. He was running proper races with the big boys and he won every one. He was up on the podium with a medal on a ribbon round his neck and Mom and Dad were bursting with pride. When it was my turn I had to do the sack race. I was so determined I was going to win like John. I remember standing in line with the other boys my age, every muscle tensed, hot with concentration, waiting for the whistle. When Miss Chalmer blew it, I made a dive forward, caught my foot in the sack and pitched over straight onto my face. My hands and knees were stinging and my nose took such a bang it made my eyes water. But I could see the other boys all right, hopping away from me down the pitch, getting further and further away. And the moisture in my eyes wasn't just from my smarting nose any more, but tears of frustration and humiliation, which of course only made it worse. John was a golden boy, a hero. I was a crybaby who couldn't even run a stupid sack race, let alone win it.

I guess that long-ago sports day more or less epitomises the whole of our lives. I never managed to match John's achievements, let alone beat them. He was captain of the school swimming team, passed his driving test first time instead of fouling up as I did and having to have another go, got his pilot's licence with ten fewer hours on his log book. I could go on, but I won't – you get the picture. And as if all that wasn't bad enough, I knew he was Mom's favourite too. Hardly surprising, but it hurt all the same – especially when Ellen, our sister, told me the reason. I dealt with it by being surly and rebellious and I guess that just made things worse. And the stupid thing is I'm doing it still.

You might think with John dead and gone the pressure would be off but in truth it's a thousand times worse. Mom's practically canonised John. If ever he might have made a mistake, got something wrong, he sure as hell won't now. He's even more golden in death than he was in life. He still haunts me.

So, what in damnation am I going to do to stay solvent? There is a solution, a proposition that was put to me a few weeks back but which I've resisted so far. It's illegal as well as immoral, and if I got caught I'd certainly go to gaol for a very long time. But

I'm beginning to think my options are reducing to one. I light another cigarette, lean against the fence, and think about it.

I've never been in any doubt but that Dexter Connelly is a rogue. There's something decidedly dodgy about the dealings that have bought him a mansion with electronically controlled security gates and a couple of bad-tempered Rottweilers in the most exclusive area on the outskirts of Varna, a string of luxurious automobiles and a lifestyle that takes in golf courses, casinos and expensive women who've had boob jobs and Botox while they're still in their twenties. He might purport to be a successful businessman but I've always thought he had a finger in a lot of criminal pies. Now I know.

From time to time Dexter Connelly hires a plane from Varna Aviation to fly him on business trips, or to Las Vegas for a weekend at the gaming tables: the Beech Baron, my pride and joy, not the Cessnas we use for lessons and sightseeing trips. I usually pilot him myself. The last time we were there, Connelly suggested I join him for an evening's gambling instead of languishing in my hotel room watching piped TV. I was sorely tempted, but for once in my life I made the sensible decision. I knew if I stepped inside the casino I wouldn't be able to resist the lure of the roulette wheel for long, and I knew what the consequences would be.

'Thanks, pal, but no,' I told him. 'I don't have the kind of dollars you do, and I can't afford to lose them.'

Connelly eyed me narrowly. He's a big, swarthy man. His muscles bulge under his expensively tailored silk suits, and he wears gold chains under his pristine white hand-sewn shirts.

'Business not so good?'

'Could be better.'

'I'd have thought you were sitting on a little gold mine there.'

'Unfortunately not.'

'Now ain't that a darned shame.'

There was something reflective about the way he said it that made me realise later that the idea had already occurred to him that he might be able to turn Varna Aviation and its financial difficulties to his advantage. At the time, though, nothing more was said, and I sloped off to my hotel room to watch the in-house movies and drink miniature Bourbons from the mini refrigerator. But the following night Connelly again suggested that I should accompany him to the casino.

'I already told you, I can't afford to lose your sort of money,' I said.

'You don't have to, buddy.' He laid a hand on my shoulder, smiled at me crookedly. 'I'll buy your chips.'

I was pretty astounded, I have to admit. 'You can't do that.'

'Why the hell not? Think of it as a gratuity for flying me. If you clean out the joint, you can pay me back. If not, that's the way it goes. I won't miss it, and I could use the company.'

I hesitated, but not for long. The thought of another night with only the television for company was not an enticing one.

I should have been more wary – I know that now. I should have realised that Connelly must have an ulterior motive, that he would never have made the offer out of friendship or the goodness of his heart. And the excuse of wanting the company didn't hold water either. With the sort of money he liked to splash about he was always surrounded by a bevy of hangers-on, men who wanted to be like him and women who enjoyed his attention and free-spending ways. But I'm not the cautious sort.

'OK, you've got a deal,' I agreed.

The pile of chips Connelly bought me was big enough to make me feel almost as wealthy as Connelly himself and attracted the same sort of attention. To begin with I hit a winning streak; then my luck changed. By the time we left the casino, I'd lost the lot.

'Don't worry about it,' Connelly said, totally blasé. 'Easy come, easy go. Don't worry, buddy, there'll be something you can do to repay me sooner or later.'

It was a couple of weeks later when I found out what that 'something' was. Connelly had booked me for a flight to Mexico, and over a drink in a quiet corner of an exclusive bar, he put the proposition to me.

'You want to make a bit extra for your business, buddy? You already run a light-freight service, don't you? Well, there's a nice little sideline I could put your way. Good for both of us. I think we'd work well together.'

I sat up and took notice. The freight contracts had been thin on the ground lately. And then Connelly told me what the 'sideline' entailed. The cargo he was suggesting I should fly in was drugs.

I had to admit it, the logic of the plan was undeniable. It's only a short hop from South America to the Keys and then in to Varna, where there's next to no control over what comes in and goes out. Especially with a well-established company like Varna Aviation. Nobody looks twice at the Cessnas with the blue and white livery. They've been part of the scene for too long, and never a hint of anything remotely suspicious. My part would just be to fly the plane – everything else would be taken care of at both ends by Connelly's associates. And I would be able to make enough money to clear my debts to Connelly with one trip alone. What I did after that was up to me.

But I felt I was in a bit of a cleft stick. On the one hand, the idea of making some easy money was darned tempting, on the other, if I carried the illegal cargo and got caught I could expect the law to come down on me like a ton of bricks. So far I've stalled, but I know Connelly won't be patient for ever. I have to give him a definite answer soon, and he won't take it very kindly if I refuse. He's a dangerous man to cross. At the very least Varna Aviation will almost certainly lose his legitimate business, and there's always the chance of more serious repercussions now that he's let on to me exactly where some of his wealth comes from. This is big, heavy stuff, and I'm not happy with it.

But I'm not sure I have a choice any more. I stare at the Beech Baron and the Cessnas, lined up side by side and sparkling in the sun. It would crucify me if I had to sell them off. I look at the new office building, remembering how proud my father and mother were to move into it, and groan when I think how the rental is crippling me now. And I think of Monica. What the hell would happen to Monica if Varna Aviation went under? How could I tell her she was out of a job?

I grind out my cigarette, push my aviator sun specs up onto my forehead, pull out my mobile and scan to Dexter Connelly's number. Then, before I can have second thoughts, I punch the dial button.

I might live to regret doing this. But I'm as sure as dammit I'll regret it if I do not.

NANCY

O h, Sarah, I can see I've shocked you. You're trying very hard to hide it, but you can't fool me. I love you too much and know you too well. When I look at you it's like looking into a mirror at myself when I was your age. Same dark hair with a mind of its own, though yours is squared off at jaw level, whereas mine was shoulder length, except when the ATA forced me to get it cut. Same too-wide mouth and small, straight nose. Same eyes that sometimes look blue, sometimes green, depending on the light. Same determined set to your jaw.

I look at it and see myself, and it turns my stomach over. Part of it is vanity, I guess. I *want* to see myself. I want to feel that gossamer thread that links the generations; regenerates like a phoenix rising from the ashes. I'm tired now – my bones ache and I've grown stiff and slow – and I need to see something of myself in your youth and vigour. Through you I have hope for the future. When I'm gone something of me will live on in you and your children.

But it's not just selfish vanity, I'm sure. There's an affinity between us and always has been. From the time you were a little girl I've recognised character traits – stubbornness, independence, fortitude – and I understood where you were coming from not just because I empathised but because your actions and reactions were like an extension of myself.

It was always there, that empathy, from the moment I saw you, a small red-faced bundle with a mop of fine hair so dark it was almost black, sleeping in the crib beside your mother's bed. I leaned over, my fingers itching to touch you, my arms aching to hold you and cuddle you, breathe in the sweet scent of baby powder and milk that surrounded you like an aura.

'Don't wake her, Mom,' Ellen warned, her voice a little tired but still managing that strident bossy tone that grates on me. But at that moment you began to whimper and wriggle, then wail, that thin pitiful cry of a new-born that tears at the heartstrings, and Ellen sighed. 'Oh, go on, get her up if you want to. You might as well.'

I held you, all wrapper and diapers, and you looked up at me with wide eyes blue as the ocean. You weren't crying any more and a feeling of love so intense it melted my bones suffused me. I've never been a baby person – I used to joke I'd rather have a puppy any day – nor a particularly maternal one. I felt more awkward with my own children when they were babies than I cared to admit; preferred it when they grew less helpless and demanding, when they began to be little people in their own right. When Belinda, your older sister, was born, I was too worried about Ellen, who'd had a hard time and a haemorrhage and was still paper-white and weak, to take proper delight in the scrap who had nearly cost her her life. But with you, the rapport was instant. I was so full of love and tenderness it was choking me.

I wasn't lucky enough to be there all the time when you were growing up – we were on opposite sides of the Atlantic. But whenever we visited that bond was still there, strong as if we'd never been apart. And I could see the characteristics I recognised as my own developing in you: the way your mouth set in a determined line when you wanted something; the impatience with yourself when you couldn't get something right; the restlessness to be up and doing. Belinda would sit quietly for hours, drawing or reading or doing a puzzle. You wanted to be outside on your roller skates, scooting up and down the lane – with a gang of boys, more often than not – and if the weather was bad your face would be dark as the storm clouds that were keeping you indoors, and your mood tetchy enough to try the patience of a saint.

I understood that perfectly. I was born a gypsy; the confines of four walls bored me rigid too.

Then there was your fierce independence.

Once when I was visiting you went missing. You'd been very quiet when you got home from school, sloped off into the garden. When your mom went to call you for tea you were nowhere to be found. Ellen was panicking, convinced she'd never see you again.

'There was a man I didn't like the look of parked up the lane today. Suppose . . . ?'

I did my best to soothe her. 'Ellen, nobody is going to come into your back yard and snatch a nine-year-old. She's probably gone off across the fields.'

'When she knows her dinner is ready?'

'Quit worrying. I'll find her.'

I went to the back of the yard, climbed the low stone wall into the meadow beyond. I was more worried about the herd of cows grazing there than I was about you. I've never been a fan

of cows in crowds – however placid they look I'm reminded of
Rawhide, stampeding cattle, flailing hoofs. I gave this bunch a wide
berth and headed for the wood at the far side of the field, avoiding
cow-pies covered in flies as I went. I knew somehow I'd find you
there – and I did. You were sitting against the trunk of a tree,
knees drawn up, arms wound round them.

'Hi,' I greeted you.

You looked up at me dull-eyed. None of your usual sparkle.
'Hi.'

'What are you doing out here all by yourself?'

You shrugged. Said nothing. I sat down beside you.

'Something's up, Sarah. Come on, you can tell me. I won't tell
your mom if you don't want me to.' You picked at the hem of your
shorts. 'A trouble shared is a trouble halved.' Your lip quivered; you
bit on it stubbornly. I waited. I knew if the silence stretched long
enough you'd fill it eventually. I was right.

'You promise not to tell anyone else?' you said at last.

Whatever it was, I doubted it was a matter of life or death. But
I don't make promises unless I'm sure I can keep them.

'Let's see if we can figure it out,' I hedged.

And you told me, haltingly at first, then all of a rush, about a
gang of girls who were bullying you at school. Nothing very serious,
just a bit of hair-pulling and name-calling and exclusion, but
persistent enough to get to you like a dripping tap. Today, one of
them had taken your homework file from your bag while your
back was turned and they'd tossed your carefully written work
around so that it got scuffed and dirty, and you'd been in trouble
with your class teacher for it.

'You didn't tell her how it came to get messed up?' I asked.

You looked scandalised. 'No! That would be sneaking.'

'I guess it would.'

'That's why I don't want Mum to know. She'd come down to school and blast off at Miss Higgins, and Miss Higgins will think I'm a wimp, and Tonia and Mandy will get back on me every time she's not looking . . .'

Very true, I thought, surprised by your perspicacity. A teacher can't be there all the time any more than a mother can. She doesn't have eyes in the back of her head. In my opinion there are some things better worked out by ourselves, even if we are only nine years old.

'Why do they do it, do you think?' I asked.

'Don't know. Because I don't do their sort of girly thing, maybe. They call me a tomboy.'

I couldn't keep from smiling. 'You are, honey. That's not a bad thing to be. It just makes you different.'

'You mean I should pretend to like their dolls and stuff?'

'No. Though you mustn't look down your nose at them either. But the most important thing is not to let them see they're getting to you. If they call you a tomboy, say, "Hey – yeah – it's great. You should try it sometime." They'll soon get tired of their silly game.'

'It's not a game, Grandma.'

'Yes, it is – to them. Why don't you give it a try?'

You nodded, wiped your nose on the sleeve of your shirt. 'OK.' Then you brightened. 'Anyway, Barney and Luke are my friends. I bet if I told them they'd biff them one.'

'Not a good idea,' I said firmly, though to be honest I wouldn't have been averse to putting them over my own knee. 'You have got friends, then?'

'Oh yeah. Barney and Luke are my *besty* friends. But the boys do different lessons from the girls – football and cricket and wood-work and stuff . . .'

I could see it all now. I wished with all my heart I could make things right for you, but you had to do that for yourself. And I knew you would, given time.

'They're just jealous, I expect, because they wish Barney and Luke liked them better,' I said. 'When they're awful to you, just try showing them you don't care – and keep me posted. Now, we'd better get back home before your mom sends out a search party for us, right?'

'Right. I love you, Grandma.'

'And I love you, honey.'

Next day when you came home from school you were much more cheerful.

'How did it go?' I asked when we were alone.

'OK. I told them, like you said. And I held out my bag to them and I said: "Here, if you want my books, have them." And do you know what? They just walked away.'

It wasn't the end of it, of course, but it was the end of the worst of it. And a couple of weeks later you got a place in the gymnastics display team and overnight you turned into a superstar that everyone wanted to claim as a friend. But I was most proud of you for toughing it out on your own with these girls who had it in for you, and showing them they weren't going to get the better of you. And, I have to admit it, I was secretly pleased that you'd confided in me when you couldn't bring yourself to confide in your mother. I treasured that affinity, Sarah. Always have. Always will.

Which is why I'm wondering now if I've made a big mistake asking for your help. Letting you into a part of my life that I've kept hidden for sixty-odd years. I've shocked you, and that's hardly to be wondered at. It's a cliché that the young think they have a monopoly on sexual love, but like most clichés, it's all too true.

Bad enough to think of your parents doing it, let alone your grandparents. A grandmother is supposed to be cosy. She can love her husband as a friend. She can love her children, her grandchildren, her siblings and puppies and kittens and canaries. But anything else is beyond the pale. The kind of love that remembers a touch that sets the heart singing and the senses swirling, that prickles over the skin and starts a fire in the soul that burns so brightly it destroys sense and reason, conscience and duty – no. That's not allowed.

It was foolish of me to have thought that you, of all people, might understand. Foolish of me to have these thoughts at all. But then, I have never been as wise as I might have been. I've listened to my heart when I should have listened to my head, and to my head when I should have followed my heart. And if I ever doubted it for a moment, the evidence is all here in front of me. In a book that I kept as a journal during the war years, and in a wallet of fading photographs.

The date stares up at me from the peeling label, 'April 1942–January 1944', and it whisks me back in time so I can almost touch the girl I once was. Twenty-one years old and desperately in love. Face to face with death, and yet truly alive. Instinctively knowing that these years were the axis of my whole life, yet not realising how they would shape not only my own future but the futures of others too.

I should have thrown it away long ago, of course, along with so much else. Keeping it was folly. But somehow I'd never been able to bring myself to do that. It meant too much to me, and though I hadn't looked at it in years, just knowing it was there, a link to the past, was comforting and dangerously titillating both at the same time.

I'd decided a few weeks back, though, that I couldn't leave it any longer to dispose of my treasures and my secrets. I am eighty-four years old; I don't want someone else clearing them out when I'm gone. It's not difficult to imagine Ritchie's impatience if he had to deal with it, the way he'd rifle carelessly through the things that were important to me, raising a scornful eyebrow at some of them, taking an unhealthy interest in others. There were things I didn't want anyone to see, but neither did I want them ruthlessly discarded into a trash sack. Hard as it was, I wanted to be the one to dispose of it all. Firmly but lovingly. And I wanted to do it while I was still able – while these stupid stiff hands of mine are still capable of tearing a letter in half, and my mind sharp enough to know what I'm destroying. I wished heartily that I'd made the effort years ago, in the days when I could sit on the floor in the midst of it all, pulling out drawers at will. As it was I'd had to ask Ritchie to bring it all in batches to the big oak table in the living room where I could draw up a chair and go through it in relative comfort.

He complained, of course; suggested he take it all direct to the town dump.

'You haven't looked at it in years – why bother now?'

'Because I want to.'

'You won't throw a damned thing away. In a couple of days I'll have to put the whole lot back again.'

I could feel the exasperation rising, both with Ritchie and with myself. I promise you, getting old is not much fun. I hate the loss of my independence, hate having to ask someone else for help with the simple things I could have done for myself without a second thought just a few years ago. And still feeling nineteen or twenty inside doesn't help matters much either. Except that back then I'd thought I was immortal, invincible, and now I know different.

'Ritchie, can't you do just one thing for me without an argument? I wouldn't ask if I could do it myself. Unfortunately, I can't.'

So Ritchie had brought through the files and boxes I'd asked him to and I began the daunting task of sorting through the detritus of my life.

There was none of the business paperwork amongst it, of course – that is all kept at the office. But there were countless envelopes stuffed full of family photographs that set the memories flowing as I pored over them. There was one of John wearing water wings and that terrible bathing costume I'd knitted him – the picture on the pattern had shown a serene smiling woman and bonny child, the perfect family, and I'd been deluded into feeling that making that costume would somehow turn me into a perfect mother too. But knitted bathing costumes are not the most sensible idea. As soon as John got into the water the wool absorbed it at an alarming rate and it ended up sagging down between his knees. There was Ellen, solemnly pressing her doll's clothes on a toy ironing board outside her Wendy house, and Ritchie on his fairy cycle, scowling because he'd been unable to ride it without the stabilisers and Joe had had to refit them.

Then there were the bits and pieces I'd kept because they made me happy and proud. There were birthday cards the children had made themselves, with stick people and flowers and bright yellow suns on the front, and uneven, childish writing inside – 'To Mom. With love from . . .' John's swimming trial time sheets – thank heaven he'd grown out of the knitted bathing costume by then! Programmes from high school drama productions when Ellen had played leading roles; a cutting from the local paper showing the rock group Ritchie had belonged to playing at a graduation ball. Ritchie had been on washboard and was half-hidden behind the boys on rhythm and base guitars, but I'd kept it anyway. John's draft papers for Vietnam were there. The guest lists for Ellen's wedding. Ritchie's first business card.

So many memories, all stuffed into drawers and box files, and stored, in recent years anyway, in the lumber room. Along with receipted bills and guarantees long since expired, recipes I'd liked the sound of but never made, instructions for gadgets long since gone to the great gadget graveyard in the sky, expired insurance policies and unused cheque books. Getting rid of all that had been easy enough.

Last of all I came to the things that were personal to me. Letters and telegrams, proficiency certificates and flight log books. Yellowing wallets of photographs taken on Box Brownie cameras. And my journals.

I started writing them when I was just a little girl, touring the country with my parents. A teacher in a Midwest school I'd attended one long-ago winter had suggested it as a way of getting me to practise my writing and spelling, which, given my erratic education, left a good deal to be desired. At first I'd kicked against the regime, much preferring to be out running wild to struggling with the hieroglyphics that seemed to come so easily to my classmates, but before long I came to enjoy it. Keeping a diary was like having a best friend to whisper secrets to, and best friends were not easily come by in my transient world.

I made a habit of scribbling at least a few words each night before I fell asleep and they were a revelation now. I'd confided so much to those pages. When I'd deciphered the misspelled entries, the tastes and smells of my childhood were all around me so that I lost myself in the little girl I once was, and the hopes and dreams and disappointments were as real to me as they had been then. I set them on one side, reluctant to let go a part of me that I had thought was gone for ever but in reality was just hiding.

I did a whirlwind tour through the years of my growing up and set the journals on one side thinking that you might like to look at them and see what life was like back then. And turned to the last one I ever wrote. The one with the label inscribed 'April 1942–January 1944'.

It took me a few minutes before I could bring myself to open it. I hesitated like Pandora with her box of secrets. The Mischiefs are all trapped within these pages; the moment I open the cover they'll fly out at me. There are plenty more Mischiefs, of course, unrecorded, in the years that followed, the years when I was too busy, too darned tired to keep up my journal. And reluctant, too, to commit to paper things that were better kept in my heart. But this one records the start of it all. The glory and the heartache. The years that finally transformed me from the little girl of the early exercise books to the woman I became and, I suppose, still am.

First I opened the wallet of photographs, but of course that was just as dangerous – maybe even more so. A photograph is not just a memory. It's a moment trapped in time like a rose frozen into a block of ice. And youth is eternal.

And there he was, reaching out to me across the years, just as I remember him. Tall. Athletic. Dark hair springing from a broad forehead. A smile twinkling in his eyes and making long creases in his cheeks.

Mac.

A nerve twisted deep inside me and there was a lump in my throat suddenly. And an ache of longing stronger by far than the arthritic pain I've learned to live with.

Oh, Mac. I loved you too darned much. And at the same time, not enough . . .

47

The next photograph was of the two of us. Buster Brown took it, I remember. Buster the joker, who could never take anything seriously. He was killed soon afterwards, shot out of the sky somewhere over the Channel. They never found the wreckage of his plane, and they never found his body. Well, they wouldn't, would they?

In the photograph Mac and I are leaning against a five-bar gate, both wearing civilian clothes, and though the print is grainy black and white, I saw it in glorious Technicolor – the sunshine yellow of my slacks and the matching ribbon in my hair, which was, of course, still thick and lustrous without even the first hint of grey. I remembered the way his shoulder had felt beneath mine, the sun-warmed scent of his skin, the curl of his arm around my waist. And felt again the way I had felt then, intoxicated by love, breathless with longing, torn apart by stifled guilt. And trying to ignore the worm of dread that crawled through my stomach because I knew it could all come to an end at any moment; the sense of standing on the very edge of a precipice that heightened every emotion.

I went through the photographs one by one. Mac with his beloved Douglas motorcycle. Me climbing into a Spitfire. A group of us having tea on the airfield veranda. And as the memories came flooding back a nostalgic longing began inside me that would, over the days and weeks, grow to a compulsion.

There was something else in the drawer too – a small leather box containing a medal. Mac's DFC, with a bar on the white and purple ribbon – and that added strength to my determination. He might have had his reasons for sending it to me, and I'd been proud to have it in my possession all these years. But it had never been mine and it was not mine to dispose of now. It belonged to him and his heirs and it should be returned to him. If he was still alive. Thinking he might not be was not only painful but also frankly unbelievable. I couldn't imagine a world without Mac in it somewhere. But facts had to be faced. He was older than me — he'd be in his late eighties now.

I knew then with absolute certainty that here was still unfinished business in my life. Just as I had needed to clear out my hoarded treasures before it was too late, there was something else I needed to resolve. Which is why, Sarah, I've taken the risk of asking for your help.

There's a veil over your eyes now, a veneer of assumed worldliness. You don't want me to know what you're thinking and feeling.

'You say his name is Mac?' you say, very blasé, very matter of fact.

I try to match your nonchalance. This is no time to admit how much this matters to me.

'That's how I always knew him. His proper name was James Mackenzie. He was a fighter pilot in the RAF. He was wounded during the Battle of Britain and for a time he was an assistant station commander with the ATA, which is when I knew him. When he was fully fit, he returned to active service.'

'Do you have an address for him?' you ask.

I smile ruefully. 'Do you count one nearly sixty years old? But I'll give you everything I have. Service number, postings . . . There must be organisations . . . and the address I have — his old family home. Maybe someone in the village is still in contact, or at least knows the whereabouts of his family. And it's not that far from you. Gloucestershire.'

You frown. 'You've never mentioned when you've been staying with us—'

You break off, afraid, perhaps, of treading on territory that is best left uncharted, and at the same moment I see a glimmer of recognition in your eyes, as if you have just remembered the time I visited and we went to Slimbridge Wildfowl Trust.

You'd not long passed your driving test and you were proud and excited that your father had let you borrow his car. Because we were in Gloucestershire I had my eyes skinned for the names of places Mac used to talk about, and I'd asked for the map so I could chart our progress and check the road signs of the villages we passed through. I remember you getting a little defensive: 'Grandma, I can find the way! Don't you trust me?' I didn't want to upset you, so I put the map away and tried to act normal. Maybe I didn't succeed as well as I hoped.

'Where in Gloucestershire?' you ask now.

'Near Stroud.' I fish in the back of the journal and pull out a sheet of paper torn from a notepad. 'Cleverley. It's not much more than a hamlet, unless I'm mistaken.'

You chew your lip, weighing it up. 'Well, I can try.' You sound doubtful. I know you're thinking that after all this time it's not going to be easy. 'What do you want me to do if I can find him?'

'I'll write a letter before you leave.' I should have done it already, but I've been putting it off. It's not easy to know how to begin after all this time. 'If you could give it to him . . . And there's something else.'

I open the little box. The DFC – Distinguished Flying Cross – is nestling on its bed of satin. It's a little tarnished, but nothing that a bit of silver polish won't cure, and it winks up at me, tugging at my heartstrings. The cross is a cross flory, just over two inches across. The horizontal and bottom bars are terminated with bumps, the upper bar with a rose; aeroplane propellers are superimposed on the vertical arms of the cross, and wings on the horizontal arms. In the centre is a wreath around the letters 'RAF', surmounted by an imperial crown.

'Mac won this – the Cross and the bar on the ribbon – which means he was honoured twice for valour while flying in active operations against the enemy,' I say. The words sound to me like a citation. 'I've kept it all these years, but I think it's time he had it back. Or his family. It would mean a lot to them.'

You're looking at the medal in awe. I don't suppose you've ever seen one before. Perhaps now you're beginning to understand why this is so important to me; no longer think I've taken leave of my senses. Though it has to be said that if there is one advantage to growing old it is that you can be unreasonable from time to time and others go along with it to humour you.

'OK,' you say. 'I'll do my best.'

I finish my sherry. Your wine glass is already empty. I ask you if you'd like another; you shake your head.

'Better not.' Then you change your mind. 'Actually – yes, I will.' The shock is wearing off; you're becoming more your usual self. 'Come on, Grandma, I want to know a bit more about this . . . Mac. I'll get us refills and then you can tell me all about him.'

Not all, I think. I owe you something, but there's a great deal better kept to myself . . .

You come back with our replenished glasses and I open the journal. There's a telegram taped into the front cover, folded several times because it is two feet long. I spread it out, remembering the heady excitement that had burst in my veins when it arrived, more than sixty years ago. A telegram from Jackie Cochran, flying ace, and already a legend in her lifetime. Addressed to me.

'Perhaps you'd like to see this,' I say. 'This was the start of it all.'

Part Two

The Past

I

The telegram was delivered to Dorothy Costello's door mid-morning on a bright day in the spring of 1942.

As Dorothy took it, Nancy felt sick with dread. A telegram meant something that couldn't wait. Which usually equated to bad news – especially with the state the world was in at present.

Until a few short months ago, the war in Europe had seemed as distant to most Americans as if it had been happening on another planet. Those who read their newspapers or listened to the world news on their wireless sets knew that Holland, Belgium and France had fallen to the invading Germans, and that British cities and airfields were under relentless attack from Luftwaffe bombing raids. They knew that American troops had been deployed to independent Iceland to relieve the British of the task of preventing the Germans from turning it into a base for harassing the vital trade routes between the US and Britain, and that President Roosevelt and Mr Churchill had met on an American cruiser off the New England coast and agreed what they called the 'Atlantic Charter'. But it was more the fact that President Roosevelt had covered up the meeting by pretending to be on a fishing trip in his yacht that aroused interest rather than the declaration of their joint war and peace aims. The war was happening half a world away. In the main, it didn't concern them.

Until 6 December 1941, when the Japs bombed Pearl Harbor. Five battleships and fourteen smaller ships were sunk or badly damaged, two hundred aircraft destroyed, and over two and a half thousand people killed. Suddenly it concerned them a great deal. Army and navy officers streamed into the War and Navy Department building, civilians began volunteering for active service.

Amongst them was Joe, who had joined the USAAF, where his experience as a pilot could be put to good use. He was flying bombers now, a notoriously dangerous occupation, and the moment she saw the telegram, Nancy was rigid with fear that it might mean very bad news indeed.

Dorothy Costello, too, was quaking with apprehension. Her flabby face had drained of colour and the loose flesh on her plump arms quivered as if every nerve had taken on a life of its own as she reached out to take the telegram. She stared at it for a moment and Nancy waited, heart hammering. Then Dorothy swung round, fear giving way to indignation.

'It's for you.'

Relief coursed through Nancy in a floodtide. If the telegram was for her it couldn't be formal notification that Joe had been killed or was missing in action. She wasn't his wife, or even his fiancée, much as he would have liked her to be. Dorothy – his aunt – was his next of kin. But Nancy was puzzled and anxious, all the same. Nobody had ever sent her a telegram before.

Dorothy peered over her shoulder as she opened it; Nancy could feel her breath, uneven, on the nape of her neck, and the heat that emanated from that quivering mountain of flesh radiant on her bare arms. Dorothy didn't believe in a person's privacy; it was one of the things about her that most irritated Nancy. That and the fact that she was always absolutely certain that she knew best. Nancy lived under her roof and she was Joe's girl. Dorothy considered that gave her the right to know everything that went on in Nancy's life and have her vociferous say about it.

The telegram was the longest Nancy had ever seen, but it was the name of the sender that leaped out at her – and at Dorothy too.

'Jacqueline Cochran?' Her voice was sharp, accusing, almost. 'Jacqueline Cochran? I've heard of her, haven't I?'

The imp of irritation pricked at Nancy again. There could scarcely be a person in the civilised world who hadn't heard of Jacqueline Cochran – beautician turned flying ace, poor white trash transformed into wealthy socialite and friend of the rich and powerful. Her photograph was often in the newspapers, wrapped in furs, dripping with jewels, and in the world of flying she was a legend.

Now, it seemed, she had turned her attention to working for the war effort.

An organisation had been set up in England, the telegram explained, to use civilians to ferry war planes from the factories where they were produced to the airfields where they were needed, so freeing up the military pilots for 'operational duties'. Already, dozens of American men had gone to swell the force and Jackie saw no reason why women should not do the same. She'd been to England to discuss her ideas with the British authorities, flying a bomber across the Atlantic. She'd persuaded them she was serious. Now she was recruiting a hand-picked team and to Nancy's astonishment she was on the list Jackie had drawn up as having the necessary qualifications and experience: a commercial licence, an instructor's rating, and almost five hundred hours on her log book. The purpose of the telegram was to invite Nancy to an interview and flight test with a view to joining Jackie's élite band.

Nancy read and reread the telegram with mounting excitement, oblivious now to Dorothy tut-tutting in her ear. Dorothy would raise every possible objection, of course. She was already bristling about the extravagance of such a lengthy missive, not to mention 'the gall of that woman, expecting you to jump when she snaps her fingers!' but Nancy was no longer listening.

Dorothy might have a lifetime's experience of running the lives of those around her, but Nancy had no intention of letting her do it this time. When it came down to it, she'd make up her own mind. In fact, she'd made it up already!

For some time now Nancy had known that she was at a crossroads in her life, though when she'd first come to Varna she'd been more than content. After years of living like a gypsy, it had seemed like heaven to have a place to call home as well as the opportunity to do the job she knew – and loved – best. And to be able to begin to put the traumas of the recent past behind her.

'You'd be delivering some light freight, running a taxi service and teaching folk to fly,' Joe had told her when she answered his advertisement for a pilot. 'Do you reckon you could cope with that?'

His voice was slow and lazy, but there was a shrewd watchfulness in his eyes. They were blue, those eyes, the bluest eyes Nancy had ever seen, in a fair-skinned face tanned dark by the elements. Joe had started out his flying career as a crop-duster, he told her, hiring himself out to any farmer who was prepared to pay for his services. Now, however, he'd decided to expand the business. He'd bought another plane, suitable for light commercial work, which would double as a trainer, and rented office accommodation at the local airstrip.

'I reckon it's time I started putting down roots, building something for the future,' he said. 'Reckon I've had enough of junketing around.'

His sentiments matched Nancy's exactly. She'd had enough of junketing around too. She desperately needed to belong somewhere. A place where she could try to rebuild a life turned sour and try to forget the things that tore her up inside, sleeping and waking. Though she suspected that however far she went, whatever she did, that was never going to happen.

Now, challenged with regard to her capabilities, Nancy met Joe's gaze squarely.

'I've been flying ever since I was big enough to reach the controls,' she told him. 'And before that I was sitting on my father's lap playing with the yoke and the throttle. I can fly anything you've got or are likely to have. Anywhere. Any time.'

He was silent, sizing her up, and she felt a twinge of unease. She'd wanted to give the impression of confidence; now she hoped she hadn't overdone it. There was a fine line to be drawn. Overconfidence in the skies could be fatal. Nancy didn't suppose Joe Costello would be overly concerned if she smashed herself up. But he certainly would care if she smashed up his plane, which very likely wasn't even paid for yet.

'Let me show you what I can do,' she offered.

'Just what I was thinking,' Joe agreed.

Nancy took off, and flew smoothly and cautiously. There'd be none of the fancy tricks she'd learned from her father today, she thought, smiling ruefully to herself. But to her surprise, when they were way out over the Everglades, Joe said: 'You gonna loop the loop for me, then?'

She glanced sideways at him, not sure if he was being serious or testing her, and he smiled a slow smile that smoothed out the creases the sun had dug in his cheeks and warmed the blue of his eyes.

'Thought you wanted to show me what you can do.'

Nancy did not need to be told twice. She put on power and raised the nose, pulled the stick back further, further, flipped the plane, and came out in a perfect roll to straight and level. Then she stole another glance at him. He was grinning.

'OK,' he said. 'The job's yours if you want it.'

Nancy liked to think that Joe took her on in spite of the fact that she was a girl. Dorothy, however, was convinced he'd taken her on because of it.

Self-doubt had never been in Dorothy's nature. She saw herself as a fount of wisdom, and considered it her duty to ensure that others benefited from what she confidently believed to be her infallible insight. She offered her advice forcefully, whether it was asked for or not, and if it was rejected, she took it as a personal slight, and then set about bulldozing a path towards getting her own way by a combination of affronted hauteur and what she termed plain speaking. 'I'm bound to say what I think,' she would proclaim self-righteously. 'It's for your own good.'

When Joe told her he proposed employing Nancy, she was instantly up in arms, convinced that no good would come of it.

'A flibbertigibbet like that ain't right for your business, Joe,' she opined loudly, careless of the fact that Nancy was no more than a few feet away, sitting in the little dining area next door to the kitchen, filling in details for Joe's paperwork. 'What can you be thinking of?'

Joe dangled teabags into the pot by their little cotton strings. 'She flies like an angel,' he said evenly. 'She's darned good at it.'

'And good at other things too, no doubt,' Dorothy sniffed, her tone laden with meaning. 'She's a sight too pretty for her own good, that one.'

In the office, Nancy's face burned. There was no way she could have failed to overhear – in all probability Dorothy had intended that she should. Her first reaction, raw as she was from events of the recent past, was a wash of hot shame – was it so obvious? Were they written all over her, the things she wanted to forget, the things she wanted to hide? Or was this disapproving woman a witch who could see right inside her? Briefly Nancy wondered if she should just get up and walk right out of here. Then anger welled up, defensive, indignant. None of that had anything to do with how well she could do her job. She wouldn't let a nasty, inter-fering old woman cheat her out of a heaven-sent opportunity like this one. And what business of hers was it anyway?

Joe listened stoically to Dorothy's objections and then, as he always did, went right ahead with his own plans. He was used to her ways – he'd had a lifetime of it – and he'd long ago discovered the best way for a peaceful life was to placate and ignore her, both at the same time. He'd learned the trick from her late husband, his uncle Walt. 'Best not to argue with her, boy,' he'd say. 'Let her think she's having her way and she'll soon cool down.' Then he would amble off to the old trailer parked on scrubland at the rear of the house, which was his refuge, Joe following, more often than not, and light one of the cigarettes Dorothy had forbidden him to smoke.

'She means well,' he'd say, puffing away. 'She only does it for the best.'

Joe knew that was true. For all her annoying ways, Dorothy had a generous heart and was fiercely protective of those she loved. She'd taken him in when he had been orphaned at the age of two by the death of his parents in a railroad crash and never once complained. He'd wanted for nothing, materially or emotionally. It had been Dorothy who had sat with him, smoothing his hair when he woke at night, crying for his mother, Dorothy who had baked his birthday cakes and darned his socks and wiped the blood off skinned knees. He had, he realised as he grew older, taken the place of the children of her own that she'd never had, but he didn't mind that. If it hadn't been for Dorothy, he'd have ended up in an orphanage. He owed her.

His gratitude was the reason he kept a room on in her house during his crop-dusting days, and when he decided to start a flying business it seemed only right that he should base it in Varna. With Walt dead a year since, she was lonely. This way he'd be home more often.

But respecting Dorothy didn't mean being her poodle. If he wanted to employ Nancy, he damned well would. Dorothy would come down from her high horse in the end when she saw opposition was useless.

When Dorothy realised that Joe was set on defying her, and that her efforts to drive the girl away with a display of tight-lipped disapproval and spiteful comments made in her hearing were not going to work either, she changed tactics. Pretending support, she suggested Nancy should move into the old trailer that had once been Walt's hideaway. She didn't care for having her in such close proximity to Joe. 'She has her eye on the main chance,' she sniffed indignantly to her friend and neighbour, Tilly Jacobson. 'We all know what she's after, don't we? Good-looking boy like our Joe, nice little business, he sure would be a catch for anybody, let alone a fly-by-night like that one . . .' But at the same time if Nancy was close by she could keep an eye on her. For Dorothy the busybody, it was a temptation she could not resist.

And when what she had feared happened and Joe fell for Nancy, she realised she had no choice but to accept that too, and re-directed all her efforts to ensuring Nancy did nothing to hurt her beloved nephew. 'If Joe's happy, then I'm happy. But I can't help worrying that she's going to break his heart some day,' she told Tilly Jacobson.

Now, peering over Nancy's shoulder at the telegram from Jackie Cochran, she was overcome with the dreadful certainty that that day had come.

'You won't go, of course,' she huffed indignantly. 'You wouldn't think of doing anything so plain damned stupid.'

Nancy folded the telegram carefully. 'Why not?' Her tone was challenging; it infuriated Dorothy.

'Why not?' Dorothy's triple chins quivered and the spectacles she'd put on the end of her snub little nose to read the telegram bounced now at the end of their chain against her ample bosom. 'Surely you don't need to ask! It's terrible in England right now. You only have to open a newspaper to see what's going on. Bombing raids every night. Rationing of just about everything – why, you'd be living in a bunker, I shouldn't wonder, with no proper food to eat and no home comforts at all. I wouldn't go near England right now if you paid me. That Jacqueline Cochran must think you're as crazy as she is. And what's more . . .' she tapped the telegram with a stubby, work-reddened finger, '. . . this is nothing but a waste of good paper. She must have money to burn, is all I can say.'

'I don't see what's crazy about it.' There was barely concealed excitement in Nancy's voice and Dorothy experienced a stab of alarm. She couldn't control this girl, never had been able to, and she didn't like it. This was all going to end in tears, just as she had always predicted.

'It makes really good sense to let civilians do the ferrying and leave the servicemen free to fight the Germans,' Nancy went on. 'Joe thought it was a good idea. He was thinking of volunteering himself if he'd been turned down by the air force.'

Dorothy snorted. 'More fool him! But it's different for him. He's a man. Women can't fly war planes.'

'They're already doing it,' Nancy said. 'Fighters – and bombers too.'

Dorothy looked incredulous. 'Well, that's as may be. But Joe wouldn't want you to do it. He wouldn't want you putting yourself in that sort of danger. And you've got your responsibilities here to think of too. Joe left you in charge of the business. You can't go gallivanting off and let it go to rack and ruin.'

'Oh, for heaven's sake!' Nancy was getting exasperated now. 'There is no business – and there won't be until the war is over. You know as well as I do that civil pilots are grounded. I might just as well be in Europe doing something useful.'

'I'm only saying what Joe would say if he was here.' Dorothy's mouth was set in a tight disapproving line. 'I can't let you go, Nancy. Joe would never forgive me.'

It was the worst thing she could have said. It scraped at the thin layer of scar tissue covering the resentment that had been growing like an infection in Nancy's blood for months now. A feeling of confinement that was anathema to her.

'Joe doesn't own me, Mrs Costello,' she said. 'If Jackie Cochran thinks I'm up to it, I'm going to England. And if you don't like it, that's just too damned bad.'

Nancy was not sure exactly when she first began feeling trapped, but she could certainly date the worst of it to when Joe asked her to marry him. Until then, she'd been content to let things rub along, trying not to notice that he was falling in love with her, or to worry about it, anyway. She enjoyed her work, every day different and challenging in some new way. She enjoyed coming home at night to the trailer that was the first settled home she'd known, and which she'd made as comfortable as she could with new cushions and throws and her own few personal possessions. She enjoyed Joe's company. He had a dry sense of humour and a philosophical way of looking at things that could put an easy perspective on any problem. Joe soothed the ripples in the pond of life – made everything seem better. 'No sense wasting time fretting,' he'd say, and he practised what he preached.

In the beginning, if she was honest, she had even enjoyed knowing that he fancied her. It was there in his eyes when he looked at her, and in the care and concern he showed for her too. He was a little too conscientious about the condition of the planes she flew, a little too ready to double-check the weather information before she took off, though he knew she always did it herself, and once he had chewed up an engineer who was rude to her, threatening to dismiss the man on the spot. Nancy had never seen him so angry – easygoing Joe, noted for his even temper – and she'd had to defuse the situation, tell him it really wasn't important and that she wasn't such a fragile flower that she would go into a decline at a few choice redneck phrases. But she'd enjoyed his protectiveness, she who had never been anything but self-sufficient. It made her feel good about herself, and after what had happened before she came to Varna, it was just what she needed. If this thoroughly nice guy cared about her, maybe she was worth something after all, Nancy thought. And his attention gave her days when she could catch a glimpse of a future bright with promise instead of dark with regrets.

Sometimes, alone in the trailer, with the heat of the day trapped inside so that the drapes smelled strong as the day the cotton they were made from was picked, and the crickets chirping so loudly they made a symphony, she even wondered if that future might be with Joe. She tried to imagine what it would be like to be married to him, with two or three children and a house that smelled of cookies baking and chicken frying, and a rocking chair on the front porch. And as long as it was just a distant dream, it was fine. As long as there was space between her and it, she could handle it.

The first time Joe kissed her was fine too. She'd been worried that when it happened she might turn and run, but she didn't. She liked the slight rasp of his stubble against her chin and the firm feel of his mouth on hers. She liked the way she seemed to melt into him. She liked the corded muscles in his arms and the broad splay of his hands where the tiny hairs were bleached gold by the sun. And later she liked laying her head against his chest and listening to his heartbeat; the way they seemed to be breathing in unison. She liked everything about him. But she didn't love him. And that was the sticking point she couldn't get past. There had to be more. Exactly what, Nancy wasn't sure. She just knew there had to be more.

Joe asked her to marry him the night before he went off to join the air force and suddenly everything changed. The future was no longer some hazy, distant country, it was the here and now. And Nancy didn't like it one bit.

They were on the front porch, leaning against the veranda rail and sharing a packet of cigarettes in the soft dusk. The air was still pleasantly warm, perfumed with hibiscus and resonant with the constant chirp of the crickets. The moon had come up, making the picket fence gleam white against the backdrop of grey-green foliage beyond, and a single star sat suspended beneath it like a diamond on a bed of midnight-blue velvet. It was an evening made for romance, and their awareness of one another was heightened by the knowledge that tomorrow Joe would be gone.

'You take care while I'm gone, honey,' Joe said. He ground out his cigarette; put his arm round her.

'Of course! But you're the one who has to take care. I'll miss you, Joe.'

For a long moment he was silent, then, all of a rush, he said: 'Nancy, there's something I want to ask you before I go.'

Nancy felt her stomach clench as if someone was squeezing it very hard. She knew suddenly exactly what he was going to say, and knew too that she didn't want him to. She didn't want anything to change. Didn't want to hurt him. She twisted away, searching for a way to stop this before it was too late.

'Joe – you don't have to say anything.'

But he was not listening. 'I want you to marry me, Nancy.' The words hung in the sweet, still air.

'Joe . . .'

'I know. I'm off tomorrow and I don't know when the heck I'll be back. If I'll be back . . .'

'Don't say that! Don't even think it!'

'It's true, though. Gotta face facts. But I'd like to think you were here, waiting for me. With a ring on your finger to show all those other guys who'll come sniffing around that you're spoken for.'

'You don't have a ring.'

'That's where you're wrong, honey. I stopped off at the jewellery store this afternoon. Got this.' Awkwardly he fumbled in his pocket, pulled out a small square box and opened it. A diamond glinted, like the star beneath the crescent of the moon. 'Will you wear it for me, Nancy?'

'Oh, Joe, it's beautiful. But . . .' Panic was not something she was familiar with, but she felt it now, knotting her stomach, closing her throat. She was touched, flattered that he should want her to be his wife. But she could feel tentacles that had not been there before closing round her, drawing her in, and she felt utterly, completely trapped.

'But you're gonna say no.' His tone was casual but Nancy could hear the undertones of hurt and disappointment all the same, and the noose tightened.

'I don't know what to say, Joe.'

'You're saying no.'

It was too dark to see his face properly and she was glad of it.

'I'm not. I'm not saying yes or no. I'm just saying . . . not now. Not like this. Maybe next time you come home. Maybe . . . Just let's see how it is for both of us while we're apart. We haven't really known one another that long . . .' She hesitated, the words that would reveal the truth about herself hovering on her lips. 'You don't really know me at all . . .'

'I know all I need to know, Nancy,' Joe said quietly. 'I don't need time, or separation or togetherness to know you're the one for me. You're all I've ever wanted.'

The tentacles twisted more tightly, suffocating her.

'I'm real fond of you, Joe,' she said, and knew it was not nearly enough. 'But marriage . . . I'm not sure I'm ready for that sort of commitment.'

'So – I should take the ring back to the shop then?' Still that light tone, a defence against his disappointment.

'What, on your way to the station in the morning?' Nancy tried to match his pretence of casualness, but inside she felt raw, a repository for his pain – the pain she was inflicting on him. She pictured him choosing the ring, full of hope; pictured him returning it, dejected, embarrassed. A kitbag on his shoulder, a woman who'd refused his proposal left behind.

'Don't take it back,' she said. 'Keep it until you come home next time. I may be ready by then.' She closed his fingers around the box, kissed his throat. 'Joe, you've got to realise, it's not you. It's me. I just hope while you're gone I'll sort myself out.'

'Well, I sure hope so too,' Joe said.

Joe left next morning and the carefree days went with him. Though Nancy had made no promises, no formal commitment, the tentacles were still there, twined around her almost as tightly as if she had. She knew she should have given him a definite answer, and that answer should have been a 'no'. If he was the one for her, she wouldn't have hesitated, wouldn't be feeling trapped and scared now at the prospect of having to go through it all again. She should have listened to her heart and been honest with him and with herself. Instead she'd taken the coward's way out. Kept him hanging on with a 'maybe'.

Guilt ate into her, corrosive as battery acid. The guilt that came from admitting she'd played selfishly with his emotions, encouraged him because his attention had filled a need in her. And from knowing she was still giving him false hope. The pressure of holding his heart and his happiness in the palm of her hand was unbearable. Something inside her shrank and shrivelled at the thought of hurting him. But she didn't want to marry him either. She didn't want to tie her life with his for ever; give up her independence; never know that elusive something that she couldn't identify but knew was missing all the same. That elusive something that yearned in an empty space around her heart and prickled restlessly in her blood.

The feeling of being trapped didn't lessen with the passing of the weeks and months. If anything it grew worse. The flying restrictions imposed on civil aircraft by the authorities meant Nancy could no longer do the job she loved; she was grounded, she, Nancy, whose freedom was in the sky. And Dorothy's fierce protectiveness of Joe meant she tried to clip Nancy's wings at home too.

As the self-appointed guardian of Joe's happiness, she became Nancy's gaoler. She nagged at Nancy to move from the trailer into the house – it made no sense, she said, to burn two lots of electricity. She complained that she was lonely. She clung to Nancy like a limpet; whenever Nancy turned around, it seemed, Dorothy was there, her beady eyes watchful as a bird's. If Nancy went out Dorothy questioned her relentlessly about where she'd been, who she'd been with, all in the name of concern for Nancy's welfare, though Nancy knew that in reality it was Joe she was concerned about. She began to feel as if Dorothy was swallowing her whole, that she would disappear for ever inside that mountain of flesh that she was coming to loathe.

And now an escape hatch had opened in the form of a telegram from Jackie Cochran. A proposition that was not only exciting but also gave her the perfect excuse to get away.

Dorothy was looking panic-stricken, at a total loss. She just wasn't used to anyone openly defying her. For a moment, Nancy felt almost sorry for her, this woman who had to define herself by managing the lives of others.

'I'm sorry, Mrs Costello, but it's everyone's duty to do what they can for the war effort,' she said.

And knew she was taking the coward's way out again. Lying to Dorothy by default, just as she had lied to Joe.

But then again, maybe she hadn't lied. Maybe it really was that she just wasn't ready for commitment. Maybe if she tasted freedom again she would realise that what she'd wanted all the time was a settled home that smelled of cookies baking and chicken frying, a swing on the front porch, a couple of children. And Joe.

For both their sakes, Nancy hoped so. But from the way she was feeling just at that moment she wasn't going to bank on it.

II

Time, Nancy thought, is very peculiar. It is measured in minutes and hours and days against the hands of clocks that move around dials at a constant speed, and in the sweep of the sun across the sky. Every minute should be equal, wherever you are, whatever you are doing. But it's not. It's fluid. A minute can seem like an hour; a week speeds by in the twinkling of an eye.

Once she had read a theory that time is not a straight line at all; that the past, present and future are all happening simultaneously. Never one for thinking deep thoughts about the meaning of life, she'd found it a bit beyond her. But she was sure there was something very odd about time. Whilst every day spent at Varna after she was forced to stop flying seemed like an eternity, and an evening alone with Dorothy stretched ahead of her like an endless desert, after she accepted Jackie Cochran's invitation to test out to join her squad of women pilots, everything began to move at a breakneck speed that left her breathless.

And yet still time played its own tantalising games. Some days rushed by in a frenzy of activity, others dragged, mired down by

73

the frustration of waiting for transport, for tests, for formalities to be completed. The entries in Nancy's journal showed that according to the calendar there were exactly three weeks separating the day the telegram arrived and the day she set sail for England, but it might have been a lifetime and it might have been a heartbeat. But whatever tricks time might play, there will always be moments that are captured for ever in the treasure house of memory. And in that special place that is ours and ours alone, time holds no sway at all.

Montreal, Canada, is half the length of a continent from Varna, Florida, but it was in Montreal that Jackie Cochran was flight-testing the women she'd selected for her élite band, and Nancy had no choice but to make the journey. Three days and nights of travelling by bus and railroad, of washing her face with tepid water that smelled of sulphur, of sleeping sitting bolt upright with her head resting into a corner where worn plush met smoke-stained wood. Three days and nights of getting dirtier and more crumpled by the hour, of hoping desperately that she'd have the chance to make herself presentable before she had to meet the great lady herself. The prospect of it had been nerve-racking enough when she'd set out wearing her Sunday-best costume, neatly pressed, with her hair freshly washed. Now, dishevelled and grubby, she dreaded to think what sort of impression she would create.

Jackie had high standards, Nancy knew. When she had won the Bendix Air Race four years previously she had been so determined not to appear at less than her best that she had kept a judge waiting on the runway while she fixed her make-up. Would a woman like that make allowances? Nancy couldn't imagine she would.

In the days since the telegram had arrived, Nancy had avidly devoured every detail she could lay her hands on concerning Jackie

Cochran and her rags-to-riches story, and it had made fascinating reading. Jackie's background was even more rackety than her own, and her life now like something from a Hollywood movie.

As a child, Jackie had been dragged from one poverty-stricken Southern sawmill town to another by the slovenly couple who had adopted her – how and why she never knew. She had run wild, rarely attending school, barefoot and dressed in old sacking. She had slept on the floor; she had hunted for crabs and clams to eat. At the age of eight or nine – Jackie was never sure exactly how old she was – she had been sent to work twelve-hour shifts in a sawmill for a pittance of a wage.

But from these unpromising beginnings, she had pulled herself up by the bootstrings and left the squalor far behind her. She had trained as a hairdresser and beautician, ruthlessly working her way up to owning her own salon in Chicago and setting up a cosmetics company at a laboratory in New Jersey. She'd learned to fly so as to further her business interests, and though she had had to take the exams orally because she couldn't read or write well enough to sit a written test, she had taken to it like a duck to water. The beautician had, first and foremost, become an aviator.

Floyd Odlum, Jackie's husband, was a Wall Street lawyer and investor who had made several million dollars by the time he was in his mid-thirties. Together they set up home at the Coachella Ranch in Southern California. Set in the middle of the desert, it was an oasis of tangerine and grapefruit trees, lush green grass and exotic shrubs. Its thousand-plus acres boasted stables, a golf course and an Olympic-size swimming pool.

A veritable army of servants waited on the Odlums and their guests – presidents and nobility, high-ranking army officers and film stars. She and Floyd each had their own secretary and personal maid. And besides their private switchboard and the telephone operator they employed, there was a separate line especially installed for talking to Howard Hughes, a personal friend and business associate, who was paranoid that the operator might listen in to his calls.

Jackie wore the latest Paris fashions. She luxuriated in furs. She dripped with jewels. Jackie had everything – and the thought of meeting her terrified Nancy. But at the same time her meteoric rise to fame and fortune was a lodestar. Jackie knew what it was like to have nothing, and to be able to rise above it. Nancy thought that if she took one look at the grubby, dishevelled girl who would disembark from the train and decided there was no way she could live up to expectations as one of the favoured few pilots who would represent their country, she would never get over it.

She need not have worried. When she stepped onto the platform, thankfully breathing the clear sweet northern air and stretching her cramped limbs, one of Jackie's aides was there to whisk her off to a hotel and the blessed luxury of a long soak in a hot bath. A maid pressed her travel-weary costume, and turned back the crisp cotton sheets on a bed that looked like heaven to Nancy. After she had eaten her first proper meal in three days, she fell into it and slept without a single care for what tomorrow would bring. She no longer looked like a hobo; all that mattered now was her ability to fly an aeroplane, and that was one thing she was confident about. She was ready for Jackie Cochran; she was ready for anyone. Most of all, she was ready for the adventure of her life.

In real life, Jackie Cochran was every bit as glamorous as she appeared in photographs, Nancy was to discover. Her curls were blonde and luxuriant, her lips a gash of scarlet, and she exuded an energy that was so overpowering the room seemed too small to hold her. She shot questions at Nancy, and issued instructions in the confident manner of someone used to getting her own way. But overawed as Nancy was, she had no intention of showing it. She answered Jackie's questions with all the confidence she could muster and flew her flight test – on a Harvard – with her usual flair. And back in the office she had commandeered, Jackie gave Nancy the news she'd been waiting to hear.

She was one of seven girls chosen to go to England. They were to sail as soon as possible from St John's, Newfoundland. And Jackie would be flying to England so as to be there herself to meet them when they landed. Nancy was so excited she could scarcely breathe. The dream was becoming reality. She was on her way.

Jackie's 'army' of seven girls were a motley bunch, with personalities as diverse as their backgrounds. They came from all corners of the States – from California and New Jersey, from North Dakota and Arkansas. Kay Butler, the only New Yorker, was the daughter of the president of a railroad company and a former debutante who had bowed out from social circles because the only thing she cared about was flying. She was a beautiful natural blonde, fair-skinned and blue-eyed, with eyelashes long enough and thick enough to look good even without a lick of mascara. She had brought with her a trunk of designer clothes that made Nancy green with envy. But despite her privileged background and the fact that she was a personal friend of Jackie Cochran, she was always more than happy to be 'one of the girls'. Julia Montgomery, small and pretty with a mop of tight curls, was a technical wizard who had worked in an aeroplane repair shop while still at school. Red-haired Liz Scott, and Bobbie Morrison, tall and dark, had learned to fly with the CPT – the government-sponsored training programme – big-boned and capable-looking Grace Williams was a former CPT instructor, and the perfectly turned out Miriam de Sousa was, Nancy thought, a conceited bore. She regaled the others with a seemingly endless catalogue of her achievements – her superior qualifications, her vast experience – and Nancy soon learned to switch off and stop listening. When the girls were allocated their cabins on the SS *Culloden Queen* Nancy was mightily relieved to find she did not have to share with her.

Miriam, Julia, Liz, Bobbie and Grace were all together in a four-bunk cabin with a mattress on the floor between them, which had to be taken up each morning, whilst Nancy and Kay were squashed into a minuscule cabin just wide enough for two narrow bunks and a tiny locker. There was no room for both of them to dress or undress at the same time, and they took turns to be first up in the morning or into bed at night. In the first days at sea Nancy was violently ill, so the bottom bunk became hers, and Kay was forced to scramble over the bucket beside her head if she needed any of her own belongings. But though the cabin stank of vomit Kay was unfailingly cheerful and the two girls struck up a firm friendship as Kay fed Nancy sips of water and teased her relentlessly. Kay's father, of course, owned a yacht, and she'd sailed for as long as she could remember. No need for Kay to have to find her sea legs; she'd practically been born with them.

By the time Nancy's bout of seasickness had passed they were way out into the Atlantic and the scene that greeted her when she was well enough to go on deck was not an encouraging one. The sky was leaden grey, merging on the horizon into gunmetal sea that was whipped into marled furrows by a bitter squall. Ahead of them and behind, the bulky shapes of the other ships that comprised the convoy belched clouds of smoke into the murk, and all around them, menacing as a pack of hunting dogs, the destroyers and corvettes circled ceaselessly. They were not the danger, Nancy knew. That was hidden from view beneath the turbulent waves – the U-boats that could sneak up unseen and let loose a torpedo to rip a lethal hole in the hull beneath the water line – but they were the outward manifestation of it, a reminder that the convoy was in dangerous territory. At the first hint of anything untoward the escort vessels went into action, their guns and depth charges making Nancy's ears sing and every nerve ending in her body reverberate with the cacophony that split the air and echoed in the resulting vacuum.

But at night it was much worse. Trapped in a tiny cabin like a sardine in a can, Nancy had never felt so vulnerable in her life. Fear assumed dimensions she had never known it had, given a sharper edge of reality that came from knowing that one ship of volunteers had already been torpedoed and everyone aboard lost. The girls didn't talk about it, but it was never far from any of their minds.

The first time Nancy was woken by the guns was whilst she was still recovering from her seasickness. She had been deeply asleep and at first, as she was catapulted into consciousness, she thought it was sheet lightning in a tropical storm that was illuminating the cabin with flashes of blindingly white light. For the moment she couldn't remember where she was, let alone understand what was happening; then her shocked body registered the throb of the ship's engines, stronger even than the trembling that comes from being jolted awake, and the boom of a depth charge and the sharp crackle of gunfire brought it all back in a flash as blinding as that of the explosions.

The sickness was not just in her stomach now, but in her blood, the sickness of fear. For a moment she lay perfectly still, feeling the thud of her heart against her ribs and the bile rising in her throat. It seemed to her that the SS *Culloden Queen* was the most enormous sitting target. Unmissable. She lay tensed and waiting for the whoosh of a missile through the murky water, the agonising scream of tearing metal, the splintering of wood. Nancy didn't know what it would sound like to be hit by a torpedo, but her imagination was working overtime.

A rustle in the overhead bunk reminded her she was not alone. 'Are you awake?' she whispered into the flickering darkness, and knew it was a stupid question. No one could sleep with all this going on.

'Yeah. You too?' Kay swung herself down, her silk pyjama-clad legs brushing Nancy's arm. 'God, I need a cigarette!' She rifled in her bag, propped on the tiny locker. 'Want one?'

'No thanks.' At the best of times, smoking in the middle of the night tasted disgusting and left Nancy's mouth unpleasantly furred; now her still-queasy stomach revolted at the very thought of a cigarette.

The darkness outside the porthole blazed again, filling the cabin with eerie blue light.

'All I can say is –' Kay paused to light her cigarette – 'if the worst happens, I only hope I get to share a lifeboat with that lieutenant who looks like Clark Gable.' She perched on the edge of Nancy's bunk, bent double so that her head and shoulders were clear of her own. 'He is – not to put too fine a point on it – a hunk.'

Nancy raised herself on her pillow; her stomach heaved with the waves. She swallowed hard, waited for the lurching to steady. 'Yes, I've seen you giving him the eye.'

'Too true!' Kay tossed her head so that her blonde hair rippled in the splintered light from the explosions. 'We might as well make the most of the beefcake while we can. There won't be much where we're going.'

'Surely there'll be plenty of pilots for you to choose from.' Nancy was trying to match Kay's nonchalance; it wasn't easy. 'Or don't you rate Englishmen?'

'Fit, healthy young ones, yes. But ATA? Haven't you heard what it stands for, sweetie?'

'Air Transport Auxiliary,' Nancy said, puzzled.

'Officially, maybe. Unofficially, it's Ancient and Tattered Airmen. All too old or unfit to be in His Majesty's Royal Air Force. Jackie told me there's one guy with only one arm and one leg. He was so determined to fly for the ATA that he got in the plane and refused to get out until they'd flight-tested him. Most of them flew in the First World War, for Chrissakes! They've been managing banks and running clothing stores since then, but oh-my-God, they've shaken out the mothballs and taken to the skies.'

'Well, if they learned to fly on those old crates, they're most likely brilliant pilots,' Nancy ventured.

'Most likely they are,' Kay agreed. 'They're also old enough to be our fathers – grandfathers, even! No, I'm afraid, my dear, there is likely to be a serious shortage of eligible talent, unless –' her tone brightened – 'unless we get posted to an RAF station. Unlikely, as far as I can make out. The ATA have their own bases, nearby to aircraft factories and maintenance units. And the girls have their own commandant, a Pauline Gower. But you never know – we might get lucky.'

The cigarette smoke, fugging up the confined space, was beginning to make Nancy's eyes sting. She rubbed them with the back of her hand.

'I can't say I mind where we are really as long as I get to fly some interesting aeroplanes.'

'H'm.' Kay got up to reach for her bag and the portable ashtray she always carried. 'Have you got a fella back home?'

Joe. Nancy ached suddenly with longing for him. To have his arms around her, to lay her head against his reassuringly solid shoulder. To have him whispering in her ear: 'It's gonna be OK, honey. Quit worrying. I won't let anything bad happen to you . . .'

And just as suddenly despised herself for her weakness. What sort of a hypocrite was she, desperate to escape the web she'd woven for herself, then wanting to run for cover the moment freedom turned sour? She was here because she'd chosen to be. She might be safe with Joe – and she had to admit, safety at that moment seemed a very desirable condition – but it was every bit as much a trap as this sardine-can cabin. Even more so, because it would imprison her not just for a few terrifying moments but for the rest of her life.

Kay was waiting for her answer. 'There is someone,' she said. 'He's in the air force now.'

'What's he like?'

'Tall, fair, crop-duster turned freight company owner. A pretty regular guy.' Another wash of longing. What the hell was the matter with her?

'He sounds nice.'

'He is nice.' *Too nice. A sight too nice for his own good.* Nancy thought of the brief phone conversation they'd had before she left. Joe hadn't tried to dissuade her when she'd told him what she planned to do, hadn't told her he didn't want her to go, just to take care of herself and that he loved her. His lack of censure had only made Nancy feel more guilty, more trapped, as if she was taking advantage of him and his good nature.

'Hang on to him,' Kay advised. 'Men like that don't come by like yellow cabs.'

Nancy said nothing. Kay was right, of course. A man like Joe was a rare treasure. But it didn't make him right for her.

The guns were silent now, the cabin dark. No more flashes, only the glow of Kay's cigarette.

'I think it's over,' Nancy said, and wasn't sure if she was talking about the attack or Joe.

'Looks that way. No adventures in the lifeboat with the gorgeous lieutenant tonight.' Kay stubbed out her cigarette, climbed back into her bunk. 'Night, Nancy.'

'Night.' The throb of the ship's engines, strangely soothing now, pulsated to the very core of her. Nancy closed her eyes and let the sound rock her to sleep.

After almost two weeks at sea the SS Culloden Queen sailed up the Avon Gorge into Bristol. The girls were on deck, watching the pilot ship guide them up a narrow channel between high, grassy cliffs, and as usual Miriam de Sousa was trying to impress with her superior knowledge.

'See that bridge up ahead? Quite a sight, isn't it? That was built by Isambard Kingdom Brunel. He built other things too . . . railways and stuff. And the first iron ship – the SS Great Britain . . .'

The bridge certainly was impressive, a vast curve of gleaming superstructure spanning the gorge from side to side with no visible means of support. That, Nancy supposed, was why it was called a suspension bridge. She thought of saying so, and changed her mind. She didn't want to start Miriam off on another lecture.

She was impressed, too, by the weather. She had always understood that England was cold and wet, but today the sky was a clear washed blue and after the biting winds of the Atlantic, the sun felt good on her face and bare arms.

Already, though, time was getting up to its strange tricks again, stretching and then snapping back like an elastic band through periods of frustrating delay and hectic activity.

When the recruits disembarked, RAF personnel were there to meet them. They escorted the girls on a four-hour journey to London, where they were to meet up with Jackie Cochran. Nancy was shocked at the devastation she saw in the capital – the water-filled bomb craters, buildings reduced to heaps of rubble, and the houses with one wall torn off to reveal the rooms inside reminded her of a doll's house she'd craved as a child. Except that sliding off the front of the doll's house had revealed miniature furniture lovingly arranged and rearranged, little beds made up with tiny coverlets, a kitchen stacked with pots and pans. These houses were a grotesque parody of the homes they had once been. The upper floors sloped drunkenly, furniture was suspended over the abyss, wallpaper was torn off and curtains billowed sadly. And the sight of them brought home to Nancy the shocking reality of a war-torn city more sharply than a million newspaper photographs could ever have done.

Jackie had arranged – and paid – for her protégées to stay for two days at the Savoy Hotel. Amidst all the devastation it seemed oddly untouched: proud, grand, thumbing its nose at the German bombers, determined to keep up appearances and old-world standards. The room Nancy and Kay shared was the epitome of luxury – after the hard bunks in the narrow cabin neither of them could resist throwing herself onto the feather beds and rolling around, laughing – but the food they'd been looking forward to was distinctly disappointing. Not even the Savoy could entirely beat the rationing, Nancy presumed. But she was in England, half a world from home, and she was determined that whatever the drawbacks, she was going to make the most of it.

'You girls are going to Luton,' Jackie said.

They were sitting in deep leather chairs in the sumptuous lounge of the Savoy, drinking Indian tea from dainty porcelain cups. On the occasional table between them was the remains of a batch of sandwiches, artistically cut into dainty triangles but tasting of nothing. Jackie, glamorous as ever in a dress that could well have been a Balenciaga, silk stockings and high-heeled, peep-toed shoes, held centre stage like a queen surrounded by courtesans.

Luton. That meant nothing to Nancy at all.

'It's a training base,' Jackie went on. 'You'll familiarise yourselves with the aircraft you'll be flying, do some technical courses at ground school and learn navigation. You'll be there for about two months in all.'

There was a sudden explosion – a splutter of indignation and the sharp chink of a teacup going down on a saucer.

'You've got to be kidding!' All eyes swivelled to Miriam de Sousa.

Jackie raised a perfectly plucked eyebrow and fixed Miriam with a cool questioning gaze. 'I beg your pardon?'

'Well, I sure hope you are,' Miriam went on, undeterred. 'If you're not, it's nothing but a shocking waste of time, and I'm not happy with it at all. I have over a thousand hours on my log book. I passed all my tech exams years ago. I came here to fly, not to hang around for two damned months while some English stuffed shirt tries to teach me something I know better than he does!'

There was a horrified silence. Nancy couldn't believe that anyone, even the brash and obnoxious Miriam, would dare to speak to Jackie Cochran like that.

'If you're going to take that attitude, you're going to be sorry,' Jackie said coolly. 'Flying in England is a very different proposition from flying at home, as you'll soon find out.'

'So what the hell was the point of testing out on a Harvard in Montreal?'

'To make sure we weren't all wasting our time signing you up in the first place. You're in the ATA now, and whether you like it or not, you'll abide by their rules.' Jackie cut her gaze, glancing at each of the girls in turn but ignoring Miriam completely. 'Now, the plan is this. I've hired a couple of cars and we'll drive down to Luton tomorrow. Your luggage will stay here in the Savoy storeroom until you get a permanent posting. We'll leave first thing in the morning, so you'll have time to settle into your billets well before blackout. Any questions?'

Most of the girls were still too stunned by Miriam's rudeness to be able to think of anything else, but Kay, irrepressible as ever, dispelled the crackle of tension that still hung awkwardly in the air.

'Yes, ma'am. Where the hell am I going to get another silk négligé in England if the Savoy takes a direct hit and my trunk goes up with it?' she asked with a characteristic flick of her shining blonde mane.

Jackie smiled. 'I'll find you one, my dear, I promise,' she said, and Nancy was in no doubt that she would. Jackie's authority was absolute, the force of her personality overwhelming. Nancy had been full of admiration for her before, now it was close to adulation. And she felt quite sure that someone who could put the dreadful Miriam de Sousa so thoroughly in her place would have no trouble at all in finding a silk négligé for Kay if the need arose, rationing or no rationing.

III

Just a few days at Luton was enough to convince Nancy that the rigorous ATA training programme made good sense. Miriam de Sousa might still consider it beneath her and be scoffing and complaining – albeit a good deal more quietly – but Nancy was more than grateful for it. As Jackie had pointed out, flying in England was a very different kettle of fish from flying back home. To begin with, there were new planes to get used to, but that was the easy part compared with navigation. Like all the other American girls, Nancy was accustomed to being able to follow wide straight roads and railroad tracks to reach a destination, and when she tried to use a map she found it was to a much smaller scale than American ones, and with unfamiliar markings and confusing symbols. There was no radio contact with the ground, which meant the use of a compass was vital. And worst of all, Morse code had to be learned. Nancy's head spun as she tried to master it.

She could not have had a better instructor, though. Besides being a very experienced flier, Norah Taft was also patient and understanding, and it was not long before she let Nancy go solo in a Puss Moth.

That night, when she went back to the lodgings she, Kay and Miriam were sharing in a pretty cottage not far from the airfield, she was still high on adrenalin and glowing with pride.

'I went solo today,' she told the others as they sat down for an evening meal of tinned meat fritters, fried potato and peas picked fresh from the cottage garden.

Miriam smirked – both she and Kay had made their first solos several days ago – but Kay raised her glass.

'Well done, kid! This might be home-made ginger beer, but we can always pretend it's champagne. Here's to you – and all of us.'

She reached across to clink her glass with Nancy's, then turned to Miriam. 'To us, Miss de Sousa!'

Miriam rolled her eyes and shook her head dismissively, but she raised her glass all the same. 'To us. And to giving that bastard Adolf a bloody nose!'

Suddenly they were all laughing, happy and exhilarated. And Nancy quite forgot that she still had a great deal to learn about flying in England.

Norah Taft was moving on. Her husband was an ATA pool commander at a base in the north of England and he had engineered a posting for her there so that they could be together. She gave Nancy the news one day as they returned from yet more cross-country practice. For all the hard work she had put in, Nancy still found navigation difficult, though she was getting better at spotting landmarks and linking them with the hieroglyphics on the map.

'I'd rather you heard it from me than from some gossip at the base.' Norah spoke in just the accent Nancy had imagined – until she'd learned differently – that everyone in England spoke, her tone crisp, her vowels cut-glass.

Nancy's heart sank. Rumours had been circulating for some days, but she'd hoped they were untrue. She liked Mrs Taft.

'You'll be moving on yourself soon,' Norah said, noticing her crestfallen expression. 'You're a good pilot, Nancy – a natural. Technically, you're one of the best I've ever taught. You've just got to get your navigation up to speed and there'll be no stopping you.'

'I've been an absolute duffer about it, I know,' Nancy said ruefully.

Norah smiled. 'It isn't your strongest point, I agree, but you're getting there. You were a lot more confident today. Actually, I think you're ready to do a solo cross-country. Would you like to have a go tomorrow?'

Nancy's spirits lifted. 'You bet!'

'OK. Work out a P-log for a triangle taking in White Waltham and Sywell. You'll land at both places and get your form signed so that I know you actually got there and didn't do anything to disgrace yourself. Get it right and I'll pass you as competent on cross-country. Get it wrong and I'm afraid it will be up to your new instructor to decide your fate. And he might not be prepared to cut you as much slack as I am.'

'He?'

'Yes. He's an RAF pilot – and he'll expect RAF standards.'

'Oh, sugar.' But Nancy knew that if she could only pass her cross-country solo there was no reason she should have any problems. She was confident that her general flying ability was good enough to satisfy the most exacting instructor and that she could handle any plane he decided to throw at her.

She grinned at Norah Taft. 'I'd better make sure I get it right then, hadn't I?'

To begin with, everything went well. Too well. Norah had approved the P-log – the pilot's log – that Nancy had prepared, working out the headings she needed to set taking wind speeds into account, and sent her off in a Puss Moth, eager and determined to get this right. She flew the first leg to White Waltham, landed and got her chit signed, then took off again heading north for Sywell. It was the longest leg and, Nancy thought, the most difficult, but she found it without too much trouble. She landed, had a cup of coffee, and took straight off again, heading for home. And then things began to go wrong.

She had no one to blame but herself for what happened, Nancy knew. She should have known that overconfidence is a recipe for disaster – she did know it, but she was enjoying herself too much to listen to the voice of caution; enjoying the freedom and the euphoria of success. She wasn't ready to go home yet. She wanted to stay up here a bit longer, purring along in the blue silence, playing hide and seek with the clouds. She flew a little detour and then another, confident she could pick up her heading again and find her way home. Only to realise to her horror that she had not the faintest idea where she was.

Nancy swore softly. How the hell could she have been so stupid? She peered down at the countryside beneath, a vast expanse of green divided by hedges into irregular squares and rectangles. Patches of darker green indicated clumps of trees, and small clusters of houses were dotted about randomly. But the roads joining them were narrow winding grey ribbons and the occasional sparkle of sunlight on water showed only a meandering stream. There was absolutely nothing Nancy could link to anything on her map so as to identify her position. In desperation she swung the nose of the Puss Moth, wondering if there was something she was missing directly underneath her. It happened; fly too accurate a course and you could end up failing to see a landmark because it was right under the nose. Not this time, though. Nancy felt the first stirrings of panic and talked herself calm again: You're not really lost. You just don't know where you are. Quit worrying and concentrate . . .

She spread the map across her knee and descended to two thousand feet. Then she tipped the wing, flying a wide orbit in the hope of spotting some landmark she could identify. Nothing. Just the vast expanse of green and a few scattered houses. Smoke was coming from the chimney of one of them, not rising straight up but wafting in bursts to make a fuzzy line almost parallel with the ground, and at this height Nancy could see the trees bending and blowing in shimmering puffballs.

That, most likely, was the cause of the problem. The wind had changed direction and strengthened since she'd worked out the compass headings. She balanced the clipboard on top of the map on her knee, unhooked the pencil and tried to make a few calculations. But maths had never been her strong point and now, with anxiety nagging at the pit of her stomach, her brain was beginning to addle and she wasn't at all sure she was getting the sums right.

Head south and pray. At least she had plenty of fuel. Sooner or later she'd come across an airfield. Then she'd land, have a cup of coffee to steady her nerves, and work out a new P-log that would get her home. But the Puss Moth seemed to move as slowly as a lazy bumblebee so that the flight she'd been so enjoying seemed interminable now, and just to make things worse Nancy could see a thick bank of black cloud encroaching on the clear blue sky up ahead of her.

A few minutes later and the first spots of rain spattered on the windscreen. Nancy gritted her teeth. Damn this English weather! There'd been no mention of thunderstorms in the met reports, but the conditions now had all the hallmarks of one. Heavy cumulus and a sudden change in wind speed and direction were not good signs. It wouldn't be the kind of tropical storm that happened back home in Florida – or at least, Nancy didn't think it would be! – but any thunderstorm is bad news for a light aircraft. The updraughts and downdraughts cause violent turbulence and the wind shear makes handling difficult. Hail can damage the airframe and windows, lightning strikes can endanger the electrical equipment.

Nancy had no intention of getting caught in a thunderstorm if she could help it. Only a fool would fly into a cumulonimbus, and that was the way the cloud ahead of her was forming up. Already the Puss Moth was being buffeted; it dropped suddenly as it hit an air pocket – maybe two hundred feet in a few seconds – and Nancy bounced so violently in her harness that her head thwacked into the roof, showering her with dust and some thick black particles of she knew not what. She banked and turned the Puss Moth away from the storm. Never mind finding an airstrip – she'd land in a field. There were plenty of them. Just as long as she watched out for cows and overhead power cables she should be fine. She levelled out at a thousand feet, chose a likely field, and checked the wind direction again to enable her to fly a circuit and land into it. She was praying now: Don't let there be any hidden ditches. Let there be a farm nearby. Or a farmer on a tractor to give me a lift to civilisation. And, please, let me get down without bending this damned plane . . .

As Nancy turned on to the base leg of her circuit she was startled to see another single-engined aircraft south of her and apparently descending. She craned forward, the clipboard on her lap digging into her ribcage as she peered out of the rain-speckled windscreen. Was this other plane putting down in a field to escape the storm as she was? Or was there something across the ridge of trees that she had missed? Another hasty glance at the dark towering bank of cumulonimbus told Nancy that she had a few minutes at most to spare before it overtook her. She made up her mind, lifted the nose and climbed again. The other plane had disappeared now behind the bank of trees along the ridge, but Nancy headed in the direction she had last seen it, lower in the sky, and definitely coming in to land.

She cleared the ridge, and could hardly believe what she saw. An airstrip, a narrow flat band cut into the darker green of the long grass, and a building, too long and low to be a house, to one side of it. Relief made her stomach go weak. She powered on, heading for the spot where she judged the other plane had begun its final descent. It had landed now; though rain was lashing her windows in a great wash of ever-widening circles Nancy could see the plane taxiing towards the building. She lined up, reduced power and put on flaps, forcing herself to concentrate on what she was doing, though the rush of exhilaration was tingling in her blood like a shot of hard liquor. She was going to make it. She could land, wait out the storm, find out where she was and plot a course home. With any luck, no one would be any the wiser.

Nancy felt the nasty gusting crosswind as she made her final approach, and the tingle of exhilaration became a tingle of awareness of danger. She crabbed in, feet poised on the rudder pedals, ready to correct where necessary. Lower, lower, with the grass speeding by beneath the wheels, lifting one wing slightly against the wind. Her hands gripped the yoke for grim death; without knowing it she bit her lower lip so hard that she drew blood. And then she was down, her wheels touching the mown grass of the runway, and she was braking, carefully, so as not to go into a skid, and slowing to a taxi. She let her breath out on a sigh of relief, headed off the runway towards the building where the other plane had parked.

And disaster struck. A sudden violent gust of wind caught the port wing, lifting it sharply. The yoke bucked under her hands, and before she could do a single thing, the whole world was turning upside down.

For a moment time seemed to stand still. Nancy was in a vacuum. Thought processes, feeling, comprehension were all frozen in utter stillness. Then the blood rushed into her head and she realised she was hanging ignominiously, still strapped into her seat, but with grass become sky and sky ground. The clipboard had wedged painfully against her ear, the map lay half across her face. Her bag was on the roof beside her, its contents scattered. Powder from her compact was everywhere, a fine layer of pink dust that made Nancy want to sneeze. Embarrassment and horror washed over her in a hot tide. Unbelievable as it seemed, she'd flipped right over!

Nancy scrabbled for the buckle of her harness, but her hands were shaking so badly she couldn't find the release catch. As she struggled with it, the door of the Puss Moth was wrenched open and Nancy found herself looking at a pair of trouser-clad legs and stout leather flying boots.

'Are you all right?' A man's voice, deep, a little rough, unmistakably English.

'What do you think?' Nancy's voice was muffled by her shirt, bunched over her mouth. Never in her life had she felt so foolish, so ashamed. 'I can't get my harness undone.'

The man reached across into the cabin, water dripping off his leather flying jacket onto Nancy's face. For a moment she was almost buried in the bulk of him, then he had released the catch of the safety harness and she tumbled out of it, landing in an awkward heap.

'Whew – it smells like a French brothel in here,' he said.

My perfume. My favourite damn perfume. The bottle in her bag must have broken. Nancy was angry now as well as humiliated. Mostly with herself. But also with this man for witnessing her humiliation.

'Get me the hell out of here!'

'OK, calm down.' He helped her scramble out of the plane; as she straightened up she went a little dizzy. She clutched at his arm to steady herself, felt even more embarrassed.

'I'm sorry.' Nancy let go his arm, leaned instead against the fuse-lage.

'No problem.' He was looking at her quizzically, hazel eyes narrowed in a sculpted, angular face. His hair, slick with the rain, was brushed away from a high forehead. Nancy wished he wasn't so damned attractive. For some perverse reason it only made her feel the more foolish. 'Let's get you inside. We'll sort this out when the storm passes.'

He turned for the low, white-painted building, glanced back over his shoulder, so that the collar of his jacket framed a strong jaw-line. 'Are you all right now?'

'Fine.' She wasn't, but she wasn't going to admit it. She walked past him as briskly as her shaking legs would allow.

The door of the hut, garish green, was ajar and another man appeared. He was older – perhaps in his late fifties or early sixties

– casually dressed in open-neck checked shirt and corduroys, with a thatch of iron-grey hair and a face that was both ruddy and weathered. When he smiled, deep creases cracked the surface of the skin like a piece of old leather. He was smiling now, his eyes, startlingly bright blue, twinkling with what looked suspiciously like amusement.

'Well, I've seen a lot in my time, m'dear, but I've never seen anybody loop the loop six feet off the ground.'

Wet through, badly frightened and with the plane she'd been entrusted with upside down on a grass strip miles from anywhere, Nancy would have told this man in no uncertain terms that she didn't find it in the least funny if she had dared trust herself not to burst into tears.

'Dear, dear, I don't know.' He spoke with a soft country burr; Nancy thought that he looked and sounded like a farmer. 'You'd best come in and have a cup of tea. I reckon you need it after a spectacular entrance like that.'

'I couldn't help it!' she protested. 'The wind just took me.'

'Ah, these things happen.' He ambled over to a card table where a brown pottery teapot stood alongside an assortment of chipped mugs. 'You'll feel better when you've got a cup of tea inside you. Lucky I'd just brewed up, if you ask me. And I should sit down, if I were you. You look proper shook up.'

He indicated a slatted folding chair beside another card table piled high with paperwork and what looked like aeronautical publications. Through the window, Nancy could see the man who had rescued her walking round the Puss Moth and inspecting it, seemingly oblivious to the rain that was still sheeting down. He walked with a limp, she noticed. She crossed to the chair and sat down, glad to be relieved of the effort to control her wobbly knees. The older man spooned sugar generously into one of the mugs, poured the tea and brought it over to her.

'Here you be. It's hot, mind.'

Nancy sipped the tea. It *was* hot, scaldingly so, and syrupy sweet, but as it hit her stomach the trembling in her hands eased. Nothing could lessen her sense of shame, though. How could she have been so damned stupid? She'd never crashed a plane before in her entire life; always been fairly scornful of people who did. Now, knowing it was an RAF Puss Moth that she'd bent made it seem a thousand times worse.

The door opened and the younger man came in, shaking the water off himself like a dog.

'Have I done much damage?' Nancy asked anxiously.

'Hard to tell before we get it righted, and in this rain . . .' He glanced towards the card table. 'Is there another cup of tea in the pot, George? I'm spitting feathers.'

'Reckon I can squeeze one out for you, Mac.' The older man shook the pot, grinned. 'You know me – I make enough to sink a battleship.'

'Why else do you think I drop in on you so often?' Mac's voice was almost drowned out by the hammering of the rain on the tin roof of the hut and an ominous crack of thunder almost directly overhead. He took a mug of tea from the man named George and in the flicker of lightning that illuminated the room Nancy noticed a livid white scar running diagonally across the back of his hand.

'So.' He raised an eyebrow in Nancy's direction. 'What's your excuse?'

The directness of the question startled her. 'I beg your pardon?'

'For dropping in on George without warning. OK – don't tell

me. The storm. But I'm still intrigued. I take it you're one of Jackie Cochran's girls.'

'How do you know that?' Nancy asked, surprised.

'You've got a Yankee accent and you're flying a Puss Moth. It doesn't take a genius to work it out. Where are you based?'

'Luton.'

He settled himself against a dilapidated glass-fronted kitchen dresser, sipping his tea. 'Tell me more.'

Nancy shrugged, disconcerted. 'Not a great deal to tell. I was doing a triangular cross-country when the storm blew up. I saw you landing and decided to do the same. I didn't want to be flying in that.'

'Quite. So what was your route?'

Nancy found herself wondering why he was asking so many questions. Perhaps it was just to pass the time until the storm blew over. But considering he had just pulled her out of an upside-down plane it seemed rude not to answer.

'Luton to White Waltham, White Waltham to Sywell, Sywell back to Luton.'

'You were well off course then.'

Nancy's face flamed. 'I was not off course!'

His eyes levelled with hers. There was something infuriatingly arrogant about his half-smile and the way he was leaning back casually against the dresser, booted feet crossed at the ankles, one hand thrust in the pocket of his flying jacket, which he had unzipped to reveal an open-necked shirt which looked suspiciously like RAF issue. Judging her, Nancy thought furiously.

'Oh, I assure you that you were.'

Nancy bridled at his tone, humiliation grating on the remnants of her tattered pride. She didn't want these men – whoever they were – writing her off as a dizzy woman pilot.

'So I flew a detour.' She tried to sound breezy, confident, but all the while she knew that before long she was going to have to admit she didn't know where the hell she was so that she could get in touch with Luton, give them her location and report what had happened.

'Do you often take joy rides on a whim?'

For Nancy it was the last straw. 'Do you always grill other pilots?' she countered. 'I was not joy-riding, as you put it, but if I was I can't see what business it is of yours.'

He raised an eyebrow, looking at her in a way no one had looked at her since she was a wayward schoolgirl up in front of the class teacher for misbehaviour.

'Who's your tutor?'

'To be honest, I can't see what business that is of yours either,' she said tartly.

'Oh, I assure you it is my business. I'd like to know which of our instructors was foolish enough to think you were competent to be let loose with a Puss Moth.'

Nancy went cold, hot, cold again. *Which of our instructors . . .* Dammit, he must be ATA. She was never going to live this down. Joy-riding, as he'd called it. Getting lost. Turning over a Puss Moth. Making it smell like a French brothel . . .

The man called George was chuckling into his tea. 'Best tell her who you are, Mac. Should have told her straight away, if you ask me.'

'I wanted to hear what she had to say for herself first.' He straightened. RAF bearing now as well as RAF-issue shirt. 'Time for introductions then, Miss . . . ?'

'Kelly. Nancy Kelly.'

'Miss Kelly. My name is James Mackenzie. I am an RAF squadron leader and at present I'm on secondment as deputy commander at White Waltham. In a few days' time, however, I shall be starting a stint as an instructor at Luton whilst a replacement is found for a certain Mrs Norah Taft.' His eyes levelled with hers. 'You are one of her pupils, I imagine, and she was trying to get you through your tests before she leaves. Nice try, but unfortunately it didn't work, did it?'

The ground seemed to open up beneath her. *Oh my God. My new instructor. The second highest ranking officer at White Waltham.* She'd really blown it now. She couldn't expect leniency from a disciplined RAF officer. She'd be sent home in disgrace, and that would be the end of her war.

'I'm sorry, sir.' It stuck in her throat. He should have told her, she thought. Keeping it from her really wasn't playing fair.

The storm was passing, the hammer of rain on the tin roof less insistent, the thunder rumbling further away.

'OK, Miss Kelly, now that we know where we stand, we'd better try to sort out this mess you've got yourself into.'

She looked at him standing there, arms folded, superiority written all over him, enjoying every moment of this, and thought he was the most arrogant man she had ever met.

And also, though it pained her to think it for even a moment, by far and away the most attractive.

IV

Nancy was a born optimist, not given to fits of depression or violent mood swings. But in the days that followed the humiliating débâcle of her cross-country a thick black cloud of shame and misery hung over her and there was a hollow of dread where her stomach should have been.

Norah Taft, understandably, was not only disappointed in her, but also furious. She had summoned Nancy to her office, a tiny room not much bigger than a cupboard, into which a desk, a filing cabinet and a couple of hard, upright chairs had been crammed. A large framed photograph of her husband stood on the filing cabinet, a smiling man with a huge handlebar moustache. But Norah Taft was not smiling.

'You do realise, Nancy, that I could make a report to the effect that you are not suited to the ATA?' Her tone was stern, her gaze steely.

'I couldn't help it, Mrs Taft. The wind just took me . . .' She'd said it so many times – to friends and colleagues, who seemed to find the whole thing amusing, as well as to critical figures of authority – that she thought she was beginning to sound like a cracked record.

'I accept that. It's very fortunate for you that the plane wasn't badly damaged and that Squadron Leader Mackenzie saw what happened and is prepared to confirm there was nothing you could have done to prevent it. That's not really the issue, though, is it? What we'd all like to know is how you came to be so far off course. I know your navigation leaves something to be desired, but it was a straightforward route. If you can't manage that after all the practice we've done . . .' She left the sentence hanging in the air, but she didn't need to finish it for Nancy to know what she meant. She was going to be written off as a failure; sent home in disgrace.

'I wasn't really lost,' she said in desperation. 'It was all going so well and I was enjoying myself and—'

'Stop right there, Nancy.' Norah held up her hand like a policeman stopping traffic. 'I don't want to hear any more.'

'But—'

'No!' That hand was unwavering directly in front of Nancy's face. 'You were trying to avoid the storm and you got lost, as I understand it. You shouldn't have, but you did. On that basis I am going to recommend further practice. You're a good pilot and it would be a pity if you were stood down because you've been a little slower than some in learning to navigate in England, because I believe you will get there. An irresponsible attitude, on the other hand, would make this quite a different matter. If I thought for one moment that you'd been using our aircraft to jazz around for your own enjoyment, then I would have no option but to recommend you as unsuitable for the service. There's no room for renegades.'

Nancy could feel the hot colour creeping up her neck. Norah

Taft knew, but she didn't want Nancy to admit to it. Once the words were said, Norah would have felt obliged to report the matter. She preferred to accept responsibility for what had happened herself, though it meant putting her own judgement in sending Nancy on a cross-country into question.

'Yes, Mrs Taft,' she said meekly.

'Good.' Norah Taft uncapped her fountain pen and pulled a sheaf of papers towards her. Nancy had an uncomfortable feeling it might be a report on her. 'What happens next will be up to your new tutor, who may well have already formed an opinion on your capabilities.'

Nancy's flush deepened. All too clearly she could hear Squadron Leader Mackenzie's sarcastic: '*Do you often take joy rides on a whim?*' He knew as well as Norah Taft what she had done. And with his RAF background he might well come down even harder on her.

'I hope you won't let me down again, Nancy,' Norah Taft said sternly. Then the hint of a smile lifted a corner of her mouth. 'You've got lots of good qualities – spirit and enthusiasm, to name but two – and your flying ability is not in doubt. Don't spoil yourself by impetuosity and a lack of discipline. Just remember either is dangerous. Together, they're a lethal combination. Put simply, they could kill you.'

Nancy nodded humbly. Mrs Taft was right, she knew.

Squadron Leader James Mackenzie arrived at Luton two days later and the story of how an RAF officer came to be seconded to the ATA preceded him. He had been wounded during the Battle of Britain and had not yet passed fit for operational flying. That accounted for his limp and the livid scar on the back of his hand, Nancy realised. He had also been decorated for gallantry – the DFC, it was said – and that added to the aura of glamour that went with his uniform.

Kay was clearly impressed. 'He's a hunk, isn't he?' she said enthusiastically as the girls ate cheese sandwiches and drank tea in the canteen at lunchtime on the day he took up his duties. 'I could fall for him in a big way.'

Miriam de Sousa raised an eyebrow. 'Isn't that what Nancy already did?'

Nancy wanted to hit her.

Kay groaned. 'Give it a rest, Miriam. It could have happened to any of us.'

'I don't think so.'

Kay ignored her. 'Have you seen him yet. Nancy? What did he say to you?'

'That he'd give me a nav test himself.'

She had gone into the briefing room quaking with trepidation, and his opening words had not helped. 'Miss Kelly. We meet again.'

'At least we're both dry this time,' Nancy countered with a flippancy she was far from feeling. 'And I'm not upside down.'

The faintest smile quirked his mouth and creased his eyes. 'Given the circumstances, perhaps it would be best if we started again from scratch. I've had good reports of you from your previous instructor – apart from some criticism of your navigation skills – so I suggest we take it from there. If that's OK with you.'

He was giving her another chance. Nancy knew she had been very lucky.

'Sure is.'

'So, let's get to know one another. You've probably heard all kinds of stories about how awkward RAF personnel can be, especially ones who were already in the service before the war began, and on the whole they're true. We were trained to very high standards. Fall below them and you'd get kicked out so fast your feet wouldn't touch the ground. I appreciate that the ATA is made up of civilians who may have been used to flying by very different rules, and that sometimes chances have to be taken and difficult decisions made in order to get the planes where they're needed for the war effort. But the ethos should be the same. If you want to kill yourself, well, that's up to you. But if you're given taxi duties the lives of other, experienced pilots are in your hands, and we don't want to lose valuable planes either.'

'I realise that.'

'But do you understand about the decisions you'll have to take daily? Perhaps a plane is required urgently in Lossiemouth.' He saw her uncertain expression and qualified. 'Lossiemouth – north of Scotland. You get the weather forecast and it's a bit dicey. But Lossiemouth are screaming for your plane. You decide to go. You run into cloud and it's getting thicker. Do you go on and hope it's clearer ahead – or higher – or do you put down somewhere and wait? It's your call entirely.'

'I'm used to making decisions.'

'Yes,' he said. 'I think you are.' He grinned at her crookedly, and something very peculiar happened to Nancy.

Afterwards, the only way she could have described the way she felt in that moment was to compare it to the way it felt to stall a plane, and that would mean nothing at all to someone who isn't a pilot.

Stalling a plane isn't at all the same thing as stalling a car – it's not engine stall, but wing stall, when the airflow over the wings that keeps you airborne breaks down. Control and height are lost and the plane is in danger of going into a spin. Wing stall should never happen by accident, but it's something a trainee pilot has to make happen so as to know what it feels like and how to recover. It's done by taking off power and raising the nose so as to alter what's known as 'the angle of attack', and gradually the plane becomes less stable.

Nancy could well remember her lessons in stalling, the eerie feeling of courting disaster, even though she knew she had taken the plane high enough to give herself plenty of time to correct the stall and get the plane flying normally again. She remembered the vacuum of silence, using the rudder pedals to keep the wings straight and level and pulling back on the control column knowing that at any moment things were going to begin to go badly wrong. When it does, the airspeed drops; the controls begin to feel heavy and unresponsive beneath your hands; the airframe begins to shudder around you: the raucous sound of the pre-stall warning buzzer shatters the silence. And then it happens. The nose drops and you start to sink so your stomach falls away and you know you're not flying any more.

You have to act quickly then, releasing the back pressure on the controls and lowering the nose. If you put on power you may drop only fifty feet, if you're recovering without power it could be two hundred feet. And then, miraculously, you're flying again.

As she looked at Squadron Leader James Mackenzie, sitting there behind the desk in the briefing room with that faintly amused smile quirking his mouth while he challenged her with his eyes, Nancy experienced exactly the same feelings as in that moment when the stall takes hold and the world shudders around you and you begin to freefall.

She looked at him and felt as if she were standing on the edge of a precipice. Her heart seemed to have stopped and the adrenalin was trembling in her veins. All her senses were screaming at her that now was the time to do something or be lost for ever. But when she was stalling a plane she knew exactly what was required of her to recover, and now her brain wasn't functioning at all.

'Right. I'll see you tomorrow then,' he said.

Nancy nodded, and left the briefing room as fast as her legs would carry her. In the ground school classroom for yet another lesson in Morse code, she stared at the dots and dashes and saw them come together in crinkles and creases around hazel eyes and a long livid scar running diagonally across the back of a suntanned hand. She gritted her teeth and warned herself to concentrate, but it was useless. And Nancy knew she was in danger of making an even bigger fool of herself than she already had.

There was no way she was going to admit that to Kay and Miriam, of course. Not even when Kay described the new tutor as 'a hunk'. No way she was even going to agree with her. It cut too close, too deep, opened a vein to the unfamiliar turmoil that had churned inside her and was still unsettling her. And it was too flip a description. Nancy had met plenty of 'hunks' in her time. She'd never felt this way before.

'You were darned lucky to get off so lightly,' Miriam said. She collected the last crumbs of her cheese sandwich on the tip of her finger and licked them off. 'You'll have to work extra hard now to impress him.'

'Don't I know it!' Nancy said, and wondered if she was talking about flying, or something else entirely.

It wasn't easy on any score. Eager as she was to impress James Mackenzie – or Mac, as he preferred to be known – most of the skills that usually came to her as naturally as breathing seemed to desert her. Or so she thought, though she consoled herself she couldn't have been as bad as she feared or he would have given up on her and sent her home after all. But she wasn't flying as well as she could, and knowing it made her edgy and defensive. The harder she tried to get things right, it seemed to her, the more stupid and clumsy she became, and when she had to work out new headings in flight her brain felt as if it were stuffed full of cotton wadding. All the while she could feel Mac's critical appraisal of every move she made. But even more distracting was the male smell of him, the brush of his arm against hers on the trim wheel and the body heat that generated between them, vibrant as static electricity and with all the power of a magnetic field.

Nancy was in constant turmoil. She'd never felt this way before and couldn't understand why she felt like it now. It was nothing he had said or done – not a word passed between them that wasn't strictly relevant to the business in hand – and sitting so close those touches were wholly unintentional and unavoidable. Yet when they were together Nancy felt heady excitement and when they were apart she couldn't get him out of her head.

She began to despair and curse the luck that had sent Norah Taft off to the north before she, Nancy, had finished her training. With Norah, she'd been getting there. Slowly but surely. Now, betwixt and between the constant criticism and the electric attraction, she felt she was getting nowhere.

'OK, Nancy. Here's a test for you.' It was a beautiful summer morning; they were out on yet another nav practice, but in a different plane – a Hawker Hart. Mac was relaxed in his seat but his eyes, ever watchful, were scanning the horizon. Nancy couldn't help but notice the craggy profile of his nose and chin above the collar of his flying jacket.

'Do you remember the airstrip where you flipped over in the thunderstorm? Let's see if you can find it again.'

'You've got to be kidding!'

'Not at all. You should be recognising landmarks by now as well as following headings. Find it – we'll land and have a cup of tea with George, if he's there.'

'I never want to see that place again!'

'I think it would do you good to lay a few ghosts. And I suggest you watch what you're doing,' he said, pointing to the altimeter.

'I am watching.' Nancy made a correction as quickly and stealthily as she could. 'I wish you wouldn't keep on at me all the time.'

'That's what I'm here for.' His voice was level, but the steely note was back. 'Come on now – find George's airstrip.'

Scanning the horizon, Nancy uttered a silent prayer. She could not help feeling her future in the ATA depended on this. And then, quite suddenly, she saw a ridge of trees she recognised. She headed for it and there, tucked into the fold beneath the hill, was the little airstrip.

She had no problems putting down on it this time. Wheels touched grass smoothly and she taxied towards the tumbledown shed and pulled up beside a light aircraft that looked as if it had seen better days. But the shed appeared to be shut up and there was no old Rover parked beside it.

'Doesn't look as if George is here today,' Mac commented.

'What is this place?' Nancy was checking her watch, pen poised over the clipboard on her knee.

'Don't bother with that.' With a gesture, Mac stopped her from recording the landing details, then answered her question. 'George flew with the RNAS in the last war and was bitten by the bug. He's from a farming family, and was expected to take on where his father left off, but as soon as he could afford it, he bought that old rust bucket and turned one of his fields into a landing strip. His flying is restricted now, of course, but he still likes to come up here whenever he can to escape from his wife and the bevy of land army girls he's got working for him these days.'

'I'm surprised he's not joined the ATA.'

'Given half a chance, he would. But he's got his farm to run. That's pretty important to the war effort too. He likes to frequent the pubs we do, though. That's how I came to meet him – over a pint in the local.' Mac opened his door of the plane.

'Are we staying then?' Nancy asked.

'No, just letting in some fresh air.' He unbuckled his harness. 'We might as well have a chat about your future while we're here. It's a pretty appropriate place really, isn't it?'

He said it unsmilingly – '*A pretty appropriate place . . .*' The scene of her disaster.

'I found it,' she said, too defensively.

'Not too great a feat when we were practically overhead.' Still no hint of praise. 'Your nav still leaves something to be desired, Nancy.'

Her heart plummeted; she felt like bursting into tears.

'You're going to fail me, aren't you?'

'Why do you think I'm going to fail you?' Something like amusement gleamed in those hazel eyes. As always, she rose to the bait.

'Because I'm rubbish at navigation, and I haven't done as well as I can with anything else either. You might as well just tell me and have done with it, instead of playing cat and mouse with me.

You enjoy doing that, don't you? You've done it right from the start. I'm a good pilot, but you make me feel like an idiot. I can't do my best when I know you're sitting there finding fault. It's just not right.'

'Have you done?' he asked.

'No, I haven't.' The bit was between her teeth now. 'I landed here that day because it seemed the sensible thing to do – the sort of necessary decision you go on about – but I wish I never had. We got off on the wrong foot and you're never going to let me forget it. To you, I'll always be the girl whose plane smelled like a French brothel. And it's not fair. Given the chance, I could have been an asset to the ATA. But you won't give me that chance. You'd rather humiliate me.'

Running out of breath, and steam, she tossed her clipboard onto the floor at her feet. 'Well, it's your loss.'

For a moment Mac said nothing at all. Then: 'Just for the record, I wasn't going to fail you,' he said. 'I was going to suggest we test you out on a Fairchild.'

A Fairchild. One of the aircraft used for ferrying pilots between airfields. Kay and Miriam had already tested out and passed; yesterday Miriam had done her first proper job, flying out as a passenger with a group of experienced pilots and bringing the Fairchild home empty herself. Kay was eagerly awaiting her turn. Mac had been on the point of testing her out too. And now she'd blown it.

Sick with misery, she reached for her clipboard. 'Oh, well, that's that, then.'

'You want to give it a go?'

Nancy couldn't believe her ears. 'The Fairchild?'

'That's the general idea.'

'Oh my God – yes! But . . .'

'I think it's time we gave you your head. That's when you do best.' His eyes levelled with hers. 'Just stop fighting me, Nancy.'

Something twisted inside her, something that had nothing whatever to do with her relief at not having been kicked out, or her exultation at the prospect of flying a Fairchild, and everything to do with that magnetic attraction she felt for him. It kicked her with the force of a bucking bronco, leaving her breathless. And for just a moment she could almost believe he felt it too. '*Just stop fighting me, Nancy . . .*'

'I'll arrange it for tomorrow then,' he said. 'Now, let's get this kite in the sky and head for home.'

She tested on the Fairchild and passed, and her delight had as much to do with the fact that she'd done well in his eyes as it did with knowing that soon she'd be flying one solo. She couldn't get him out of her head, any more than she could forget the excitement of what she was doing daily. Flying planes she'd never thought she'd get her hands on. Helping the war effort. And all in a country an ocean away from her old familiar life.

Nancy did her first ferry flight as a 'stooge' – sitting in the co-pilot's seat while a more experienced officer ferried half a dozen pilots to Filton to collect new planes from the BAC factories nearby, and flying the Fairchild home alone. She bought a bicycle that she saw advertised for sale on a card in a shop window as she thought it would be useful for getting around. And she felt her stomach tip each time Mac looked at her and their eyes met. Still nothing untoward had been said; there was nothing between them that went beyond the professional, and yet, when he looked at her she could almost believe he was feeling what she was feeling – that electric attraction so strong it was almost tangible. She couldn't stop thinking about him; there was a shininess about ordinary everyday tasks and she wished she was sharing them with him. She woke in the night from erotic dreams and pictured him flying his Spitfire in the Battle of Britain; wrapped her arms around herself and imagined they were his.

Back home in Florida, stifled by Joe's devotion, Dorothy's controlling ways, and a restriction on the flying that was her life, Nancy had longed for adventure. Now, in every possible way, it seemed she had found it. It was a package, this new life, a whole parcel of new experiences and emotions that was making her feel more alive than she'd ever felt before, nerve-tingling, intoxicating, unreal, a hiatus carved out of time. Nancy wanted it to go on for ever.

The dream came to an abrupt end one evening when she and the other girls were enjoying a well-earned drink at the local public house.

It had been an exciting day – at long last their new uniforms had arrived; they would no longer have to fly wearing the civilian slacks they had brought with them. The girls had tried them on and pranced around the living room of the cottage where they were billeted, admiring themselves and each other.

'Oh my God, do we look the business!' Kay had exclaimed.

The uniforms were dark blue, cut and styled like an RAF officer's, and the girls had been supplied with both trousers for practical purposes and a skirt for ceremonial parades. The shirt was light blue, the tie black, and there was a pair of black gloves which were to be carried or worn at all times. Nancy was less enamoured of the sensible regulation lace-up shoes, but they were more than compensated for by the USA flash on the uniform sleeve. She could just about see it when she looked at herself in the overmantel mirror, and it made her glow with patriotic pride. She liked the dark blue service cap with its ATA badge too. It suited her, she thought, and it sat jauntily on the newly bobbed hair, which she'd had to have cut to above shoulder length in line with regulations.

With some reluctance, though, they'd changed back into civvies to go to the pub, where they clustered around the bar drinking the cider and joining in the chatter about flying and the war in general. Spirits were high – news was coming through that the Allied forces were wreaking havoc against Rommel's troops at El Alamein, and 'Bomber' Harris, chief of Bomber Command, had warned the German people to expect devastating air raids on their industrial cities 'every night and every day, rain, blow or snow', which was the boost everyone badly needed.

It was hot in the bar and the air was thick and fuggy with cigarette smoke.

'Let's get some fresh air,' Kay suggested, and she, Nancy and half a dozen others went out into the still-warm night.

It was not yet dark, but the soft grey twilight that comes when the sun has just sunk below the horizon and the brightness of the day has faded to an echo of gossamer. The girls were sitting on a low stone wall, sipping their drinks, when Nancy saw a tall and instantly recognisable figure heading along the road in their direction.

Mac. As always, awareness prickled in her veins like a shot of Joe's Jack Daniel's, and she looked quickly away, pretending she hadn't noticed him.

'Evening, ladies.' His voice was deep and lazy. He was in civvies too – light-coloured slacks and a white shirt, open at the neck, with the sleeves turned up to elbow length.

'We don't often see you out here,' Kay said. Her tone was flirtatious; Nancy noticed she had rearranged her position on the wall so that her skirt rode up provocatively, exposing one knee and a little shapely thigh.

Mac grinned. 'Perhaps I should make it more often. Well, now that I am here, how about I get you all a drink? It looks as though your glasses are nearly empty, and this might be the last chance I get.'

'Oh my God, you're not leaving?' Kay said.

He laughed. ''Fraid not – not yet, anyway. A few more new recruits will have to put up with me yet. No, you're the ones who'll be moving on. You've more or less finished your familiarisation now, and it's time for you to do some more advanced training. As a matter of fact, the first orders came through this afternoon.'

They were all agog now.

'Whose?'

'Where are we going?'

'Oh – not Hamble, for goodness' sake!' That was Kay, reverting to type. Hamble was an all-female pool.

'All of us?'

Mac shook his head. 'Sorry, ladies, you'll have to wait for tomorrow for the details. Right now, I'm off duty. Now, how about these drinks? The offer's still on the table.'

'Well, if you're buying, mine's a whisky and black,' Miriam said.

'Cider, please.'

'Cider.'

'Nancy?'

He looked directly at her. In the soft pearly light it felt as if his eyes were caressing her. Dear Lord, she thought. I've had too much to drink already.

'Bitter lemon,' she said.

'Nothing stronger? Are you sure?'

'Sure as dammit. You know the saying – eight hours between bottle and throttle.'

Bobbie Morrison laughed. 'You planning on flying at five in the morning then, Nancy? Or are you so squiffy already you can't add nine and eight?'

'Oh, for Pete's sake! I just fancy a bitter lemon, OK?' She could feel herself blushing.

Mac wrote the orders down on the inside flip of a Players packet. He always smoked Players. To Nancy, they embodied his Englishness and she was fascinated by the bearded sailor in the picture on the front of the pack.

'Need some help carrying all that lot?' Kay offered.

He grinned. 'I'll manage.' And disappeared inside the pub.

'What a hunk.' Her tone was wistful.

'Nancy certainly thinks so, don't you, Nancy?' Why did Miriam always manage to sound spiteful, Nancy wondered.

'He's OK.' Dusk was falling rapidly now and she was glad of it. She didn't want anyone to see the colour that was heating her cheeks.

'Aw, come on! You never stop talking about him! Mac this . . . Mac that . . . And only a blind man could miss the way you look at him.'

'I do not!'

'You do! Like a moon-sick calf.'

'Admit it, Nancy. You do.' That was Bobbie.

This was awkward, Nancy thought. It was about to get worse.

'Unlucky for you that he's not available,' Miriam said. 'From what I hear, he already has a wife.'

'He's *married*? How do you know that?' Kay asked, stunned.

'Oh, just something I heard.' Miriam was enjoying herself. 'Why shouldn't he be married? Half the men on the base are. Why should it be such a surprise? He's hardly wet behind the ears. And wives aren't camp followers any more. Anyway, it's no good you getting starry-eyed about Mac, Nancy. He's already spoken for.'

'For the last time, I am not starry-eyed about Mac,' Nancy snapped, too sharply. Lying in her teeth. Lying to save face. Lying to hide from herself that she'd gone into freefall, her dreams disintegrating around her.

'Shh! He's coming back!' Bobbie, sharp-eyed. The subject was changed hastily.

Mac had the drinks on a tin tray, balanced waiter-like on the flat of his hand. Nancy took hers and muttered her thanks without looking at him. She wished the ground would open up and swallow her. If the other girls had noticed the way she felt about him, he'd probably noticed too. She thought of all the times when they'd been alone together, sitting closely side by side in a plane, facing one another across the briefing-room table, and burned up inside with embarrassment. She'd made a complete and utter fool of herself. For the moment that was her overriding emotion, and it left little room as yet for disappointment.

She only hoped she was one of the girls due to move on tomorrow. The greater the distance she could put between Mac and herself the better.

V

Nancy got her wish. Along with the other girls she was to move on to White Waltham for the next stage of her training. But it was, she soon discovered, a double-edged sword. Relieved as she was not to have to face Mac, the thought of not seeing him was a dull ache of regret that not even knowing he was already spoken for could obliterate, nor the thrill of getting her hands on bigger aircraft and perhaps even doing a proper job quite make up for.

Besides this, White Waltham was the ferry pool where Mac had been second in command before being seconded to Luton, and Nancy didn't know whether to be glad or sorry about that either. His ghost was everywhere; she could not escape it. She had thought his memory would fade with so much else to occupy her, but it didn't seem to be happening. She heard the deep burr of his voice in her ear as she struggled in ground school to master obscure technical details; he was beside her in the co-pilot's seat when she flew her first ferry job from Hullavington to South Cerney. It was as if, in the short time she'd known him, he'd crept under her skin, become a part of her. He was every beat of her heart, every breath she breathed. A stupid, futile obsession, she knew. But not one, it seemed, that she could conquer.

Compared with Luton, White Waltham was a bustling metropolis. Before the war, it had been used by the RAF; now it was the headquarters of the ATA, and besides being a busy ferry pool, it was home to the school where pilots could be trained on the more advanced aircraft.

Nancy and the other girls were billeted in a rambling country house surrounded by parkland, and the Stockley family who lived there treated them as honorary daughters. After the ex-army cots that had been provided for them in the commandeered cottage in Luton, it was bliss to sink into a comfortable bed at the end of a long day, and Mrs Stockley took it upon herself to send them off each morning on a breakfast fit for a king. As for the dinners that were served, they were nothing short of gourmet cuisine. There were eggs from the flock of hens that clucked around the barnyard, rabbit and pheasant from the estate, and fresh trout from the stream that ran through an orchard where the trees were laden with ripening fruit.

When they first arrived, the girls attended a ten-day course of ground school where they struggled with a plethora of technical information – hydraulic systems and retractable undercarriages, flap systems and different kinds of constant speed propellers and superchargers. Since gaining her licence, Nancy had never bothered much with technicalities – if a plane flew, that was good enough for her – but somehow she mastered the details and passed the written examinations. Then it was time to begin flying new aircraft types and Nancy felt far more at home.

Her instructor was a dry Scotsman named Sandy Bruce. At first she struggled with both his accent and his sense of humour, but Sandy was patient and thorough, and soon Nancy had Masters, Martinets, Hurricanes, and even an Oxford on her log book.

The social life at White Waltham was good too. Number 1 Ferry Pool buzzed, old-timers rubbing shoulders with trainees, men and women from all walks of life thrown together in one great melting pot. There were a number of Americans on the base, which made Nancy feel at home, and often they would go to Skindles Hotel for a drink and a snack, or to the American Club in Maidenhead, where they could swim in the pool. Sometimes they went up to London, where Nancy experienced her first air raid, and was shocked to discover she found it more exciting than frightening. And one balmy afternoon she, Kay and Miriam took a two-hour boat trip up the river and rounded it off with a meal of ham, egg and chips at a riverside pub.

By now Nancy had grown used to Miriam's little ways; she would never be a close friend, but Nancy had learned to ignore her sharp jibes and constant boasting, and admired her flying skills and the seemingly effortless ease with which she absorbed every new bit of information that was thrown at her. Miriam was her compatriot; it was only right that American gals should stick together.

Between her studies and her leisure activities, Nancy made time to write to Joe. She had a stack of letters from him, tied together with a ribbon, in her locker. Though more often than not a whole bunch would arrive together after a hiatus of several weeks, it was clear from the dates, entered in Joe's neat, sloping hand, that he wrote almost every day.

Knowing it made Nancy uncomfortable. It was good to get those letters, though they were so heavily censored they told her very little about what Joe was doing or even where he was. They were a link to home, and gave her some status too – a man who cared enough to write to her. But at the same time they reminded her of how trapped she had felt before Jackie Cochran had offered her a means of escape – and made her feel dreadfully guilty. She'd led him on, left him with the impression there was a chance for him, and it had been very wrong of her. Though there was nothing flowery or sentimental about the letters – that wasn't Joe's style – the very fact that he sat down and put pen to paper almost daily was evidence that she was on his mind a great deal more than he was on hers. Sometimes Nancy glowed with warmth towards Joe, sometimes she was consumed with impatience. Why couldn't he meet someone else and forget her, leave her free to do the same? But that rebounded on her too. She *had* met someone, and the cords of her own making held her more securely than the ones Joe had imposed ever had. She wrote back to him, unsure as to whether her letters would ever reach him, but knowing that if they did it would make his day. That much, at least, she owed him.

She worried about him sometimes. He was flying bombers, she knew, and bombers were horribly vulnerable. And when she did she recognised that a small selfish part of her was holding on to him for her own ends too, and the guilt worried at her again.

She began ferrying work, just a few short hops in the easier planes to begin with, then gradually more and more. Every day began with a sense of anticipation. The girls would walk through the manor grounds and along the orchard-lined lane, which had once been a rural idyll but was now busy with buses transporting in pilots and engineers. At the airfield they would sit around small, café-like tables drinking tea and coffee as they waited for 'Whitey', the ops officer, to line up the day's work. The moment word got around that the chits were out, the girls would head for the corridor outside the ops room where the chits were laid out on a long polished shelf, and fall on them eagerly. Next stop would be the met office to check weather conditions, and Maps and Signals for operational details of the airfields to which they would be flying. A taxi aircraft would be waiting for them, its route carefully worked out, to transport them to the airfields where their planes were waiting to be ferried. They would climb in, laden with parachute, blue-covered pocket book of *Ferry Pilot's Notes*, and a float that would enable them to buy a drink and a meal if they should happen to get stuck out. But that did not happen to Nancy in those early days. More often than not the Anson would arrive when she expected it. She would be able to enjoy the ride as it racketed around putting down at various airfields to pick up other pilots, and still be home in time to go out for a drink at the Riviera or Sunny's Club.

Little by little the crazy obsession that had been Mac began to fade. The sharp urgent knife-thrusts of longing came less often, the unreal aura of sad sweetness that had surrounded her like a cloud of perfume from the last of the summer roses dissipated and Nancy scarcely noticed its loss. She was herself again, her own person, no longer the slave to a futile dream.

And then one day she walked out across the tarmac to the taxi Anson and there he was, sitting in the pilot's seat. Nancy felt her knees go weak and her heart pounded so loudly that it drowned out even the roar of the engine as he ran his pre-flight power checks. And she knew that nothing had changed. She hadn't got over him at all. The attraction that was akin to madness was as potent as ever.

*   *   *

123

Mac was concentrating on what he was doing; Nancy wasn't sure if he'd seen her. She folded herself into her seat, self-conscious, yet at the same time unable to tear her eyes away from the back of his head and the way the collar of his flying jacket ruffled into his hair. Mac finished his power checks, exchanged a few words with Bert Tyndall, a veteran ATA flyer who was sitting behind him, then rotated further and raised an eyebrow at Nancy.

'Well, Miss Kelly!'

'Mac.' She hoped she didn't sound as awkward as she felt. 'What are you doing here?'

A corner of his mouth quirked up. 'This is my station. They've got a replacement for Norah. So I'm back.'

Nancy searched for some bright, witty rejoinder; failed dismally. The last ferry pilot had clambered aboard now and Mac turned his attention to taking off. Nancy felt the wheels lift, looked down on the sprawl of huts and new building, the thick dark green of orchards and the lighter palette of fields, watched the scatter of residences take on the proportion of dolls' houses and felt as queasy as a novice on a first flight. An elbow in her ribs; beside her Kay was grinning broadly.

'Return of the gorgeous Squadron Leader Mackenzie! Watch yourself, Nancy.'

'Oh, for heaven's sake!' Nancy was glad there was little opportunity for conversation above the noise of the aircraft engine.

How she managed her ferrying that day without incident, Nancy would never know. She agonised over whether it would be Mac who would come to collect her from Kemble, and if it was, what she could say to him without giving herself away; cringed as she wondered whether she'd given herself away already. But at the same time she was ridiculously happy, a swell of pure joy bubbling inside her. And she was ridiculously disappointed, too, when the Anson touched down at Kemble and she saw that it was not Mac at the controls, but Bill Jenson, ex-BOAC captain, the nicest man imaginable, but certainly not one to make her pulses race. She'd been granted a breathing space, time to muster her defences and plan her strategy.

That night she and Kay went to the club and Nancy flirted outrageously with a group of Americans they met there. One of them bought her a couple of drinks, and when they left she let him kiss her in the blacked-out car park. She tried very hard to rustle up some enthusiasm for this tall, good-looking man with a familiar accent, but long before his hands began to wander to the buttons of her blouse she had had enough. She pushed him away, demanding curtly to know what kind of girl he thought she was, and silently answering the question herself.

She should have felt guilty for cheating on Joe. He would be so hurt if he knew she had been kissing someone else, even if it was an American serviceman she would probably never see again. But worryingly Nancy was having difficulty conjuring up Joe's face, and strangely it didn't feel as if it was Joe she was cheating on at all. Bizarrely, it felt as if she was cheating on Mac.

For a few days their paths seemed not to cross at all, and Nancy was beginning to relax her guard and actually believe she was getting her feelings under control. It was, after all, a ludicrous situation. He was married, for goodness' sake. Not so much as a word out of place had passed between them. He was a senior officer, she had been his pupil. Very soon one or the other of them would be posted elsewhere. End of story.

Except, of course, that it wasn't.

* * *

125

September that year in England was bright blue and clear. The heat had gone out of the sun but it was still pleasantly warm. The brambles in the hedges were heavy with blackberries, the trees beginning to turn colour. Dawn came later and dusk earlier, making the flying day that much shorter.

Nancy had ferried a Hurricane to St Athan, an RAF air base in South Wales. The taxi pilot who came to collect her was Mac. As she was about to clamber aboard she saw that he was making hand signals at her and shaking his head. – *Stay where you are.* Then he jumped down onto the tarmac.

'Technical problems. I'm going to have to get it checked out before we go anywhere. I'd go back to the mess and get another cup of coffee if I were you.'

'Oh shucks.' She and Kay had planned to go to the flicks that night – Fred Astaire in *Holiday Inn.* 'Is it going to take long?'

'No idea. Depends what they've got on – and what the trouble is.'

He went off in search of an engineer and as he had suggested Nancy went to the mess for a coffee. She was still sitting there, surrounded by her paraphernalia with the remains of a bitter-tasting brew gone cold in front of her, when he came through the swing doors and headed for her table.

'Could be a long job. We mightn't even get away tonight. I'll know more in an hour or so.' He nodded in the direction of the remains of her coffee. 'You want another one?'

Nancy made a face. 'No, thanks – it's disgusting. It tastes of nothing but chicory.'

He grinned. 'The joys of wartime England. Powdered egg, tinned meat and dishwater coffee.'

'And dry cheese sandwiches. I never want to see another cheese sandwich as long as I live.'

'Better than nothing, though. Are you sure you don't want another coffee?'

He was poised to head for the urn and Nancy relented. If he was going to have one, then it seemed more sociable for her to have one too. More – normal.

'Go on then.'

He fetched the coffees and sat down opposite her.

'What about the other pilots you're supposed to be picking up?' she asked. 'Won't they be wondering where you are?'

'I've talked to White Waltham, asked them to make alternative arrangements. Bill Jenson won't be best pleased at having to turn out at this time of day – he's probably giving the poor old ops officer some stick at this very minute – but that's how it goes.' He stirred sugar into his coffee; sipped it. 'You're right about this. It's bally disgusting.'

'I did warn you. Will Bill Jenson come for me then?'

'Shouldn't think so. All the other pick-ups are around Brize Norton.' He grinned over the rim of his cup. 'I reckon you're stuck with me.'

'Stuck with me.' For an hour, or maybe all night. Her heart lurched treacherously.

'Where will I sleep?'

A look of surprise, a twist of amusement. Women! He didn't say it aloud but she could hear him thinking it.

'Don't worry about it. They'll sort you out something. If it comes to that.'

Flustered, Nancy hid her face as best she could behind her coffee cup. She didn't even taste the bitterness of the brew this time.

They made small talk for an hour or so, Mac checking his watch at regular intervals. Eventually he pushed back his chair and got up. 'I'm going to get an update. Are you going to stay here?'

'I think I'll get a breath of air.'

They went out together into the deepening dusk. Mac headed off in the direction of the workshops and hangars, Nancy perched on a low wall watching him go. The air was heavy with the smell of aero fuel, but she fancied she could also make out the perfume of the countryside – mown grass and silage. It seemed to encapsulate the world she was inhabiting. War and peace. Adventure of widely differing kinds. Heartache and happiness. But at that moment, she decided, mostly happiness.

A while later he was back with the news that repairs to the Anson would not be completed until next day.

'They're arranging accommodation for you in the WAAF billet,' he told her.

'What about you?'

'Oh, don't worry about me. I'll get my head down somewhere. But I think I could put away a pint and a half-decent meal. I suggest we adjourn to a hostelry. Are you up for that?'

Again, that treacherous lurch of her heart. 'Yes . . . why not?' *Why not?* A thousand reasons, none of which she was about to elaborate to Mac.

'There's a reasonable place about half a mile down the road, I'm told. I had hoped to get my hands on a car, but nobody seems to be offering.'

'Never mind. It's a nice evening for a stroll.' How could she sound so relaxed, so normal, when her emotions were churning? Excitement. Nervousness. A feeling that she was skating on very thin ice.

They parked their kit and set out. At a guess, Nancy thought, half a mile was a conservative estimate for the distance they had to walk, but she wasn't complaining, and when they found the pub they were both agreed it was well worth the effort. The smoky bar was crowded with civilian workers from the aircraft repair shops, but there was a small dining room where the tables were set with chequered cloths, ornamental plates were arranged on a wooden dresser, and the mantelpiece boasted a collection of toby jugs. It was quintessentially British, and Nancy was fascinated by it.

'Looks as if we've got the place to ourselves.' Mac got out his packet of Players and offered her one. 'I don't suppose many people are taking holidays these days, and all the commercial travellers are in the forces.'

Nancy took a cigarette. 'Commercial travellers?'

'Salesmen. Brushes, insurance, nuts and bolts, pharmaceuticals . . .' He leaned forward to light her cigarette. The lighter was heavy silver; it smelled of petrol. 'This is the sort of place they'd be likely to stay overnight once a month or whatever. Must be the same in the States, though I imagine their areas would be a lot bigger.'

'I guess so.' Commercial travellers had not figured in her life.

The landlord came to take their order. He was a big, bushy-browed Welshman, and Nancy had as much trouble understanding what he said as she had her Scottish instructor.

'Why can't they speak English?' she asked, exasperated, after Mac had translated for her and they'd ordered ham and chips.

Mac laughed. 'It's all double Dutch to you, isn't it, Nancy?'

'Sure is.' The expression 'double Dutch' was new to her too, but she could guess its meaning. 'It's a whole different language.' She thought of the story the girls had laughed over – a GI who had misunderstood an English girl's request to 'knock her up' and got his face slapped for his pains – but decided against repeating it.

'Whereabouts is it you come from?' he asked.

She told him about Florida, but she did not mention Joe, and she did not ask any questions of Mac either. She didn't want to hear about his wife, didn't want him telling her of any children they might have. This was her stolen time; the ghosts were there lurking in the shadows, but she didn't want them to become any more real. Without any prompting from her, however, Mac volunteered some information.

'This isn't far from home for me.'

'Wales?'

'No, but just the other side of the Bristol Channel. Gloucestershire, actually. God's Own County.'

Gloucestershire – Kemble and Aston Down. Bristol – Whitchurch, famous for its CO's refusal to have female ATA on his station, Filton, home of the Bristol Aeroplane Company, makers of Beaufighters and Blenheims. Nancy was surprised – and proud of – how much she'd learned in her few short months in England. Her grasp of the language might still leave something to be desired; her geography was definitely much improved.

The ham and chips arrived, deliciously thick slices that Nancy thought might well have come from a pig who had once been a resident of St Athan. They tucked in ravenously – it had been a long day – and though there was no time for conversation the silence between them was companionable. Nancy had begun to feel more at ease in Mac's company than she'd ever imagined she could be, given the feelings she had for him.

They rounded off the meal with huge slices of home-made

apple pie and cups of coffee that tasted only faintly of the dreaded chicory.

'Well, I suppose we had better be making tracks.' Mac ground out his cigarette. 'I'll settle the bill.'

He slid some notes out of his wallet, laid it open on the table in front of him while he rifled in his pockets for loose change. There was a photograph behind a Cellophane window, a couple of inches square, a head and shoulders studio shot of a woman. His wife. He carried a picture of his wife in his wallet. And why wouldn't he, for goodness' sake? Most men did. Nancy tried surreptitiously to see what she looked like, but the light from the overhead lamp was splintering on the Cellophane and in any case the photograph was upside down to her. All she could see before Mac closed the wallet and put it back in his pocket was that the woman had long dark hair that framed her face in thick bangs. She would probably be excruciatingly pretty, Nancy decided – any woman who could ensnare a man like Mac must be – but she would never know.

A shard of pain pierced her heart, her relaxed, happy mood dissipated as if it had never been as reality came flooding in.

'OK,' Mac said, unaware that her world had fallen apart. 'I'll see you safely back to your billet.'

And before she could stop herself Nancy said sharply: 'Wouldn't your wife mind?'

The moment the words left her lips she regretted them and her embarrassment was compounded when Mac raised an eyebrow at her, said in a faintly amused tone: 'I'm offering to walk you back to the base, not making an improper suggestion.'

'I know! I meant—'

'In any case,' Mac said, 'my wife is not in a condition to mind about anything. She's been in a coma for almost two years.'

Nancy stared at him, her embarrassment forgotten. Mac was toying with his lighter, turning it over and over between his fingers.

'A coma?' Nancy repeated, shocked. 'But – what happened to her?'

'This damned war happened.'

'You mean . . . an air raid?'

'No. An accident in the blackout. She was cycling home from work and a car went into her.' His voice was flat, totally lacking in emotion, as if he was simply repeating a mantra he'd recited many times before and his eyes, opaque, revealed nothing of what he might be feeling.

'Oh my God, that's terrible! How could something like that happen?'

'All too easily. She wasn't the first to be hit by a car with its lights half-blacked out and she won't be the last.' The same flat tone, no anger, no apportioning of blame, just stating facts.

'Oh my God,' Nancy said again.

Mac pulled another cigarette out of his packet and lit it, this time not offering her one.

'You can see how it happened. It wasn't the driver's fault. Dark road, dark clothes, dark bike. He just didn't see her. If anyone's to blame it's me. I'd been home the weekend before and she told me she was having trouble with her rear light. I thought I'd fixed it. Obviously I hadn't. It was still on the blink. Wonky bulb, perhaps. We'll never know – it was smashed to smithereens by the time I saw it again. And Judy . . . well, Judy was smashed up too. She's never regained consciousness.'

'Mac – I don't know what to say . . .' Nancy pulled the packet of Players towards her across the table and took one. Mac leaned across, flicking his lighter so that the flame flared, and lit it for

132

her. The familiar grin crooked one corner of his mouth, but his eyes were dead, unsmiling.

'Nothing you can say, is there?'

'Except that I am so, so sorry.' She touched the hand holding the lighter, then hastily withdrew. She knew instinctively he did not want pity – hers or anyone else's. The shell he had built around himself was an almost tangible barrier, his pain too private.

Mac pushed back his chair, got up. 'Shall we go?' He shrugged into his jacket, cigarette held in the corner of his mouth.

Nancy nodded. They walked back to the base in almost total silence. Mac had retreated into a world of his own and Nancy was still stunned by what he had told her; she could think of nothing else. For the moment all her own churning emotions were stilled, smothered by a blanket of aching sympathy.

Mac carried the burden of this awful tragedy with him every day, and she had not known. He did his job, hid his pain deep inside, where no one else would see it. Suddenly, Nancy felt very humble.

The Anson was ready by early afternoon the following day. Back at White Waltham, news of a fresh posting awaited Nancy. She, along with Kay and Bobbie Morrison, were to go to Ratcliffe with immediate effect.

Once again she was leaving Mac behind. But he was on her mind more than ever. His revelations had stirred a whole new raft of emotions; though she scarcely realised it, infatuation and sexual attraction were deepening to love.

VI

He missed her. Bloody hell, he missed her!

Mac, sitting in the CO's chair – the CO was taking a few days' well-earned leave – capped his fountain pen, pushed the pile of paperwork he detested away from him and lit a cigarette.

It was a week now since Nancy had left for Ratcliffe, and he'd been relieved to see her go. Her presence was just too unsettling, though for the life of him he couldn't work out why she affected him so. She was chippy, she was overconfident, she was a little bit brash – like all the American girls, he thought wryly. All things he disliked in a woman. But something about her had got under his skin, awakened feelings he'd never thought he'd have for anyone but Judy, and it was giving him sleepless nights.

There had been the odd woman, of course, in the two years since Judy's accident – usually when he'd had too much to drink. The night-club singer who'd wound herself all round him after she'd finished her nightly stint in a dimly lit Soho bar; the pretty sister of a fellow RAF officer who'd been in a group of girls invited to a party in the mess. But they'd meant nothing. A few hours when he could forget his sorrows, a few minutes of physical release. Nancy was different.

He'd known that almost the first time he'd laid eyes on her, if he was honest. He should have come down on her like a ton of bricks for joy-riding and smashing up a Puss Moth. If it had been anyone else he would have done. But he'd felt himself melting under the hard shell he wore like chain mail. She'd amused him and touched him, and he hadn't had the heart to give her the carpeting she deserved. But he hadn't realised how dangerous it was to allow a chink in his armour. She'd slipped through it un-noticed, curled up inside it with him. He'd only realised it when he found himself watching out for her, looking forward to seeing her, and finally dreaming about her. The morning he woke, remem-bering that she'd been there with him as he slept, was when he knew for certain that Nancy Kelly was more than just an engaging pupil, more than just another pretty girl. And he didn't like it one little bit.

In a world gone bad, Mac was the most honourable of men, and to him having feelings for anyone other than Judy was dishon-ourable in a far more fundamental way than the rushed couplings with the one-night stands. He'd felt disgust with himself after the event, then forgotten it quickly enough. But this was different. Thinking of Nancy as he had begun to was betrayal of the worst kind.

Judy was his wife. The fact that she had not smiled at him, nor touched him, nor even looked at him for almost two years was neither here nor there. He'd married her for better or for worse. And he still loved her. Even though it was becoming harder to hear her voice in his head, see her clearly in his mind's eye. He thought of her now as she had looked the day he married her. He could build the picture piece by piece as if it were a jigsaw: the orange blossom in her hair, her dark eyes sparkling behind the lace of her veil, her lips reddened more than he would have chosen – Mac preferred the natural look – the pearls at her throat, the trailing bouquet of deep red roses that matched her lipstick. He could put it all together, just about, but it was still nothing but an unreal snapshot of a girl who no longer existed, and his wedding day an event that might have happened to someone who was not him, if it had happened at all. The reality now was a still, waxy face against which that blood-red lipstick would have been garish and ugly, a sweep of eyelashes from bluish lids permanently closed like a sleeping doll's, and dark hair spread out across a white pillow. The scars and blemishes the accident had caused had long since faded; Judy was now immobile perfection.

In the beginning, when it was touch and go whether she would survive, he had scarcely left her bedside. He'd held her hand and prayed to a God he wasn't sure he believed in not to let her die. And his prayers had been answered. Judy had clung to life, and sometimes he wondered if he was to blame for that too, whether it wouldn't have been better for her if he'd prayed for her to slip away.

'She's like a Sleeping Beauty,' her mother had said once, tears running down her cheeks, and Mac had turned away, sudden anger welling. No kiss from a prince was going to waken her, and if it did . . . He heard again, all too clearly, the words of the doctor who was caring for her.

'There is a chance that she'll come out of it one day if the pressure on her brain eases. But even if that happens, there's no guarantee you'll have your wife back as she was. Her vital functions are likely to have been damaged beyond repair. You should prepare yourself, Mr Mackenzie, for the fact that Judy may be severely mentally and physically disabled.'

Mac had felt his stomach tighten. His lovely Judy. Dear God, Judy was warm and funny and kind. She loved life. The thought of her pretty mouth drooling, her expressive eyes blank and uncomprehending, was unbearable, worse by far than death. But somehow he'd steeled himself to ask: 'What do you think is the most likely outcome?'

The doctor, faceless, dispassionate, authority in a white coat, had refused to be drawn.

'It really is impossible to say. She could remain in a coma for years – it's not unheard of. She could, as I say, make a partial recovery. Or she could slip away. We simply don't know. In the meantime, there will be decisions to be made . . .'

Mac had dug his hands deep into the pockets of his flying jacket, grasping the keys of his Douglas motorcycle so tightly that the metal cut into his fingers.

'I want her to have the best possible care. Money is no problem.'

That wasn't strictly true. In his own right Mac was no better off than any other RAF officer. But he would get funds. It would certainly mean making peace with his father; eating a good slice of humble pie. It would probably mean he'd have to give up his career in the RAF when the war was over and go into the family business as the old man had always wanted – one of the reasons they'd fallen out in the first place – if Judy was still alive and still in need of care then. But he'd do it. He'd have worn sackcloth and ashes and swept streets if it meant he could do the best for Judy. And in the meantime he would have to ensure that she would be provided for in the event that anything happened to him. The odds of survival for a Spitfire pilot weren't ones a betting man would care to take. Mac had thought how ironic it was that he, who risked getting shot out of the skies every day, should be standing there unscathed whilst his wife, who should have been safe in the comparative peace of rural Gloucestershire, was hovering between life and death.

And he damned near had bought it too, soon afterwards, when his Spitfire had been shot down. Well, not shot down, exactly. If it had been he'd certainly have been killed, or badly burned like some of the others from his squadron. Charlie and Tigger and Nobby, all lost without trace. Dennis, whom he'd visited in hospital, unrecognisable beneath the layer of white gauze covering his face. Dennis had been suspended on straps, just clear of the bed, his arms, stiff with hard-set tannic acid, stuck straight out in front of him, his hands looked like nothing more than claws. Rumour had it that he was likely to be blind. Fire was Mac's worst nightmare, and it could well have happened to him.

They'd already got the Heinkel between them, he and Bill Ward – seen it spiral down towards the sea and explode in a ball of flame that turned the mist fiery – and were looking for more bombers when the Messerschmitt came out of nowhere. Mac saw it on Bill's tail; radioed him: 'Watch out! You're being followed!' Bill rolled to one side, the Messerschmitt went after him. Mac's teeth clenched. Bill was a relative novice; there was no way he was going to get away. Mac's instincts took over. He went for the Messerschmitt, trying to draw it away, firing round after round. And he got it. But not before the Messerschmitt got him too. A burst of gunfire holed the fuselage and his port wing, dazing him briefly. The Messerschmitt had gone into a spin, but Bill was still there, a few hundred feet away, seemingly unharmed. 'Yes!' Mac shouted through gritted teeth, but his exhilaration was short-lived. The Spit was flying erratically, and he could feel a warm river of blood coursing down his face. For a split second Mac considered ejecting, decided against it. He didn't fancy ending up in the drink. And the stubborn streak in his nature was urging him to try to get the plane home.

Somehow, he limped back to base, and the sight of the flare path had never been more welcome. But when he tried to lower the undercarriage nothing happened and the red warning light on the control panel showed it was locked up. Tired, bleeding badly, and fighting to maintain control over a damaged aircraft, Mac did everything he could to free it. No luck. In the event there was nothing for it but to attempt a belly landing. He alerted the tower as to his predicament, waited until he saw the fire engines take up their positions at the end of the runway, and came in onto the grass. For seemingly endless moments the underbelly jolted and scraped, then the nose dug into the ground and the Spitfire flipped and crumpled. The fire engines had been following him; they opened their jets and willing hands somehow freed Mac from the wreckage. He was badly injured. Blood and bone protruded through the torn fabric of his uniform trousers from the double compound fracture he'd sustained, the tendons of his hand had been ripped open in a jagged diagonal gash, and besides the scalp wound, he was concussed. But he was alive – just. Dimly he heard the voice of one of his rescuers: 'You're a lucky bastard, Mac!' and gritted through his pain: 'You really bloody think so?' And then the world went dark.

He'd drifted in and out of consciousness in those first days, and when he'd come round properly he had the impression that he and Judy had communicated somehow, been together. He'd dismissed it, of course, as some kind of fever-induced hallucination – Mac wasn't a believer in astral planes and all that esoteric nonsense – but the impression had remained, and with it the feeling that he'd let her down again, abandoned her in that murky waste-land between life and death.

As soon as he was fit enough he'd got a pal to drive him to visit her – an awkward, painful journey because his leg was still in plaster – but there was no change in her condition, and the deepest of depressions had descended upon him. What the hell was there to live for? Judy was beyond his reach, and his injuries meant he couldn't return to his squadron – not for the foresee-able future, and possibly never.

Being seconded to the ATA had saved his sanity. It gave a purpose to his life, and as he recovered from his injuries he was able to fly again, albeit non-operationally. The pressures of the job prevented him from going home to Gloucestershire to visit Judy very often, but with a creeping sense of shame he realised that was quite a relief. Sitting beside her bed when she had no idea whether he was there or not had been something of an ordeal. But it didn't mean he loved – or thought about – her less. She was still in his heart and on his mind every waking moment.

And then Nancy had come along and invaded the space that had belonged to Judy and Judy alone. Nancy, with her elfin face and that irrepressible hair that never quite conformed to service regu-lations, however often she got it cut; Nancy who could be rebel-lious and defiant, who gave the impression of bubbly confidence but who, for some reason he couldn't quite fathom, seemed rather vulnerable in spite of it. Nancy, who was warm and resilient and truly alive. She'd given him a lift somehow; when she was around he felt good, felt like a whole man again. And he wanted her. No question of it.

It was a dangerous situation. Many was the time he'd jumped on his Douglas, opened up the engine and roared around the lanes, trying to get her out of his system. Well, she'd gone now – for the time being anyway – though almost certainly at some stage she'd be back for further training on the Class 3 planes – the light twin engines such as the Oxford and the Dominie – and it should be a case of out of sight out of mind.

Except that it wasn't. He missed her, dammit. Mac slid his wallet out of his pocket, flipped it open to display the photograph of Judy that he carried in it, stared at her lovely face and felt his heart contract with longing for what had been and was no more. But the moment he put the wallet away it was another face he was seeing, the face he'd seen so many times set into an expression of determined concentration as she struggled to master some complicated bit of ground school or find her way by map and compass to a destination she'd never been before, but which could equally light up with mischief. Only this time he was seeing Nancy as she had looked when he'd told her about Judy, the pert features gone soft with compassion, lip caught between her teeth as if she was trying not to cry. He saw it through the curling haze of his cigarette smoke, felt the touch of her hand on his before she'd drawn it quickly away. And thought again that it was a damned good job Nancy was out of reach for the time being. If she were here, he wasn't sure how much longer he could resist her.

Nancy was not in a good mood. Somehow she had managed to mislay her copy of Ferry Pilot's Notes – a crime almost akin to 'breaking' an aircraft – and could only think she'd managed to leave it in the canteen at St Meryn where she'd grabbed a cup of tea whilst waiting for her transport back to Ratcliffe. Without much hope she went through her kit one last time, then headed for the ops room to report the loss.

With nightfall the fog had come down, thick and clammy, shrouding the hangars and stores that clustered on the edge of the airfield, and it did nothing to improve Nancy's mood. Shivering, she turned up the collar of her greatcoat and burrowed into it. If this pea-souper didn't clear there'd be no flying tomorrow.

'Nancy!'

She swung round, surprised, peering into the murk, and made out the dark shape of a utility van parked beside the white office building.

'Annabel, is that you?'

A figure wearing a forage cap materialised. 'Yeah – me.' Annabel was one of the MT drivers; once, not so long ago, in another life, she had been a débutante. Now, like all the other drivers, she worked eleven- and twelve-hour days without a word of complaint. 'I've got something for you.' She ducked back into the car, rummaged inside and handed Nancy an envelope.

'What is it?' Nancy asked, unable to make out what was written on it.

'A letter. For you.'

'I can see that. But who's it from?'

'How should I know? I had to drive a pilot who's stationed at Prestwick. He asked me to give it to you.'

'But I don't know anyone at Prestwick.'

'Sorry, can't be any more help. I've got to go.' She climbed back into her van and started the engine.

Glancing over her shoulder as she went towards the office block, Nancy saw the taillights disappearing into the murk. She pushed open the door, looked at the envelope by the glare of electric light within.

Joe. There was no mistaking the neat sloping writing. She had

143

a stack of letters addressed to her in an identical hand. Except that there was no postage stamp on this one and no franking to indicate that this letter had been checked by the censor.

A nerve jumped in Nancy's throat. What the hell was Annabel doing couriering her a letter from Joe? But this wasn't the time or the place to open it and find out. Nancy folded the envelope in half, slipped it into her greatcoat pocket and headed for the ops room to make her confession regarding the lost *Ferry Pilot's Notes*.

By the time she tore the envelope open in the privacy of her room, Nancy had already more or less worked out the scenario – and the letter confirmed that she'd guessed correctly.

Joe had been posted to Prestwick, an airfield in Scotland that was not only a USAAF base, but also the most northerly of the ATA ferry pools. He'd seen the chance to get a letter to Nancy without the censor's heavy blue pencil obliterating great chunks of it by simply asking around the ATA at the base for a pilot who was going to Ratcliffe. He'd talked the man into delivering it, probably rewarding him with chocolate or cigarettes or silk stockings for his girlfriend. That much Nancy had guessed. What took her totally by surprise was the reason for Joe's secrecy. He had written:

I don't know how your outfit works, but from what I can see of it, it's a whole lot more free and easy than the air force. So how about you try and get a posting up here? It's a good place to be if it weren't so darned cold, and the best of it is we'd be together. Jeez, Nancy, I've seen too many good buddies go out and not come back. Last week we lost three Flying Fortresses in one night, and I've got this yen to see you, honey, just in case my number comes up like theirs did. I sure hope it don't, but you got to face facts. A Flying Fortress is a sitting duck. Ours is called Rita – after Rita Hayworth, y'know – and she's looked after us so far. But there's only so much luck in the pot, and the bung's got a few holes in it. Could start running out at any time. Think about it, Nancy. See what you can do, honey . . .

She could hear his voice speaking from the page, his slow, gentle drawl, and her heart twisted. But at the same time panic was knotting her stomach – the panic that came from tentacles twisting around her, drawing her in, trapping her. The period of separation hadn't done anything to change the way she felt; if anything it had made things worse. She loved Joe – she did! – but in the way she'd love a brother if she had one. She knew that now that she'd experienced all-consuming passion. Nothing had happened between her and Mac, nothing ever could, but she'd looked at a man and felt as if she'd been hit by a bomb, felt herself melting inside whilst every nerve trembled with desire. Maybe no one else would ever affect her that way, but she couldn't settle for less. It was not fair to Joe, and it was not fair to herself.

But the pressure now was greater than ever. Death was not some shadowy fate that happened to other people, it was real. It sat on the shoulders of pilots and aircrew every time they took to the skies. The sense of obligation to Joe was a ligature squeezing tight around Nancy's heart. If she hurt him and he was killed, she would never forgive herself. If only he'd never written this letter, put her on the spot! But he had.

Crossly, Nancy folded the letter and put it away with the others, wondering what on earth she was going to write to him by way of reply. It was unlikely, of course, that even if she requested the transfer she'd get it. But then again she might, and she did not want to risk that.

A day or so later, when she'd had the chance to think things through, Nancy put pen to paper.

Dear Joe. It's a lovely thought, but there's no way I can ask for a transfer. I'm needed here. And in any case, you might get a posting. There are lots of USAAF bases round here and in the south of England. It would be pretty silly if I moved to Scotland and you weren't there any more. Let's leave things as they are, OK?

Whether Joe saw the sense in her argument, or whether he was afraid to push her for fear of what her response would be, Nancy never knew for sure. But whatever the reason, Joe did not raise the subject again.

The English weather she had so dreaded closed in with a vengeance, hampering flying as well as depressing spirits. Nancy, used to the sunshine of Florida, shivered and shrank. Ratcliffe, high up along the Fosse Way to the north of Leicester, occupied an exposed position that made it prone to dense fog and thick snow.

It had its compensations, though. Once again, Nancy found herself billeted in a magnificent country house, Highfields Grange, and the hospitality there was even more lavish than it had been at White Waltham – when there was time to enjoy it. Nancy was now working harder than ever, and was often too late home to eat dinner with the family. But invariably there was a plate of something cold left out for her, and Hetty, the cook who had been employed at the Grange for more than thirty years, would heat a bowl of soup to bring the warmth back to her frozen limbs.

Christmas came and went. Nancy had thought she would have no excuse not to try to meet up with Joe since she had a couple of days of well-earned leave. But a nasty bout of flu intervened, which she attributed to the damp and none-too-clean sheets she'd been forced to sleep between in a dingy third-rate hotel one night when she'd been 'stuck out' and unable to get back to base. Instead of making her way to Prestwick or some midway meeting point if Joe had leave too, she had spent the festive season in bed, snivelling miserably and shivering in spasms that seemed to make every hair of her head stand on end, and aching all over. New Year had come and gone too before the medical officer pronounced her fit enough to resume flying. And then it was back to the busy round once more.

But Nancy was not complaining. She was flying aircraft she'd never dreamed she'd fly, she was helping the war effort. And she was having the time of her life.

VII

Nancy craned forward, peering over the long nose of the Spitfire and desperately looking for a break in the cloud. Normally she loved flying Spitfires – 'the best plane I ever flew!' she'd written to Joe – but today she was far from happy. She'd already climbed to six thousand feet hoping to find a clear patch but there was none and when she'd descended again, heavy icing had begun to form on the windscreen, wings and airscrews.

She was in a cleft stick and she knew it. Unless she descended further she'd never be able to find a safe place to land, but the icing could only get worse, and if that happened she was going to lose control. A nerve jumped in Nancy's throat, and she acknowledged that for one of the few times in her life, she was frightened.

And it had all started so well, dammit!

Three days ago she'd left Ratcliffe in a Mustang, bound for Woodley, an airfield just south of White Waltham, and had expected to be back at Ratcliffe the same night, with any luck. But a batch of urgently needed Spitfires had come on line at the Vickers factory at High Post. Hamble, the ferry pool usually responsible for clearing the planes to the Wiltshire maintenance units where they would undergo their final preparation, was badly overstretched and put out a call for help. Nancy had no onward flight lined up, and the ops officer at White Waltham had asked if she'd be prepared to do the job.

Nancy had jumped at the opportunity. She loved flying Spits; the Vickers factory at Castle Bromwich was close to Ratcliffe, so she'd already notched up her fair share. And when she and the other two pilots who had been assigned the job walked out to the taxi plane, it was Mac at the controls.

Nancy had felt a surge of elation. All very well to tell herself she had to forget him – her heart wasn't listening. And just seeing him there, sitting at the controls and running his power checks, resurrected all her latent feelings. He turned, giving her a crooked smile and a wink, and she settled into her seat bathing in a rosy glow.

The weather, already dull and overcast when they took off, worsened rapidly, and by the time they reached High Post it took all Mac's skill to land safely. They sorted out accommodation for the night, spent a convivial evening all together, and went to bed early, hoping the weather would have improved by next day.

It hadn't – nor the next. Nancy, Mac and the other two pilots could do nothing but sit in the draughty airfield hut, watching the rain trickle down steamed-up and grime-encrusted windows, and wait for a break in the thick blanket of cloud. They played cards, they ate the dry, tasteless sandwiches provided for them, and the other pilots grumbled, chafing at the bit. But Nancy had enjoyed every precious stolen moment.

On the third day there was hope of an improvement. Though visibility was still down to thirty yards, the forecast predicted a break by midday. They talked it over between themselves and the men declared their intention of trying to get away if it was at all possible. Nancy was less certain – she knew her capacity for getting lost. But when the break came she was reluctant to be the only one to refuse to fly. Her pride wouldn't allow it.

'Yeah – let's give it a go,' she said with more bravado than she was feeling.

Mac's eyes levelled with her. 'Are you sure?'

'Yep.'

In the last resort the decision whether or not to fly was down to each individual pilot. If Mac was doubtful about the wisdom of Nancy's choice, he said nothing. The three Spitfires took off and he watched them go.

For a while the break in the weather held and Nancy set course for Colerne. It wasn't far, for goodness' sake, just a short hop of thirty miles or so. But before long she was in cloud again, thick and totally disorientating.

Shit, why had she attempted this? She was going back, and to hell with her stupid pride. She turned 180 degrees, heading back the way she had come, but the cloud had closed in behind her; if anything it was even more dense than up ahead. Nancy thought of the airstrip at High Post as it had been the past two days with the visibility down to a couple of hundred feet or less. There was no way she'd be able to get back in safely.

She turned again, wondering what the hell to do. There was a bright patch over on the starboard side – perhaps the cloud was thinner there. She climbed to two thousand feet and headed for it. But before she could reach it, it had disappeared, and to her horror she realised the plane had begun icing up. Determined to get out of the cloud, she climbed again, this time to six thousand feet, and broke through to the blessed relief of clear sky. But her elation was short-lived. Beneath her a thick grey carpet stretched from horizon to horizon. There was not a single break to be seen. Panic gnawed at Nancy's stomach; she fought it. Panic helped no one.

She flew a wide orbit, giving herself time to think. The only time she'd deviated from her heading had been when she'd done that 180 degree turn, and when she'd found conditions behind her even worse than ahead she'd turned a full 180 back again. Nancy checked her watch. Judging by the time she'd been in the air she should be pretty well over Salisbury Plain by now. That – as its name suggested – was flat. And empty. Mile upon mile of open country broken up only by the odd dry-stone wall, a number of airfields, an army barracks. Perhaps the best thing would be to go down and try to find somewhere to land. Just as long as she didn't manage to run into Stonehenge. A bubble of nervous laughter tickled in Nancy's throat. Wouldn't it be just her luck to collide with the centuries-old standing stones? She could see the headlines now: 'Girl Pilot in Spitfire Demolishes Ancient Monument'. What a disaster that would be!

Don't be so damned frivolous and concentrate! she told herself. This is serious.

The icing was getting worse all the time, reducing visibility even further, so that the cloud now had a mystical sparkle. It was making handling heavy and awkward too. And then the engine began to splutter.

Oh God – no! Nancy thought, horrified. Don't do this to me, please! But she knew it was too late for prayer. The narrow cockpit, snug around her shoulders, felt like a coffin suddenly. The engine was going to die and she didn't think there was a damn thing she could do about it.

Under normal circumstances engine failure was not the end of the world; it was something all pilots trained for. Kept in trim the plane would glide quite well enough to establish wind direction, look for a suitable site and land safely. But the conditions today made it quite a different matter. She had to make a decision, and quickly. She could use what little power was left to gain enough height to bail out safely, open her parachute and pray. Or she could remain at the controls and do her best to choose the spot the Spit came down. Out here the chances were that, unmanned, the plane would simply nose dive into open ground, but there was no way she could be sure of that. She thought of Stonehenge again – damn Stonehenge! – they'd just have to lever the blasted stones up again. But supposing the Spit crashed onto an isolated house or farm? A school even? There must be hamlets, however scattered, and hamlets meant people. Nancy knew without a second thought that she couldn't risk it; couldn't live with the knowledge that she'd been responsible for killing someone. There was really no decision to be made at all.

The engine had cut out completely now; she was in a bubble of silence. Floating, then gliding, except that it wasn't the usual smooth, manageable glide. The icing was playing havoc with stability; nothing was happening the way she was used to. Fighting to keep the plane in trim, there was no more time to be afraid. Nancy gritted her teeth as the plane lost height and still she had no idea what was beneath her. Then, at perhaps less than a hundred feet, she made out the ground, rushing up to meet her. Rough, undulating, with what looked like a stone wall immediately ahead. But no houses, no farms, no road. Hallelujah! The wing, heavy with ice, tipped alarmingly, the muddy green and the grey stone disappeared under the sloping nose. A jolt. A splintering crash, ear-shattering in the silence. Tearing. Grinding. A shock wave reverberating through her, rattling her bones. And the world disintegrating around her.

'Where the hell is she?' The anxiety that was consuming Mac made his tone angry, aggressive; for the hundredth time he strode across the small ops room, peering out into the thick grey gloom that was darkening towards murky nightfall.

None of the other men in the room answered him. The same thought was in all their minds; they didn't want to voice it. It was almost four hours now since the three Spitfires had taken off. One had turned back almost at once, one had somehow managed to reach Colerne. From Nancy there had been no word.

'Conditions were bally awful,' Eric Faulkner, the ATA pilot who'd turned back, ventured, as much to excuse his own failure to get through when Eddie Bristow had managed it as to explain Nancy's loss. All very well to know it had been the sensible thing to do; it was still galling to feel that his own ability was inferior to Eddie's and his courage less than Nancy's. 'It wasn't fit for flying at all. You shouldn't have let her go, Mac.'

'The met reports promised improvement,' Mac snapped. 'And you all make your own decisions – you know that. It's not for me to make them for you.'

But he was cursing himself all the same, blaming himself for not having intervened. He'd not been happy about it; his instincts had been that they'd all turn back before long – the reason why he'd waited himself. But he should have known Nancy would do no such thing. She was too damn proud – and stubborn. Too determined to prove that anything the men could do, she could do as well, if not better. Their natural caution and the fact that they were not driven by testosterone made the other women he'd taught some of the safest pilots in the air, but Nancy was different. She was too competitive by half, and her desire to do well could make her reckless. He knew that, and he'd still let her make her own decision and go. If something had happened to her . . .

If . . . There was no 'if' about it. She hadn't called in to say she'd landed. And she almost certainly couldn't still be flying. Her fuel would have run out by now. Which left only one alternative. She'd come down somewhere.

In the first couple of hours when he'd acknowledged Nancy was overdue, he'd tried to console himself that she'd maybe gone off course looking for a break in the cloud, maybe headed back for White Waltham or the Midlands, where the terrain was more familiar to her. But from what he could make out the weather was almost universally bad and wherever she'd been trying to reach she should have made it by now. The only faint hope left to him was that she'd made a landing somewhere isolated and had no way of calling in to report her position. But even that wasn't a great deal of comfort to him. If she was stuck out all night in the middle of nowhere in this weather the chances were she'd suffer hypothermia, maybe even freeze to death if the rain turned to snow. He was fairly sure there was sleet in the rain already, and certainly the latest met reports were forecasting it. But there was not a thing he could do to help her. Flying in this weather was impossible, and even if he got a plane into the air there was no way he could carry out a search. Especially since he hadn't the first idea where to look. There were hundreds of square miles of open country within the scope of the fuel the Spit had been loaded with. It would be like looking for the proverbial needle in the haystack.

Frustration boiled in Mac, along with the anxiety and the guilt. Nancy was out there somewhere. He didn't know if she was dead or alive, injured or just frightened, cold and alone. And it was eating him up, getting to him in a way that went far beyond professional concern for one of his pilots.

This wasn't just any pilot. This was Nancy. And he'd failed her, just as he'd failed Judy. He'd messed up fixing the rear light on Judy's bike, and she was in a coma. He'd failed to stop Nancy taking off when he'd known very well she shouldn't be flying, and she was missing. What sort of a man was he?

Mac thudded his fist hard into a metal filing cabinet and the resulting crash reverberated around the room.

'Bloody idiot!' he growled through gritted teeth, and though the others thought it was Nancy he was castigating, it wasn't. It was himself.

The telephone shrilled; Paddy, the ops officer, snatched it up. Mac froze, still nursing his sore knuckles, and saw Paddy's eyes narrow, his mouth set in a grim line.

'Yes . . . Yes . . . Where?' His barked responses told Mac nothing – and everything. His stomach clenched. Paddy replaced the receiver and sat for a moment with his hand resting on it, head bowed.

'What?' Mac demanded.

Paddy looked up. 'Not good, Mac. A farmer on Salisbury Plain has reported a plane down on his land. He saw a glow in the sky and went out to investigate on his tractor. He thinks it was a Spit.'

'Thinks?'

'It's burned out. He couldn't get close enough to be sure.'

Fire. His ultimate horror. Mac felt physically sick.

'And the pilot?'

'No news. But the farmer didn't see anyone.' He took in Mac's stricken face and added: 'It's possible she bailed out, Mac. She could be anywhere.'

She could, it was true. But somehow he couldn't see Nancy baling out. She was the sort who'd cling on to the bitter end, looking for a way out of the mess she'd got herself into. Though he was numb with shock and dread, Mac's natural response was action. At least they had a location now. At least they knew where to start looking. In case she'd got out alive.

'I want transport,' he said.

'We can't fly, Mac. You know that.'

'You've got those things that run on four wheels, haven't you?'

'Well, yes, but . . . wouldn't it be better to leave this to the chaps on the spot? It's forty miles, and in this weather—'

'For Chrissakes, are you going to lend me a car or not?'

'OK.' Paddy raised his hands in submission. 'There's a utility van – or you can take my car if you'd rather.'

'I don't care which it is as long as it goes.' Mac was shrugging into his greatcoat. 'Look, I'll find a phone box on the way and call back to see if there's any news. But I'm not hanging around until we hear whether or not the pilot got out. If she did, she's out there somewhere on the Plain. And we've got to find her – fast.'

Paddy pulled out the keys to his Hillman, pushed them across the desk in Mac's direction. 'I'm parked right outside. Keep us informed, won't you? And good luck.'

Mac nodded abruptly. The door slammed after him and the other men exchanged grim glances.

'Good luck,' Eric Faulkner called after him, and added in a low tone, 'All I can say is – he'll need it.'

He'd been right, there was sleet in the air and it was turning to snow, coming out of the murk in a shimmering miasma that was almost hypnotic and building up behind the sweep of the windscreen wipers. The Hillman's headlamps, half-blacked out, were coming back at him too and the concentration required to negotiate the narrow, undulating road was keeping him from thinking too much about what might have happened to Nancy. But the dread was still there, a leaden weight in his stomach, and the sense of urgency was pure adrenalin in his veins. But progress was frustratingly slow, and Mac cursed the foul weather that was preventing him from putting his foot down hard to the floorboards and keeping it there, and the Hillman for its limitations. After an hour or so he spotted a phone box as he passed through a village and thought about stopping to put in a call to High Post as he'd said he would to check if there was any further news, then decided against it. It would only delay him, and if Nancy was, by some miracle, alive somewhere out on the Plain, he wanted to join the search for her the soonest he possibly could. Others would be out looking for her, yes – men who knew the terrain a whole lot better than he did – but with the best will in the world, they wouldn't be searching with the same zeal as he would. To them, the missing person was just another pilot. To him, it was Nancy. His Nancy – no, not his Nancy. But she might as well have been, for the compulsion that was driving him now, and that all-pervasive dread that was aching in his bones. Time was of the essence if she was out there in this weather, injured maybe, burned maybe, perhaps even unconscious. And if she hadn't got out, if she'd perished in a burning plane . . . well, he didn't want to hear it out here in the middle of nowhere, didn't want to have to turn round and drive back to High Post with all hope gone. Not that he would have turned back anyway. If the remains of a body had been found in the burned-out Spitfire he wanted to be there when they got it out. Wanted to make sure she was treated with proper respect. Wanted to be the one to bring her home.

His stomach clenched as it had when he'd first heard the news; he glanced at the telephone box, snow already building up in the corners of the windowpanes, and drove on.

The call to High Post had come from an RAF camp close to where the Spitfire had come down; they were coordinating the search with the aid of army personnel in the area. Mac intended going directly there. It took him another hour or so before he was at the gates, presenting his credentials to the officer on guard duty, who was very young and very officious, reluctant to allow in anyone without authorisation, and unwilling to make the necessary call to get it.

'For Chrissake, do I look like a German spy?' Mac snapped. 'Make that call and let me in now, or I'll see you're up on a charge so fast your feet won't touch the ground.'

And still the boy hesitated, eyeing Mac with suspicion. 'I mean it. I'm an RAF squadron leader and the friend of an air vice marshal,' Mac, who had never before in his life pulled rank, grated.

The unfortunate lad retreated into the guard room. Mac shifted and stamped impatiently, watching him through the window as he made a telephone call to his superiors. His face was pinched with the cold, Mac noticed – a droplet of moisture was suspended precariously from the end of his reddened nose. For some reason it exacerbated Mac's irritation with him.

'OK, sir, you can go through.' The boy came back, raising the barrier.

'I should think so too. And wipe your ruddy nose!' Mac snapped.

By the time he reached the office block the commanding officer himself was waiting, stamping his feet against the cold. Mac's heart sank; it didn't look good. He allowed the CO to usher him inside, along a narrow, brightly lit corridor into an office filled with a haze of tobacco smoke and the smell of paraffin from a small Aladdin stove, which had been wheeled in to supplement the heating.

'This is a bad business.' Group Captain Reg Brock shifted his pipe from one corner of his mouth to the other. He was a slight, bowed figure; he looked as if he carried the weight of the world on his shoulders.

Mac steeled himself. 'I take it the plane that came down was our Spit.'

'Looks like it, yes.'

'And the pilot?' His jaw clenched.

'No sign.'

For a moment Mac thought he'd misheard. He'd been ready – as ready as he ever would be – to hear that Nancy was dead. The thud of relief that reverberated through his body shocked him as much as the words.

'She wasn't with the plane?'

'No. We've got teams out searching, and the army are helping, but in this weather . . .'

'Give me some directions. I'm going out to help.'

'Christ, man, she could be anywhere! If she bailed out—'

'She wouldn't bail out.'

'The Spit caught fire.'

'She must have got out somehow. Wherever that plane is, she'll be somewhere in the vicinity. We've got to find her. It's freezing out there.'

Reg Brock shook his head. 'It's a wild-goose chase. She'll have bailed out somewhere.'

'She did not bail out,' Mac retorted furiously. He didn't know why he was so certain, only that he was. 'It's the area around the crash site you've got to concentrate on.'

'If you're right, she'll have crawled into a ditch somewhere.' *To die.* He didn't say it, but Mac knew what he was thinking.

'I don't give a damn. Just give me directions.'

'Well, that's up to you.' Brock tugged with his teeth on the stem of his pipe and sighed. This was a man obsessed; there was no reasoning with him. He couldn't understand it, though. Nobody liked to lose a pilot, but you couldn't allow yourself to get so personally involved. As he rattled through directions, Mac listened, eyes narrowed, committing them to memory with the efficiency and precision that made him such a good pilot. Then, barely pausing to thank the CO, he headed for the door.

He was back with the Hillman with the engine running, knocking the covering of snow that had accumulated in the few minutes he'd been inside from the windscreen when the CO appeared, silhouetted against the light from the open doorway.

'Hey! Wait!'

Mac turned his head, still brushing at the snow with his gloved hands. 'What?'

'She's been found. You were right. She must have stayed with the plane.' He sounded bemused.

'They've found her?' The rush of joyous relief almost choked Mac. He strode back to the office block, feet crunching and slipping in the fresh snow. 'Where? Where is she? Is she all right?'

'I don't know any details. But the landlord of the Traveller's Rest has phoned. It seems she's fetched up there.'

'The Traveller's Rest?'

'On the Salisbury road. About five miles . . .'

Mac waited for nothing. He leaped into the car, and gunned the engine, letting the wipers finish clearing the windscreen.

She was alive. God alone knew what sort of state she was in, but she was alive. For the moment nothing else mattered.

How he made it to the Traveller's Rest without running into a ditch, Mac would never know. He drove like a man demented, tyres skidding on the icy surface, barely able to make out the road through the swirling snow and even less able to read the signposts along the way. But by religiously following the directions the CO had given him he found it – a squat old building miles from anywhere that had probably once been a coaching inn. Nowadays, presumably, it catered for tourists and the summer trade, of which there would certainly be none tonight. Given the terrible visibility and the fact that only bare chinks of light showed behind the blackouts at the windows, it was a miracle that Mac did not miss it altogether, but his headlamps, poor as they were, caught and reflected from a creaking inn sign. Mac swung into the pristine virgin white of the broad frontage which served as a car park, switched off the engine and leaped out, not bothering to lock the car and almost forgetting to turn off the headlamps. He had to go back and do that; it would not help Nancy if the battery went flat. Then he threw open the door and hurried inside.

She was in the bar, huddled in a chair before an open fire, an empty brandy glass on a small table beside her. Someone had draped a blanket around her shoulders and her back was turned towards him so he could not see her face. A burly man was crouching beside her, a big-busted bottle blonde hovered anxiously. They both turned as Mac burst in. He ignored them, hurrying towards Nancy.

She lifted her head, twisting in her chair, and the blanket slipped off her shoulders. 'Mac.' Her teeth were chattering; she attempted what might have been intended as a wan smile, but her face looked stiff and the chattering teeth bared her lips into a rictus grin. There was a huge egg-shaped swelling over her right eyebrow, which had already begun to discolour badly. Blood had trickled down the side of her forehead and dried in thin rivers on her cheek; her face was devoid of colour – her skin had a bluish grey tint to it.

Mac pushed the table aside and hunkered down beside her, covering her hand with his.

'God, Nancy, you know how to put the wind up a man, don't you? Are you all right?'

Her eyes fell from his. 'I lost the plane.' It was a shamed, agonised whisper.

'Never mind the damn plane! What about *you*?'

'She just turned up here,' the landlord said. 'Gave me the shock of my life, she did. I opened the door to have a look at the weather, and there she was . . .' His voice tailed away as he realised neither of them was listening. They were totally wrapped up in each other. He might as well have been the ghost he'd thought for a moment Nancy was, materialising as she had from the swirling snow. He pulled himself to his feet, leaning on the arm of Nancy's chair, exchanging glances with his wife.

'I iced up and lost all power,' Nancy said. 'I got down, but I had no control. The Spit crashed and . . .' her eyes filled with tears, '. . . it caught fire. Oh, Mac, I'm so sorry!'

'Don't be daft.' Her tears were affecting him more even than her bruised face and her pallor. He'd never seen Nancy cry before; it just wasn't her.

'I don't know how I got out,' she went on, ignoring him. 'I thought I wouldn't. I could smell burning. But I did, somehow.

And then it went up. Just a little trickle of fire at first, and then – oh God, Mac, it was just horrible! An inferno! And they needed it so badly . . .' She was crying in earnest now, the tears mingling with the dried blood on her cheeks. 'And I . . . There was nobody about. Well, there wouldn't have been! That was the whole point. I wanted to make sure it didn't come down on a house or something. But I just . . . well, all I could do was to walk . . . and keep walking . . . and I thought I was never going to get to anything . . . and it started to snow . . .' This last was punctuated with small hiccuping sobs.

'Nancy, we'll talk about this later.' He pulled himself up. 'I'm going to get you to hospital.'

'I don't need—'

'You're half frozen and in shock, besides whatever injuries you might have. Don't argue with me now.'

She brushed her nose and face with the back of her hand. He noticed it was trembling. And when she stood up she looked unsteady on her feet too. The blanket slipped down into the chair; the landlord stepped forward to retrieve and offer it to her again.

'Take this with you. She needs something . . .'

'It's OK.' Mac unbuttoned his greatcoat. 'She can have this.'

Nancy's eyes looked up into his. 'But, Mac . . . you—'

'I'll be fine.' He shrugged out of the coat. There was no need really – the landlord would have let them borrow a dozen blankets if they asked. But this was something he wanted to do. Nancy was his responsibility. He'd failed her once today; he wasn't going to fail her again.

As he helped her into the greatcoat she staggered slightly, falling against him. He steadied her, aware of her hair brushing his face, her head against his chest, something he'd wanted for a very long time. But now he could feel nothing but overwhelming relief that she was here, more or less in one piece, and the pressing need to get her warm and looked at by a doctor.

He buttoned the greatcoat around her; in it she looked small and lost. Then he supported her out to the car and helped her in. The landlord, anxious to do his bit, had followed them out with the blanket draped over his arm.

'Look, have this too. Just in case you get stuck. You can bring it back any time . . .'

Mac thanked him and tucked the blanket around Nancy. Then he started the engine and turned on the headlights. The landlord's words were a stark reminder that in barren country like this there was every chance of becoming snowbound. Better get going – fast.

He glanced at Nancy, her face pinched and looking tiny above the enveloping collar of his coat, and sent up a prayer of thanks that she'd come through this alive.

He'd thought he'd lost her. Now, along with the sense of urgency to get her to warmth and safety and medical treatment, was another compulsion, just as strong.

He'd thought he'd lost her. Whatever happened, he wasn't going to let her go again.

VIII

Nancy was dreaming, a warm, pleasant, fuddled dream. She'd dreamed a lot these last few days – heck, she'd slept a lot! In fact, since Mac had taken her into the RAF hospital at Wroughton she'd done little else. It wasn't that she'd been badly injured; she'd needed a few stitches in the gash on her head, but apart from that and an assortment of cuts and bruises and suspected concussion, she had escaped very lightly. But they'd insisted on keeping her in for observation and, settled in a comfortable bed in a little private room, Nancy had discovered just how tired she was. The weeks of continual, endless ferrying, the constant pressure and the living on one's nerves had taken their toll; now the exhaustion weighed heavily in her bones and she relaxed into the bliss of not having a single thing to worry about – no decisions, nothing whatever expected of her. Her room was off a corridor adjoining two surgical wards and in the beginning the patients who were up and about had popped in for a chat, but Nancy, normally gregarious, wanted only peace and quiet. She kept her door firmly closed to discourage them and to shut out the sound of the wireless on the ward churning out *Workers' Playtime* and *ITMA*, and slept.

Sometimes, drifting and dozing, she relived those moments when she'd known for certain the Spitfire was going to crash and she had thought she was going to die.

Sometimes she saw it explode in a ball of flame, sometimes she relived the trek through the snow across a bleak, featureless landscape, hurting, bleeding, despairing of ever reaching civilisation or seeing another human being again. But mostly she floated in contentment, hugging to her the memories of Mac crouching beside her, looking at her as if he really cared; wrapping his greatcoat round her; tucking her into the seat of the car; driving with the same dogged concentration as he flew a plane; supporting her into the hospital and demanding a doctor for her *now*. He'd stayed with her until she'd been seen, and Nancy had thought that once her wound had been stitched she'd be able to leave with him, but the doctor had insisted on admitting her. She hadn't seen Mac since, but every time she closed her eyes she could feel his fingers on her forehead, brushing her hair away from the dressing in a gesture of concern that was the closest thing to tenderness that she could imagine, and his hand squeezing hers when he left.

She could feel it now, his fingers wrapped around hers, a part of the dream that was fading into wakefulness. Mac. He was here, beside her bed. A rosy glow of happiness warmed her.

'Hi,' she murmured lazily.

'Hi yourself.' The voice was all wrong but she couldn't work out why. Puzzled, she opened her eyes, and was suddenly wide awake.

'Joe! Joe — what are you doing here?'

'Come to surprise you, honey.' In his USAAF uniform he looked like a big cuddly bear; his face was furrowed with anxiety.

168

'Joe – I don't believe this!'

He smiled, the slow smile she knew so well. 'They gave me a couple of days' leave to come visit you. So, here I am.'

'Oh my God, Joe!' Emotions were churning, welling up. Pleasure at seeing Joe, disappointment that it was not who she had thought it was.

'There's no need to cry about it, honey. I'm here, and you're here. That's all that matters.'

'I'm not crying.' But she was; she could feel the tears wet on her lashes. 'How did you get here?'

'Got a lift in a Walrus. Gee, what a peculiar plane that is! More like a ship than a plane.'

'That's because it's amphibious.'

'Ambidextrous, more like, the way she swings about!' Joe laughed at his own joke. 'But never mind about aircraft. How are you doing?'

'I'm OK.'

'You don't look OK.'

'Gee, thanks!'

'You look as though you've gone ten rounds with Joe Louis.'

'Don't remind me.' The bruise on her forehead had drained down; Nancy now had a black eye, though why it was called a black eye she could not imagine – hers was mutating from purple to greens, blues and yellows. 'I'm fine really, though. I shouldn't be taking up a bed here. I feel a complete fraud.'

'They want to keep an eye on you,' Joe said. 'From what I can make out it was a close thing, Nancy.'

'Sure was. But I'm fine now. Just tired. A few more days and they'll sign me up as fit to fly, I'm sure of it.'

'I want to talk to you about that, honey,' Joe said. His face had gone serious; she knew what he was going to say.

'Don't try telling me to go home, Joe Costello,' she said. 'Because I'm not going.'

'Nancy, you came *that* close to being killed. I've not said anything before, but I'm saying it now. I don't want you doing this, honey. It's too damned dangerous.'

'Oh, phooey! Accidents can happen anywhere. What I'm doing is no more dangerous than flying at home.'

'You don't get icing at home,' Joe said reasonably.

'No, but the tropical storms are pretty spectacular.'

He ignored that. 'The whole point is, Nancy, you're under pressure to fly when you know you darned well shouldn't. They need the planes moved, so they send you out whatever. They don't give a damn about you.'

The criticism of Mac stung. She leaped to his defence.

'That's just not true. And nobody *sent* me out. I chose to go.'

'Because you felt obliged to. I don't want you feeling obliged to fly in dangerous conditions, or when you're tired out, or not well.'

Her lips set in a tight line. 'Somebody has to.'

'But not you, Nancy. I want to know you're safe at home, waiting for me.'

The tentacles again, twining around her.

'It's not what I want, though.' She saw him wince, saw the hurt in his eyes, hated herself for doing this to him when he'd come all the way from Scotland to South-West England just to see her. She should have told him long ago that things between them weren't the way he liked to think they were. She shouldn't be leading him on like this. But she felt too weak to be able to face going through all that now.

'Don't let's argue,' she pleaded. 'And I don't want to lie here in state, either. I'm allowed up. If I wrapped up we could go out on the balcony. It's a nice day . . .' She swung her legs over the edge of the bed, and for the first time noticed what looked like a bunch of flowers wrapped in tissue paper on the floor beside Joe's chair. 'Oh, are those for me?'

'Oh – yeah.' He picked them up and gave them to her, strangely awkward. She tore the paper away and saw the cheerful yellow of daffodils.

'Best I could do,' Joe said apologetically. 'It's hard to get flowers in England right now, what with the war and it being winter. I don't know where these came from, but wherever it is, spring must be coming.'

'Oh, Joe, they're beautiful.' The flowers touched a nerve that Joe's person had not; getting himself from Scotland to Wiltshire to see her – that was Joe all over. Buying flowers was not. He would have been hugely embarrassed to be seen carrying them, she knew. No wonder they were wrapped so thoroughly. But he'd done it for her. Guilt flooded her; she filled up again. 'Joe, I don't deserve you . . . I'm not a nice person . . .'

'Don't talk such rot. And you've got me, honey, whether you like it or not.' He stood up, putting his arms round her, and the feeling of being trapped returned, more strongly than ever. She pulled away.

'You're squashing the flowers! I'll go find a vase . . .'

'Never mind the flowers.' He took them from her, put them down on the cabinet beside her bed. 'Come here, honey.'

He pulled her to him again. She buried her sore face in his shoulder, biting down hard on her lip, fighting the rising panic. And wondering what the hell she was going to do.

* * *

In another private room in another hospital Mac sat beside his wife's bed, feeling the same anger and frustration that he always felt when he visited, though the grief had dulled a little and he no longer felt shock at seeing her lying there like a beautiful wax doll. It had become the status quo now, and an acceptance he didn't care to acknowledge had begun to take the place of denial. He still felt awkward, though, self-conscious, as unsure of how to behave as if Judy had been a stranger, not the woman with whom he had shared his dreams, his body, his life.

'Talk to her,' the doctor had urged him, long ago, and he had tried – he really had tried. But at the best of times Mac was not a conversationalist, and the total lack of response was unnerving. It made him feel foolish, as if he was talking to himself. But from a sense of duty he went through the motions, reciting accounts of what he had been doing and how the war was going, and giving her messages from her family: 'Your mum and dad send their love . . .' 'Jenny,' her sister, 'says to tell you she thinks she's in the family way again . . .'

Today, however, there were things he desperately wanted to say, and could not. The need to tell her about Nancy, to ask for her understanding and forgiveness, was all-consuming – and futile. He wanted her blessing, but he couldn't ask her for it. He didn't think she'd hear him, but he couldn't be sure. How would she feel if she could? If her mind was receptive in a paralysed body? She might interpret what he said as an intention to abandon her. He'd never abandon her, as long as she drew breath. But if she thought there was someone else that was how it would feel to her. She could be weeping inside that prison of hers and he would never know. Mac gazed at her sleeping face and felt inner turmoil wrenching him in two.

He loved her and he always would, but it was time to move on. These past two years he had spent in a lonely limbo, his capacity for living lost with Judy. How many more years would pass before there was any change in her condition? He had long since realised it was highly unlikely that he would ever have back the wife he had loved, and he had come to terms with it. But since he had never wanted anyone else, it had never occurred to him to wonder what would happen if he did. Now the purely hypothetical had become reality. Now, there was Nancy. If he did nothing and let her go he could spend the rest of his life regretting it. Yet to take her into his life without Judy's knowledge seemed the ultimate betrayal. He had to share it with her, and at the same time reassure her.

Mac took Judy's hand in his, her lifeless, unresponsive hand that was still as warm to his touch as if she were merely sleeping, and bent his head so that her wrist lay against his forehead. His jaw clenched; he closed his eyes.

I'll never leave you, my love. I'll never forget you, or what we shared. You are here in my heart till the day I die. But I can't go on like this for ever. I have to start living again . . .

There was no sound in the room but the rise and fall of her breath, a little laboured, a little rasping, and the distant clank of a trolley somewhere on the other side of the closed door.

'Oh, Judy, forgive me.' They were the only words he spoke aloud.

And clear in his head, so clearly that he thought by some miracle she'd woken up, he heard her voice.

'There's nothing to forgive.'

His eyes snapped open; he raised his head to look at her. But Judy lay motionless as before. Nothing had changed. Except that he fancied there was the faintest smile on her lips. He kissed her fingers, rearranged her hand on the covers, bent over and kissed her forehead too.

'Thank you,' he said. And felt a weight lift from his heart.

Nancy came back to White Waltham at the beginning of March. The doctors had pronounced her fit to fly, the enquiry into the loss of the Spitfire had found her not guilty of negligence, and the order had come through that she was to go back to the Training School to learn what she needed in order to qualify as a Class 3 pilot. The course was intense, and, assigned to a lady instructor, Joan Hughes, Nancy saw little of Mac, and never alone. But whenever their paths crossed the atmosphere was electric. As it always had been, she thought, but now, with the shared experience of Nancy's crash, there was an added dimension. She couldn't put a name to it – didn't even try – but it was there all the same. A sense of destiny, of inevitability. A feeling of anticipation. Of waiting. It reminded her oddly of the days immediately after the arrival of Jackie Cochran's telegram, the days when a life-changing experience was just over the horizon. And Nancy buzzed with it.

She flew Ansons, the mainstays of the taxi fleet, and looked forward to the day when she'd be able to fly a plane load of pilots to their destinations as a captain, not as a 'stooge'. She flew Oxfords, practising spinning and flying on only one of the two engines under the watchful eye of Joan Hughes, and then two or three solo flights. On one of these a side window jammed open and as she grew steadily colder, Nancy was uncomfortably reminded of her trek over Salisbury Plain. For a moment her confidence faltered, then she tossed her head impatiently and told herself to forget it. She'd learned an important lesson, and she was alive to tell the tale. That was really all that mattered.

174

Nearing the end of her course, Nancy's sense of anticipation regarding Mac began to spiral into urgency. A few more days and she'd be headed back for Ratcliffe. And then one afternoon as she left the classroom after a debriefing, Nancy came face to face with him.

'Nancy.'

'Hi.' She had the strangest feeling he'd been lying in wait for her.

'How's it all going?'

'Oh – fine.' She tried to sound nonchalant. 'I've just done a solo on a Magister.'

'You're not too overburdened with homework now?'

She frowned, puzzled.

A corner of his mouth quirked. 'I just wondered if you might fancy a night off. A drink, maybe? But I wouldn't want to interfere with your very important studies.'

Her heart soared. 'Oh, blow my studies! I think I've done more than enough to earn an evening off.'

'So you fancy a drink?'

'I'd love a drink! In a proper pub.'

Mac grinned. 'You're beginning to talk like a native. OK, then. I'll pick you up – say about seven thirty?'

'What do you mean, you'll pick me up?'

'On my bike.' He raised a quizzical eyebrow at her. 'Ever ridden pillion?'

'No!'

'Want to try it?'

'Yes!'

'Wrap up warm, then. And you'd better wear slacks.'

'This,' Nancy said, 'is unreal.'

*   *   *

And so it was, the whole, magical evening. She adored the Douglas, sitting perched behind Mac with her arms wrapped tightly around his waist and the wind blowing her scarf back from her head to whip her hair into frenzied curls, and the throb of the engine reverberating through her body. She loved the pub he chose, way out in the country, and reminiscent of the one where they'd had a meal the night they were 'stuck out' – all oak beams, ancient farming implements and horse brasses, and a roaring log fire to bring the life back to her limbs, which, she found when she tried to get off the Douglas, were stiff with the cold, though she'd never even noticed in the excitement of the ride. And she loved every moment of being alone with Mac in a private oasis in the middle of the throng of locals. She chattered happily, and they were on their second drink when she noticed that Mac was very quiet. In itself that was not so unusual – Mac was never the most talkative of men – but she suddenly sensed something close to preoccupation, and having noticed it, became more and more aware of it. Yet he'd seemed his usual self earlier on.

'What's wrong?' she asked.

He seemed to come back from a long way off, but it was still a moment before he answered her. He offered her a cigarette and lit it for her, his hand cupping hers. Then he lit his own and looked at her through the haze of smoke.

'How would you feel about a permanent posting to White Waltham?'

Nancy's eyes narrowed. 'I'm supposed to be going back to Ratcliffe.'

'I know. But if I could swing it . . .'

'I'd love to be based at White Waltham.' With you. She didn't say it, but she didn't need to.

'OK. I'll see what I can do.' He drew deeply on his cigarette, stubbed it out and nodded at her glass. 'Do you want another?'

'Oh, why not?' Nancy drained the remains of her cider in one long pull.

'Steady on,' he said. 'I don't want you falling off the back of the bike on the way home.'

'As if! I shall be holding on to you for grim death.'

'Good.' There was a twinkle in his eyes; her heart leaped. He was back with her.

She watched him go to the bar, easing his way in between the locals, and thought about it. The preoccupation had been about the suggestion he'd just made. He hadn't been sure how she'd take it, been wondering, maybe, how to raise it. It had mattered to him, and that could mean only one thing . . . Why not go for broke? Nancy thought, two pints of cider and the thrill of the motorcycle ride making her reckless.

Mac returned with the drinks.

'Why do you want to get me posted to White Waltham?' she asked, looking at him mischievously over the rim of her glass.

He matched her gaze. 'Because you're a danger to yourself. I want you where I can keep an eye on you.'

'The nerve! And there was I thinking it was because I'm the best pilot in the whole of the ATA.'

'Nancy.' His face went serious; he lowered his voice. 'I think you know as well as I do why I want you at White Waltham. And it has nothing whatever to do with how well – or how badly – you fly.'

A nerve jumped in her stomach. 'I know,' she said softly. 'Or at least, I hoped.'

'You've got under my skin, Nancy. From the minute I saw you hanging upside down in that Puss Moth, and smelling—'

'Like a French brothel – I know. Won't you *ever* let me forget it?'

'Probably not.' He treated her to a wicked grin, then turned serious, embarrassed even. 'Anyway, the fact is . . . I don't want you to go. Only I wasn't sure how you'd feel about it.'

Nancy smiled faintly. 'I think you know very well how I feel. I'm not exactly subtle, am I? No matter how hard I try not to make a complete idiot of myself, I still do. I just can't help it.' She pressed her fingers to her mouth, studying the beer mat on the table top intently without noticing a single detail. Then she looked up, meeting his eyes directly. 'I want to be with you, Mac, more than anything else in the world. There – I've said it. I warned you I'm not subtle.'

His mouth quirked. 'You're Nancy.'

''Fraid so. And I'm not likely to change.'

'I sincerely hope not!' He reached across the table, covering her hand with his. The touch was electric to her; more than simply the contact, it seemed to her to have enormous significance. It was the first time he had touched her intentionally – unless you counted the night when he'd rescued her after the crash, and that had been in the spontaneity of relief and possibly to comfort her. This was different – this was deliberate – an expression of something he couldn't put into words. Yet – if ever. She turned her hand over; their fingers entwined.

'Mac . . .'

'Are you sure about this, Nancy?' He was looking at her intently.
'Yes.'

'You know I can't give you anything?'
'Yes.'

'No promises. No commitment . . .'

She swallowed hard. 'Yes. I know the way things are, Mac. And . . .'

'You're happy to go along with that? Until such time . . .' His voice tailed away.

She knew what he meant, saw the bleakness that was there briefly in his eyes. Her throat closed. It wasn't ideal, but it was more than she'd dared expect. Nancy would have been prepared to settle for far less if it only meant seeing him, being with him. She loved him. She knew that now. She loved him more than she'd ever imagined she could love anyone. Totally. Unconditionally.

'Mac, I'm more than happy,' she said. And knew it was nothing less than the truth.

IX

In the spring of 1943, a cautious optimism began to grow along with the buds and new leaves. The terrible air raids by the Luftwaffe were a thing of the past now, and pressure was growing for the blackout restrictions to be lifted and the church bells to be allowed to ring again. And at last the Allied Bomber Commands had enough suitable aircraft at their disposal to begin a serious programme aimed at destroying the German military and the big industrial sites on the Ruhr.

Nancy worried about Joe. She knew that he would be flying daily – the Americans, with their heavily armed Flying Fortresses, preferred daylight raids, whereas the RAF attacked mainly at night. Besides the obvious dangers, she had heard horror stories of aircraft running out of fuel because bad weather, or a crash on the runway, had prevented them landing at their own base and they had been forced to stack elsewhere. But at least he was no longer in Scotland, far too far from the targets for comfort; he was now based near the south coast, and Nancy tried not to think too much about the dangers he faced.

For the most part, she was happier than she had ever been in her life. Mac had found her a little flat in White Waltham, and she was thrilled to have a place of her own, cramped and dingy though it might be. The first thing she had done was put a coat of fresh emulsion on the walls and a lick of sparkling white gloss paint on the woodwork, and she had bought bright yellow oilcloth to line the shelves and cupboards. She managed to find bright cushions and even an orangey-yellow glass vase that stood in its own matching dish, and seemed to reflect what sunlight managed to creep in at the little windows. She bought cushions, and a hand-embroidered cloth to cover the ring-marked table, and at a village fair to raise money for the Spitfire fund she acquired little matching pots for honey and jam fashioned to look like miniature cottages. In her mind's eye she saw herself and Mac lingering over breakfast with these exotic crocks on the table between them, though as yet he had scarcely set foot in the place. He still had his own accommodation in Maidenhead, and there was precious little time in any case for anything but flying. But she could dream, and she did. She began collecting recipes that she could cook for him, she who had never had to do more than boil an egg in her entire life. And she laundered the sheets with the greatest care, imagining that one day he would perhaps share the bed with her. It was a time of utter exhaustion and breathless anticipation, and she wished it could last for ever.

Nancy, writing pad balanced on her knee, chewed on the end of her pen and wondered how in the world she was going to break the news to Joe that she was in love with someone else. It wasn't the first time she'd tried, and failed. Each week when she sat down to write to him she was determined to find the words; each week she chickened out. Sighing, she reread what she had already written.

Dear Joe,

Hope this finds you well. The weather is much better now – I really think spring is coming – and I've been flying every day.

I really love my little flat here at White Waltham. I'm trying to make it really homey, like I did the trailer. Looking out for bits and pieces is fun, though the shops are pretty empty, really.

So far, so good. But then things began to get difficult. Joe would expect some report of what she was doing in her spare time, and that was mostly spent with Mac.

'Went to the cinema and saw *Casablanca*,' she wrote. 'Humphrey Bogart and Ingrid Bergman were just marvellous.' But she made no mention of how she'd tucked her arm into Mac's as they'd walked home and teased him, 'Here's looking at you, kid!' in her authentic American accent. 'A few of us went for a drink last night . . .' – but not a word to let on that she had travelled to the pub on the back of Mac's Douglas. And the omission was a weight of guilt sitting inside her like a poorly digested meal. She was deceiving him because she couldn't bear the thought of hurting him, but wasn't that even worse?

'He deserves the truth, Nancy,' Mac had said when they'd talked about it the previous evening. 'I wouldn't want to think you were being less than honest with me just to spare my feelings. It's an insult really.'

And he was right, she knew in her heart he was. Yet still, when she imagined how hurt Joe would be, she shrank from finding the words that would break his heart.

'I will do it, Mac. I will,' she had promised.

They had been sitting together in a corner of the pub, oblivious to the raucous laughter of the crowd they'd come with. Funny how they could disappear into a world of their own. Funny, but wonderful. Last night he'd talked for the first time about his family and now Nancy allowed her attention to wander, mulling over his descriptions of his childhood in rural Gloucestershire, long summer days roaming the countryside with his two brothers, winter evenings when they'd make piles of toast in front of a roaring fire, and play dominoes or fight battles with their toy soldiers.

His family, it seemed, were pretty well off – they owned a brewery – and though he didn't go into details, she got the impression that his father had not been best pleased when Mac had chosen to join the RAF rather than the family firm. Whatever, it was a very different background from Nancy's own, and it fascinated her, as did everything about Mac, if the truth be told.

With an effort she put aside her drifting thoughts and tried to concentrate on the letter to Joe. She should tell him about Mac. She really should. But the moment she began to pen the words her stomach clenched with an almost superstitious knot of dread. Supposing something should happen to him right after he received her Dear John? She'd never forgive herself for hurting him so much. Wasn't it better by far to let him down gently?

After a moment's hesitation, Nancy ripped the letter in two and began again.

Nancy had had a long and tiring day. The taxi Anson taking her to her first job – a Martinet from Heston to Little Rissington – had left White Waltham just after ten that morning, and thereafter she had spent the day ferrying Spitfires to and from various repair units and airfields. The longest time she had been on the ground was at

Chattis Hill, where she had to wait for an hour for her plane to be made ready, and the shortest at Castle Bromwich, where the team were only too anxious to be rid of the repaired aircraft so that they could pack up and go home, and she had a break of only ten minutes. By the time she landed back at White Waltham just before six in the evening, Nancy was shaking with exhaustion and a dull headache was starting behind her tired eyes.

Mac was nowhere to be seen – he was doing a taxi run, someone told her. Nancy debriefed, dumped her flying kit, and managed to bag a lift home with an engineer who was going her way.

Back in her flat, she investigated the contents of the larder without much enthusiasm. Half a loaf of stale bread, a couple of onions, a tin of Spam and an egg. Hardly the ingredients for a banquet, and she didn't feel like bothering to cook anyway. The headache was getting worse, a dull throb in her temple interspersed with a sharp stabbing pain that made her feel a bit nauseous. She pressed the sore spot with her fingertips, wondering anxiously if she'd done some damage to herself when she'd crashed the Spitfire that the medicos had failed to pick up on. She couldn't remember having headaches like this before the accident. In fact, she could scarcely remember having a headache at all, unless she'd drunk too much alcohol. Now, however, they seemed to come with monotonous regularity.

Nancy slapped the tin of Spam down onto the counter and squeezed the bread to see if there was any give in it at all. There wasn't. 'I do not want a dry bread Spam sandwich,' she said aloud. 'In fact, I don't think I want anything at all.'

Except a bath. She could die for a bath. She went into the tiny bathroom, filled the copper and lit the gas under it. Then, while she was waiting for it to hot up, she went back to the living room, took a couple of aspirins, ate one of the precious chocolate bars that were issued to pilots to combat hunger and low blood sugar when they were flying, made a cup of tea, and sat down. The moment she put her feet up, however, the tiredness overwhelmed her, and with no warning whatsoever she fell asleep. She woke an hour later to find the flat full of steam and the copper bubbling as furiously as a witch's cauldron.

'Oh, sucks!' The sleep hadn't refreshed her; it had made her feel thicker and woozier than ever, and the thought of having to bail the water out of the copper was as unappealing as cooking a meal had been. But she couldn't waste the hot water, and she thought a bath would do her good. She opened a window in the living room to let out some of the steam but it still hung in a thick fug in the bathroom, and she had no intention of opening a window there and having to bath in a cold draught. Using her biggest saucepan under the tap of the boiler and a smaller one as a dipper, she transferred the hot water to the bath, ran enough cold in to make it the right temperature, and climbed in.

Oh, bliss! In just a few minutes the hot bath had done for Nancy what the sleep in the chair had failed to do. Her headache was easing, her tired limbs were relaxing, and she began to feel refreshed.

And the doorbell rang.

For a moment, Nancy considered not answering it, then it rang again, too loud and insistent to ignore. Muttering to herself, she clambered out of the bath, wrapped herself in a towel, and dripped her way across the living room.

'Who is it?' she called from behind the still closed door.

'It's me.'

'Mac?' She opened the door a crack.

'Yes – me! Can I come in, or not?'

'Oh my God – no! I'm not dressed! I was in the bath . . .'

'You'd better go and put some clothes on then. Unless you want to be ravished.'

A nerve jumped deep inside her; a twist of reckless desire. *Oh, yes, please, I want to be ravished. You have no idea how much* . . . But she couldn't be so brazen as to open the door to him wearing nothing but a towel.

'I'll only be a minute.' She padded into the tiny bedroom, struggled into her art silk kimono, which stuck to her since her skin was still damp, and tied the sash securely. 'OK, I'm decent now.'

She opened the door, smiled up at him, expecting – waiting for – him to kiss her. Instead, he gave her a grim, narrow look that was almost a glare and abruptly averted his eyes. Then he marched across to the ring-marked dining table and plonked a quarter-bottle of whisky down on it.

'I came by this today. I thought you might like to share it.' His tone was short too.

'Yes, great!' Nancy tried to sound enthusiastic, though his mood was making her uncomfortable. 'I'm not sure I should, though. I haven't had anything to eat. I was really tired when I got home. Not feeling too good. And I haven't got anything worth eating anyway.'

'Perhaps we should go out then.' Mac was still avoiding looking at her, busy uncapping the whisky. Nancy stared at his unyielding back, bewildered.

'But I'll have to get dressed again.'

He didn't reply, just went to the cabinet where the glasses were kept, took one out and poured himself a generous measure of whisky. 'Do you want one or not?' Still not looking at her, he tossed back the drink.

'No, I've got a headache.' She went to him, winding her arms around his waist, and felt him stiffen. 'What's wrong, Mac?'

'Oh, I heard today another of my pals has bought it. Shot down in flames. Old Johnny Westwood. Shouldn't come as a surprise, of course. There aren't many of my squadron left. But it still gets to you.'

Nancy had come to know all too well the blasé way flyers talked when one of their colleagues was lost. The insouciance, the façade of breezy acceptance, as if a pretence of not caring could make it so. They didn't let on their true feelings; grief was pushed into a dark corner, along with the knowledge that next time they could be the one who did not return. She didn't know how close a friend of Mac's this Johnny Westwood was, but she did know that the loss of any of his old squadron would have hit him hard, and beneath his deliberately matter-of-fact manner he would be grieving privately.

'Oh, Mac, I'm so sorry.' She laid her face against his broad back, pressing the full length of her body against him. She could feel the tension in him and she slid her hands up to his shoulders, massaging them gently as if unknotting his muscles could ease the pain in his heart.

His response, however, was not as she expected. He stiffened still more, slammed the glass down on the table and spun round to face her.

'For God's sake, Nancy! What are you trying to do to me?'

Nancy took a step back as if he'd struck her, bewildered, hurt. 'I'm only trying to comfort you.'

'Well – don't. OK?'

The aggression in his tone shocked her. He'd never spoken to her like that before. It was as if there was a wild animal there,

inhabiting his skin and barely under control. Nancy felt her lip wobble, and realising that she was close to bursting into tears made her own hackles rise.

'I know you're upset, but don't take it out on me!' she flared. 'Take your darned whisky and go drink it with somebody who understands you – or on your own, for all I care. But on second thoughts, I'll have one first. I damn well need it now!'

She grabbed the bottle, poured some into his glass and downed it in one quick gulp. As she reached for the bottle again she felt his arms go round her.

'Nancy, I'm sorry . . .'

She turned to him, her anger dying as swiftly as it had risen.

'Oh, Mac . . .' His mouth was on hers, cutting her off mid-sentence; she was crushed against him so tightly she could scarcely breathe. Her body was melting into his, the first sharp twist of excitement spiralled deep within her, her flesh, magnetised, prickled with awareness, and the world shrank to a bubble where nothing mattered but the two of them and the chemistry sparking between them. Nancy felt his hands caressing her through the thin silk of her kimono; his mouth slid down her throat, a slight rough stubble on his chin scratching the tender skin as he burrowed down into her shoulder. Her knees felt weak; she pressed closer, both for support and because she wanted to feel every inch of his body against hers. And suddenly, with a groan, he pushed her away.

'Christ.' He was making for the door, not even looking at her. 'I'm going home.'

'But . . . why?' She was trembling, confused. 'What have I done?'

He didn't answer her. The door slammed after him and Nancy was alone. She stood frozen for a moment, shocked by the violence of his reaction, feeling as though the ground had been cut away from under her. Then her breath came out on a small shaky sob, first one, then another and another, reverse hiccups that rose and fell in her chest. She pressed a hand to her mouth, staring over it at the closed door as if even now it would open again and he would walk back in.

She couldn't believe he'd gone like that. Her body ached with desolation. She'd wanted him so much – still did. Every bit of her was crying out for him. And she'd thought he wanted her too. He'd kissed and held her with such hunger she'd been sure . . . But then, in an instant, he'd turned cold. Thrust her away as if she was repellent to him. And gone. Gone without a word of explanation or even a goodbye.

'You bastard!' she exploded. 'How can you treat me like that? Good riddance is all I can say!'

She pounded the air with her fists, wishing it was his face she was pounding. The face that could set into hard lines, shutting her out. The face that could look so arrogant, so self-assured. The face that went into deep creases when he smiled, the mouth quirking, the eyes warm and teasing . . . And suddenly she was crying, anger dissolving, wretchedness a physical pain melting her bones. She folded in on herself, bending double as the sobs racked her body and the tears coursed down her cheeks.

She loved him. Loved him desperately. But he didn't love her. Didn't want her. Not really. As a distraction, maybe. An amusement. Somebody to while away a free hour. Nothing more. That was all she'd ever be to him. And now – maybe not even that. After the way he'd walked out on her she couldn't imagine there was any way back.

As she straightened Nancy realised her kimono was gaping open at the neck, exposing most of one breast. Well, it didn't matter now. Nothing mattered except that it was over, and she'd never be with him like this again. She felt the tears threatening once more and angrily yanked the neck of the kimono back into place and retied the sash.

The whisky bottle was still on the table, uncapped. Not much left in it now, but enough. Nancy emptied it into the glass they'd both used, stared at it for a moment, then drank. She'd probably have a filthy headache tomorrow – but who cared? Right now she wished there was enough left to drink herself into oblivion.

Mac opened the throttle of the Douglas and rode like a man possessed. But he couldn't leave behind the grief and anger he felt at the loss of Johnny Westwood – another young life cut short, another face he would see no more, another pal he'd never again share a drink and a joke with. And he couldn't escape the image of Nancy, thin silk skimming her curves, damp hair curling round a face rosy from her bath and lying in tendrils at the nape of her neck. He could still smell the fragrance of her skin and feel the tantalising curves of her body against his. Christ, he wanted her! Wanted her so much he was consumed by it. But at the same time . . .

He couldn't do it. Couldn't give in to the desire that flared in him like a forest fire. It wasn't simply a conscious decision, it went far deeper than that. Reason told him that Judy could not be hurt by him making love to Nancy. But the fidelity he'd promised in his marriage vows and practised ever since were too deeply ingrained. He'd never cheated on her, apart from those couple of drunken lapses, which scarcely counted. This was different. Nancy was in his blood. In his heart. To make love to her would be to betray Judy at the most basic level, and to do so now, when she was utterly helpless, more vulnerable than she had ever been, was utterly abhorrent to him. He couldn't do it, no matter how he wanted to. He was at war with himself, and it was tearing him apart.

He'd known, of course, the minute Nancy had opened the door to him what he should do. The minute she'd said she was undressed. The minute he'd smelled the warm, damp scent of her. He should have turned around and left there and then. But he'd thought he could handle it. Joked, even, about ravishing her.

And then she'd come back and let him in, wearing nothing but that damned silk dressing gown thing, and he'd known he was in trouble. He'd tried his best to shut her out. Bury his desire in anger at Johnny Westwood's cruel and senseless death. But his grief had also made him vulnerable. When she had put her arms round him and he had felt her body pressed against his, ratcheting up his need, he'd turned that anger on her, and even that hadn't worked.

God Almighty, he'd been that close . . . until the habit born of three years of marriage and two years of virtual celibacy had kicked in. The self-imposed restraint. The sick guilt. It had sobered him like a bucket of ice-cold water. He had to get out. Get away from the temptation that was Nancy. No stopping to explain – heck, he couldn't even explain it to himself. He only knew he wanted her too damned much, and he couldn't have her. Not now. Possibly not ever.

Mac hunched over the handlebars of the Douglas and opened the throttle fully in a vain attempt to exorcise the frustration and despair that were tearing him apart.

She didn't know how she was going to face him again, but she had to. Avoiding him for ever was impossible. Though she certainly did her best to!

The way she turned and high-tailed it in the opposite direction if she saw him approaching, and stuck her chin in the air and pointedly ignored him when there was no other option but to come face to face might even have been comical, Mac conceded, if he didn't care so damned much. As it was . . .

'Nancy, I owe you an apology.' He'd cornered her in the kit store where she was off-loading her parachute after a day's ferrying.

Her shoulders moved in a small shrug; she didn't turn round, just went on with what she was doing.

'Hey, come on,' he said. 'We can't keep this up for ever. We're going to have to fly together sometime.'

Another shrug. 'I thought you'd have had me transferred elsewhere by now.'

'You know that's not what I want.'

She swung round now, clutching her kitbag to her chest like a breastplate, chin jutting, eyes defiant. 'You could have fooled me.'

'Nancy.' Mac spread his arms helplessly, resisting the temptation to turn round and walk away from this. 'I've said I'm sorry. What more can I do?'

'You always make a fool of me, don't you?' she blazed. 'You always have. Right from the first time we met.'

He groaned impatiently. 'Nobody is making a fool of you.'

'No?'

'No.'

'Well, I guess I make a pretty good job of it all by myself.'

'Oh, you're just being silly now.'

'There you are! It's what you think of me.'

'It's not what I think of you at all. You know perfectly well how much I think of you.'

'Well, you've got a pretty funny way of showing it.'

'Nancy . . . I shouldn't have walked out on you that night. We should have talked it through there and then. I just didn't trust myself to stay a minute longer.'

'What's to talk about?' she interrupted him. 'You made yourself pretty clear.'

'You've got it all wrong.'

'Really?' she snorted. 'I might be a brash Yank, but I know a brush-off when I see one. You didn't want me. End of story.'

Mac was holding on to his patience with difficulty now. Why did she have to be so dense – so exasperating?

'Of course I wanted you,' he said roughly. 'Too much. But I told you, Nancy, right from the start, I couldn't offer you anything. You know the way things are.'

'I didn't know that meant you'd cut me dead and leave me cold.'

'I'm trying to explain. If I'd stayed . . . you were driving me crazy, Nancy. Another minute and I'd have—' He broke off.

Nancy's lip wobbled. 'And would that have been so wrong? Isn't that what people who are in love do? Except that you don't love me, do you, Mac? You're still in love with your wife.'

'Of course I still love her. You can't just switch off because it's not convenient any more. And I can't be unfaithful to her either. But that doesn't mean I don't love you too. Oh . . . !' He half turned away, running a hand through his hair and leaving his forehead resting on the heel of his hand. 'I can't expect you to understand, Nancy. I don't understand myself . . .'

She was melting inwardly. He'd said he loved her. He *had* said it, hadn't he? Or had she imagined it?

'Did you say you loved me?' she asked, half afraid that she was just making a fool of herself again.

'Yes, dammit. You know I do.'

'Oh, Mac.' She could feel tears pricking her eyes, the tears that for her inevitably followed anger. But this time they were tears, not of happiness, exactly, but the most profound, overwhelming sense of relief. She touched his arm. 'Oh, Mac . . . I love you too. What the hell are we going to do?'

He shook his head, his shoulders bowed. 'I don't know, Nancy.'

'But you do want to be with me?'

He nodded wordlessly, slumping now beneath the defeat and despair. Nancy, on the other hand, felt invigorated and powerful suddenly. If Mac loved her half as much as she loved him, anything was possible.

'OK,' she said, 'here's what we'll do. We'll go on seeing each other, but we'll make sure we're not alone together in the sort of situation . . . well, a repeat of the other night. At least – until you're ready.'

He turned; his eyes met hers. 'I don't know how long that will be. I told you – no promises, Nancy.'

'I don't care!' she said passionately. 'However long it takes . . . I'll wait for you, Mac. I wish it were different, but . . . we've just got to make the best of it, haven't we?'

'Oh, come here.' He pulled her into his arms, no passion this time, just a warm bear hug. 'I thought I'd lost you.'

'No chance,' she murmured against his chest.

As she'd said, she wished with all her heart that it could be different. But beggars couldn't be choosers. And she felt proud and blessed that the man she'd fallen in love with was honourable and faithful and strong. Right now, those qualities were against her. But maybe one day . . .

Judy, she thought, had been a very lucky woman.

X

'This is just the stupidest thing ever!'

Nancy, on her hands and knees in the middle of the airstrip, straightened her aching back and let out a grunt of frustration. All around her, also crawling along on all fours, were practically the entire staff of Number 1 Ferry Pool – pilots, cloakroom attendants and waitresses from the canteen, each armed with a cardboard box or a bucket. Even the CO himself was amongst the motley army that had been assembled to cope with the strangest emergency ever to affect White Waltham.

Mac, working alongside her, raised a rueful eyebrow and tossed a rusty tin opener into his bucket, where it landed with a loud clunk on the assortment of nails and screws he had already collected.

'Got to be done, sweetheart, if we want to get the planes flying.'

Nancy snorted. 'I just can't believe anyone could be so stupid as to dump rubbish like this on an airfield! A monkey would have more sense than the people who run your Ministry.'

Mac smiled and said nothing, but privately he agreed with her. This was a cock-up of the first order. When the airfield had been resown earlier in the year in preparation for the enlargement that was planned, some bright spark had decreed that a top layer of soil should be laid over the seed to act as a mulch for the growing grass. And so it did – the grass had grown beautifully. Unfortunately, the top soil had been contaminated with rubble from bomb sites, and only when one plane after another punctured tyres on take-offs and landings was it discovered that the entire field was covered with a fine sprinkling of broken glass, nails, screws, and even the odd tin opener or rusty knife.

White Waltham, normally a hive of activity, had become a ghost station overnight. The only planes that left the ground flew out of the nearby Forty Acre Field, and it was all hands to the pump in an effort to clear the airfield of the offending debris. For two days now from dawn to dusk they had crawled in a line like an organised search party, and the monotony of it was driving Nancy mad.

'It's never going to work,' she said dismissively. 'We can't possibly clear every last bit. It's just impossible. And the next plane that lands will find what we didn't – you can bank on it.'

'We just have to be thorough.' Mac was continuing to work steadily. 'Come on, keep up, Nancy.'

'I bet you've missed some – I bet you have!' She broke line, scrabbling about in the ground Mac had just covered. 'There you are – look! A six-inch nail and a piece of broken glass.' She overtook him again and waved her finds triumphantly under his nose. 'See! Even you, Mr Perfect, managed to miss these, so I sure as hell wouldn't want to land on the strip that drippy waitress with acne and adenoids covered – what's her name?'

Mac, annoyed at having been found wanting, snatched the shard of glass from Nancy so abruptly that he cut his finger.

'Well, have you got any better suggestions?'

'Actually, yes. What you want – for the metal stuff anyway – is a magnet.'

'Oh yes, great.' Mac sucked on his cut finger. 'I can just imagine the Ministry's response if we indented for a couple of hundred magnets.'

'Not a couple of hundred,' Nancy said scornfully. 'Just a few really big ones. And you need something wide and low to attach them to, like one of those sowing machines the farmers use to plant their crops.' She was warming to her idea. 'They cover the field in broad sweeps, don't they?'

Mac, initially scathing, stopped work and looked at her narrowly. 'You know, you might have something there . . .'

'Well, anything has got to be better than this.' Nancy dug out a door hinge and dropped it in her bucket. Mac got up, brushing rubble from his knees. 'You're breaking line, sir,' she said mischievously.

He cast her a withering look. 'I'm going to talk to somebody about your suggestion,' he said.

Nancy watched him walk away, stopping to speak to someone – probably the CO – and went back to work feeling mightily pleased with herself, and with life, as she almost always did these days.

It had been a wonderful few months, working and playing along-side Mac. They'd stuck to their bargain not to spend time alone together in the kind of situation that might all too easily end up with things getting out of hand, and it had worked. They socialised with the others from the base, drinking at the Coach and Horses, eating chunks of delicious bread pudding at Mrs Cook's Restawhile Café in Cherry Garden Lane, taking the ATA bus into Maidenhead for a dance or cinema trip, and it was fun. There were plenty of times, of course, when Nancy yearned for more, but she was determined to make the most of what she had. She recalled all too clearly the utter desolation she had felt when she'd thought she'd lost Mac to want to risk such a thing again, and in any case, life was too short – and too uncertain – to waste a single moment on regrets or frustration for what might have been. To her shock and dismay, Nancy had heard that Norah Taft had been killed when her plane had suffered a total engine failure on take-off and she had thought how ironic it was that Norah, one of the best and most meticulous pilots she had ever met, should have died, whilst she, with all her faults, had survived – so far. Then, only recently, a pupil and his instructor had been killed right here in White Waltham when two Blenheims collided shortly after take-off. Measures were being taken now to set up some kind of air traffic control, but even if it worked – and Mac, for one, was doubtful it would – there would always be other hazards. It was a dangerous business they were engaged in – it could not be otherwise – and Nancy knew that her world could all too easily be torn apart, her life or Mac's ended abruptly in a pile of twisted metal or a watery coffin.

She kept up her diaries, recording all her happiest moments in detail and mentioning the tragedies only briefly. She bought a Box Brownie camera and took scores of photographs, much to Mac's amusement – and irritation when she tried to snap him. Mac didn't care for having his picture taken. And she hugged to herself the love that they shared. Unconsummated it might be, but at least they were together. And for that Nancy was truly grateful.

Even if it did mean spending two boring days on her hands and knees scouring an airfield for anything that could cause a puncture in an aeroplane tyre . . .

She was still beavering away, doing her best to keep pace with the line and ruing the damage to her fingernails, when Mac came back.

'I reckon you'll soon be able to call it a day,' he said.

'It looks as if you already have!'

He grinned. 'Where's the good in being second in command if you can't use your influence sometimes?'

'To get out of a horrible, backbreaking job.'

'No, to be able to take suggestions right to the top. Looks like they're going to come up with a way to make use of your idea, Nancy.'

'No way!' Nancy could scarcely believe it. Then she smiled, all her natural ebullience coming to the surface. 'See, you have to admit it. We Americans are absolutely brilliant!'

'And so modest!'

The air-raid siren began to wail suddenly; the entire workforce scrambled to their feet, casting anxious glances at the sky and heading for the air-raid shelters. There were no enemy aircraft to be seen, but daytime raids were not uncommon.

As they made their way across the open ground Nancy felt no fear, only a strange, unreal exhilaration. She actually enjoyed living close to the edge, she realised. It sharpened the senses and heightened emotion; made one feel truly alive. She glanced at Mac, walking briskly beside her, and felt the now familiar swell of warmth, tenderness and desire.

She'd wanted excitement, and she'd sure as heck got it. She'd wanted a man to sweep her off her feet, and she'd got that too. It might not be perfect, but what in this life ever was? She was, she thought, the luckiest girl in the world.

In that summer of 1943 Nancy felt proudly patriotic.

'What would you do without us, eh?' she demanded when shipping losses in the Atlantic fell dramatically. 'It's all down to our destroyers that the U-boats are on the run.'

'And our bombers.' Mac could be equally patriotic.

'We've captured Palermo without even a struggle! They knew when they saw the Yanks they might as well wave the white flag.'

'And we've done pretty well in Africa. The Germans and Italians have surrendered there too.'

'Because you had the help of the New Zealanders.'

'And what about the raids on the dams? That's one success we managed all on our own.'

It was also one she couldn't argue with. In May, 617 Squadron, led by Wing Commander Guy Gibson, had successfully ruptured the dams on the Ruhr and Eder, causing mass destruction to much of Germany's industrial heartland. And the man who had dreamed up the 'bouncing bomb' that had inflicted all the damage was English too. How could he not be, with a name like Barnes Wallis?

'OK, I'll give you that one,' she agreed with an impish grin.

'I should hope so too.'

'But you've gotta admit, you'd be in trouble without us.'

'I am admitting nothing,' Mac said, and kissed her.

August 1943. Long blue days of summer, fruit ripening on the trees, roses blooming in the gardens, horse-drawn wagons laden with bales of harvested hay meandering along the lanes. Perfect flying weather. The bitter cold of winter, the fogs, the snow, seemed like a bad but distant dream now and Nancy found it hard to believe that it would, inevitably, come again.

She was a second officer now, qualified to fly advanced twin-engined types such as the Blenheim and the Wellington, and was inordinately proud of new stripes, one broad, one narrow. Kay had come to White Waltham for her Class 4 training too, and the two girls had enjoyed the chance to spend time together and catch up with all the gossip.

'I always knew you two were sweet on each other,' Kay said when Nancy confided her relationship with Mac. 'You could see that a mile off.'

'So I recall,' Nancy said ruefully.

'Joe couldn't have been very happy about getting the brush-off.'

Nancy bit her lip, unwilling to admit she was still procrastinating.

'He is going to be so hurt, Kay. I just can't bear the thought of breaking his heart,' she said guiltily.

'You mean you haven't told him?'

'Not yet. I mean – anything could happen.'

'I guess, but still . . .'

'I'm going to do it. I just have to pick my moment. When he gets some leave, maybe, and I know he isn't going to be flying. I'm scared he's going to take it real hard. If he's all upset, he might lose concentration, do something rash. If he crashed right after I told him, I'd never forgive myself.'

'Well, I reckon you ought to give him more credit, and make it soon,' Kay said bluntly.

'I know,' Nancy answered. And felt the familiar weight of guilt and dread settle in her stomach.

The staff car pulled up alongside Nancy on the perimeter road as she was heading home after a long day's ferrying. To her surprise, she saw it was Mac in the driver's seat, leaning across to open the passenger door. Unusual. Generally the staff cars were chauffeured by one of the girl drivers. She climbed in, grateful for the lift.

'Hi! This is nice.'

'I borrowed the car. Nancy, we need to talk.'

A frisson of alarm shivered inside her. Mac looked, and sounded, serious.

'What's wrong?'

'Let's get away from here. Find somewhere quiet.'

'Mac?' He didn't answer. 'Mac, what's going on?'

'I'll tell you in a minute.'

He was heading for the open country. Nancy glanced at him; his face told her nothing. When they met a herd of cows being driven in for milking he drummed his fingers impatiently on the steering wheel as the udder-heavy animals barged their way past the car. Nancy's imagination ran riot. What the hell did he want to talk to her about? Had something happened to Judy – or Joe? To Kay? Had the powers that be decided she should move to another pool? The possibilities chased one another round inside her head.

There was a copse up ahead; Mac slowed, pulled up at the side of the road and reversed up the track that led into it. Deep in the trees, he stopped, switched off the engine and turned to her.

'I've been passed fit for active duty. I'm rejoining my squadron.'

Her jaw dropped; she felt her heart drop with it.

'Mac! When?'

'I saw the MO today.'

'No, I mean, when are you going?'

'With immediate effect.'

'Oh my God.' She felt numb. 'But I thought . . .'

A corner of his mouth quirked. 'I suspect I'm in pretty good shape compared with most of the pilots they've got left. And certainly a whole lot more experienced than the boys they're taking in now. Time for me to get back in the hot seat, Nancy.'

A bolt of sheer terror made her feel sick. This wasn't just about separation. This was about Mac resuming operational flying. Leading a squadron. Escorting bombers into enemy territory. Dodging ack-ack. Being fired at. Maybe being hit again. Last time he'd been lucky. This time . . .

'Oh, Mac!' She buried her face in his shoulder, trying to shut out the vivid image of a Spitfire spiralling down, trailing black smoke.

He put his arm around her. 'Come on, it's not the end of the world.' *It might be.* 'I'll be OK.'

'I . . . I don't want you to go.' Her voice was muffled by his uniform jacket.

'No choice, I'm afraid.'

'Oh, I hate this war!'

'You don't. You love it.'

'Not any more.' This was her punishment for falling in love with a man who belonged to somebody else. For betraying Joe – and deceiving him. For all her past sins – the ones nobody knew about, and which she had thought she'd finally left behind her. Mac was going to be taken away from her and there was not a darned thing she could do about it. She raised her head, eyes bleak, chin trembling, looking at the planes and angles of his face, shadowed by the overhanging trees, and felt her heart breaking. 'I love you! I don't want to lose you.'

'Sweetheart – don't . . .'

His mouth was on hers, the smell of his skin in her nostrils – musky soap and tobacco. She clung to him, agony giving birth to urgency, sweeping away the caution and restraint of the last months.

Oh, Mac, Mac . . .

He moved away slightly; as his face came into focus she saw her

205

longing mirrored in the darkness of his narrowed eyes, an intensity he'd hidden from her before.

'I've got a week's leave.' His voice was low, urgent. 'You must have some leave due too.'

'Not a week.'

'I couldn't spare a week either. I need to go home, see my family, spend some time with Judy. But maybe we could snatch a couple of days . . .'

'But I thought . . . we agreed . . .'

'Nancy,' he said. 'I want you.'

It was all she needed to hear.

Two days. Two wonderful stolen days. It was all they could manage, maybe all they would ever have.

'I love you so much, Mac. I never thought I could feel this much love . . .'

They were lying, limbs entwined, in the deep feather bed in the secluded hotel where he had booked a room. Secluded – and discreet. Not an eyebrow had been raised when Mac signed the register 'Mr and Mrs'. If the receptionist suspected for a moment from the way Nancy blushed as she watched him do it, then she did not show it. This was wartime and the man was in uniform; usual proprieties were thrown to the winds.

Perhaps she thinks we're on honeymoon, Nancy thought, and felt her flush deepen.

An elderly porter had shown them to their room, summoned out of retirement when his younger counterpart had been called up, no doubt, Nancy thought as they followed the scrawny, bent figure up two flights of carpeted stairs. She could see Mac watching the man anxiously. He hadn't felt right about letting such a decrepit character carry his bag for him, she knew, but he had respected the man's pride and let him do it anyway.

As the porter unlocked the door for them she felt a rush of embarrassment. All very well to plan this, want it desperately – but the sight of the double bed made up and ready for them, the two stacks of towels piled neatly on the counterpane, made her self-conscious suddenly. And with the self-consciousness, a little dart of nervousness. She was far from experienced in this sort of thing, didn't really know what he would expect of her. Suppose she got it all wrong? Or, even worse, what if he suspected the secrets she hugged so closely to herself that even thinking about them now made her cringe inwardly? She'd thought once, long ago, that Joe's Aunt Dorothy had been able to see right through her, just by looking at her. Intimacy with Mac could be far more revealing. One day, if they ever got together properly, she'd tell him the truth about herself. But this was not the moment.

Mac was searching in his pockets for money to tip the porter; Nancy crossed the room, dumped her handbag on a fluffy stool and fingered a plastic-covered notice that lay on the dark polished wood dressing table beside it. Instructions as to what to do in the case of an air raid. She smiled faintly. If there was an air raid and the hotel suffered a hit, she and Mac would be caught out good and proper! Everyone would know – and they wouldn't be around to explain themselves.

The door clicked shut behind the porter. Nancy went on studying the 'Information for Our Guests'. She felt Mac's arms go round her; glanced up and saw the two of them reflected in the bevelled mirror, heads close together, her body obscuring most of his. Breath caught in her throat; a nerve jumped deep inside her.

'This tells us what we have to do . . .'

'I don't need telling. Do you?'

'. . . if there's an air raid.'

'There won't be an air raid.' His mouth was on her neck, covering the pulse point, his hands cupped her breasts. She shivered, desire and nervousness all mixed up together.

'There might be.' Anything to put off the moment. Anything to hide the way she felt.

'Trust me, there won't be.' He was unbuttoning her blouse, watching in the mirror as inch by inch it revealed more flesh.

'Mac . . . it's the middle of the afternoon . . .'

'So?'

His hands on the waistband of her skirt, unhooking the fastener, easing it over her hips until it slid down to the floor revealing French knickers, a wisp of suspender belt and dark stockings. Nancy stared at the reflection of this wanton woman, a little shy, and yet at the same time aware of a breathtaking feeling of excitement, abandonment.

'You are beautiful,' Mac said. His arm slid down behind the back of her knees; he lifted her bodily, holding her for a moment so that her forehead brushed his cheek, then turning towards the bed and setting her down on it.

Another little twist of panic. Last time they'd been this close to making love he'd suddenly remembered his marriage vows to Judy. For some reason, even now, Nancy had to be sure this was what he truly wanted.

'Mac, what about . . . ?' She didn't have to finish. She could see in his face that he knew what she had been going to say.

He laid a finger over her lips. For just a brief moment his eyes darkened – with pain, she knew, not lust. Then he said gruffly: 'Nancy, right here, right now, there's only you and me.'

And then his mouth was on hers and there was nothing more to say.

He took her gently at first, and only when he was sure she was ready, then again, with less restraint. He took her to places she had never dreamed existed, and afterwards, as she lay replete, floating in a cocoon of bliss, she realised that not once had she had to wonder what to do, or wanted to stop anything he had done to her. It had just been so right – still was.

'I'm so glad,' she whispered, meaning not only that she was glad that they'd fulfilled the desire that had overwhelmed them both, but also that they'd waited until now, which somehow made it all the more special. This was what was meant by love, this total oneness of body and spirit, this giving to one another and receiving so much more in return. The closeness had made them easy in one another's company, not awkward as she had feared, and if just once or twice she had sensed a withdrawal in Mac, it was quickly over, as if he were determined not to let anything spoil this special, stolen time. He had thought it all through, she realised, and come to a decision. For these two precious days she, and what they shared, had become his priority. Knowing it thrilled her and satisfied her; for the moment it was more than enough.

On the second day, though, with the end not only in sight but rushing towards her like a flood tide, Nancy began to feel the stirrings of panic and sharp painful glimpses of the desolation to come.

'I will see you sometimes, won't I?'

They were having breakfast in the hotel dining room – at least, Mac was having breakfast. Nancy, whose stomach was a churning nest of emotions, had no appetite at all.

'I don't know,' Mac said. 'It all depends.'

'But we hop around the country like crickets! I might have to deliver a plane to your station . . .'

'And what chance will there be for socialising?'

'But you'll get leave. You're bound to . . .'

'Much of which I will have to spend going home to Gloucestershire.'

Jealousy, sharp as acid, pricked her. Judy doesn't need you, she wanted to say. I do! But she knew she must not. He'd come this far, buried his scruples and his guilt to allow these special days to be, but it didn't mean he'd forgotten Judy. And it didn't mean he would abandon her either. If he felt it was his duty to continue his visits to her he would do it, and nothing Nancy could say would make any difference. Correction – it would make a difference, but not in a good way. If she upset the apple cart she had the most uncomfortable feeling that she would be the loser.

'How was Judy?' she asked. It was the first time they'd actually mentioned the three or four days Mac had spent at home; now it felt right to do so.

The bleakness flared in his eyes, but this time his face did not go shut in.

'The same.'

'Oh, Mac.' She reached across the table, covering his hand with hers. 'It's so terrible for you.'

'No worse than for plenty of other people.'

'I don't care about other people. I care about you.'

'I know. And for that I count myself lucky.'

'Lucky?'

'A lot of men live their whole life and never find what they're looking for. I've had Judy. And I have you.'

Her stomach wrenched. She was still sharing him. But she must try not to mind. She was lucky too. That was what she must hold on to.

'What are we going to do?'

The bleakness again. 'I don't know.' Followed by a look of resolve. 'All we can do, Nancy, is take one day at a time.'

'I can't bear for you to go.'

Their bags were packed and ready, stacked beside the door. Nancy and Mac lay on the bed, fully clothed, but in one another's arms.

'Nancy, don't.'

'But I can't. I can't bear it.'

He rucked up her skirt, rolled on top of her. As he entered her she wound her legs around his waist, nails biting into his shoulders, and felt his teeth raking her breast at the open neck of her blouse. For the moment nothing mattered but the movement of their bodies in urgent unison.

And then it was over. Not this time the bliss of burrowing into him, falling asleep in his arms. The bed shifted as he got up and fixed his clothing, his back turned towards her. He'd left her already, she realised. Their stolen time was over.

'We'd better be going.'

'Mac . . . thank you.'

He glanced at her over his shoulder, a grin creasing his chin.

'Any time. My pleasure.'

No, not any time. Maybe never again . . . She wanted to weep, to hold on to him and never let him go. Inwardly she was screaming. But all she said was: 'I'll never forget.'

Another quirk of his mouth. For a moment she thought he was going to say, 'Neither will I', but he did not. He wasn't a one for flowery sentiment and in any case the time for intimacy was gone. Mac had become a fighter pilot again – a squadron leader – a husband.

By tomorrow morning he would have gone, in person as well as in spirit.

It was over.

Part Three

The Present

Part Three

The Present

SARAH

We're somewhere over the Atlantic in that strange juddering limbo-land that is a Boeing 747. Already I've endured four hours of sitting in an armchair that feels like a straitjacket, four hours of enforced inactivity and meals that taste of plastic, and clattering trolleys and a never-ending stream of passengers squeezing past on their way to the loo, and the bored child behind me kicking the back of my seat, and there are still another four hours to go. By now I'm heartily sick of it; the time till we land stretches away into infinity. I love flying, but not as a passenger in a jumbo jet. Never that.

I've flicked through the in-flight magazines and I've tried to read the Sarah Waters novel that I started on the outward journey and haven't looked at for the whole three weeks I've been in Florida, but I seem to have lost the thread and can't summon the concentration to begin again. I've dozed a little and been woken up each time by a stewardess or a restless passenger, or that weird tinging noise that regularly punctuates the silence, or the captain giving us an update on our position and weather conditions. And I've cursed myself, just as I always do on the flight home, for not upgrading to club class where I could have had more leg room and more peace and quiet. Why is it that it always seems so much more tedious than the flight out; why do I mind all the petty irritations so much more? Because, I suppose, on the way to Florida I'm buoyed up with the anticipation of the weeks ahead of me, whereas now I can feel the shackles tightening round my wrists and ankles, the problems and stresses of everyday life closing in around me with every long minute, every throbbing mile.

It's dim in the cabin now; they've pulled the shutters and lowered the lights to a soft bluish glow, and the screens that show the in-flight movie or the graphics of a little aircraft over an endless sea of blue are lifeless and dark. I pull the lightweight cellular blanket up to my chin and try to find a comfortable position to rest my head, but I know that if I begin to drift off, something will happen to bring me back to sour-mouthed wakefulness, so instead I close my eyes and give myself up to my thoughts.

I have plenty to think about, that's for sure. More than enough to keep me occupied all the way back to Heathrow.

First and foremost, Grandma Nancy and the task she's set me – to find this Mac that she knew when she was flying with the ATA in England sixty-odd years ago. She said she wanted me to return a medal that he'd given her either to him, if he is still alive, or to his family. That it belongs rightfully to them and she doesn't want Ritchie disposing of it when something happens to her and he has to go through her things. But to be honest I think there's more to it than that. There was a glow about her when she talked of him that I've never seen before, and not a little wistfulness. I think she wants to contact him for herself, maybe even see him again, or at least know what became of him.

It's pretty unsettling, that thought. It has never before occurred to me that there had ever been anyone for her but Grandpa Joe. Now I'm not so sure. Correction. I am sure, as sure as I've ever been of anything. She was in love with this Mac. She's carried him in her heart all these years and we knew nothing about it – well, I certainly didn't. And now, with the end of her life coming closer, he's the one she's thinking of, the one waiting for her in the shadows.

It shocked me rigid at first. Nancy has always been just Nancy to me – kind, nice, fun to be with, my beloved grandmother, but somehow I'd never imbued her with the passions and foibles and failings of ordinary human beings. I saw her as timeless, as if she had always been as she is now – wherever 'now' might be. As a child, I'd loved to hear her stories about her own rackety childhood, buzzing round the country with her parents and the air circus, and of how she'd flown in the war with the ATA in England. But to me they were just that – stories, only as real as the books I read or the films I saw. And she was the heroine, a one-dimensional character, an image in the old photographs she showed me, and who bore little relation to the Nancy I knew – or thought I knew. I'd never stopped to scratch the surface, look deeper. I'd seen only what she'd allowed me to see, never knitted complications into the pattern.

Perhaps I hadn't wanted to. It doesn't sit comfortably to realise that Grandma Nancy might share the same turbulent emotions as me, the ones that I wouldn't care to expose to the public gaze; that as a young woman she had felt the same dark passions and uncertainties, the same ecstasies and despairs. And even less so that she might experience them still, more muted perhaps, but none the less potent, the longings of her youth that have followed her down the years into a body that has withered and grown stiff. That they have been there all the time in the secret heart of her as she cooked and cleaned and raised her family, as she went through life as Grandpa Joe's wife and my mother's mother, was an enormous shock to me.

I think now of the tiny signs I've seen and attached no significance to, a faraway look that might come into her eyes for no apparent reason, a half-smile that might curve her mouth, making her suddenly young again. There's one time I remember in particular.

It was 1995 and she was visiting us in England. I know it was 1995 because there were endless programmes on TV and radio celebrating fifty years since the end of the war. This particular programme was on local radio – interviews with veterans interspersed with the music of the era – Vera Lynn, Gracie Fields, Glenn Miller. Dad, always a radio fan, as in fanatic, had turned it on and then gone out to mow the lawn. Mum bustled in like a whirlwind, tutting, and went to switch it off.

'No, leave it,' Nancy said. She was arranging some dahlias she'd cut from the garden in a pottery vase I'd made when I was at school and by some miracle Mum had actually kept. She's not normally sentimental, my mother.

'That loud? They must be able to hear it in the next street.' Mum turned the radio down a fraction, bustled out again, tight-lipped, impatient.

I was searching in my bag for an emery board to smooth off a nail I'd snagged; I glanced at Grandma Nancy and our eyes met and engaged for a moment, an unspoken twinkle of shared amusement tinged with exasperation. Chill, Mum. I found the emery board, began filing off my broken nail.

I wasn't really listening to the radio; it was washing over me, though I recognised the song that was playing – 'For All We Know, We May Never Meet Again'. A few moments later when I looked up, Nancy was still there at the sink, in body at least, but she seemed to have gone into a trance. She was unmoving as a statue, scissors in one hand, purple spiked dahlia in the other, head tilted to one side, eyes half closed, one half of her mouth curved up into what was not quite a smile and not quite a grimace.

'Grandma – are you all right?'

She didn't seem to hear me, or if she did, she didn't answer, though her lips were moving. She was mouthing the words of the song, I realised, and I began to listen. It was a sweet, sad song, and it seemed to be about love and loss, and making the most of the moment.

'Grandma!'

She came back into focus then, the dreamy wistfulness replaced by something that might have been embarrassment.

'Sorry, honey. What was that?'

'Oh, nothing . . .' I was the one who was embarrassed now, that I'd somehow intruded on a private moment.

My first thought was that she'd been reminded of John, her son and Mum's elder brother, who was killed in a flying accident. I'd never known him; he'd died before I was born, before Mum came to England, even. But Mum had said that Nancy still mourned him and always would. 'He was her favourite,' she said, not without a touch of resentment. 'She'll never get over losing John.'

Then I wondered if Nancy had suddenly felt lonely for Grandpa Joe, and was worried something might happen to him while she was in England. He hadn't come with her; he rarely did. He was always too busy with the business and he wasn't keen on travelling too far from home. Strange for a pilot, but, 'I've had enough

219

of all that,' he'd say. 'I've seen the world. I'll stick to my own little corner of it now, if it's all the same with you.' Besides which, he'd had a health scare a couple of years back, a heart attack. He'd made a good recovery and the medication they had him on had put him back on a pretty even keel, but ever since he'd been more reluctant than ever to travel, and I knew Nancy worried about him. Perhaps she was secretly afraid she would never see him again.

'I'm sure Grandpa's fine,' I said. 'And you'll be home in a couple of weeks.'

She looked puzzled, startled even. 'Yes, I'm sure he is, honey.'

So it hadn't been Grandpa she had been thinking about. It must have been John. I wasn't going to mention him. Close as we were, we never talked about John.

Now, however, in the darkened cabin of the 747 I remember that morning and the song that spirited Nancy to a place that, wherever it was, certainly was not the kitchen of my old home, and I wonder. A wartime song with soulful words and a haunting melody. Had she been seeing the face of the man whose photograph was tucked into my bag along with the DFC? I'd seen much the same expression on her face a couple of days ago when she showed them to me and asked me to find him.

I remember something else too, something she said to me just before I left Florida. Fergus had phoned me, the third time he'd done so during my stay. We were eating dinner, just Nancy and me. Ritchie was still at the airfield, or had stopped off for a drink at his favourite bar as he so often did; the latter, Nancy seemed to think. I'd rustled up a spaghetti Bolognese – I like to cook for Nancy when I'm in Florida – and we were halfway through it when the phone rang.

Nancy reached for it. She likes to keep the phone within easy reach when she's alone, so as not to have to hurry protesting muscles when it rings, she says, and even though I was there now, she stuck to the habit.

'Nancy Costello.'

I couldn't hear the voice on the other end, but a smile spread across Nancy's face and leaked into her voice.

'Yes, indeed I am . . . Well, that sure is nice of you to say so . . . Yes, she's right here. I'll put her on.' She held the phone out to me, still smiling, raising an eyebrow at me. 'Your young man.'

I've known Fergus since for ever. Once upon a time he was engaged to Belinda, my sister – they'd met at college and were inseparable for a couple of years. When they broke up and Belinda married Ben, he'd somehow gravitated to me, turning up at my flat with a bottle of wine and the cheeky grin that made it impossible to throw him out. I was pretty sure he was still besotted with Belinda, and I was the closest he could get to her, but somehow we'd become firm friends, perhaps because I was in an unhappy relationship too, and breaking my heart over a man who was never going to leave his wife and children for me. He'd lent me his shoulder to cry on, and I'd found it easier, somehow, to talk to him about my troubles than it was to talk to any of my girlfriends. They were judgemental, and rightly so; Fergus was just Fergus, sweet-natured and kind, breezy and as comfortable as an old shoe. He never castigated me for falling in love with a married man; I think he knew I already felt guilty enough without him rubbing it in. He just helped me pick up the pieces when I decided enough was enough, and I had to make a clean break of it.

We enjoyed one another's company, Fergus and I, not a doubt of it. We had some really good times. But somewhere along the line he had decided that he wanted to marry me, and for all that I was very fond of him, I wasn't at all sure that I wanted to marry him.

Now, I put down my fork and took the phone, feeling guilty that I had scarcely spared him a thought these last few days. 'Hi,' I said through a mouthful of spaghetti.

'Hello, Sarah. Fergus here.'

'Yes, so I hear.'

'Thought I'd give you a call. See how you are.'

'Fine. And you?'

'Missing you like hell. It's nearly midnight here and all I've got for company is a glass of single malt and the bloody cat.'

'Cat? Fergus, you haven't got a cat.'

'Next door's. Seems to have adopted me. Every time I open the bloody door or leave a window open it comes sneaking in. I'm beginning to wonder if I've got mice – or rats. Since the council have only been collecting the rubbish fortnightly instead of every week the street's been infested with bloody rats.'

I couldn't believe he was paying transatlantic phone call rates to have a conversation about rats.

'Fergus,' I said. 'Are you drunk?'

The slight delay on the international line made it appear he was hesitating, but when his reply reached me it was pure Fergus, frank and unabashed.

'Probably.'

'Then I think you ought to go to bed and sleep it off.'

'I will. I will. Wanted to speak to you first, though. Bloody hell, Sarah, I can't stop thinking about you. Counting the days till you're home. Marry me, Sarah. Have my babies. Grow old with me.'

I could feel the familiar tightening in my stomach. The longing for the babies, the claustrophobia that came from the prospect of being tied to Fergus.

'In a rat-infested flat?' I said, determinedly flip.

'We'll get a place out in the country. Roses round the door. Stream at the bottom of the garden. Village pub down the lane.'

'I thought it wouldn't be long before the pub came into it,' I said drily.

'Think about it, Sarah.'

'Good night, Fergus,' I said firmly, and disconnected.

Nancy had laid down her fork and was watching me shrewdly. I felt obliged to offer some explanation.

'That was Fergus.'

'So I gathered. He sounds kinda nice, honey.'

'He is. Very nice.' My tone was flat, unenthusiastic.

'He said I didn't sound old enough to be your grandmother.'

'He would. That's Fergus all over. And anyway, you don't. Sound old enough to be my grandmother, I mean. You sound about twenty.'

'He's got a real nice voice. Do his looks match?'

'He's quite good-looking, yes.'

'But he's not the one.'

I pushed spaghetti around my plate. 'He wants to marry me.'

'But you . . . ?'

'I'm thinking about it. I'm thirty-six years old, Grandma. I want to have a family before it's too late, and there aren't too many good men around. By the time you get to be thirty-six, most are either married already, or are never going to be, or carrying a hell of a lot of baggage, or looking for a girl ten years younger, or at least not one with a degree and a career. I wasted close on ten years on a relationship that I should never have embarked on and which was going nowhere – you know all about that. Fergus is a really nice chap. A bit of a Jack-the-lad, perhaps, but if he had a proper relationship and a family, I'm pretty sure he'd settle down and make a go of it. He says he loves me, but . . .'

'He's not still in love with Belinda, is he?' Nancy asked, looking at me narrowly. I'd forgotten that she knew that Fergus was Belinda's boyfriend before he was mine.

'I don't think so. Still a little bit fascinated by her, maybe. Belinda has that effect on men.' I saw Nancy's eyebrow quirk; funnily enough she's never had a great deal of time for Belinda, though everyone else seems to think she's the bee's knees. Maybe their personalities don't gel the way hers and mine do.

Nancy sat back in her chair, studying me. 'What does he do for a living?'

'He works for one of the big insurance companies in Bristol.'

'And when he's not working?'

'Plays golf. Works out at the gym. Goes skiing a couple of times a year. Enjoys a drink.'

'A pretty regular sort of guy, then.'

'Well . . . yes. I suppose he is.' I poured some more wine into her glass and mine, took a slurp. 'What do you think, Grandma? Do you think I should go for it and marry him?'

Nancy reached for her glass, curling her puffy fingers round the stem. She wore no rings now; she'd had her wedding ring cut off a year or so ago when it had begun biting into the flesh. Her eyes levelled with mine.

'If you have to ask me that, honey, then the answer has to be no.'

'Even if he's my last chance?'

She smiled then, that sweet smile of hers that softened the lines time has etched into her cheeks.

'Sarah, honey, thirty-six isn't old these days. In my day you could be on the shelf by twenty-four, but now . . .'

'You think there's hope for me yet?'

'There's always hope.'

I thought of Monica, sitting behind her desk at the airfield, comforting herself with Krispy Kreme Doughnuts.

'Tell that to Monica.'

Nancy tutted. 'Monica's obsessed with Ritchie – more fool her. She's let it blind her to opportunities just like you did when you were hooked on that married man – what was his name?'

'Mark.'

'And now you're doing it again. Letting somebody else get in the way of you meeting the right man.'

'No I'm not.'

'Of course you are. Open yourself up, Sarah. But don't be too desperate. Nothing puts a man off faster than desperation. Just go with the flow, honey, and when the time's right, it'll happen.'

'Well,' I said, 'if it doesn't, I suppose I've got a few years yet to go it alone. I've thought of that too. Getting myself pregnant on purpose. Plenty of women are single mothers.'

I thought that would shock her, given the generation gap. But nothing much shocks Nancy. I should have known that.

'I guess. If there's no other way,' she said. 'It's not ideal, of course, but it's a damned sight better than tying yourself to a man you don't love. Fairer on you – and fairer on him. Fairer on the child too.'

'So you're saying I shouldn't marry Fergus.'

And then Nancy said the thing I'm thinking of now, in the semi-darkness of the 747.

'You may regret it sometimes if you don't, Sarah. I can't promise

225

you that. But you certainly will regret it if you do. Sooner or later, honey, if you marry someone you don't love, you will regret it.'

There was a set to her face I can picture now in the lines and swirls behind my eyes, and I grow cold beneath my airline blanket as I realise what it meant. Nancy wasn't just talking the sound common sense of worldly wisdom gathered at second-hand. She was speaking from experience. She knew what it was like to feel the regret she spoke of. She'd had moments – perhaps more than moments – when she'd regretted marrying darling Grandpa Joe, the man I'd always thought of as her soul mate.

Another shadow had followed her down the years, lain between them, closer than her own skin, maybe kissed and caressed her in the darkness. Another man was in her heart.

And his name was Mac.

I don't have the easiest of relationships with Ellen. I love her, of course I do – she's my mother. There's no escaping the bonds of nature and nurture. But I also find her intensely irritating, and more often than not we just rub each other up the wrong way.

Perhaps the trouble is that we're too much alike. We're both stubborn and independent, a bit feisty. We both like to do things our own way, and when they don't run according to plan we get impatient and take it out on those around us. We're both busy people who hate to be idle. But there are aspects of my mother I really don't like very much, and I keep a vigilant eye on myself to try to avoid falling into the trap of turning into a clone of her as I get older.

One of the things I desperately want to avoid is her habit of trying to manage everything and everyone, of giving the appearance that she knows best and if you go against her advice, on your own head be it. She can be bossy and controlling if you allow her to be, opinionated, very sure of herself, and not afraid to speak her mind. As a teenager I had to fight hard not to allow her to run my life, and as a result there were plenty of rows over what she saw as my rebelliousness.

'Why do you make it so hard on yourself?' Belinda, my sister, would say. 'There's no point fighting Mum; she'll always win.'

'It's all right for you, Miss Goody Two-Shoes,' I'd say. 'You get away with murder.'

And it was true, she did. If only because she avoided confrontation, smiled sweetly, played submissive, and did exactly as she pleased anyway. I couldn't do that. I had to argue and protest openly, and as a result there was this state of constant warfare.

Then there is the way that once Ellen gets an idea in her head, she just can't let it go. If she takes a dislike to a person, they've had it. She can be tolerant and forgiving, and make excuses for them for months or even years, but one day they'll go too far and it's as if something snaps in her, a spring coils and flies off in the opposite direction. After that point, there's no going back. She turns against them as thoroughly as she previously defended them and nothing they can say or do will change her mind.

But for all that Mum gives the appearance of being strong and together, there's also a needy side to her. Perhaps it stems from the fact that she's virtually cut herself off from her family in Florida, and Dad, Belinda and I are the only ones she's got. I really don't know why she's estranged from Nancy and Ritchie, I can only assume that something must have happened that made her go into that state of being unable to forgive that I mentioned just now, though she's never said what it was, and I'm not sure Nancy knows either. It's just as if somehow, somewhere, they crossed the line and Mum put up barriers and cut them out of her life.

227

Whatever, I am aware that she wants more from me than I am able to give, and that makes me feel bad. It would be easier, I guess, if Belinda lived nearer, but she doesn't, and the whole darned guilt trip falls on me. I know Mum thinks I should visit more often, but I have a very demanding job, and in any case, whenever we're together we seem to end up in an argument about something: my job, my relationships, the fact that I don't phone her often enough, the state of the world in general.

One of the things that really gets to me is the way she seems to think Dad is vegetating. She can't seem to accept that after working in a pressured environment all his life, he's enjoying his well-earned retirement. She thinks he should be dashing around as she does, with every minute of every day filled, and looking like an advertisement for Saga holidays into the bargain. She never appreciates what he does, either; he always manages to get something wrong. If he buys paint to redecorate, it's not quite the right shade; if he tidies up the garden he's dug up a clump of something she wanted to keep; if he cooks a meal he's used the freshest veg, not the ones that needed using first. Unsurprisingly, he's taken to spending more time at the golf club and leaving her to get on with it.

I adore my dad; he's the best in the world. So I get prickly on his behalf, just as I get annoyed that she's still trying to run my life for me, and I react badly. Then, afterwards, I feel even more guilty. I'm a rotten daughter, as intolerant as she is, etc., etc.

Just at the moment, this guilt is exacerbated by the fact that I've just spent three weeks in Florida, and I know she thinks I should have spent at least part of my holiday at home with her and Dad. For some reason, Mum has never liked me going to Florida, and she seems resentful of the bond I share with Grandma Nancy. I don't understand it, but I feel the burden of it like a millstone round my neck, and the irritation that causes completes the vicious circle.

Which is why I'm here now, at home, drinking coffee with Mum in the well-ordered kitchen of the spacious, five-bed des-res in a small, exclusive development that somehow got built on what everyone thought was green-belt land, and where I grew up. I'm hearing how well Ben, Belinda's husband, is doing – another promotion; God, much higher and he'll be wearing a cloud for a hat – and telling her yes, I have to go back to work on Monday, and no, I am not about to get engaged to Fergus. Then I have to listen to her bringing me up to speed on the births, marriages and deaths of people I remember only vaguely, or not at all.

'Little Mr Bunting who used to be on the council – of course you know him! His wife served on Saturday mornings in the baker's in the High Street. Knocked down by a motorcycle on the pelican crossing last Wednesday week on his way back from the post office! Poor man is in hospital with a fractured hip. It'll be the end of him, I wouldn't be surprised.'

Mr Bunting. The name rings a distant bell, but I can't picture him at all. Or his wife. To me, all the ladies in the baker's shop were indistinguishable from one another in their blue and white checked nylon overalls and jaunty little caps. Except for one, rotund and beaming, who used to slip me bits of sugary topping from the lardy cake when no one was looking. But I don't think she was Mrs Bunting.

'Annaliese Taviner had twins – again. You must remember Annaliese. You were at school with her . . .'

Oh, yes, I remember Annaliese. She had dreadfully red patches of dry skin on her cheeks that made her look as if she'd been out in a high wind or too much sun, and she was asthmatic. I can see her now, wheezing painfully and puffing on her atomiser. But Annaliese has managed two sets of twins, four children, and I haven't got even one . . .

'So, how was your grandmother?' Mum asks at last, and it seems to me the question, which should have been her first, has actually ranked lower in importance to her than Mr Bunting and Annaliese Taviner and other newsworthy residents of Norton Handley. Or perhaps she's been deliberately delaying the subject.

'She's getting more frail,' I say. 'I don't think she'll ever come to England again. You really ought to go over and see her.' I don't add: 'While you still can,' but it hangs in the air, unspoken.

Mum combs her fingers through her hair, short-cut and sassy, elegantly casual with not so much as a hint of grey. She takes good care of herself, and I admire her for that. But though she could easily pass for ten years younger than her real age, she never falls into the trap of looking like mutton dressed as lamb. She has the knack of nodding in the direction of current fashion whilst remaining true to her own style, and she never makes the mistake of going too heavy on the make-up. Tinted moisturiser, natural-coloured lipsticks that don't bleed into the fine lines around her mouth, a lick of mascara, are all she ever wears. She told me once she considered herself lucky she'd left Florida before the hot sun had the chance to scar her skin with wrinkles and sunspots; I think she inherited Nancy's youthful looks, and I only hope she's passed the same genes on to me.

There's a flicker of something I can't read in her eyes now; could it be the same guilt I feel when I find an excuse not to visit her? Her words confirm it, and I feel a moment's rare empathy.

'Perhaps I should . . . It's just finding the time . . .' Then her mouth hardens. 'I'm sure she'd much rather see you, though. You and she . . .' She reaches for the cafetiere, tops up our cups. 'How about Ritchie? He's not married *again*, I hope?'

I smile. 'No. Mary-Lyn was his last mistake, I think. He can't afford to make another. The business isn't doing well enough to support any more ex-wives. In fact, I get the impression he's struggling to keep it afloat.'

'I'm not surprised.'

We talk a bit more about Nancy and Ritchie and Florida. And we've reached the point where I feel I can no longer avoid mentioning the mission Nancy set me.

I could, I suppose, say nothing. But if Mum should find out I'm trying to trace someone for Nancy without telling her, she'll accuse me of going behind her back and the fallout will not be pleasant. Better to mention it but play it down. And in any case, there's the faint chance she may know something that will help me.

'Grandma asked me to do something for her,' I say. 'She's been turning out and she came across a medal belonging to someone she knew in the war. Heaven knows how she came by it or why she's kept it all these years. She'd forgotten about it, I suppose. But she's having a guilt trip now. She wants me to try to find him or his family and return it.'

Mum has suddenly gone very still. Her face is frozen into an expression of shock, her coffee cup poised midway between table and mouth. She grasps it now with both hands, as if she doesn't trust one alone to hold it, lowers it very carefully to the saucer.

'You're not going to, of course.'

I frown. 'I'm going to try.'

'Sarah, it's ridiculous. How on earth can you hope to track down someone after all these years?'

'There are ways and means,' I say. 'Grandma gave me service numbers, postings, addresses. He was called James Mackenzie, and he came from Gloucestershire, apparently.'

'I can't believe you are going to waste your time. Which you always claim is so precious.'

I ignore the jibe. 'It won't be a waste of time if it makes Grandma happy.'

Mum snorts impatiently.

'I might not have any luck, of course,' I concede. 'But the internet makes research pretty painless. And Gloucestershire is hardly Timbuktu. I can drive there and back in a couple of hours. I was thinking of going this afternoon. Why don't you come with me?'

'Certainly not!' Mum snaps. 'And I don't want you to go either, Sarah.'

It's the old Mum, the control freak. My hackles rise as instantly as if she'd hit me.

'I'm sorry, Mum, but I'm going. I promised Grandma.'

'I don't want you to,' she repeats.

I stare at her, startled by the ferocity of her tone. 'Why ever not?'

Mum is totally buttoned up, her face a rigid mask. For a moment I don't think she's going to give me an answer, that she's going to fall back on the old 'because it's best' routine. Then, instead of replying to my question, she asks one of her own.

'What did your grandmother tell you about this man, this James Mackenzie?'

'Just that he was an RAF pilot – a squadron leader, I think she said. And that she knew him when she was flying with the ATA.'

'Nothing else?'

'Not really.' It's no less than the truth. Bare facts are pretty well all Nancy gave me, and I'm certainly not going to embellish them

232

with the bits I've filled in for myself. It seems, though, that Mum has trodden the same path of supposition before me, and come to the same conclusion.

'A wartime romance.' Her mouth twists into what is almost a sneer. 'And you thought – how sweet. How romantic.'

'Well, isn't it?' I counter defensively.

She snorts again. 'Maybe you'd be less generous if she'd told you the whole truth.'

I'm growing a little angry now on Nancy's behalf, but I'm also curious.

'Mum, what are you talking about?'

Again I think she's going to clam up, tell me she doesn't want to discuss this any more. I can see the indecision in her face as her reluctance to explain fights with outrage at my plans which, as she sees it, only the truth will put a stop to. The outrage wins.

'No, I didn't think she'd have told you *that*.'

'*What*, Mum? What didn't she tell me?'

And her reply completely knocks the wind out of my sails. Whatever I'd expected, it wasn't this.

'That she had a child with this Mac,' Mum says.

MONICA

'**F**ancy a drink, Monica?' Ritchie says.

We've just finished up for the day. I've closed down the accounts file I've been worrying over for the past hour and Ritchie has seen off his last pupil and tied down the plane for the night. Now he's sprawled in the client chair on the opposite side of my desk, collar undone, black tie loosened – unusually, he's wearing one today – swinging his aviator sunspecs between his fingers over the arm of his chair.

I switch off the computer, push the keyboard to the back of the desk.

'I should be getting home.'

'What for?'

What for indeed. There's nobody expecting me. Hasn't been since Brad, my youngest son, left for college, and that's ten years ago now. They all have their own lives, my three boys, and that's as it should be. But it doesn't mean I don't get a mite lonely once in a while, hanker after the days when the house was overflowing with them and their friends, cluttered with sneakers left in the kitchen and dirty socks and sweatshirts scattered in a trail from bathroom to bedroom, and throbbing with that damned garage music they used to play so loud it drove me crazy. And I wonder how things would be different if Don hadn't taken sick and died all those years ago when the boys were just kids. A brain haemorrhage, they said, though they used some fancy name for it. All I really took in at the time was that he had a raging headache, collapsed, and died. He'd be heading for sixty now if he was still alive. Maybe taken retirement. We could have been enjoying life together, taking vacations, maybe playing a little golf. Not that I've ever touched a golf club in my life, but heck, who knows what we might have done together?

Still, it's no use hankering after what might have been. That's just a damned waste of time. Always has been, always will be. You have to pick up the hand you're dealt and do the best you can with it. That's the way I try to live. No sense doing anything else. Even if I do wish every now and then it had fallen different. And that there was a guy in my life.

Correction – not just any guy. I guess if I hadn't been so damned choosy I might have found someone to hook up with. But in the beginning nobody measured up to Don, and I doubt any of them would have fallen over themselves to take on three growing boys as part of the package anyway. And then, darned fool that I am, I got this soft spot for Ritchie.

Now I know better than anyone, Ritchie ain't the kind of guy it's sensible to fall for, and you'd think I was old enough and wise enough to know better. He's had three wives, for Chrissakes, and as a marriage bet he's not one I'd care to lay odds on. He's too darned free with his money when he's got it – it burns a hole in his pocket – and dependability sure as heck is not his middle name.

He can be scratchy and downright miserable. He's got a chip on his shoulder the size of the Empire State Building. He has an eye for the womenfolk, and he's a sight too fond of a bourbon.

But there's something about him all the same. He can be real sweet, and kind of vulnerable. I guess I've seen a side of him he doesn't put on display too often. Brash, short-tempered, too darned sure of himself, that's the way he appears if you don't know him. But I can see beneath that and I see a guy who's been badly hurt sometime, and is still hurting. Like I said, I try to make the best of the hand life's dealt me. Ritchie finds it kinda hard to do that. He's hidden away like a clam in a shell. I've raised three boys, remember. I know that boys are a whole bunch softer than girls. A hell of a lot more tender, for all they try to play the big tough guy.

To tell the truth, I'm surprised Nancy doesn't know that and make allowances for it. I can't quite work out why they don't get along better. But the fact is, they don't. Could be it's Ritchie's fault, I guess. I'd have had him down for the kinda guy who dotes on his mom, and I think deep down he does. But for some reason he has trouble showing it and I reckon it goes back to that chip on his shoulder. He had an older brother, John, who was the golden boy, or so I've heard. I never knew him – he was killed in a flying accident before I came to work for Varna Aviation – but by all accounts John was the apple of his mom's eye. And Ritchie has it in his head that his mom would rather it had been him that ended up dead.

He said as much to me once. He was in one of his black moods and he'd been drinking. I knew he was in a black mood from the way he stomped in to the office and unhitched the keys for the plane from their hook without so much as a word or even a glance in my direction, and I could smell the drink on him from three feet away.

'Ritchie,' I said, 'are you sure that's a good idea?'

He didn't answer, just carried right on as if I hadn't spoken.

'Ritchie,' I said, 'get your ass back here.'

'Butt out, Monica. I'm going for a spin.'

'You're in no fit state,' I told him. 'You don't fly drunk. You damned well know that.'

Ritchie muttered something unrepeatable under his breath.

'You'll wind up killing yourself, Goddamit,' I said.

'Well ain't that a shame.' Ritchie's tone was heavily sarcastic. 'Reckon that'd solve a lot of problems for a lot of people.'

'Not for me, you asshole. I'd be out of a job.'

'Yeah, right.' He headed for the door.

I had one last stab at making him see sense. 'Ritchie, for Chrissakes, your mom already lost one son. Do you wanna make her lose the other?'

And that's when he said it, the thing I've never forgotten.

'She wouldn't give a shit. You know what? She wishes it was me that was dead instead of her precious John.'

I've never forgotten the look on his face when he said it either. The bitterness. The hurt.

'Ritchie Costello, that is a terrible thing to say!'

'True, though.'

'It is not true! She's never gotten over losing John, maybe, but that doesn't mean she wishes it had been you. She's your mom, for Chrissakes. Moms love their children all the same. She'd never wish one dead to have the other alive.'

'You reckon?' He swung the plane keys. 'Well, I reckon different. I reckon she'd be mighty relieved she didn't have to look at me

238

any more. I reckon she'd think it was poetic justice. That's what I reckon, Monica.'

And he walked out. There was not a damned thing I could do to stop him. Ten minutes later I saw him take off.

I spent the next two hours worried out of my mind and thinking about what he'd said. It was a load of shit, of course. Every one of your kids is special and irreplaceable. OK, so maybe I get on better with Brad than I do with Troy or Russell, but that don't mean that if anything happened to Brad I'd blame the others for being alive when he was dead. It doesn't work like that. But shit or not, Ritchie believed it all right, and that was what mattered.

By some miracle he got himself home in one piece that day. I was still there, standing at the window and watching the sky, when I saw him come back into the circuit and I don't mind admitting I damn near wept with relief when I recognised the blue and white livery. He got down with a bit of a bounce, but when he came back into the office I could tell at once he'd got some of the black mood – and the alcohol – out of his system.

'You still here?' he said, jamming his sunspecs up onto the crown of his head.

'Yeah, I had things to do,' I lied. No way was I going to admit I couldn't have rested easy not knowing if he'd got back safe or not.

'You work too damned hard, Monica,' he said. 'We don't deserve you.'

There was a warmth spreading through my veins and a lump in my throat, but I'm not given to signposting the way I feel if I can help it. I just fixed him with a hard stare.

'Any more capers like today and you sure as heck won't have me. I'm going home.'

I don't believe we ever mentioned that incident again, but it kinda stuck with me. I'm real fond of Nancy as well as having this stupid soft centre for Ritchie, and it bugs me that the two of them do such a fine job of tearing one another apart. I've tried my damnedest to keep the ball in my own park, but sometimes I just can't keep quiet.

It's like that right now. Maybe I don't have anyone at home waiting for me. But Ritchie does, and I reckon he should pay her a little attention once in a while.

'Why don't you spend some time with your mom?' I suggest. 'She's feeling lonely, I shouldn't wonder, now that Sarah's gone back to England. I reckon she'd appreciate your company.'

I'm half-expecting Ritchie to bite my head off, and he doesn't disappoint.

'Give me a break, Monica. I've done a hard day's work. I need a drink.'

'You could have a drink at home,' I point out.

'Well, so I could. But I also need to relax. I don't need Nancy looking at me disapproving when I crack open a bottle. She just winds me up.' He gets up from the client chair. 'Are you gonna join me or not?'

I sigh. 'OK. Somebody better be there to keep you in line, or you'll be out till God only knows what time and fit for nothing in the morning. If it's not going to be your mom it might as well be me.'

'You know what, Monica? You're as bad as she is.'

'I guess I am,' I say evenly. 'But a darn sight less trouble than any of your ex-wives. OK, sunshine, let's go.'

Sometimes Ritchie drinks in dives. I know, I've been there with him. It's like he thinks he can lose himself in the murk and the soulful throb of country music and the inane introspective conversation of a crowd of guys as desperate to find some purpose in their sad lives as he is. And none of them has a clue as to what it is they're looking for. Tammy Wynette belts out 'Stand By Your Man', and they gaze in their drinks and wish somebody – anybody – would stand by them. They play the slot machines, imagining they might hit the jackpot, and the bandits whirr and whine, and every so often there's the clatter of dimes and quarters cascading down the chute and for a minute or two the sucker with the flashing lights reflecting in his eyes thinks he's gonna be rich. And at the end of the night they're more damned miserable than when they came in, and a good deal poorer, with nothing to look forward to but a thumping head in the morning.

Ritchie doesn't take me to ZzaZza's Bar tonight, though, or any of the other shitty dives hidden away in the back streets and industrial estates. Instead, when we've crossed the bridge, he heads towards that area of town where the golf course sits like a great green lily pad, and the plots off the network of streets would take half a dozen houses the size of mine. He pulls into the driveway of the Island Club. I follow, and park alongside him amongst the BMWs and the Mercs, just the teeniest bit surprised at where we're headed. I know Ritchie was a member here at one time when he'd been in one of his free-spending phases, but I'd thought his membership had lapsed a while back. He must have renewed it, but I surely haven't seen the payment go through the books. The Island Club is a classy place and the subscription would stick out like a sore thumb. No, the business wouldn't stand covering the membership any longer, and from what he's said, I wouldn't have thought Ritchie's personal finances were in any shape to cover it either. But heck, when it comes down to it, what do I know? Maybe some rich widow has taken a shine to him and paid the membership for him.

'We're doing it in style tonight then,' I say, grabbing my purse off the dash and locking my car.

'Reckon we've earned it,' he says. 'There's somebody I want to see, anyway. Are you hungry? Do you want to eat?'

'Ritchie, I'm always hungry. It's been a long day. But I can't afford their prices.'

'It's on me, honey.' Ritchie smiles at me. I register the first twinge of unease, and stare at him. The smile shifts a little off-centre and I glimpse what might just be a shifty look hiding behind it. 'It's OK. Trust me.'

'I guess if you're paying, it has to beat warmed-over chilli.'

'Attagirl.'

I'm still not at all sure how I feel about this. For one thing, I'm not really dressed for the Island Club. Most places around here are pretty relaxed, but I can't believe the other women in the place will be wearing the same pair of shorts they've been stuck in all day, or that they fixed their face in two minutes flat in a restroom where the mirror is lit only by a fluorescent strip on the ceiling.

But it's not just that I'm looking less than my knockout best that's making me uneasy. Ritchie is up to something. He can't fool me – I know him too darned well. And I've learned the hard way that when Ritchie's up to something it usually ends in tears.

I wish the hell that just once in a while when I get a gut instinct that something is wrong, it could be me. That when unease starts pricking under my skin like a poison ivy rash I could console myself it's nothing more than that I'm tired and low and imagining problems that don't exist. Trouble is, I know from bitter experience I'm usually right to be worried. That even if I can't put my finger on why I'm feeling that way, there's something my subconscious knows that I don't. I've proved it too often.

Take the time when Russell was just a baby. He kept vomiting and sleeping, sleeping and vomiting, crying a bit and sleeping some more. Don reckoned he was just off colour, that Troy had acted up much worse plenty of times and I was getting myself all worked up over nothing. But I knew it was more than that. I knew Russell was real sick and I wouldn't rest until we took him to the infirmary. To start with, they said the same as Don, that it was just a virus and he'd be fine in a day or two. But, thank God, they kept him in for observation and it saved his life. Turned out he had meningitis, and when it developed they were able to get his treatment going right off. If he'd been home, in his crib, we'd have lost him. As it was, at least he had a fighting chance. There were a couple of weeks when we didn't know whether he'd live or die, and an agonising wait of months before we knew for sure he hadn't wound up brain damaged or deaf, but he pulled through, more or less unscathed. Thanks to the doctors and medical science – and my sixth sense that something was real wrong.

It's happened plenty of times over the years. Big things and small things. I get this kind of black foreboding and I know something bad is going to happen. I got it when Troy trashed his car in a pile-up on the freeway, couldn't settle, though he wasn't even that late home, just watching for him out the window and kinda waiting for the phone to ring, or a knock on the door. I've had it just before the mailman delivers a letter with unwelcome news in it, or an unexpected bill. The only time I never got it, not an inkling, was when Don had his brain haemorrhage. Not so much as a notion. But when I do get it, it's never wrong.

And I've got it now. It's the wee small hours – the clock on my nightstand shows a quarter after two – but I'm too damn tense to sleep. Every time I think I'm drifting off, this naggle somewhere inside my head wakes me up again.

I push back the covers, go to the kitchen, and stick a cup of milk in the microwave to warm. As I drink it, I try to rationalise the way I'm feeling.

OK, it's about Ritchie, no question of that. I'm wondering why he took me to that swanky club, and I'm worried that he had a wad of bills in his wallet as thick as a paperback in the Plaza bookstore. And there's more.

He'd told me right off there was someone he wanted to see at the Island Club and when we went in, he had a good look round, but whoever it was couldn't have been there yet, and we'd finished eating before I found out who it was.

I was having a good time, I gotta admit it. It's hard not to at the Island Club. By the time I'd put away Hawaiian chicken, followed by Key lime pie, I sure as heck wasn't hungry any more, and a piña colada and my fair share of a bottle of Pinot Grigio helped me forget I was wearing crumpled shorts and sneakers. And Ritchie was in a pretty good mood, kinda funny and charming, the way he can be when nobody's bugging him.

The alcohol had made me careless about the dough he was spending too. I told myself it was no business of mine how he'd come by it, and certainly none of the rich dames there seemed to be taking a proprietorial interest in him. I even allowed myself to feel a little optimistic about the fact that he was sharing this luxury with me, wondered if maybe after all this time things were looking up between us and he was seeing me as something more than just the gal who minded the office for him and listened to his gripes and dusted him down from time to time.

We were on the coffee – Colombian, with frothy milk, brown sugar and a shot of bourbon – when I came down to earth with a bump.

'You OK here for a minute, Monica?' Ritchie said. 'I've got a bit of business to take care of.' He didn't wait for me to answer, just slid out of his seat and headed for the bar area.

The layout of the Island Club is mostly open plan; I only had to swivel round a quarter-turn on the bench to get a view of the bar. And that prickle of unease started up again the minute I saw who it was Ritchie was talking to.

I've known Dexter Connelly for years. Well, maybe to say I know him is stretching it; the fact is he'd pass me on the sidewalk and not so much as pass the time of day. But I know him in the sense that we've had business dealings with him when he's hired a plane to fly off on one of his business trips or a weekend in Las Vegas, though Ritchie usually dealt with him himself. I know him by reputation too. Most folk in Varna do. He lives in one of those mansions with electronically controlled security gates that the tour trolley bus slows down to pass so the visitors can get an eyeful of how the other half live, and he generally has an expensive-looking woman hanging on his arm. But it's how he's gotten his wealth that people wonder about, and most decide they're better off not knowing. It's my opinion he's a rogue, who'd most likely be behind bars if he hadn't made things sweet for the chief of police, or threatened him – one or the other. And though Varna Aviation has never been able to afford to be choosy about clientele, I've never felt comfortable dealing with him, or taking his money.

I felt less comfortable than ever now. I saw him greet Ritchie like a long-lost friend, clap him on the back, buy him a drink. Then he patted his pocket, pulled out what looked like a pack of cigars, and the two of them disappeared out the French windows onto the patio area, for a smoke, I supposed, and the privacy to talk about whatever it was they wanted to talk about.

They weren't gone long, and I was glad of that. I was feeling mighty uncomfortable sitting there alone among all those dressed-up folk with their surgically taut faces all made up and their gold and diamond jewellery flashing enough to give an epileptic a fit. The women were casting curious and disapproving glances in my direction, and one or two of the men were giving me the glad eye. I thought about moving out into the bar area, but figured that would be even worse, since there was a group of guys there who looked like they belonged to the horsy set from the equestrian centre up on the mainland, and we all know they can be as frisky as their high-strung thoroughbreds. Anyway, like I say, it wasn't long before Ritchie was back.

'All set then, Monica?' He didn't make any attempt to sit down again.

'Yeah, sure.' Any hopes I'd maybe entertained that Ritchie might have had some kind of romantic intention disappeared faster than a double whiskey down the throat of an alcoholic. He'd come here to see Dexter Connelly; I was just the window dressing.

Connelly was in the bar as we passed through, chatting to the equestrian set. It crossed my mind he looked for all the world like a Mafia godfather – dark suit, dark glasses, slicked-back hair, profile like it's been carved out of rock. He and Ritchie didn't so much as acknowledge one another.

'So what's with Connelly?' I asked as the warm night air washed over me like a Turkish bath.

'You don't wanna know, Monica.'

The warm night air turned chill on my skin. 'Ritchie . . .'

'I'm doing a little business with him. He'll be calling in a day or two. If I'm anywhere about on the premises, I'll take it, OK? If I'm not, tell him I'll call him back. This is between him and me, nothing to do with Varna Aviation.'

The misgiving prickled deep in my veins. 'I hope whatever it is is all legal and above board,' I said.

'Have you ever known me get mixed up with anything that wasn't?' He sounded hurt, as if I'd accused him of kicking the cat's butt or robbing old ladies of their life savings.

'Well, no, but . . .'

'I've got a business to keep afloat, and I'm doing it the best way I can. OK by you?'

'I guess.'

'Trust me, honey.' It was the second time that night he'd used that phrase. It didn't sit well with me. But I wasn't going to get any more out of him, that was plain.

I drove home and I went to bed and I fell asleep, no trouble. The food and the alcohol, I guess. But an hour or so later I was awake again, with all kinds of worries chasing circles in my head. Which is why I'm in my kitchen at three in the morning, staring at the remains of a cup of milk and worrying myself sick instead of being tucked up in my bed and dreaming.

There's something going on and I don't like it one little bit. I don't even need that damned sixth sense of mine to know that – just eyes and ears and a dose of good sound common sense.

Right now I don't know what that something is, but I sure as heck intend to find out. 'You don't want to know,' Ritchie said, but I do. 'This is nothing to do with Varna Aviation,' Ritchie said, and I'm not sure I believe him. 'Trust me,' he said. And, God help me, I can't.

I've seen Ritchie make a darned fool of himself too many times before. I don't want to see him do it again. But if he's doing whatever it is he's doing for Varna Aviation, then I have to be with him all the way. If he lost the business, it would destroy him. And it would destroy Nancy too.

What the hell am I going to do? That's the sixty-four-thousand-dollar question.

ELLEN

James Mackenzie. Mac. I never expected to hear that man's name again, ever. I certainly didn't want to. God, he has a lot to answer for! All the troubles that beset my family are down to him. My mother must know that every bit as well as I do, and yet she has the gall to ask Sarah to find him. I can't believe she'd suggest it, risk exposing all the skeletons in the cupboard that we've locked the door on for all these years. That she would open old wounds and inflict new ones; burden Sarah with a whole load of stuff she need never have known. I can only think she's becoming senile. There's no other rational explanation.

I've lived getting on for forty years knowing things I'd rather not have known, about my mother and John and Ritchie. I've tried to put it out of my mind, and for the most part I've succeeded. Forty years is a long time, especially when you are on the other side of the Atlantic from the major players in the story. That's the way I wanted it; the only way I could live with it. It's one of the reasons I was only too happy to move to England when Bob asked me to. I was in love with him, yes, but I might not have been so ready to leave home and live on the other side of the world if I hadn't wanted so much to escape my demons.

And now here is Sarah informing me Nancy wants to rake it all up again. She's looking at me with that barely concealed impatience with what she thinks is my intransigence and my over-reaction to her grandmother's request; judging me without having the first idea as to why I'm horrified by the suggestion, and I am outraged.

'Why shouldn't I go to Gloucestershire?' she asks – no, demands – in that irritatingly sanctimonious way she has, and I can see I'm being cast again as the unreasonable harridan.

Then, before I can stop myself, I'm doing the very thing I always promised myself I would never do. I'm telling her the truth – or part of it, anyway.

'I dare say Nancy didn't tell you she had a child with this man,' I say.

I see her eyes go wide with shock, and I can't help but feel a moment's grim satisfaction. Sarah has always had Nancy up there on a pedestal. Perhaps I should have disenchanted her a long time ago.

But the trouble is it won't stop there. Sarah can be like a dog with a bone. She won't be satisfied until she has the whole story. And then like me, she'll probably never want to go to Florida again, which is a pity really, because it means a lot to her. And besides, knowing she visits takes the pressure off me.

I don't want to go home. I don't want to see Mom and I don't want to see Ritchie. I don't want to be reminded of all the things I'd rather forget.

But it's too late now. What's said is said; it can't be taken back. I'll have to take the consequences and do my best to sort things out. Just as I always do.

*　　*　　*

I knew, the minute I got out of bed this morning, that it was not going to be a good day. Well, maybe not the minute I got out of bed exactly, but certainly by the time I poured milk straight from the plastic bottle into my tea and saw yellowish-white flecks and blobs rise to the surface. It was off, and I hadn't got any more on my way home yesterday afternoon as I'd intended. Court had sat late – I'm a magistrate – and I'd shied away from calling into the supermarket, but when I got to the eight-till-eight shop in the High Street there was no parking space, just an endless row of cars bumper to bumper at the kerb. Half the town had decided to get a takeaway from the Chinese chip shop next door, judging by the customers waiting three deep inside. I'd decided to take a chance on the half-full bottle I knew was in the fridge – I was too tired to bother driving round and round the one-way system until a space came free – and this was the result. No milk for my tea and none for Bob's cornflakes either. And I wasn't even sure how much bread there was left, or how fresh it was.

I poured the mug of tea down the drain and made a coffee instead – luckily I like it black – and managed to cut enough slices off the half-loaf to make toast for Bob and myself, inspecting it carefully to make sure it wasn't growing green mould round the edges. Already I felt irritable; I hate being less than well organised – usually it's my forte. And I knew Bob would be less than happy about it. He's not keen on toast, says it's too dry first thing in the morning, even though he lathers it with enough butter to raise the cholesterol levels of an entire regiment and uses a dessertspoon to pile on the marmalade. But that was just too bad. There was no reason on earth why he couldn't have gone out for milk yesterday instead of leaving it to me. He has nothing to do all day that I know of but watch the test match on Sky or go to the golf club or just potter aimlessly.

The bread was in the toaster when I heard him lumbering down the stairs. I glanced up as he came into the kitchen and sighed inwardly. His hair, what's left of it, was standing on end as if he'd been out in a high wind, and he was wearing baggy jeans and an old sweater that I've been trying to persuade him to throw out for years.

'Morning,' I said. It was the first time I'd seen him today – we sleep in separate rooms and have done now for a year or more. I like to read in bed; he wants to go straight to sleep. He says he doesn't mind me having my reading light on, but I always feel too guilty looking at his hunched back to be able to take much pleasure in my book. And then there's his snoring. He maintains I snore too, but I'm sure that's just his way of getting back at me. Whatever, since there are five bedrooms in the house and only the two of us in residence, it seems far more sensible to have separate rooms so we can do as we like.

'Morning.' Bob yawned, rubbing his jaw so that the bristle – silver now – rasped.

'You'll have to have toast,' I said. 'The milk is off.'

Bob pulled a face, went over to the digital radio, perched on the window ledge, and switched it on. I winced. I hate the radio blaring away first thing in the morning, and Bob has it on so loud these days. I've told him he should get a hearing aid, but he refuses to accept there's anything wrong with his hearing.

'Are you in court today?' he asked over the strains of 'Have a Nice Day'.

'No. I'm helping out in the charity shop today.'

'Right.' His tone was bland enough, but I knew what he was

thinking. The hospice shop – just another of my commitments. When he retired last year he suggested I gave some of them up so that we could spend more time together, but I have no intention of doing that. I'd go stir-crazy, moseying around all day as he does, and I like to feel I'm filling my days doing something useful. Being necessary to someone.

I'm not necessary to Bob, that's for sure. I doubt if he'd notice if I wasn't there. He'd miss his clean shirts, I suppose, that I always iron and put on hangers in a neat row in his wardrobe, colour-coded and sorted because he doesn't seem to be able to tell the difference between blue, green and grey, or between cotton and flannel. Provisions would soon run low – not just the milk – because he hates shopping and the supermarket is his idea of hell. But he'd manage. In most respects he's almost frighteningly self-sufficient. He'd probably get himself a dog. He's suggested it a few times over the years, but I've talked him out of it; I couldn't cope with the mess it would make. But mostly he'd simply drift on exactly as he does now. He says he's making up for the fact that he was weighed down by responsibility most of his working life, but I can't understand how he can bear just messing about with no clear plan of how to fill his days.

No, I'm not necessary to Bob, and I'm no longer necessary to the children either. I loved being a mother. I taught both girls to read and write long before they started school. I ferried them to ballet classes and riding lessons, I was chairman of the PTA, sewed costumes for Nativity plays, baked cakes for bring-and-buy sales, sat on poolside while they learned to swim, and stood on touchlines when they played netball and tennis. Later I provided a taxi service to discos, hosted sleep-overs and parties, and sat in car parks outside cinemas and bowling alleys. Life was hectic, and wonderful. I didn't mind that Bob was never there to share the duties. I enjoyed them, every one, and I was happier and more fulfilled than at any other time in my life.

But of course, children grow up and become independent. Belinda married quite young and moved to Oxford, Sarah went to university and on to a demanding career. Without them I felt as if I'd had an arm or a leg amputated. I'd heard of empty-nest syndrome, but I'd never for one moment imagined how awful it would be.

It was then that I applied to become a magistrate. And started helping out at the hospice charity shop. And went on the rota as a hospital driver. And took out a gym membership. All these things filled my days, but they couldn't fill the empty place inside me. And never have, though heaven knows, I should be used to it by now.

It would be different, I suppose, if Belinda lived closer. She has two children, a boy and a girl, and I could help out with baby-sitting and do things with them without having to make an excursion of it. Sarah's not that far away, only fifteen miles, but she's always too busy to spend much time with me. To be honest, I don't think she wants to. I can hear the evasive note in her voice if I phone and suggest she comes over. 'Oh, Mum, I'm up to my eyeballs right now . . .'; 'I didn't get home from work until gone eight last night . . .'; 'I've got a meeting tomorrow in London . . .' Busy, always busy. I dare say she is, but she finds time to go to Florida for three weeks each year. And though I try not to let it, it rankles with me.

So, it's just me and Bob and a forty-year marriage that seems to have gone stale. It makes me sad sometimes, when I remember the things we used to share, the laughter and the love, and I wonder if we grew apart when his work kept him away from home so much. Or perhaps it would have happened anyway. Whatever the reason, Bob does his thing and I do mine, and I'm not sure how happy either of us is about it.

We ate breakfast in near silence, if you don't count Radio Two. 'Why don't you at least listen to the *Today* programme?' I urged him sometimes. But Bob would reply that he'd had enough of world affairs, and it was all too depressing. So Terry Wogan it was.

When I'd finished my toast and coffee I showered, dressed and fixed my face. Bob was still sitting at the kitchen table and reading the newspaper when I came back downstairs and told him I was off.

He barely glanced up. 'OK, see you later.'

Already it felt warm outside and the air smelled fresh and sweet. Bob had mowed the lawn yesterday, I noticed, and the blackbirds that live in the hedge that separates our garden from the house next door were busy looking for worms. They barely moved as I crossed the patio, just fluttered far enough away to watch me from a safe distance. They really have become very tame over the years.

My mood lifted a bit. But when I went to get my car out of the garage, I realised it wasn't handling properly. I stopped, got out and checked my tyres. The rear nearside one was pancake flat.

Fuming with exasperation, I went back into the house.

'Can I borrow your car? I've got a flat tyre.'

'I was going to the golf club today.' Bob folded the *Independent*, and got up. 'I'll change it for you.'

'Oh shit! I'm going to be late . . .'

'They won't miss you for half an hour, surely?'

I followed him outside, still fuming. Maybe I wouldn't be missed for half an hour. Truth to tell it wasn't necessary for me to go in today at all; we were fully staffed. But Norma Benson and Josie Chalmers are not the last word in efficiency. Only last week they let a designer coat go for one pound fifty and almost sold a customer's bicycle that he'd brought into the shop for safety's sake while he was browsing. As for the tyre, I rather suspected the damage might be deliberate. I'd had a gang of local yobs up in front of me yesterday and I wouldn't put it past them to have stuck a nail in my tyre after they'd left court with their community service orders. They'd know my car if they saw it in the car park and they'd very likely decided on revenge.

As it happened, though, they had actually done me a favour, because whilst Bob was changing the tyre, Sarah phoned and said she was coming over, which of course is a rare treat. Bob delayed going to the golf club long enough for us all to have coffee together – he and Sarah have always got on like a house on fire – and it was quite like old times, sitting around the kitchen table and chatting. Almost the family we once were, except that Belinda was missing. I was really enjoying it. But then Bob left and Sarah and I got talking about Florida and everything went horribly wrong.

She dropped this bombshell about Nancy asking her to try to find James Mackenzie and I've done the unthinkable. I've opened the Pandora's box that we have managed to keep tightly closed all these years. And God alone knows what Mischiefs are going to escape.

Sarah is beginning to recover herself a bit now. She's fixing me with that sceptical look that I find infuriatingly patronising, and I can see she doesn't quite believe me.

'Mum – are you sure?'

'Well, of course I'm sure!' I snap. 'I'd hardly be likely to make up something like that, would I?'

'But Grandma would have said.'

'Would she?' I can hear the bitterness in my voice. 'Your grand-mother likes her secrets, Sarah. She's very good at them. She's had years of practice.'

Sarah shakes her head, clearing it. 'So where is this child now?' A thought strikes her, her eyes widen. 'Is *that* the real reason she wants me to find this Mac? He knows what happened to the baby? She was in England when she had it, and it was adopted over here?'

I sigh. 'No, Sarah. The baby wasn't adopted, and it wasn't born in England.'

'Then what . . . ?'

'She kept it.' I can feel all the muscles in my neck and jaw taut as bowstrings. 'She let Grandpa Joe bring him up as his own. Oh,' I snap suddenly, 'surely you can work it out for yourself. Her favourite? The one who could do no wrong? It was John, of course. Your uncle John. This James Mackenzie was his father.'

'Oh-mi-God.' Sarah claps her hand over her mouth. Above it her eyes hold mine, wide with shock. Then a look of compassion softens the little creases that are beginning to form round her eyes. 'Oh, poor Grandma! No wonder she's never got over John being killed. Her love child, and she lost him. All she had of Mac.'

I splutter with indignation. *Love child . . . all she had of Mac.* What the hell has she been saying to Sarah? But I can guess. Oh, I can guess.

'For God's sake, Sarah, don't you start romanticising it. It was a sordid wartime affair with a married man, that's all.'

Sarah shakes her head. There are tears in her eyes. Tears, for Chrissakes!

'I think it was more than that. Oh, Mum, it's just awful. All this time she's been keeping this to herself – mourning both of them – and I never knew. Did Grandpa know? That John wasn't his?'

'I don't know,' I say impatiently.

'But he must have known, surely, if you know.'

'It was never talked about.'

'Then how do you . . . ?'

I knew it. I knew Sarah would keep on and on, worrying the details out of me. She won't be satisfied until she has it all – and then she'll wish she hadn't.

'I need a drink,' I say. I fetch Bob's bottle of Grant's from the drinks cabinet in the lounge, pour two fingers into a tumbler, and wave the bottle at Sarah. 'Do you want one?'

She indicates 'no', with a tiny shake of her head. 'I'll have a glass of wine, if you've got a bottle open,' she says.

'You can open one. You know where it is.' I'd do it, but I don't trust myself with the corkscrew. Sarah will see how my hands are shaking. I gulp at the whisky, neat.

'Mum?' Sarah pauses beside me, bottle in hand. She's looking concerned now. 'Mum – are you all right?'

'Not really, Sarah, no. I can't imagine why your grandmother has dragged all this up now. Why she should involve you.'

'It is a bit of a shock, I must admit,' Sarah says. 'Especially that John wasn't Grandpa's. I can hardly believe it. You are sure, are you?'

'Oh, yes, Sarah, I'm sure.'

The whisky is sour in my throat, and I can feel the same sickness in the pit of my stomach as I felt all those years ago when I first learned the truth of why my mother was so besotted with her first-born. Except that it is even worse now, because I know the tragedy that discovery spawned, the way it shaped and overshadowed all our lives.

There's a nagging guilt too for the part I played in what happened, but I won't go there. It was my mother's fault, all my mother's fault, because she couldn't let go of her obsession for a man who wasn't my father. God knows, I've tried to understand, tried to forgive her. But some things are beyond forgiveness. The sustained deceit is one. The destruction of my family is the other.

Part Four

The Past

Part Four

I

Once or twice in every lifetime there comes a pivotal moment, a turning point after which nothing is the same again. For Ellen, that moment came in the summer of 1960 and for the rest of her life certain triggers had the power to whisk her back through time, recreating the exact aura of that moment, albeit fleetingly. The rustle of silk through her fingers, the sun slanting through the window just so, the scent of Californian Poppy perfume. Most of all the scent of Californian Poppy. She hadn't encountered it now for years. It had disappeared, she supposed, into the great perfume graveyard in the skies. Consciously, she could barely conjure it up. Yet sometimes a perfume wafting past, elusive as a dream forgotten on waking, would stir in her a memory she could not quite catch and she thought it harked back to that day.

The silk, her mother's underwear stacked neatly in the drawer of her dressing chest. The sun dappled by the leaves and blossom of the mimosa tree outside the window. The Californian Poppy perfume aromatic on her own moist skin, the perfume that in her dreams and aspirations would transform her from gawky high school girl into the sophisticated woman she longed to be.

They led her irresistibly, those triggers, back through time to the discovery of the letter that would change her life. She would find herself reliving the overwhelming curiosity that had driven her to pry, the shock and confusion that had flooded through her when the Pandora's box was opened and the Mischiefs flew around her, dark and darting in that shaft of sunlight, like a flock of disturbed bats. Her world had tilted on its axis, shattering certainty and security, and yet at the same time the debris falling like the scattered pieces of a jigsaw puzzle had formed a pattern and slotted into place, explaining conundrums, making sense of things she had wondered about.

Ellen had been racing eager and impatient towards womanhood. That day the ground had rocked beneath her feet as the realisation hit her that her growing up had occurred in quite a different way from the one she had anticipated. It had happened whilst she was quite alone, within the safe confines of her home. She could never be a child again.

Collier County Junior High Spring Hop. Ellen had been looking forward to it for weeks. She was head over heels in love with Ken Kelsey and, miracle of miracles, he'd asked her to be his partner. She wasn't at all sure how it had happened; they'd barely spoken a dozen words to each other since he'd joined her class as a new boy to the area in the fall, though when she'd sneaked longing glances at him she'd often caught him looking at her too, and in the brief moment before they both blushed and looked away a kind of communion flared between them that had no need of words. Afterwards her heart sang for the whole of the rest of the day, and when she was alone at night, tucked up in her bed with the patchwork quilt that Nancy had let her choose herself pulled up to her chin, she would take the memory of their shared glance out and relish it, whilst prickles of fluid warmth darted deep inside her.

Katy Johannson, her best friend, reckoned that Ken 'liked' Ellen, and she prayed Katy was right. But she couldn't imagine that he would ever ask her out, and she wasn't at all sure that her mother would allow it if he did. Which would be the most embarrassing thing in the whole world. Truth to tell, Ellen trembled at the prospect of asking Nancy's permission to go on a date. Nancy had made her views on the subject abundantly clear. Ellen was far too young to be thinking about boys. She should be concentrating on her schooling. When she was sixteen she could begin dating, if the boy was 'suitable'. Ellen felt sure Ken would pass muster in that respect. He'd never been in any kind of trouble that she knew of, and his father was a doctor at the infirmary, which was about as respectable as you could get. But it was two whole years and a bit before she would be sixteen, a lifetime away. Ellen veered between longing for Ken to ask her out and being terrified that he would and she would have to tell him 'no'. She'd lose him then for sure. There were plenty of girls whose parents were less strict – not strict at all, in fact. Betty Cross, for one, who had already developed a figure to die for, and who everyone knew was 'fast'. She sometimes went out with older boys, the ones who had their own set of wheels or were allowed to drive their fathers' automobiles, and it was rumoured she'd 'gone all the way' with one of them. Ellen found that shocking. She couldn't imagine how anyone could be so shameless. She'd die before she would ever let a boy get to 'first base' – hands under her sweater – let alone any further. But oh, she did so want to go out with Ken Kelsey! She imagined how it would feel if he held her hand, or put his arm around her, and when she thought of how it would be to kiss him, her stomach melted like warm chocolate and a pulse of excitement throbbed deep inside her. But always a cloud of black depression hung over her imaginings. If Ken should ask her out, Ellen just knew there would be a battle royal at home.

In the event, however, it had been much easier than she had feared. The Junior High Hop was a different matter altogether from a walk or a cycle ride or a drive-in movie. It was accepted tradition that the girls should be partnered, and it was well chaperoned by the teachers and some parents. Ken had said that his father would chauffeur them and though Nancy had at first insisted that Joe should drive Ellen there and back, a phone call from Dr Kelsey with a promise to take good care of her had changed her mind. As she said to Joe, if you couldn't trust a physician, who could you trust?

For days now Ellen had felt so sick with excitement and nervousness she could barely eat a thing and her mood swung violently between sheer joy and stomach-trembling apprehension.

What would they talk about, she and Ken? Would he try to kiss her? If he did he'd be bound to know she'd never kissed anyone before. How did you actually manage it without bumping noses? What if he put his hand somewhere he shouldn't – what should she do? And worse – oh, a thousand times worse – what if he had only asked her to the hop as a convenient cover? Perhaps he'd abandon her after a dance or two and go off with someone else. She'd seen Betty making eyes at him, and everyone knew that boys liked the girls who let them do things.

She worried about whether her hair would go fuzzy and flyaway if she washed it on the day, or look greasy and flat if she didn't. She worried that her dress wasn't grown-up enough. It was new, and she'd been delighted with it when she'd tried it on in the store, twirling round so that the three-tiered skirt fanned out over the paper-nylon petticoat beneath; now she wondered if flower-patterned white seersucker was babyish. Katy had a bright red circular skirt with black felt dice appliquéd round the hem and a black top with a stand-up collar. She was also borrowing a cinch belt from her older sister to make her waist look smaller. Ellen didn't have a sister to borrow such things from, and she knew Nancy would never sanction her buying one. It wasn't that her waist wasn't small, it was, quite. But her breasts were small too, and a cinch belt might make them look bigger, give her more shape. Katy had advised stuffing her bra with cotton batton, but that just looked lumpy and she couldn't get the two sides to match.

On the afternoon when her life turned upside down, she had decided to do a trial run on getting ready for the big day. She was alone in the house; Miss Jackson, her teacher, was off sick with a dose of influenza, and the class had been let out early for private study. Ritchie, not so lucky, wouldn't be out of school for another hour. Nancy and Joe were both at the airfield, and John was away at college.

Ellen took off her school skirt and shirt and folded them neatly. Unlike the boys, she never left her clothes in a tangle on the floor or looped over a chair. She kicked off her sensible school under-pants and dumped them in the laundry bin, then reverently removed her new white panties and brassiere from the tissue paper they were still wrapped in and slipped them on. The brassiere felt a little tight. Was she beginning to develop at last? She fervently hoped so. When the little mounds had first appeared she had hated them with a passion, covering them with her nightdress as quickly as possible. Now, however, every night before she went to sleep she willed them to grow; she just wanted to look more rounded and grown-up like Katy and Betty Cross.

Ellen unhooked the new dress, which was hanging on the door of the closet, and put it on. She untied the ribbon that held her hair in a ponytail and shook it out so that it fell to her shoulders in a shining golden curtain, slicked on a little pink lipstick that Nancy had reluctantly allowed her to buy, and dabbed Californian Poppy perfume on her pulse points and around the base of her neck. Then she slid her feet into a pair of candy-pink pumps with kitten heels and peep toes, and surveyed herself in the mirror.

The dress did look pretty on her, just as it had in the shop. She didn't look sophisticated, but she did look older. Ellen did a little twirl and the skirts fanned out satisfyingly. She hoped they'd be allowed to rock and roll so that she could show them off. But even if the modern waltz was insisted upon she wasn't going to complain. At least with the modern waltz she would have Ken's hand planted firmly in the middle of her back.

No, she definitely looked OK; she only hoped Ken thought so too. There was only one slight problem; the paper nylon of the petticoat felt scratchy around her waist. It might bring her out in a rash, she thought. Not that anyone would see it, but she wanted to be comfortable. This was an occasion when everything had to be perfect.

What she needed was a camisole. Ellen didn't own one, of course, but she knew her mother did. It was made of cream silk and edged with ecru lace.

I wonder if she'd let me borrow it? Ellen thought. She went into Nancy's bedroom, the one at the front of the house that looked out on the mimosa tree, and pulled open the drawer of the chest where Nancy kept her underwear. She had to rummage a bit before she found the camisole; Nancy had little occasion to wear it these days, she supposed. As she pulled it out something came out with it and fell to the floor. An airmail envelope; the red and blue chevron pattern around the edges was distinctive, the paper thin and fragile between her fingers when she picked it up. It was addressed to her mother in a firm sloping hand. There was no stamp – that came as part of the package – but the postmark was Gloucester, England.

Ellen stared at it, the camisole forgotten. Who had been writing to her mother from Gloucester, England? Ellen had never so much as heard Nancy mention it. On the point of replacing it in the drawer she hesitated, curiosity burning. She shouldn't pry, she knew, but the temptation was overwhelming. Who would ever know? She unfolded the letter and began to read, hastily at first, picking out odd sentences, with a weather eye on the drive in case Nancy should come home unexpectedly. Then, with utter disbelief sending shock waves through her, she read it more thoroughly. Everything else was forgotten now – the dance, the camisole, the possibility of discovery here, in her mother's room, with her mother's secrets.

Ellen's secure world, as much taken for granted as the air that she breathed, disintegrated around her. Nothing could ever be the same again.

It began formally enough, that letter that was meant for no one's eyes but Nancy's.

'Dear Nancy.' Not 'My Darling', or any of the other endearments you might expect to precede what the letter went on to say. And the first paragraph was about the weather. 'How are you? Enjoying

269

glorious sunshine, I expect. It's bitterly cold here. We had heavy snow all day yesterday. Roads are blocked, and the farmers are struggling to get feed out to their cows.'

And then, without further preamble:

There's something I want to tell you, Nancy. I'm thinking of getting married again. Elizabeth is a great girl and I don't want to be on my own for the rest of my life. But neither do I want to ask her to marry me if there's a chance you might change your mind. I've never stopped hoping we could be together one day – and I would so much like our child to be a part of my life. I've missed most of the growing-up years and I'd like to make up for lost time.

I guess there's not much chance of it happening, though. Seems like fate has it in for us, and there will always be someone between us to whom our first loyalties lie. But the fact is I still love you, Nancy, just as I always have. Won't you reconsider?

Hoping to hear from you soon.

Yours always,

Mac

'Ellen? Where are you, honey?' Nancy's voice, calling up the stairs. Ellen hadn't heard the car on the drive; her world had shrunk to a flimsy sheet of airmail paper. She thrust it to the bottom of the drawer, colour flaming in her face.

There was something else there, concealed beneath the carefully folded underwear, a small leather box and what looked like another letter. But Ellen had no time to investigate it.

'Up here, Mom. Trying on my outfit for the dance,' she called shakily.

'Let's look at you then.'

Ellen shrank into herself. Her chest felt tight, every bit of her seemed to be trembling, not violently, not so as you'd notice, but as if the cells that made up her flesh had all come loose. She didn't want to face her mother. Didn't want to see her even, not knowing what she knew now. She felt sure the knowledge was written all over her in indelible ink. But what choice did she have? Her reluctant, shaking legs took her to the top of the stairs.

'Come on now, honey, don't be shy! Wow – you look a million dollars! Is that really my little girl?'

No, not your little girl. Not now. Not ever again.

'It scratches,' Ellen said. Her voice seemed to come from a long way off, as if it didn't belong to her at all, but her mind was working overtime, remembering that the camisole was still lying on Ellen's bed where she'd left it. Could she replace it in the drawer as it had been without Nancy noticing anything? She doubted it. Nancy didn't miss much. 'You know that camisole of yours?' Ellen said. 'The silky one with lace. Do you think I could borrow it?'

'I don't see why not.' Nancy started up the stairs.

'It's all right. I found it already.'

'That's OK then.' Nancy sounded utterly unfazed, as if she had forgotten what she had hidden in that drawer. How could she forget something like that?

Ellen stared down at her, at her smiling face, achingly familiar yet utterly changed. A smile that concealed secrets. A face that belonged to a woman who had become a stranger Ellen did not know at all.

My mother had a lover. She had a child with him. 'Our child', 'I would so much like our child to be a part of my life. One of us is not who we think we are. One of us is different. No, not one of us. John. It has to be John. John is not my proper brother at all. This man who signed himself 'Mac' is his father.

She'd known it the moment her numbed brain had begun to function again. She'd stared at the letter that had devastated her world and known. Her mother had been in England in the war; John had been born the year she had come home. And shocked though Ellen was, it explained so much that had puzzled Ellen since she had been old enough to wonder about such things.

'How come you and Daddy got together when you were both away at war?' she had asked Nancy once, looking at a photograph of their wedding, Joe in the uniform of the USAAF, Nancy in a neat dark navy-blue dress and wide-brimmed hat, holding a posy of lilies of the valley.

'We met up in England,' Nancy had replied. 'I was with the ATA, as you know, and your father was posted to an American air base there. We decided to get married.'

'That is real romantic,' Ellen had said. But it didn't answer all her questions. She knew the date her mother and father celebrated their wedding anniversary each year, and she knew John's birthday. She could do sums. She might not be the greatest math brain in the class, but you didn't have to be a genius to count up nine months.

It was no big deal, she'd told herself, feeling quite grown up. Mom and Daddy wouldn't be the first to get ahead of their wedding night and they wouldn't be the last. And it had been wartime, when you never knew if a wedding night would ever come. But Ellen couldn't help wondering about the logistics of it. How had they managed to do it when they had been stationed miles apart? Had they snatched a romantic night in a hotel room, or had it been a rushed encounter in a dark corner behind some barracks hut? Ellen had thought about it and decided she didn't want to know. It was just too embarrassing.

Then there was the way that Nancy always seemed to favour John, like he was special somehow. Ellen hadn't attached too much importance to it until now; she'd always told Ritchie he was being silly when he complained that John was given special privileges, allowed to do things he wasn't. 'He's older than you,' Ellen would say. 'Of course he can do things you can't. When you're his age you'll do them too.'

Ritchie had scowled. 'Wanna bet? Mom likes him better than me. You know she does. She never even seems to tell him off. And I've never known him grounded.'

'Of course she doesn't like him better. It's just that he doesn't do stupid things like you do. He gets home when he's supposed to and he doesn't talk back to her. You're always doing things she's told you not to, and ripping your shorts, and scuffing the toes out of your sneakers. John—'

'Yeah, yeah, I know. John's always perfect. It's like he came down from another planet.' His face had brightened. 'Perhaps he did. Perhaps he's an alien from Mars.'

'You are so stupid, Ritchie.'

'I know I am.' The scowl was back. 'I don't need you to tell me.'

She thought of that conversation now. John might not be from Mars, but it seemed like he was an alien after all. The older brother she adored, hero-worshipped almost. Who had given her rides on the crossbar of his bicycle before she had one of her own, shared his candy with her, washed her top and shorts in the river when she'd got all muddy one day and hung them on the branches of a bush to dry so that Nancy wouldn't know she'd wandered into the swamp where she had been expressly forbidden to venture. Whom she cheered until she was hoarse when he was playing football for the school team, or swimming in a gala. Who made her burst with pride when he stood on the winner's podium with a medal round his neck. He'd given her one of his medals; it hung over the mirror on her nightstand beside the rosette she'd managed to win at Pony Club. Only a third, and though she'd never admitted it to anyone who wasn't actually present on the occasion, only three had competed in that particular novelty race anyway. Not a winner's medal like John's.

John, who was tall and handsome and clean-cut looking. Who was clever and seemed to excel at everything he touched. John, kind and funny and patient. John, who was not her brother at all. Well, not properly.

Tears swam in Ellen's eyes. Nancy had deceived her. Deceived them all. Did John know? She didn't think so. Did Joe? He must, surely he must. Yet he'd never so much as hinted by a word or a gesture that he did. He never made any difference between them as Nancy did. Ellen could see it now, the pride, the tenderness, the reluctance to admit to even the smallest fault, the readiness to over-look misdemeanours, however rare and insignificant. John was Nancy's love child. He was special to her. 'Our child'. Hers and Mac's.

'Mom, I've got to get out of this dress before I mess it up,' Ellen said. She scuttled back up the stairs, to her own room. She slammed the door behind her, covered her face with her hands and burst into tears.

Ellen told no one about her discovery. Once or twice it hovered on her lips when Nancy castigated Ritchie for his latest misde-meanour, or praised John for some fresh achievement, but she said nothing, though the unfairness of it burned in her like a forest fire and smouldered for long afterwards. She hugged the knowledge to her like a guilty secret, which, of course, was exactly what it was. She became moody and withdrawn, resentful beneath the weight of it, and resentful too that her pleasure in going to the hop with Ken Kelsey had been spoiled beyond redemption. For her, the new dress with its scratchy petticoat would forever be associated, not with trembling anticipation and happy memories of a special night, but with the awful discovery that nothing in her family was as it seemed.

It had coloured everything, that discovery. It hung around her, a cloud that refused to go away, even though she tried not to think about it, for that special night, at least. At first it had worked – almost. She had looked at Ken, smart and scrubbed in a new and very grown-up tux, standing on the doorstep and waiting for her, and felt the excitement twist deep inside. She had felt pride too, going with him into the school hall, which had been decorated with balloons and banners for the occasion. 'Look!' she wanted to shout. 'Ken Kelsey asked me to be his partner!' But when they started chatting and he asked her about her brother, who had been cleaning his bicycle in the drive when Ken and his father had arrived to collect her, she'd clammed up instead of talking eagerly about John as she would have done a few short days ago. And when they played Elvis Presley's 'It's Now or Never' for the last dance, and Ken pulled her close so that the beat seemed to throb between them, all she could think of was her mother in the arms of someone who wasn't her father. Her cheek was almost resting on Ken's shoulder, she could smell his soap and the faintest odour of fresh sweat, feel his hand firm on her waist and her breasts pressed against his chest, and suddenly it was all too much, too evocative of what it had been like for her mother with this other man, this Mac. She pulled away, holding herself stiff and awkward, panic rising like nausea in her throat, claustrophobia suffocating her. Ken had become stiff and awkward then too. And when at the end of the evening he'd plucked up the courage to ask if she would go to the movies with him, she panicked again, and said: 'I don't think my mom would let me.' 'Oh, right,' he'd said, offhandedly, as if it couldn't matter less, and she had known he wouldn't ask her again

Sometimes in the weeks and months that followed Ellen found herself studying John to see if she could spot features or traits that didn't relate to any of the rest of her 'proper' family, but she couldn't be sure. He didn't look like Nancy or Joe, and certainly not like Dorothy, her great-aunt on her father's side. But then, neither did she and Ritchie. Not really. There didn't seem to be any strong family likeness at all that she could see. And again and again she wondered if either Joe or John himself had any idea that they were not related.

She pumped John gently when the opportunity arose. 'How come you're so good at everything when Ritchie and I are such idiots?' she asked one day, watching him slyly.

'You're not idiots.'

'We are. If it had been left to me, we'd have gone up river back there.'

They were on vacation in North-West Florida, and they were doing a trip down the Wekiva River from Longwood back to Sanford. Ellen had never canoed before and it had been decided she should team up with John, whilst Ritchie went with Joe. Nancy had stayed behind; they'd left her in the shady car park at Katie's Landing to enjoy a quiet day. The tour Jeep had taken them upriver, the operator had seen them safely into their canoes and driven off, leaving them to their own devices.

At first they had stayed more or less together, enjoying the hot sun dappling through the overhanging trees and screeching at one another to see the turtles that slid hastily off rocks and disappeared beneath the water as they approached. The Little Wekiva was narrow and almost blocked in places by fallen trees; Ellen was happy to sit in the canoe whilst John got out and waded, knee-deep, to pull them clear, though both Joe and Ritchie shared the task with their canoe, hoisting it between them over the debris. Once, Ritchie let out a shriek that had Ellen convinced he was being attacked by an alligator, but it was only a dead fish, washed up on a fallen branch, and Ritchie had trodden on it barefoot.

They stopped for a while to picnic in the boats in a small lagoon. They had brought packets of sandwiches and flasks of water and juice with them, and Ellen, needing a bathroom stop, had clambered ashore to a spot where the trees would afford her some privacy.

'You go on ahead,' John had said to the others. 'We'll catch you.'

It was a natural enough remark, but to Ritchie it was red rag to a bull. Desperate as always to prove that anything John could do, he could do better, he set off at a cracking pace.

'Hey, fella, where's the fire?' Joe asked, but Ritchie was not listening. John catch him? Never! By the time Ellen was back in the canoe, Joe and Ritchie had disappeared around a bend in the river.

'Where are they?' she asked, a little alarmed.

'Oh, you know Ritchie. He couldn't wait. It doesn't matter. There's only one way home. We'll have them in our sights again when the river straightens out.'

'I guess.'

The river was becoming wider all the time. There was another island up ahead, bigger than the ones they had already circumnavigated, and covered with dense foliage that blocked out any view of what was on the other side.

'Left or right?' Ellen, who was in the front of the canoe, asked, but she had already begun to pull to the left.

'Right.'

'Oh, I'm going this way now. Surely it doesn't make any difference?'

'If you want to get back to Katie's Landing, go right.'

'Why?'

'Because I reckon this is where we join the main Wekiva River. Go left, we'll be going upstream.'

'No. It's just another island.'

'Have it your way.'

But after ten minutes' hard paddling and getting nowhere she conceded defeat. When they stopped she could see, just, by the gentle ripples around the canoe he'd been right all the time.

'Oh shucks. It's not fair. How did you know?'

John shrugged. 'Just a hunch. Look at where the sun is and get your bearings, Ellen.'

They paddled back, past the island that had thrown her. Ellen thought she was getting blisters on the palms of her hands, and when they hit a bank of reeds they stopped to rest. Ellen pulled in her paddle, resting it across her bare legs, and turned to John whilst she massaged her sore hands.

'How come you're so good at everything?'

'I'm not.'

'You are.'

'Ellen, you're talking rubbish.'

'I'm not. You are so much smarter than Ritchie and me. It's like you're from a different planet.' Ritchie's words, haunting her.

'Yeah, sure. Are we gonna get going or not?'

He didn't know. She was as sure of it as she had ever been of anything. Her own knowledge prickled on her skin along with the bites of the predatory insects that abounded on the river, and grumbled in her empty stomach. But Ellen said nothing. John might not know the truth, but it was not her place to tell him.

II

Vietnam. Ellen hated the conflict with a vengeance, and so did most of her fellow students at the University of Southern Florida. In between lectures and cheering on the Golden Braham baseball team they held protest meetings and attended rallies, and Ellen herself had even managed to hitch a lift with Joe to Washington where she'd joined with 35,000 others to circle the White House and march to the Washington Monument.

It hadn't ever been thus. In the beginning most Americans had supported President Johnson's decision to bomb, Nancy and Joe among them.

'There's times when you just gotta stand up and fight,' Joe had said stoically. 'Otherwise folks just think they can walk right over you.'

But Ellen had hated the idea of war right from the start. She hated violence of any kind, and she was sickened by the pictures of Vietnamese villages bombed by the marine rifle company which flashed across the TV screens; she recoiled from the thought of the suffering of innocent women and children who were losing their homes and their lives; she was horrified by the rising death toll of American servicemen. Most of all she couldn't bear that. A boy she'd known at High School had been killed quite early on. She didn't know exactly how or where; she hadn't cared to ask the details. But she'd been home from college when his funeral took place, and like everyone else in Varna had turned out to line the streets as his cortège passed by, attended by a posse of fellow marines, grim-faced and impossibly young-looking, like little boys whose game of soldiers had suddenly gone tragically wrong. She hadn't known the boy well – Alan Swain, his name was. He'd lived with his mother in a shack on the wrong side of town and his father drove a truck when he wasn't in prison, so his circle and Ellen's hadn't really touched. But she could picture him clearly, his jet-black hair longer than most of the other boys' and swept back in a DA from his handsome, swarthy face, his pants 'far too tight to be decent', Nancy had once said, sculpted to long muscular legs. He'd come home in a body bag, Joe had said, a term that had made Ellen shudder. She had looked at the white coffin draped with the Stars and Stripes and topped with his uniform cap, and felt sick. It was just too awful to think that he was dead and would never again fool around with his friends, or strum a guitar, or kick a football. And he was far from the only one. Almost everyone knew someone who had gone to Vietnam and come back, in Joe's awful terminology, in a body bag.

Ellen had begun to be scared, very scared, that John would have to go to Vietnam. His draft had been deferred whilst he was in college, but she knew they'd hit him with it the minute he graduated, and John being John wouldn't try to avoid it by going for further education or by burning his draft papers at a protest rally as some people did. He'd consider it a matter of honour that he should go and do his bit.

And so it had turned out. John had graduated from college the same year she was a freshman, and joined the USAF. Because he was already a qualified pilot it wasn't long before he was flying Phantom jets, and then it was only a matter of time before he was sent to Vietnam.

The atmosphere in the house on the day John left American soil was a cauldron of tension and unexpressed emotion. Joe was never one to display his innermost feelings, but there was no mistaking the dark cloud that surrounded him. Nancy was snappy and bad-tempered, but looked as if she might burst into uncharacteristic tears if anyone said a wrong word, and even Ritchie was subdued. Ellen was distraught. She was trying very hard not to think of the terrible images of Vietnam that she saw daily in the newspapers and on television, but there was no escaping the sick dread that sat heavy in her gut and pumped with her blood in her veins.

Supper was a wretched meal; they were all too conscious of the empty space at table where John had sat during his pre-deployment leave. They didn't want to talk about it but they couldn't stop thinking about it either. Nothing else was important enough to warrant their attention.

As she helped clear the dishes, Ellen set one too close to the edge of the counter. Nancy, plonking a pan down beside it, managed to dislodge it. It went crashing down, shattering into a dozen pieces and depositing corn kernels and gravy all over the floor. Instantly, Nancy exploded.

'Oh, no! One of my best plates! Look at the mess! Why did you put it there, Ellen? It should have been stacked in the sink. Oh, I just don't believe this!'

'It's only a plate, honey,' Joe said placatingly.

'It is not only a plate. It's one of my set. I won't be able to put out six alike any more,' Nancy retorted.

'There are only five of us,' Joe pointed out.

'And what if one of them has a friend over?'

'Honey, no one's going to notice.'

'I'll notice. Why couldn't you think what you were doing, Ellen, and take more care?'

'I'm not the one who broke it,' Ellen protested.

'Don't talk back to me!' Nancy snapped.

Ellen, already on the edge of her nerves with worrying about John, felt tears gathering.

'Oh, leave me alone, can't you?' she sobbed, and ran out into the yard, burning with indignation at the unfairness of it all.

The evening air was cool on her hot cheeks, but it couldn't dampen the burning behind her eyes. She sat down heavily on the swing seat, crumpled into herself and let the tears come.

'Ellen, honey?' She hadn't heard Joe follow her out, but the seat rocked again as he sat down beside her. 'Don't cry now. Your mom didn't mean it. She's upset. We all are.'

'She doesn't have to take it out on me,' Ellen gulped. 'It wasn't my fault.'

'I know that and you know that. And so does your mom. She's just not herself. She's worried sick for John.'

'Oh, Daddy.' Ellen began to cry harder at the mention of her beloved brother. 'I'm so scared for him. Suppose something happens to him? Suppose it was an omen?'

'How d'you mean, honey?' Joe asked, puzzled.

'Oh . . .' Ellen could hardly bring herself to say it, the awful superstition that had settled in her stomach and was worrying at her ragged nerves. 'Mom likes to have a spare plate and you said,

"There are only five of us." But supposing it means that with only five plates, we're still going to have a spare? That we're not going to be five any more, only four?'

'Aw, come on, honey, that's just nonsense and you know it.' Joe put his arm round her and she buried her face in his shoulder as she had done when she was upset ever since she was a little girl. Except that whereas Daddy had always seemed able to make things right in the past, she wasn't so sure of his power to work magic this time. Keeping John safe was not something he had any power over.

'I couldn't stand it if anything happened to John,' she sobbed. 'I just couldn't.'

'Nothing's gonna happen to him. Trust me.'

'How can you be so sure?'

Joe didn't answer, just fished a handkerchief out of his pocket and handed it to her. 'Here, honey, dry your eyes. Everything'll turn out right, you'll see.'

Ellen took the handkerchief and snuffled into it. It smelled comfortingly of Daddy, of the soap he used and tobacco and petrol from his lighter. Ellen blew her nose.

'Better?' Joe asked gently.

'Mm.' She wasn't really, but his strength was comforting.

'That's my girl. You coming back inside now? It'll only upset your mom more if she knows you're upset.'

How could he be so calm, Ellen wondered. Even given his pragmatic nature, how could he not be falling apart too? Or was he just better than the others at hiding it?

And then she remembered. John wasn't his. Not really. Did that make a difference?

Suddenly, in this bubble of intimacy they were sharing, she

285

wanted to talk to him about it. 'Daddy, I know.' The words hovered on her lips. She looked into his face, the face she loved so well, lined now, with the anxiety he took such care to hide as well as the passage of the years, into his kind, honest blue eyes, and her courage deserted her.

John might not be his son, but it made no difference. Just as it made no difference to her. He'd raised John along with her and Ritchie, and loved him just the same. He was as worried as she was. He was just not showing it. She couldn't raise the subject of John's parentage with him now. And probably never.

'Let's go get a cup of coffee, honey,' Joe said.

Ellen blew her nose again and wiped her eyes. But she didn't return the handkerchief to Joe. She kept it screwed up in a ball in her hand, her own personal comfort blanket.

Ellen worried about John every minute of every day and some-times woke at night in a cold sweat too, the anxiety gnawing at her gut, her imagination working overtime.

She followed the news daily, half afraid to open a newspaper or switch on the TV or radio because every mention of fresh casual-ties made her stomach turn over, yet driven obsessively to do so all the same.

She listened to President Johnson's State of the Union Address hoping desperately for some light at the end of the tunnel and was instead chilled by his words.

'War in Vietnam is unlike America's previous wars. Yet finally war is always the same. It is young men dying in the fullness of their promise. It is trying to kill a man that you do not even know well enough to hate . . . therefore, to know war is to know that there is still madness in this world.'

286

The anti-war protests were mushrooming now; there was scarcely a major city that hadn't seen gatherings and marches by people as sickened by the carnage as she was, and yet still it went on. B52 bombers were being used now to flatten towns and villages, each carrying a hundred bombs that were dropped from an altitude of six miles. Ellen was glad at least that John was flying fighters; she knew he would be as appalled as she was at the mass destruction inflicted by the bombing – he'd said so, very forcefully.

'I hope to God I never have to inflict that on innocent people,' he'd said. 'I sure don't want that on my conscience, even if I am doing it for my country.'

But there was plenty else to worry about. The Tan Son Nhut air base was attacked with the loss of twelve US helicopters and nine aircraft; it was reported there were a hundred and forty casualties. A hundred and forty – dear God! And Phantoms, the jets John flew, were involved in dogfights over Hanoi, though they were prohibited by Washington from attacking the MiG air bases in the north.

Ellen followed the news and trembled. She could see no end to it. No end at all. And the knowledge that John was out there in the thick of it was a suffocating cloud that followed her around and cast a damper over what should have been the happiest, most carefree, time of her life.

It was that same spring that Ellen met Bob Lintern. He was five years older than she was, English, and an engineer; it was nothing short of a miracle, Ellen thought, that their paths had crossed at all. But certainly Bob provided a welcome diversion from the anxiety for John that pervaded her life.

She first set eyes on Bob in the T-Bone Steak House where she and a group of her friends from the School of Business Studies

287

had gone to take advantage of the 'special' that the T-Bone sometimes put on for students. The T-Bone was a cross between a diner and an old-fashioned saloon bar, rough wood panelling offsetting Formica counters, cushions softening the hard benches in symmetrically aligned booths, candles spilling sculpted fountains of wax over the necks of dark green bottles, the glow they cast rendered impotent by the harsh glare of overhead neon strips. A pungent aroma of onions and French fries wafted in waves from the kitchen area where the Mexican chef sweated over the griddle in full view of the diners, and collected in a dense cloud around the red-checked gingham curtains; through the medium of the juke box, the Righteous Brothers belted out 'You're My Soul and Inspiration'.

Ellen noticed Bob the moment he came in. He stood out as being different as well as being tall and good looking. Where most of the guys were in jeans or shorts, he was wearing brown pants she would later learn were called cavalry twills and his hair, light brown, fell in a loose bang over his forehead instead of being slicked back or chopped into a crew cut.

'Who's that?' Ellen whispered to Barbara Foley, her closest friend and room mate.

'Don't know. Never seen him before. You want me to find out? I will if you like.' Barbara, known for her ebullient personality, was already sliding towards the edge of the booth.

'Don't you dare!' Ellen hissed.

The T-Bone was filling up rapidly; a Student Special night always attracted a large crowd. The stranger and his friend approached the booth where Ellen and Barbara were sitting.

'Are these seats taken?'

Oh-mi-God, it was him. Ellen was so flustered she barely noticed at first that his accent was not American, but English. She shook her head mutely; Barbara answered for both of them. 'No, you're OK. Be our guests.'

He was looking at her. Ellen knew it. She glanced up from the menu card and their eyes met for an awkward moment. She looked away quickly, feeling a flush spreading up her neck and into her cheeks. She was glad she was wearing her new Madras plaid pinafore skirt, and that she'd washed her hair that morning and rollered it into a sleek pageboy. She hoped she hadn't gone overboard on the kohl eye-liner; if she had it was Barbara's fault. She was always trying to persuade Ellen to make up her eyes more heavily, though Ellen protested it made her look like a panda. Barbara, irrepressible as ever, was chatting to the boys; Ellen chewed on her steak and from behind those panda eyelashes watched the stranger watching her.

He wasn't a college student, Ellen learned. He was on a six-month exchange with an electronics company in Tampa who were making a name for themselves in the specialised field of flight simulators and who had links with the aero industry firm he worked for in England. He had met Ted O'Leary, who was, like Ellen, majoring in business studies, when Ted had been working on an assignment that had taken him to the electronics factory in downtown Tampa, and the two had struck up a friendship. Beyond his colleagues, Bob knew few people in Tampa. And Ted, sensing he was lonely, had started hanging out with him. Tonight he had invited him to the 'special', flashing his student card briefly to get them both in.

The talk turned to Vietnam.

'Ellen's brother is there, flying jets,' Barbara offered. 'Did you have to do draft, Bob?'

'National Service, we call it in England. And no, we don't have it any more. I missed it by a couple of years.'

'Lucky for you.' Ted was sweating on being drafted when he graduated next year.

Bob looked a little shamefaced, as if he had somehow been found wanting, and, feeling sorry for him, Ellen said: 'What you're doing is really important, though.'

Bob looked surprised, as if he'd never considered the reason for what he was doing beyond that it interested him, but he smiled at Ellen all the same and she felt her tummy tip.

At the end of the evening, Bob followed Ellen out of the T-Bone.

'I was wondering . . . could I see you again?'

And Ellen, who was already more than halfway in love, didn't hesitate. 'If you like,' she said.

They dated through what was left of spring and into early summer, and the closeness growing between them was her salvation. Loving Bob opened a whole new dimension for her; when they were together the electricity between them was tangible, prickling on her skin and magnetising her every nerve ending; when they were apart he was constantly in her thoughts. She'd never felt this way about anyone before; the excitement, the poignant ache of longing to be close to him, both physically and emotionally, was new and all-consuming. He made her happy too in a more complete way than she had ever imagined possible.

Just one shadow hung over everything they shared; fall was approaching too fast, and in the fall Bob was due to go home to England.

'Can't you get a job out here permanently?' she said one night. They were cuddling in the back seat of his car at the drive-in movie. Neither of them had the first idea what the film was about.

'I don't know.' Bob nibbled her ear. The fall was months away; it was tonight he was interested in.

Ellen pushed free and wriggled round to look at him. 'You could, I bet. Aviation electronics is huge, and they're building new test bays and taking on more workers, you told me so. It would be really great if you could stay in Tampa. Oh, find out about it, Bob!'

Bob said nothing. The shadows cast by the flickering of the film chased one another across his face.

'Go on – why don't you?'

'I'm not sure that I want to.'

That hit her like a mule kick in the stomach. 'What do you mean, you don't want to? Don't you like it here?'

'It's OK. It's fine. But my home is in England.'

'The sun shines here! You can't rather have rain and cold than sunshine!'

'I don't mind it. I'm used to it.'

'You have to be here for Thanksgiving! We have a turkey like you wouldn't believe, and—'

'We have turkey at Christmas.'

'Bob, you can't go back to England.'

'Well, I'm sorry, but I am.'

Tears pricked behind her eyes. 'And you don't care about leaving me.'

'Well of course I do.' He scooped her close again.

'You don't. If you cared about me you wouldn't want to go back to England.'

'You could always come with me.' His mouth was against her

291

hair so the words were blurred and she thought she couldn't possibly have heard aright.

'What did you say?'

'I said you could always come with me.'

Her heart had begun to beat a tattoo. She tried to feign nonchalance.

'Oh yes, right. Like I just walk out on my studies and take off with no money and no job and nowhere to live . . .'

'I've got a job. And a flat . . . well, it's not mine, it's rented, and I do share the bathroom . . . but I should be due a pay rise when I get back and I reckon I could afford something bigger and nicer. Bristol's a great city. You'd like it.'

'Bob.' Her heart was hammering now so hard she could scarcely breathe. 'Are you saying what I think you're saying?'

There was a silence that seemed to stretch into infinity. Even the film seemed to have gone quiet; if either of them had cared to look at the screen they would have seen the hero and heroine in a romantic clinch. Then Bob said slowly: 'Yes, I suppose I am.' He sounded stunned, as if he could believe what he was saying even less than she could. 'How about we get married, Ellen?'

'Oh, Bob!' she said. 'Oh, yes!' And in that moment she had no doubts at all.

They came later, the doubts. Not about Bob – Ellen knew she was in love with him – but certainly about abandoning her course and leaving home to live in a cold, wet country halfway across the world. What had seemed incredibly romantic and exciting in a private oasis under the stars at the drive-in movie seemed less so in the harsh bright light of day.

'You gotta be kidding!' Barbara said when Ellen told her about it. 'He's good, I know, but no guy's that good, Ellen. Not to just give everything up for. Gee, honey, give it a break! You'll soon meet up with someone else when he's gone.'

Nancy and Joe were less than delighted too, though Joe seemed more resigned than Nancy. 'I hadn't realised my little girl was all grown up,' he said, what looked suspiciously like tears misting his blue eyes. 'I'll miss you, y'know that?'

'Don't talk such rubbish,' Nancy said briskly. 'She's not going anywhere. At least, not for a long while yet. You hardly know the guy, Ellen. You don't know what sort of a home he comes from, or how he behaves when he's back there.'

'I know enough,' Ellen said defensively.

'And what about your education? You have to finish that before you even think of getting married. Tell her, Joe.'

'An education's a fine thing, Ellen,' Joe said, but he didn't sound convincing. Nancy set great store by education, all too aware, no doubt, that it was something she had missed out on, but Joe was less convinced of its importance. A husband, a home, a family, that was what a woman should aspire to in his opinion.

'I love him!' Ellen said fiercely. 'And anyway, I've said yes. He's going to buy me a ring. He has already, for all I know.'

'Well, let him buy you a ring if he must, though I'm not sure even that's a good idea. But let's hear no more talk of following him to England yet awhile. Keep in touch, finish college, and then, if you're still set on it, we'll talk about it again,' Nancy said.

'I will be.' Ellen did not want to concede defeat, but at the same time she was oddly relieved to have the decision made for her. She loved Bob, she was excited by the prospect of marrying him. But she wasn't sure she was ready to leave everything dear and familiar and start a new life on the other side of the Atlantic just yet. It was an enormous step and she was just a little apprehensive about taking it. Besides, if she held out, there was always the chance Bob would give in and see things her way. Perhaps she could yet persuade him to seek a job here in Florida. If she trotted behind him to England there would be no hope of him doing that.

III

John was coming home on leave. Ellen was so excited she could scarcely bear it, and every time the happiness rose in her it somehow made her afraid. Being so happy was tempting fate. Supposing something happened to him now? She closed her eyes, held her thumbs, and prayed.

It was summertime now, and she was on vacation. She and Bob still managed to see quite a lot of each other; he drove down to Varna each weekend and sometimes, on a weekday evening, she borrowed Nancy's car and they met up halfway. A zircon ring sparkled on the third finger of her left hand. Bob had wanted her to have diamonds or sapphires, but she had liked the colour of the zircon. It didn't matter to her, as it did to Bob, that it was only a semi-precious stone. She was happy with it. She frequently stretched out her hand to admire it, and Barbara had teased her that she was fast becoming ambidextrous. She couldn't wait to show her ring to John; she thought at least he would be happy for her. Certainly he'd written his congratulations as soon as he'd got the letter telling him of her engagement. Ritchie, on the other hand, had simply

295

grunted and raised his eyebrows, and in the beginning he had done his best to avoid Bob. They seemed to be getting along better now, though, and as Ellen had said to Bob by way of embarrassed explanation – what else could you expect from your kid brother? What she didn't tell him was that Ritchie poured scorn on Bob's conservative dress sense and lack of knowledge in the matter of popular music, and mimicked his accent for the amusement of his friends.

For days before John was due home Nancy was in a fever of preparation. The house was spring-cleaned from top to bottom, and the larder filled with John's favourite foods. Never the world's greatest cook, she embarked on a programme of slow simmered casseroles and baking that a professional chef would not have been ashamed of. Ellen helped with the preparation of vegetables and Dorothy came over to ice a homecoming cake, such artistry being far beyond Nancy or Ellen's capabilities. Dorothy was plumper than ever these days; since a heart scare years ago, when John was just a baby, she had taken no exercise at all. When she was forced to move from one place to another she hobbled on short fat legs like a mountainous Jello. But she was as acerbic and bossy as ever, criticising Nancy's efforts and directing operations from the bar stool at the kitchen counter, which she overflowed in every direction.

She was excited in her own way too at the prospect of having John at home again, Ellen realised. Like everyone else she adored John. Ellen wondered briefly what she would say if she knew he was not her flesh and blood, but it was a fleeting thought only. John's parentage wasn't something she dwelled on much these days. Nor did she want to think for even a moment that all too soon John's leave would be over and they'd have to say goodbye again. For the moment it was all happy anticipation.

John flew into Fort Myers airport, and Nancy, Joe and Ellen went up to meet him. Nancy had wanted Ritchie to go too, but he said it would be too much of a crush for all of them in the Chevvy. Ellen suspected it was just a ploy to have the place to himself with Diane, the girl he'd been dating since they were in Junior High. She knew they got up to things they shouldn't when they had the chance; she'd found a packet of rubbers in his room once when she was looking for a record he had borrowed and failed to return.

When they saw John walking towards them they were all in tears, Nancy and Ellen unashamedly, Joe wiping his eyes surreptitiously with the back of his hand and beaming fit to bust.

John looked older and thinner. There was a gauntness about him that hadn't been there before and there were dark shadows around his eyes. But he was here. Nancy and Ellen hugged him as if they'd never let him go, and Joe clapped him on the shoulder and then stood back, watching benignly as the women enveloped him again.

John was here, in one piece. For the moment, it was all that mattered.

For Nancy, however, the joy of holding John in her arms again was tempered by the realisation that this wasn't the John who had gone away. With a mother's intuition she saw that although, physically, he was with them, there was a barrier in his eyes, a distance about him that was, to her, almost tangible. She'd met it before with the men she had known who were fighting in a war. It hadn't struck her so forcibly then, since she had not known them before they went on active service. Often they coped with the loss of friends, and the realisation that they too might have the life expectancy of a day lily, with an almost manic zest for the moment, so there was no room left for grief or fear. But sometimes there was that withdrawal that she saw in John now, the shutting out of anyone who had not shared their experiences and could not know the dark thoughts and emotions that tormented them in the dead of night, the ever-present knowledge that each day might be their last.

Nancy recognised the signs of battle fatigue and wept silently for the loss of youth and innocence, and for her own inability to reach her beloved son. So many young men had been destroyed by Vietnam, and for many, being killed in action was a fate almost preferable to the physical wounds and psychological scars they would bear for the rest of their lives. The short fuse, the reflex action that led to them harming those they loved through the momentary delusion that they were the enemy, the scream in the night, the drinking to forget. At least John was a pilot, not a marine; he would never have to look into a man's eyes as he shot him or bayoneted him in the guts. But he would have doled out death and seen his friends shot down in flames. And he was not a tough guy, hardened by a background of gang wars and street violence. He was chivalrous by nature, sensitive and vulnerable. There were facets to his character that would make it harder for him in many ways. Knowing him as she did, Nancy trembled for him.

Would she ever get back the John who had left? She didn't know, and didn't want to waste energy on speculation. She needed to give her all to supporting him now, and cocooning him in a warmth and normality that he could take back with him to the killing fields of Vietnam.

In the days that followed, as Nancy lavished attention on John, Ritchie found to his shame that his brother's return had stirred up all his old feelings of jealousy and inadequacy.

With John out of the picture, it had been as though a weight had been lifted from his shoulders. Not having to compete with his brother on a daily basis had relieved him of a lifelong struggle with his perceived inferiority, and his confidence had received a further boost when Joe had agreed that he could begin working for Varna Aviation straight from High School. Ritchie had been fretting that he'd never get grades good enough to be accepted by a college as highly regarded as the one John had got into with effortless ease. It did occur to him to wonder if Joe too didn't think he was college material, but he was too relieved to let it bother him too much. He didn't mind that Joe had insisted he learn the business from the bottom up. He quite liked working with Don Rivers, the engineer and maintenance man, and he accepted that it would be useful to know how a plane flew as well as how to fly it, and to be able to check out more than just the oil, fuel and fuselage and run power checks.

Altogether, he had relaxed into himself during the months when John was not there, an ever-present shadow. Now, with his return, and the fuss everyone was making of him, it all came flooding back. And something else was bothering him too, gnawing away at him like a sour apple in his gut. That something was Diane.

Ritchie had been dating Diane for almost four years now, and she was considered something of a catch. Pretty, hair that fell in waves and curls to just below her shoulders, a figure that had every guy in their year drawing descriptive curves in the air when she passed by and itching to get their hands on the real thing. And her father, so it was rumoured, had played bass guitar in a group that had had a chart hit back in the fifties, though to look at him now, balding, sporting a beer gut and driving a cab for a living, it was hard to imagine.

Though he sometimes felt a little restless, Ritchie was very proud of Diane. She was, he thought, the one thing he'd got right. And

Diane seemed as happy to be his girl now as she had been in the beginning, something he never ceased to marvel at. She never so much as looked at anyone else, and the boys who ogled her knew she and Ritchie were an item and never made a move on her. But she was looking at someone now, and that someone was John. When she came to share their family meals, Ritchie could see her watching John under her eyelashes, and when he smiled at her she went ever so faintly pink. She dimpled at John too, the way she'd used to dimple at Ritchie when they first noticed one another, and hadn't done now, he realised, in a very long time.

The old demons stirred in Ritchie's gut. John was better-looking than he was, and cleverer, and good at everything he touched, and now he had the added glamour of being a combat pilot fighting for his country in Vietnam. It had never occurred to him to worry about John in respect of Diane before, but he realised now that she was no longer a kid. She was seventeen years old and the age gap between her and John had dwindled.

Ritchie felt sick. If John took Diane away from him it would be the last straw. The restlessness he had sometimes felt disappeared like magic; all he could think of was that he just couldn't stand for her to transfer her affections to John. Who he knew, with sinking certainty, could take her with no trouble at all if he wanted to. Just as he had taken everything else, for the whole of his life.

The catalyst for catastrophe happened almost by accident, and looking back years later, Ellen could never quite understand how she had come to tell Ritchie the truth about John. It had been a stupid, stupid thing to do. For years she had kept it to herself and never once been tempted to share it with anyone, least of all Ritchie. She was good at keeping secrets. She prided herself on it.

And then one day in that summer of 1967 she broke her silence and disaster followed as surely as night follows day.

There had been something of an upset that morning, and as a result Ritchie was sulky and disgruntled. He'd wanted to borrow Nancy's car to take Diane out; Nancy said she had already promised it to John, who wanted to go up to Naples to look up an old friend. She had pointed out that if Ritchie was so keen to see Diane, he could ride over to her house on his bicycle, and that since John's time at home was limited, his needs should take priority. Ritchie had muttered something to the effect that John's needs always did, Nancy had overheard and castigated him. Ritchie had sloped off, miserable and muttering, and it had been left to Ellen to try to cheer him up and make the peace.

'Why does she always have to treat John as though he's special?' Ritchie said, and before she could stop herself, Ellen replied: 'Well – to her, he is.'

The minute the words were out she wished she could snatch them back. But it was too late for that. Ritchie was staring at her.

'What are you talking about?'

'Oh . . . nothing . . .' But her face, shut in suddenly, and the deliberately casual tone that failed to hide the fact that she was flustered, told a different story.

'No, what did you mean? Come on, Ellen, tell me what you meant.'

Ellen sought desperately for a way out of this; failed miserably.

'Why is John special to Mom?' Ritchie persisted.

'Ritchie, please don't ask me. I can't tell you,' Ellen said. 'Forget it, please just forget I said it.'

'As if! For Chrissakes, Ellen . . .'

She took a deep breath, knowing there was no way he was going to leave this until he'd ferreted out the truth.

'Joe's not his father.' There, it was said. Ellen glanced at Ritchie from beneath her lashes, terrified of the consequences of what she had done. Ritchie had become utterly still. He wore an expression of shock, as if he had just been struck in the face by a baseball but didn't yet know what had hit him.

'Say something,' Ellen pleaded.

Ritchie shook himself. 'I still don't know what the hell you are talking about.'

'Joe is not John's father. Mom had him as a result of a wartime romance. That's why he's special to her. She kind of feels she has to protect him.' She caught at Ritchie's arm. 'Ritchie, you have to promise me not to tell anyone about this. I don't think John knows. I'm not even sure if Daddy does.'

'So how come you know? This is a leg-pull, Ellen, isn't it? You're winding me up.' But his face told her he was clutching at straws, and her face told him this was no wind-up. 'How come you know?' he repeated.

'It's a long story.' Ellen rubbed her eyes with her fingers, already bitterly regretting her indiscretion, trying to excuse it to herself, and to Ritchie. 'Ritchie, I really think it's the reason Mom treats John the way she does. It's not that she doesn't love us – you and me. It's nothing to do with us at all really. Like I say, I think she's protective of him because Joe isn't his father. He's kind of hers alone. And there's more to it than that. John reminds her of someone who meant a great deal to her. Maybe he even looks like him, I don't know. But when Mom favours him, it's not because you've failed somehow. It's that whatever you did you could never match up because he's . . . well, special.'

'Oh, yeah, sure.' Ritchie had walked too long in John's shadow to be fooled into thinking it changed anything, even if it was true.

John was still better-looking, cleverer. It wasn't only Nancy who treated him like a hero, it was everyone – teachers, family, friends . . . Diane. None of them knew the secret, they had no emotional stake in who he was, or wasn't. They only judged him and Ritchie on what they saw. And found Ritchie wanting.

They talked some more, then Nancy was calling up the stairs.

'Hey, you two, come on down! There's food on the table.'

Ellen grabbed Ritchie's arm. 'Don't say anything! Please, Ritchie, just act normal.'

Ritchie chewed on the inside of his lip, his eyes narrowed. For the first time in years, perhaps ever, he felt powerful and enabled. This was something he needed time to think about. He wouldn't say anything. Yet.

'Gee, John, it sure is good to have you home.'

It was rare for Joe to put his feelings into words, rare enough that the rest of the family gathered around the table for dinner sat up and took notice.

Instinctively Ellen shot an anxious glance in Ritchie's direction. He'd been quiet all day, brooding, she guessed, over what she had told him, and she was tight as a coiled spring, afraid he might let the cat out of the bag. But Ritchie seemed preoccupied with Diane. She had joined them for dinner – Nancy had roasted a chicken and made the corn fritters John loved – and Ellen had not failed to notice she was paying a little too much attention to John. There was something in the way she looked at him that set alarm bells ringing and it escalated the tension Ellen was feeling. If Diane were to transfer her affections to John it would destroy Ritchie.

It was Nancy who picked up on Joe's sentiment.

'Amen to that. I guess it makes me sound like some old biddy, but it's a real treat being all together. John back from Vietnam. Ellen home from college. Ritchie . . .' Her voice tailed away. What was there to say about Ritchie?

'Just as long as you don't go off to England with Bob, Ellen, please God it won't be too long before we're all together again,' Nancy went on. 'I know it seems like for ever just now till John's home for good, but it'll pass. Then things will settle down in no time. Never mind that we want you back safe, John, your father can't wait to be able to take things a bit easier. He's finding running Varna Aviation a bit of a strain, isn't that right, Joe?'

'Sure is. Things have moved on since I started out with just the one little plane.' Joe shovelled more potatoes onto his plate. 'Flying I can handle, though I could do with another good pilot I can trust so I could run another twin-engine. The business side . . . well, it's all getting too much for me. I never was that good at it anyway. The sooner I can get you in charge of all that, John, the better. You haven't changed your mind, I hope, since we last talked about it? You haven't gotten other plans?'

'I've got no plans at the moment beyond getting out of the air force as soon as I can,' John said easily. 'Right now keeping the family flag flying sounds pretty good to me.'

'And you'll find it worth your while. It'll be yours one day – well, yours and Ritchie's. I reckon with your business training and the way you get along with folk you could turn it into a little goldmine. And I can retire and leave you to it.'

Ritchie had gone very still. He'd never heard before of any discussion between Joe and John about John going into the business. He'd assumed John would want to make good use of his fancy qualifications by making a career with some high-falutin' company or other. It stung, knowing they'd talked this over and never mentioned it to him. And in a flash he could see the way it was going to be. One of these days he'd be drafted to Vietnam and by the time he got back, John would be settled in, in charge. And he, Ritchie, would be the dogsbody, fixing planes, flying whatever John told him to. Doing all the routine stuff while John ruled the roost and took the glory. Second-best again.

Nothing had changed, it never would.

He glanced at Nancy, beaming happily, swivelled his eyes to Diane, and saw the look on her face, the way she was dimpling congratulations across the table at John. Ritchie laid down his fork, covered her hand with his. She jerked it away, still smiling at John.

Fury born of years of resentment and jealousy flared in his gut. God, how he hated John! How he hated the ease with which he sailed through life, the way everything fell into his lap. He even hated the fact that John was so darned *nice*. If he'd been a self-satisfied bighead, if he threw his weight about and traded on the blessings life handed him, it might have been bearable. But he didn't. He remained likeable and reasonable and easy-going, and somehow it made the bitter pill the harder to swallow. Tears of jealousy and rage burned behind his eyes. One day he'd get even with John. He'd show him. He'd show them all.

'Are you OK with that, Ritchie? We can run it together, you and me.' John looked a bit awkward now. He had seen the look on Ritchie's face and realised he was upset.

'Yeah, cool,' Ritchie said, as nonchalantly as he could manage.

But the evening was set to go from bad to worse.

When he drove Diane home she was off-hand with him, and when he pulled into a deserted dark spot and tried for a smooch,

305

she wasn't in the mood. He felt her stiff and unresponsive in his arms, and as his hand slid up under her skirt she slapped it away.

'Stop it, Ritchie.'

'Aw, Diane, come on! What's the matter?'

'I just don't feel like it. Can't you ever think of anything else? I'm tired, Ritchie. Just take me home for once.'

John, he thought, angrily starting the car and pulling away with a screech of tyres. She's got the hots for John. Despair flooded him and he put his foot hard down to the floorboards.

'For goodness' sake, slow down before you kill us both!' Diane squealed, and Ritchie thought that it was not him and Diane who should be killed, but perfect John, the bane of his life.

Ellen was waiting for him when he got home. Like John, she had noticed how fed up Ritchie had looked at supper and she felt dreadfully sorry for him. It wasn't his fault that he couldn't compete with John. It wasn't his fault that he didn't have the genes that made John a golden boy, nor that he was not a love child who would always have a special place in his mother's heart. He was hurt, so hurt, Ellen knew, and it just wasn't fair. Why couldn't anyone but her seem to see beyond the truculence and make him feel special once in a while? She had decided she'd have a word with him and try to find something – anything – to say that would comfort him and make it all a little more bearable.

'You OK?' she asked, sitting down on his bed and cuddling one of his pillows in her lap. 'No, don't answer that. You're not, I know. But you mustn't take things so hard. Daddy said the business was going to be yours and John's equally and I'm sure that's how he means it to be.'

'You reckon?' Ritchie retorted, scowling. 'Well, that's not how it sounded to me. He wants someone he can trust. He said it right in front of me, like I don't count at all. I'm fit for nothing but doing repairs with Don to keep an eye on me. I've worked my butt off, and he wants John to walk back in and take over. Bloody John. I could kill him. Everything falls in his lap. I'm just the afterthought, scratching around for his leavings.'

'Oh, come on, Ritchie,' Ellen cajoled. 'Dad didn't mean it like that. But you've got to admit, John's older, he's got more experience and a degree in business studies and hours of flying different types on his log book. It's only natural Daddy should cut him in if he's willing.'

Ritchie seemed hardly to be listening.

'And Diane fancies him rotten,' he went on bitterly. 'She's gone cold on me and I see the way she looks at him. And Mom . . . well, we've already been there. Bloody John. I wish she'd given him away, or strangled him at birth. I wish he were—' He broke off, but the word he hadn't spoken hung in the air, and the resentment turned to hatred was spine-chilling.

'Ritchie, you've got to stop this,' Ellen said, shocked. 'John's your brother. You mustn't wish him dead, especially not when he's in danger of his life every day in Vietnam. If anything happened to him, you'd never forgive yourself for saying such things, thinking them even.'

Ritchie snorted and let fly with his fist, sweeping a photograph of him and John on a long-ago fishing trip off the shelf. It crashed to the floor, the glass cracking in a wide V around John's smiling face and cutting him off from the catch he was proudly holding aloft. 'He won't be killed in Vietnam, not he,' he said scornfully. 'He's too darned lucky for that. He always comes up smelling of roses, or haven't you noticed? He'll be back again taking all the prizes, you can bet on it.'

'Ritchie!' Ellen pleaded.

And he looked her in the eye, his face twisted with hatred and despair, and said the thing she would never forget.

'You want to know why I wish John was dead? If he was dead, I'd be free.'

John's leave had shrunk so fast it seemed it was only hours ago they had been driving to Fort Myers to meet him; now there were only two days left before they would have to drive him back again. Knowing it lay heavy in Ellen's stomach like a steak and fries eaten too late at night. But at the same time she was aware of a feeling of relief. Ever since she had told Ritchie her secret she had been on tenterhooks, afraid he would spill the beans, or perhaps had done so already. John had grown increasingly quiet and withdrawn and she worried that Ritchie might have said something to him. But perhaps it was just the prospect of returning to the war zone that was weighing him down; bad enough, but not as bad as learning the truth just now.

On the last day he disappeared into his room and was gone a very long time.

'Are you OK?' she asked him anxiously when he finally re-appeared.

John shrugged. 'What do you think?'

'Oh, John.' She didn't know what to say.

'I'm going up to the airfield, take one of the little planes for a spin. I checked it out with Dad before he left. He said he'll get Ritchie to have it ready for me.'

'You want me to come with you?' For Ellen, it was the supreme sacrifice. She hated flying and always had. A crash she'd seen up at the airfield when she was tiny had frightened her, her mother always said. Ellen couldn't remember it, she only knew that she got a sick feeling in the pit of her stomach when she was around planes, and she was relieved now when John declined her offer.

'No, you're OK. I just want to be on my own for a bit. Flying something that doesn't have a cargo of bombs. But thanks for offering. You're a good kid, Ellen.'

'Hey, less of the kid!' She tried to make her voice light, but the weight was still there in her stomach.

John punched her arm playfully. 'All grown up, eh? Yeah, I guess you are. We had some good times when we were young, though, didn't we?'

'We sure did. And still will. It'll be over soon, John.'

There was a shadow in his eyes, defeat in his voice. 'It'll never be over.'

Ellen shivered involuntarily. 'Don't talk like that! You're frightening me.'

'Ellen, you don't know . . . I hope to Christ you never do.'

She had never felt more removed from him. It was as if he had gone away to another place where she could not follow and he didn't want her to. But she couldn't give up on him. She wanted so much to share his pain. She didn't want him to be alone in the hell he was living. 'Tell me about it, John. Please.'

Indecision flickered in his eyes. Then he shook his head. 'I'm going flying.'

Ellen gave up. 'OK, see you later.'

He nodded, punched her arm again, and was gone.

The morning passed much the same as any other. Ellen spent it catching up on some required reading that had been set for the vacation, but she wasn't really concentrating. Half of her was thinking that if she decided to go to England with Bob she'd never finish her course anyway, and the other half was busy dealing with the horrible knowledge that tomorrow John had to go back to Vietnam. Early afternoon she was still in her room, the books open in front of her, a half-eaten sandwich and an empty lemonade glass at her elbow, when she heard the telephone begin to shrill. She waited, expecting Nancy to answer it. When she didn't, Ellen ran down the stairs and picked it up.

'Hello. Costello residence.'

'Ellen.' Joe's voice. But he sounded odd somehow. 'Is your mom there?'

'Somewhere. You want me to find her?'

'If you would, honey.'

The first twinge of alarm pinched Ellen's stomach. 'Mom?' she called.

'Here.' Nancy came in through the garden door, pulling off her gardening gloves. 'I've been pruning the roses.' She nodded at the telephone Ellen was holding out to her. 'For me?'

'Daddy.' Ellen handed her the phone, hovered in the background.

'Hi, Joe,' Nancy said.

Still Ellen hovered, not quite sure why. And saw Nancy stiffen.

'What? And he's not answering his radio?'

Ellen felt her stomach dip. She stood frozen, hands clenched at her sides, breath trapped in her lungs.

'You'll let me know as soon as there's any news.' Nancy's voice was dangerously flat and expressionless. She put the phone down, stood for a moment with her hand resting on the receiver. Ellen could bear it no longer.

'What?' she said. 'What's the matter?'

'It's John,' Nancy said. She turned round and Ellen saw the fear naked in her eyes though her face was as blank as her voice had been. 'He should have been back an hour or so ago, and they can't raise him on his radio.'

Ellen went cold. 'Mom?'

'Oh, it's probably nothing. He's gone further than he meant to and he's out of range. Or doesn't want to talk to anyone. He's preparing himself to go back to Vietnam. You know how he was this morning . . .'

'You think?'

'Well, of course.' Nancy's tone was brisk.

Fear was gnawing at Ellen's stomach, icy shivers darting through her veins.

'John would never worry us like this,' she burst out.

'He's not thinking straight,' Nancy said. 'He'll be back soon enough. But your father is calling out the Search and Rescue just in case he's hit a problem and had to make a forced landing somewhere. He'll let us know as soon as there's any news.' She pulled on her gardening gloves. 'I'm going to finish those roses. You'll be here if the phone rings.'

'Mom!' Ellen could feel her jaw trembling. She had to set it to keep her teeth from chattering. 'What if something has happened to him?'

'Don't be silly, Ellen. John is an experienced pilot. Of course nothing's happened to him.' But her eyes were telling a different story. She was real worried, Ellen knew. And Daddy must be worried too. He'd never call out the Search and Rescue if he wasn't.

'Mom, leave the roses – stay here, please!' Ellen begged.

Nancy hesitated. Then: 'Let's go down to the airfield, honey,' she said.

* * *

311

The hours dragged by, every minute a lifetime, marked by the relentlessly turning hands of the clock. They watched the skies and listened for the phone. They paced and drank coffee and slugs of bourbon from the bottle that Joe kept in a drawer of the filing cabinet. And John did not come back.

Ritchie and Don Rivers joined them. Ritchie was white-faced and tight as a drum, and he drank more of Joe's bourbon than the rest of them put together.

It was past six, and a thunderstorm was threatening, when the news came. Wreckage had been spotted out in the Gulf of Mexico. There were no signs of life.

'It might not be him,' Joe said. He looked weary and shrunken somehow, aged ten years in a day.

Nancy was standing alone, her arms wrapped around herself as if to hold all the bits together, but she was still curiously, unnaturally calm.

'And how many light aircraft are missing, I'd like to know? It's him, Joe, it has to be.'

'No!' Ellen screamed. 'No – no!' She ran to her father, beating his chest with her hands. 'It isn't John! It isn't! He'll be back like you said. It's not him! Oh, please, oh, please, say it isn't him!'

'Honey . . .' There was nothing he or anyone could say to make this come right. Joe held Ellen until her screams became sobs and the sobs wore themselves out into snuffles and gasps. Lightning flickered and flashed out over the Gulf; he stared at it over the top of her head, nature's salute to his son. And though she didn't want to accept it, Ellen pressed her face against the rough cotton of her father's shirt and knew John was never going to come home again. He was dead.

*   *   *

How? How the hell had it happened? As Nancy had said, John was an experienced pilot. In the long dark and lonely hours of the night Ellen asked the question of herself over and over again and could come up with only one answer. Ritchie was to blame. He was the one who'd got the plane ready. There must have been something wrong with it, and he'd missed it. John should have checked it over thoroughly before taking off, of course, but the mood he'd been in had probably made him careless. He'd assumed Ritchie had made sure it was airworthy, and it hadn't been. He'd trusted Ritchie, and, as Ritchie himself had said, he couldn't be trusted.

Ellen thought of the other things Ritchie had said too, the things that had horrified her so. Ritchie had wished John dead and now he was. Just as if the wishing had made it happen. Even if he hadn't fouled up over some important bit of maintenance on that plane, she still couldn't help feeling that it was his fault that John was dead. 'Be careful what you wish for . . . for wishing can make it so.' She wasn't sure where she'd heard that, but she couldn't stop thinking about it now.

And neither could he, she felt sure. He hadn't been able to look her in the eye since they had heard the terrible news. She didn't think he'd looked Mom and Daddy in the eye, either. They must know, as she did, that it was likely to be Ritchie's omission that had been the cause of the tragedy, but they had not spoken one word of recrimination. Perhaps that was even worse punishment for Ritchie than if they had ranted at him that he should have been more careful. That Mom and Daddy, shocked, grief-stricken, should be unwilling to lay any blame on him.

But Ellen blamed him, though she would say nothing. Ritchie had been the cause of John's death, one way or another. So had she. She should never have told him the truth about John. And so, in a way, had Nancy. If she hadn't favoured John, Ritchie wouldn't have had that enormous chip on his shoulder. He wouldn't have been so filled with anger and hate that day that he hadn't checked the plane out properly.

There was another thought too, one that she could hardly bring herself to think, but which she couldn't quite get out of her head either. Supposing it hadn't been an accident at all? Ritchie's words, his almost tangible hatred of his brother the night before he died, were worrying at her on an almost subconscious level, and try as she might, the awful suspicion remained. Had Ritchie done something to the plane that had made it crash? It was too terrible to contemplate, much less believe, and yet she couldn't quite rid herself of it; it hung like a dark shadow at the edges of her mind.

She couldn't believe it of Ritchie. She wouldn't. But at the same time, she didn't think she could ever forgive him either.

Bob was her salvation. She would have gone crazy without him, she thought. Crazy with her own grief and guilt for the part she had played, crazy from having to see the terrible grief of Nancy and Joe too. And crazy from blaming them all for John's unnecessary and untimely death. She shouldn't be harbouring it, she knew, but she simply couldn't help it.

When Bob asked her again to go with him to England, Ellen agreed. She couldn't bear the thought of being left here without him. Or even of being here at all any more, where the reminders of what had happened were inescapable.

Ellen and Bob were married in the fall and when they left Florida for England, Ellen hoped she could leave some of her grief and bitterness behind. She couldn't, of course. Time and distance only entrenched her resentment of the way her family, and the secrets

314

they had kept, had all contributed to John's death. And her own guilt for the part she had played ate into her too, though for reasons of self-preservation she came to see that through a prism.

Better to leave the past where it belonged. Better to cut herself off and start a new life.

Ellen had done just that.

Part Five

The Present

SARAH

People who were born and bred in Gloucestershire often refer to it as 'God's Own County'.

I once heard a man from Scarborough say the same thing about Yorkshire; I really couldn't pass an opinion on that. I've only been to Yorkshire once and it poured with rain the entire time. But beginning the descent of the steep and winding road that is Frocester Hill, I catch my breath at the panoramic vista spread out beneath me, and I can't help but feel it's a pretty good way to describe Gloucestershire. You don't have to be religious to see God's hand in the sweep of tree-studded hillside, quintessentially English, that rolls down to the valley floor where the River Severn winds towards the Bristol Channel. Dappled green, from emerald through dark moss, sparkling sapphire, burnished silver, as far as the eye can see; rural Gloucestershire is a little piece of heaven on earth, an idyll lost in time. It's balm for the spirit, and balm for the spirit is just what I need at the moment.

I'm headed for a village called Monkshaven – I'm guessing that once upon a time there must have been a priory or abbey in the vicinity – but it's not the history of the place I'm interested in.

I'm going to find out what became of Grandma Nancy's Mac. And truth to tell, I'm as nervous as hell. A week ago, before I talked to Mum, I was all set to go, and it was no big deal.

I'd done as much research as I could, without much success. I'd gone on line and trawled every site from Services Reunited to the telephone directory, but there was no match for Mac on the register of former pilots, and though I'd taken the bull by the horns and called each of the J. Mackenzies listed in the telephone directory for the Stroud area, none of them was him. Given that he would now be in his eighties, I wasn't really surprised. It was possible he was no longer alive, and if he was, he could have moved away, be living with relatives, or even be in a care home. I'd decided the best option was to go to Cleverley, the village Nancy had named as being Mac's old home, and ask around. Village life is pretty incestuous, plenty of locals live in the area that was home to their parents and grandparents even, and there was a good chance that someone would remember the Mackenzies and be able to point me in the right direction. I'd intended to go that afternoon. Next week I'd be back at work, up to my neck in all the paperwork and problems that had piled up during my absence, and probably not leaving the office until eight or nine at night.

But after Mum dropped her bombshell I'd put my plans on hold. I was in no state to go ferreting around asking questions and maybe having to answer them too. I needed time to regroup, think about everything she'd told me. And in any case, I didn't want to upset Mum any more that day. She was more distressed than I ever remember seeing her, and it's no small wonder.

'And you never said anything to anyone?' I asked, incredulous, when she had finished telling me.

'What good would it have done?' she said, and there was a

bleakness in her face that made me horribly aware of all the pain she's borne secretly all these years. 'I just wanted to put it all behind me. But it isn't that easy.'

'Oh, Mum . . .' I was at a loss for words. I put my arms around her and as she sagged against me briefly I felt her vulnerability. Then she stiffened and drew back, rejecting her moment of weakness like a snake sloughing off its skin.

'Anyway, now you know.' She was herself again, at least on the surface, brisk, matter-of-fact. 'Now you can understand why I don't want you to try to find this man.'

'I do understand,' I said.

'And you won't think any more about it? Please, Sarah, promise me you won't go stirring up things that are best left well alone.'

'Oh, Mum . . .' Now, on top of everything else, I was being torn apart by opposing loyalties. I didn't want to hurt and upset Mum, but I'd made Nancy a promise. 'I don't know what I'm going to do,' I said wretchedly.

But I did. In my heart, I already knew.

This meant so much to Grandma that she had risked involving me. I'd seen how frail she had become and I had a horrible feeling she wasn't going to be with us much longer. If I could find this Mac or his family and it made her happy, then I would. It might well be the last thing I could do for her.

My flat in Bristol is my haven. It's in Redland, a first-floor, two-bedroom apartment in a big old semi with a good-sized parking area equipped with security lights at the rear. I bought it five years ago, and it's pretty well doubled in value since then. I have a spacious living room, and use the second bedroom as an office unless I have friends staying. There's a bathroom which I absolutely

321

love, with scented candles lined up along the edge of the bath and a watercolour print above. And a lovely little kitchen I designed myself, all stainless steel and scrubbed pine.

That evening, when I got home, I went into the bedroom-cum-office, switched on my computer and went on line. I now knew that Mac had been intending to marry a woman named Elizabeth so I went back into the telephone directory and tried 'E. Mackenzie', but had no more success than I had before. Truth to tell, if I had found someone who might be her I'd have been a bit wary of ringing her out of the blue as it was possible she knew nothing of her husband's affair with Nancy and a carelessly worded enquiry could set the cat among the pigeons. But as it was, the decision was made for me. If I wanted to find Mac, it seemed that my original plan of going to Cleverley was still probably the best option. And I would have to go this weekend or leave it for another week.

Saturday was a pretty full day; I had to do a big shop and get myself ready to go back to work on Monday, and in the evening Fergus and I went out for a meal in a little Italian we both like. I didn't mention anything about the mission Nancy had entrusted me with, or what Mum had told me. It wasn't something I wanted to talk about to Fergus or anyone.

The biggest problem was that he was set on spending the night with me.

'Come back to my place, Sarah.'

'With rats scuttling round?' I joked. 'No way.'

'Yours then. Aw, come on, Sarah. You've been away the last three weeks. A man can get desperate, you know.'

'Oh, Fergus, the last of the great romantics.'

He looked crestfallen. 'You know me. Not very good at saying what I mean. I've missed you like hell, Sarah. I don't want to let you go again.'

A nerve jumped in my throat. I really couldn't let this go on. For all his flippancy, Fergus really cared about me, and he didn't deserve to be strung along when I knew I was never going to feel the way he wanted me to. It wasn't fair on him, and however hurt he was, and I knew he was going to be dreadfully hurt, at least he would be able to begin to pick up the pieces and find someone who would love him back.

'Fergus,' I said, 'we have to talk.'

I could see from his face that he knew what I was going to say, but he pretended he thought this was just about tonight.

'OK, OK,' he said. 'You're tired and jet-lagged, I know. I'll take you home, leave you to get some sleep. There's always another day.'

I shook my head, feeling sad and guilty. 'No, Fergus, there's not. I've been thinking a lot about us, and I've made up my mind. I don't feel the way I should about you. I really like you . . .' I cringed when I said that; how crass, how patronising! '. . . but it's not enough. You deserve someone who really appreciates you. And that someone isn't me.'

'You're tired, Sarah. You'll feel differently tomorrow.'

'No, I won't,' I said. 'Listen to me, Fergus, I have to do this, for both our sakes. I'm really sorry, but it's over.'

For a horrible moment I thought he was going to cry. He didn't, thank God, but he did argue and reason what seemed like for ever. And I remained firm. And had no doubt whatever in my own mind but that I had done the right thing. When we parted I was exhausted and sad, as wrung out as a wet dish rag, but at the same time I felt as if a weight had lifted from my shoulders, and shackles from my feet.

The weather was great on Sunday, warm sunshine, a perfect day for driving up to Gloucestershire. I set out mid-morning, and found Cleverley without much trouble. I drove past a sprawl of old Cotswold stone houses interspersed with thirties-style bungalows, a couple of modern detached, and a short rank of what looked like council-built properties. There was a hairdressing salon, a pub named the White Horse and a shop. The news boards outside indicated that it was open, so since it was not yet midday, I decided to try the shop first.

I parked at the kerb, manoeuvred my way past a lad on a skateboard who was racketing around on the forecourt doing 'wheelies', or whatever such tricks are called on skateboards, and went inside. Behind the counter a woman wearing a blue and white tabard over jeans and a vest top was sorting through a pile of magazines. I asked if she knew a James and Elizabeth Mackenzie, but she screwed up her face into a blank expression and shook her head.

'No, sorry. Doesn't ring any bells with me. Mackenzie. There's no one of that name in Cleverley that I know of.'

'It was back in the war that he lived here,' I said. 'Is there anyone still in the village who was here then?'

The woman snorted. 'Well, my father-in-law, but you won't get much sense out of him. He's gone a bit doolally. Though it's true he's better at remembering things from years gone by than he is when it comes to something that happened last week. I reckon your best bet would be the White Horse. There's folk go in there that have lived here all their lives.'

'The pub down the road? Thanks, I'll give it a try.'

'I would. And if you don't have any joy come back. I'll see if I can get anything out of my father-in-law.'

I thanked her again, turned the car and drove back to the White

Horse. There were a few people sitting at rustic tables on the fore-court but I didn't bother asking them if they knew the Mackenzies. They looked more like incomers from town than locals, in their trendy summer casuals, long shorts and vest tops, designer sunglasses and sharp haircuts. Maybe I was doing the locals a disservice, maybe these days city fashion has reached out to rural Gloucestershire, but in any case they looked too young to be able to help me.

I went into the bar. This seemed more promising. A group of middle-aged and elderly men perched on bar stools, engaged in conversation with a burly bearded figure I assumed to be the land-lord. They stopped talking as I walked in and stared at me, not bothering to hide their curiosity.

The landlord approached me, finishing his conversation over his shoulder before giving me his full attention.

'Yes, my dear. What can I get you?'

'Tonic with ice and lemon, please.'

'We haven't seen you in here before, have we?' he asked as he fixed my drink, and I realised he was as curious as his regular customers. 'Meeting somebody, are you?'

'No, but I am looking for someone. It's a long shot, but I'm hoping you or one of your regulars may be able to help me.'

'Oh, yes? And who's that then?' He put down the glass on the bar in front of me. 'That'll be one fifty.'

I waited until I'd sorted out the coins before answering. 'His name is – or was – James Mackenzie. He'd be in his eighties now; he flew Spitfires in the war. He was actually a squadron leader, I understand, and he used to live in Cleverley.'

'Sorry, can't help you. I've only been here the last five years.' The landlord picked up the coins, deposited them in the till and nodded in the direction of the men on the bar stools. 'These are

325

the ones you should be asking. Hey, Bill, do you know anybody called Mackenzie who used to live in Cleverley?'

'Mac Mackenzie. Now there's a name from the past.' Clearly the men had been listening to what we'd been saying. One of them, a large, raw-boned man with thinning grey hair and the weathered face of one who had spent most of his life outdoors, wiped a slick of beer foam from his mouth and swivelled round to face me full on, and the others followed suit.

'Mac Mackenzie?'

'You can mind him, surely? Lived up at Apple Tree Cottage when we were nippers. Used to ride a darn great motorbike, go roaring up the hill kicking up the dust. Had a pretty wife – she died. Got knocked off her bike in the blackout, if I remember rightly. You can mind Mac Mackenzie.'

'Ooh ah, the squadron leader. Haven't thought about him in years. He moved away, didn't 'e?'

'Well, o' course he did, otherwise he'd be here now, wouldn't he? I reckon Gerry Cootes and his missus have lived up at Apple Tree Cottage for the last twenty years, and there was that man that was retired from a petrol company before that. Came here from abroad, Bahrain, I think it were, but he weren't here long . . .'

'Never mind him. This young lady's asking about Mac Mackenzie. What's your interest, my love?'

'My grandparents knew him in the war.' I didn't want to say 'grandmother'; it gave away too much. 'I promised to try to find out what happened to him.'

'I think he went London way.' The men were enjoying themselves now.

'Didn't they used to come down here for holidays, him and another woman? I got a feeling I can remember that . . .'

'Oh, ah, you'm right. Didn't have his motorbike then, though . . .'

'Didn't they rent a place over Minchinhampton way . . . ?'

'Well, well, Mac Mackenzie . . .'

I was beginning to despair. I'd come up against a brick wall, it seemed.

'Excuse me.' A couple of young women had come in and were standing at the bar behind me. The one who spoke was, I judged, about my own age, fresh-faced and buxom. 'Did I hear you say you were trying to find out about someone called Mackenzie?'

'Yes.'

'We've been telling her, Lisa, he's been gone years.'

'Probably dead by now.'

'But none of us knows where he went, not really . . .'

'Try Dr Mackenzie at Monkshaven.'

I swung round. 'Dr Mackenzie?'

'Yes. He should be able to help you.' She smiled. 'Well, if he can't, no one can. I think you'll find that the James Mackenzie you're looking for is his father.'

To say I was astonished would be an understatement. I'd all but given up hope; now here was someone saying they knew Mac's son. It was surreal. And I think the men I'd been talking to were as surprised as I was.

'Mac's son?' one of them said wonderingly. 'How d'you know that, Lisa?'

'Freda Parker was telling me when I called in to dress her leg the other day. Her daughter Penny lives in Monkshaven, and he's her GP. Freda was staying with Penny when her ulcer flared up, and she saw Dr Mackenzie. When he noticed her home address, he said his father used to live in Cleverley.' She glanced back at me.

'I'm one of the district nurses here. You'd be surprised how much we get to know. People who live on their own like Freda like to chat about anything and everything when they get a captive audience. And it probably does them more good than anything that comes out of a bottle or a tube. Anyway . . .' She turned away, fumbling in her bag for her purse and raising her hand to attract the attention of the landlord.

'Let me buy you both a drink.' I owed her, big time.

'No, you're all right.'

'Please. Let me.' I hadn't finished asking questions yet; by the time I had she'd probably wish she hadn't volunteered the information in the first place.

Her friend grinned. 'You don't turn down the offer of free drinks, Lisa! Go on, mine's a Stella. And Lisa's is a Chardonnay, unless she fancies a change.'

'No, Chardonnay will be fine.' Lisa cocked her head to one side; reddish brown hair that probably spent most of its life swept up in a scrunchie tumbled in waves to her shoulder. 'I expect you want to know how you can find Dr Mackenzie.'

'Well . . . yes. I suppose if I ring the number for his surgery I'll be put through to an out-of-hours service. And I've only got the rest of the day before I'm back at work . . .'

'You realise you want me to do something highly unprofessional?'

'I know it's a lot to ask, but . . .'

'Tell me why you want him.'

I did. This time I was strictly truthful. Lisa fished in her bag again, came out with a mobile phone.

'I'll see what I can do.'

She took a sip of her wine and headed out the door. Either the

328

signal was stronger outside, or she wanted to make a call in private. I didn't know which it was, and didn't much care as long as she came up with the information I wanted.

She did better than that. A few minutes later she was back.

'OK. Monkshaven is about eight miles from here. Head for the motorway and you'll see it signed. It's more of a long cul-de-sac than a village. You want Monkshaven Cottage. Follow the road pretty much as far as you can go and it's on the left-hand side. Dr Mackenzie is expecting you, and I think you owe me another drink.'

'You know something, Lisa?' I said. 'I think I do.'

Which is why I'm heading down Frocester Hill, nervous as a day-old kitten, but not so nervous I can't appreciate the view. I've got a better lead than I ever dared hope for. Another quarter of an hour or so and I'll be talking to the man who is Mac's son. I can't believe I've done it. I don't know what he's going to tell me, but whatever it is, it will be closure for Grandma Nancy. And I can give him the medal she entrusted to me, the one she's looked after all these years. I won't have let her down, and that means the world to me.

When Lisa the district nurse described Monkshaven as a long cul-de-sac rather than a village, she had it spot on. It straggles for maybe a couple of miles from a 'No Through Road' sign, most of the houses on the left as you drive in, with open fields opposite them. Apart from a short terrace of three cottages, they are mainly substantial properties, set well back and half-hidden behind hedges, fences and creeper-covered walls. Apart from what appears to be a farm track arcing off at an angle at one point, there's nowhere to go but straight on, so I keep on going. And eventually see a long, low house with a sign that reads 'Monkshaven Cottage'. There's a good-sized square of grassed-over parking at the side, bordered by a strip of garden filled with shrubs and herbaceous plants, and I pull onto it. My heart is hammering. I can't ever remember being so nervous in my entire life.

The front door of the house is hooded by a little porch of trellis with a white rose winding through it. As I approach the gate, the door opens and a man appears. He's tall, around six feet, I estimate, as he brushes against a trailing stem of the roses, loosening a few mature petals which drift down to lodge in his hair and on the collar of his polo shirt. Yellow polo shirt, dark hair with a few flecks of silver, receding a little at the temples. He's clean-shaven and quite good-looking in an unshowy way. Though he's casually dressed today he looks like a doctor somehow, though I'd be hard-pressed to say what a doctor should look like. My heart does another stupid thud that echoes in my throat so that I have to swallow quickly. Too late to back off now. He's coming down the path towards me, hands stuffed casually into the pockets of his chinos.

'Ms Lintern?'

'Yes. It's really good of you to see me, Doctor.'

How stupid does that sound? *Good of you to see me, Doctor. A bottle of linctus and a course of antibiotics, if you please . . .*

A corner of his mouth quirks as if the same thought had occurred to him.

'My name's Chris when I'm off duty.'

'Sarah.'

He nods. He's looking at me intently now, eyes narrowed as though he was peering into a microscope. It's pretty unnerving. 'You want to talk to me about my father, I understand.'

'Yes. My grandmother knew him in the war. She came over from America with Jacqueline Cochran to ferry planes for the RAF—'

'Nancy Kelly,' he interrupts.

I'm taken by surprise, but pleased. 'You know of her?'

He smiles. It's a nice smile, a bit crooked. 'Oh, yes, I've heard of Nancy.'

No secrets then, it seems, in Mac's family. How different from my own! But it certainly makes this a whole lot easier.

He turns back to push the door open wider and another shower of rose petals festoons his shoulders. This time he notices and brushes them off.

'Come in, or at least, come through. I was in the garden – it's the best place to be on a Sunday afternoon in summer, in my opinion. Can I get you something to drink? Glass of wine? Cup of coffee?'

'It had better be coffee,' I say regretfully. 'I don't drink and drive.'

'Tell you what, I've got a bottle of low-alcohol Sangria in the fridge. Someone brought it for a party I had a few weeks ago and it never got used. I haven't a clue what it's like; it's not my thing. But if that would fit the bill, you're welcome to it.'

'Sounds good to me.' I'm relaxing a little already. Mac's son is very easy to get along with, though there's still a wire pulling taut in my stomach.

I follow him through a small interior porch, a big kitchen breakfast room, up a couple of steps and across a tiled lobby that leads to a garden door, which is open. Beyond it is a lawn, a patio area with garden furniture and a barbecue, and a couple of mature trees; beyond a low fence, nothing but open fields. Nice. But no scattered toys, no mini trampoline, no tree house. It doesn't look as if Dr Chris Mackenzie has any children. And there's no wife in evidence either. That surprises me. I'd expected there to be a Mrs Mackenzie. Chris looks to be somewhere in his early forties, an age by which most men have acquired a family.

He leaves me sitting at the patio table while he fetches the Sangria for me and a can of beer for himself, returns to the kitchen and comes back with a bowl of corn chips and a jar of spicy salsa. 'Help yourself.'

I don't want to start nibbling, but the Sangria is acceptable enough. More than acceptable, actually it's quite nice, or maybe it's just me in need of a fix.

'So,' he says, chomping on a corn chip, 'you are Nancy's granddaughter.'

'Yes.' I go through my explanation, though it's pretty clear he's heard it from Lisa, the district nurse. 'I promised I'd try to find him,' I finish. 'So here I am.'

Chris Mackenzie says nothing for a moment. Then: 'It's not good news, I'm afraid. My father died two years ago.'

It was what I'd half expected, but it still hits me hard. The taut wire in my stomach snaps and coils into corkscrews, leaving me flat and empty inside. I had so much hoped that I could magic up a happy ending for Nancy, but it's not going to happen. In two short sentences, Chris Mackenzie has destroyed the dream.

'Oh, I'm sorry,' I say mechanically.

'Me too. He was a great chap, and in pretty good health until the last six months. It's the way he'd have wanted it, and I'm grateful for that. At least I didn't have to watch him lose his faculties one by one. As it was, he managed to keep his dignity and his independence. No care home for Dad. He was able to bruggle on more or less to the last.'

'And your mother?'

332

'She's been dead for ten years now.'

I nod sympathetically, but I'm thinking: what irony. If Nancy had looked for Mac a few years earlier she might have had that happy ending.

'No one seemed to know what had happened to your father, and I'd practically given up when the district nurse pointed me in your direction,' I say.

'Lisa Timbrell, yes. A string of coincidences really. She's not my practice nurse, and she'd have been unlikely to make the connection if we hadn't shared a patient. I've only been in the area for the last eighteen months or so. If you believe in fate, it seems to have given you a helping hand.' He grins at me, that engaging crooked smile. 'Actually, it was after my father died that I decided to look for a position in this part of the world. I'd always fancied it. We used to take holidays here when I was a lad, and as you know Dad came from round here. But when I was married, I had my wife to consider, and her career, her whole life, really, was in the Maidenhead area. Then, by the time we divorced, Mum had died and Dad was on his own. I never let on that I stayed where I was for his sake – he would have been outraged. But you know how it is. I didn't like the idea of being too far away in case he needed me. But when I no longer had any ties I started looking around. This came up, and I jumped at it.' He takes a long pull of his beer. 'Anyway, enough about me. That's not the reason you're here. You want to know what happened to Dad so that you can tell Nancy.'

'I'd be grateful, yes.'

'How is she doing, by the way?'

'Amazingly well, for her age. I saw a big change in her this last time I visited. But like your father, she prides herself on being independent. She's not going to give in easily.'

Chris Mackenzie chuckles. 'I'll bet she's not. They were a tough bunch, that generation. They don't make 'em like that any more. Anyway, to get back to Dad. What do you want to know?'

I sip my drink and sit back. 'Anything you can tell me about his life after the war.'

'The abridged version, presumably.'

Actually I want to know everything there is to know about the man Grandma loved so much she has never forgotten him. But I can't impose too much. Chris Mackenzie is already giving up a sizeable chunk of his presumably precious free time to indulge me.

'The abridged version, yes,' I say.

After the war, it seems, Mac went into civil aviation. He became a pilot for BOAC, flying passengers long haul out of Heathrow, and moved from Gloucestershire to Maidenhead to be closer to his work base. He knew the area well, in any case, having been stationed there with the RAF, and liked it – open countryside within easy reach of the metropolis.

It was whilst flying with BOAC that he met Elizabeth, Chris's mother. She had been a stewardess in the days when they were called 'air hostesses' and the term 'trolley dolly' had yet to be invented. She came from a solid business family and she had done a course at the Cherry Marshall School of Modelling before putting on her glamorous uniform and flying the world.

In later years, when Mac had tired of piloting a plane that virtually flew itself for an eight- or nine-hour stretch, he had taken on the training of new jet pilots and continued in that role until his retirement. His life seemed to have settled into a comfortable pattern, the adventures and traumas of his early life firmly consigned to the past.

But: 'He never forgot Nancy,' Chris Mackenzie said. 'I especially remember him talking about her when the airlines got their first woman captain. "Nancy would have loved it," he said. "She was always up for proving anything a man could do, she could do better."' He smiled. 'I doubt she'd have had any more patience than Dad did, though, with sitting for hours on end with an autopilot doing the work for you.'

'She probably wouldn't,' I agree. 'And I don't think I would either. The fun comes from being in control. Doing a crossword puzzle over the Atlantic wouldn't be my idea of flying.'

'You fly?' He looks surprised.

'When I can. But mostly when I'm in Florida, in one of Grandma's Cessnas. It's so damned expensive to hire a plane over here, and with all the commercial traffic you can almost write a blank cheque to burn money while they keep you waiting at a holding point or make you orbit Cheddar Lake for half an hour while the big boys come in.' I can see he doesn't really know what I'm talking about. 'You haven't followed in your father's footsteps, I take it.'

He grins ruefully. 'No. I don't know why really. I never had the time to learn, I suppose. I was too busy qualifying in medicine. A junior doctor's hours aren't really compatible with doing anything but working and sleeping, and by the time I'd moved up the pecking order, I guess the moment had gone. Dad did take me up a few times, though. He used to enjoy hiring a little plane and going for a flip. And when he gave up flying commercially he joined a gliding club. I have thought of doing that; there's a good outfit not far from here. Have you ever done any gliding?'

I shake my head. 'I can't say I'm crazy about the idea of only one go at landing. I like to get it right first time, but I also like the option to go around if needs be.'

'Dad used to say that riding the thermals was exhilarating. Back to basics and all that. Do you know, I think I might just do something about it. You've inspired me.' He looks at me narrowly. 'You ought to think about it too. It would be a lot cheaper than a powered plane. And no being held over Cheddar Lake.'

'Perhaps I will.'

The conversation has wandered away from Mac and Nancy; I think it's time to draw it back. I reach for my bag, propped against the leg of my chair, and hoist it onto my lap. I fumble inside and pull out the small box Nancy entrusted to me. I don't open it, just rest my fingers on the leather, warm and smooth to the touch, then, with surprising reluctance, I push it across the table towards him.

'Grandma asked me to return this to Mac, or to his family. It's his DFC. He gave it to her for safe-keeping, she said, though I think it may have been more than that. But she feels that now it's time to return it. She doesn't want it to go astray when she's no longer there to look after it, and . . .' My voice wavers a little. Talking of Nancy no longer being there is a painful nod to the reality of what the future holds.

Chris doesn't look surprised. He knew what had become of his father's medal, I realise, and again I'm struck by the differences between his family's openness and the secrecy inherent in mine. He flips up the lid and the silver of the cross flory that Nancy polished before giving it to me gleams in the sunlight. Chris's eyes narrow and for a moment there's a faraway expression in them; he may have known of the medal's existence, but he's never seen it before, never seen his father wearing it. I imagine it's stirring all kinds of memories and emotions. Then he snaps the box shut and pushes it back into the centre of the table.

'I'm not sure I should have this. Dad gave it to Nancy. I think he wanted it passed on to their child.'

Another bolt of surprise jolts me. He knows about John, and presumably his mother knew too. What he doesn't know is that John is dead.

'I'm afraid John was killed in a flying accident,' I say. He frowns, a puzzled frown. Clearly he doesn't recognise his name. His knowledge doesn't extend that far. Perhaps Mac never knew what Nancy had named their child.

'Nancy and Mac's son was called John,' I explain. 'Unfortunately he died when he was in his twenties. Ironic really. He was serving in Vietnam, but he was killed whilst he was on home leave.' I'm pushing to the back of my mind what Mum told me. I don't want to think about it, let alone tell Chris her suspicions of what happened. 'Ritchie is the only one still in Varna – he's my mother's younger brother. He runs the business for Grandma these days. But . . . he doesn't have a lot of time for sentiment. I think Grandma is afraid that when she's gone he'll get rid of all her things without bothering too much about what happens to them. That's why she wanted the medal returned to Mac or his family. If John was still alive, she might not have felt that way. She'd probably have liked him to have his father's medal. But as things are . . .'

Chris is silent for a moment. His face is a blank canvas, not betraying anything of what he is thinking or feeling. Then he fixes me with a direct, narrow look.

'What makes you think that John was Mac's son?'

'Mum told me. Years ago, when she was in her early teens, she came across a letter from Mac to Grandma—' I break off, regrouping. I don't want to tell Chris that that letter was a last-ditch attempt on Mac's part to persuade Nancy to leave Joe. I'm all too aware that if he had been successful, Mac would have walked away from Chris's mother. As a family, they might be big on having no secrets, but I couldn't believe Mac's policy of openness would stretch that far. It was one thing for a woman to accept a lover and a love child in her husband's past, quite another to know she would have been jilted practically at the altar if Nancy had said the word.

'The letter mentioned John,' I go on. 'It was a terrible shock for Mum; she had no idea that he wasn't her full brother. But at the same time it explained things she'd always wondered about, such as how Grandma and Grandpa had managed to conceive him when there was a war on and they were stationed hundreds of miles apart. And Grandma had always seemed to treat John differently from her and Ritchie too, as if he were special in some way. When she found the letter it all made sense. She realised Nancy had had a forbidden wartime romance and become pregnant. And that Grandpa Joe, for love of her, had brought up her illegitimate son as his own.'

'Didn't your mother ever mention it to Nancy?' Chris asks.

I shake my head. 'I know it sounds pretty odd, but you don't know Mum. She's very . . . self-contained. She kept it to herself.'

Apart from telling Ritchie and setting in motion a terrible chain of events . . . But I'm not going to go there.

'I've only known about it a few days myself,' I say instead. 'Mum only told me when I said I was going to try to track down Mac for Grandma. She was totally against it, and when I asked her why, it all came spilling out.'

'Right.' But he's looking at me very oddly, eyes narrowed, brows furrowed, and I get the impression there's more that he wants to say but doesn't quite know where to begin. There's something going on here that I don't understand and I don't like it.

'What?' I say.

'I'm not happy with this, Sarah.' He doesn't look it either; he looks the way I imagine he might look when he's faced with giving a patient a grim prognosis. He pushes the medal further across the table towards me, relinquishing it. 'I can't take this just now. I think you should talk to Nancy again. Tell her you can't return the medal to Mac because he's no longer with us. Ask her what she wants done with it. If she still wants me to have it, then I will, and I shall be very proud to take care of it. But it's her decision. Everything from here on in is her decision.'

I'm totally puzzled. 'You've lost me. What the hell are you talking about?'

He hesitates. Then: 'No, it's not my place. You need to talk to Nancy.'

He gets up. The interview is at an end. I want to press him, but I can tell from the set of his jaw that I'll get no more from him.

There's a tension between us now, heavy as the pregnant air before a thunderstorm. And without analysing it, I know it's not just because he knows something I don't, but is not going to tell me what it is. I'm sorry for the loss of the easy rapport we had enjoyed until I brought out that medal. I really like Chris Mackenzie and I regret the sudden distance between us.

I put the medal back in my bag. We walk through the house.

'Thanks for seeing me,' I say awkwardly.

'Talk to Nancy, OK?' The ghost of a smile twists his mouth. 'And keep in touch.'

'I will.'

I walk to my car, look back. He's standing in the doorway, watching me. A tall, good-looking man with a fresh sprinkling of rose petals in his hair.

A man who apparently knows a great deal more about my family than I do. A man who is not going to enlighten me.

I'm driving, not really concentrating on the road or thinking about where I'm going. I'm a cauldron of churning emotions and fractured thoughts. I'm trying to make sense of what Chris said – or didn't say – and getting nowhere. I feel as if I'm fighting my way through the sticky fibres of a spider's web. I'm confused, puzzled and anxious. None of the possible explanations for Chris's reaction that occur to me make any sense. And besides that, a dull, leaden weight has settled in the pit of my stomach. Mac is dead, has been for the past two years. I'm going to have to break that to Nancy, and though I suspect it's no more than she half expected, I'm not looking forward to that.

For a moment I forget about the riddles Chris has set me and glimpse what it must be like to be eighty-four years old and be the one who's left. The loneliness of losing your contemporaries, one by one, until there is no one who shares your memories of the experiences that shaped your past. I taste briefly the desolation of plodding on alone across a bleak landscape with nothing but failing faculties and, ultimately, death to look forward to, and I feel so unutterably sad that I want not so much to weep as to howl, like a wolf, at the moon.

I see too how fleeting is a lifetime. To Nancy, I suspect, it seems but a heartbeat since she was young, much younger than I am now. When she was pretty and vigorous, with a heart full of dreams. Because she opened up to me, I can see her as she was then, and the realisation of what a very little time ago it really was has shaken me rigid and, frankly, terrified me. Year upon year we see the cycle of nature unfold, the fresh green buds of spring blossoming to full growth and then withering and dying. Year upon year I feel melancholic as the leaves turn colour and begin to fall; for me there is no glory in the russet and gold of their final brave defiance. I want them to be fresh and green again!

A lifetime, in the end, may seem just as short – or even shorter, as the days and the months and the years rush past at breakneck pace. Another birthday. Another Christmas. Already? No, impossible! Time contracts, so that a lifetime is not so much a succession of seasons as the fleeting beauty of a rose, one day dew sparkling on a tightly furled bud, the next full glory, and the next blown and faded, drooping petals like tears. Already I am halfway through my allotted span, and I don't know where the years have gone. Inside I am still seventeen, impatient and eager.

I suspect it is no different for Nancy. Except that her hopes and dreams have nowhere to go now. And I am going to be the one to destroy the last of them. It's my main concern at the moment, how it's going to affect her. Will she lose the will to live and go into a decline? Should I somehow rustle up a bit more leave and fly back to Florida to tell her myself, in person? Should I try to persuade Mum to come with me? I do think she should make the effort to see Nancy at least once more, and perhaps sort out the differences that have marred their relationship these past forty years.

And now, just to complicate matters, Chris Mackenzie is suggesting there's more to it than we know. I'm already shrinking from telling Mum that, but I know I have to. And we have to talk to Nancy.

Why the hell did she have to be so damned secretive? But I suppose it was a different age back then. There must be plenty of other people with skeletons rattling in the family cupboard.

Whatever, it's just another reason for seeing Nancy again whilst there is still time. I don't want her secrets to die with her, even if that's what she always intended. I can't live the rest of my life wondering what they are.

I need to know the truth about my family.

MONICA

It's been one hell of a day and I'm worried sick. Not just a bad feeling any more, full-blown gut-wrenching anxiety I can't get away from however hard I try. Ritchie is up to something with that asshole Dexter Connelly and if I was playing poker and the evidence I've piled up were the cards in my hand, I'd go for broke that it's something illegal and be as sure as I can be I wouldn't lose my shirt.

For starters, though he doesn't come through me on the office line, I know Connelly calls Ritchie on his cellphone. Ritchie steps outside to take the calls and when he comes back after one of them he's kind of hyper, strung as tight as a violin, but with a manic gleam in his eye.

'That wasn't a new lady, I hope,' I said after one of them, though I knew darned well who it had been.

'Maybe it was and maybe it wasn't,' Ritchie hedged.

'Well, if her boobs are as big as her voice is deep, she's quite a dame,' I quipped. 'Sounded like Dexter Connelly to me.'

'OK, you've got me.'

343

'Since when were you and Mafia Man best buddies?'

'Monica,' Ritchie jabbed a finger in my direction, 'butt out!'

'Sure thing,' I said, amiably enough, but I wasn't going to. No, siree. I wouldn't trust Dexter Connelly any further than I could throw him, and I sure as heck ain't gonna be wearing a USA vest in Olympic field events any time soon.

The phone calls just kept coming, and after one of them Ritchie said he'd booked in a job flying down to the Windies for a man by the name of Jack Pele. Claimed he'd taken the call while I was out of the office on a bathroom break. I'd never heard of the guy and alarm bells went off in my head like rockets on the Fourth of July. I did a bit of surreptitious checking, came up with zilch. As far as I could ascertain the guy didn't exist. But Ritchie made the flight all right, in one of the twin-engines, leaving midday-ish. He hadn't returned when I left work that night, but next morning the plane was back where it should have been, all tied down and tidy, and Ritchie made an appearance later than usual and looking like he'd had a rough night. I checked out the log and he'd been to the Windies, no question, but I couldn't get a lot of sense out of him as to what it was all about. Then he took off for Houston in the same plane he used yesterday.

Dexter Connelly went a mite quiet for a bit after that, and I dared hope that was the end of it. But yesterday he called Ritchie again and there's another trip booked for Mr Jack Pele tomorrow, and one pencilled in for next week with follow-up trips the next day to Houston, and I don't like it one little bit.

On top of all that, Ritchie's too damned chipper about the future of Varna Aviation. It's only a couple of weeks since he was real worried about how we were going to keep the outfit from going bust. All of a sudden he's like got a song on his lips. The one about being sure to wear a flower in your hair if you go to San Francisco. Music from his youth, for Chrissakes. And Mary-Lyn's looking pretty pleased with herself too. She was out here a couple of days ago driving a brand-new cabriolet. Last I heard, Ritchie was moaning about having to get her air conditioning repaired; now he's treating her to new cars. Carry on that way and they'll be an item again. Mary-Lyn never could resist having a few dollars spent on her. And where will that leave me? Just where I always was – no darned where.

This morning, though, just confirmed that Ritchie's quit worrying about money. There was a letter in the mail from the outfit who operate out of Fort Myers. They're doing pretty well, it would seem, and they're looking to buy out Varna Aviation. From what I can see of it, it's an offer Ritchie ought to look at at least. The terms are too generous to ignore.

Not that I want to see the end of Varna Aviation as an independent concern. Christ no! It's been my life for too darned long and I'm sentimental about it. But I've got my head screwed on right too. Looks like they'd be happy to keep Ritchie and me and Stu Taviner, the mechanic, on the pay roll but they'd combine the operations. Bigger. Better. More twenty-first century. I'd be sad to see our blue and white livery go; I'd mourn for the days when Joe and Nancy were the bosses. But I sure as heck wouldn't miss trying to make the books balance. I sure as heck would like somebody else to pay the bills.

But do y'know what Ritchie did? He tore the letter across, screwed it up into a ball and aimed it straight in the wastepaper bin with the kind of shot that would have earned him a place in a basketball team of merit if he was thirty years younger.

'They can go stuff themselves,' he said.

'Ritchie, don't you think you ought to at least consider it?' I said. 'We're only just holding this together. This is a darned good offer and it would solve all our worries.'

'No way. No fucking way!'

'Ritchie, watch your language. There's ladies present.'

He smirked. I expected him to come back with some insult. Instead, he said: 'We're gonna be OK, Monica. We've turned the corner. Trust your uncle Ritchie.'

I rolled my eyes. 'I've been doing these books for nigh on twenty years. I haven't seen any sign of a turnaround yet. I think you should at least talk it over with Nancy.'

Ritchie snorted. 'She'd agree with me. She wouldn't sell. Not Joe's baby. No way.'

'Well, I reckon you should at least give her the chance to turn it down. Nancy's shrewd. Varna Aviation might be Joe's baby, but she's the one with the last word now, whether you like it or not. I reckon she'd rather sell out at a reasonable price if the conditions are right than see you struggle and maybe go under.'

I should have known better. I should have known I was tickling Ritchie's weak spot. His face went dark.

'She'd sooner trust the business to anyone but me, you mean?'

'No, Ritchie, I didn't mean that.'

'Sure you did. And you're right, more than likely. Well, I don't care for the idea of going back to being a jobbing pilot in somebody else's outfit. I like being my own boss, OK?'

'And maybe go broke?' I snapped.

'Trust me, Monica, I am not gonna go broke. Just don't you say anything about any of this to Nancy, OK? I don't want her worried with it. Not at her age. She's had her crack of the whip, now it's my turn. And I'll run Varna Aviation the way I decide.'

'It's your call.' I know better than to argue with Ritchie when he's in that mood.

But it doesn't mean I give in so easy. Maybe Ritchie is nominally in charge these days, but Varna Aviation belongs to Nancy as long as there's breath in her body. Christ, she is Varna Aviation, just as Joe used to be, even if she doesn't come here much any more. And it goes against the grain real bad for me to keep something like this from her.

My mind is made up. I'm going to go see Nancy and fill her in. And if Ritchie doesn't like it, that's too darned bad. I'm just waiting my opportunity, that's all.

It comes Monday evening. As we're closing up for the night Mary-Lyn arrives in her snazzy new car and Ritchie's all over her like a rash. Honest to God, I don't know what he's playing at. I'd have thought he'd have learned his lesson by now. It hurts like hell when they go off together, Ritchie driving the cabriolet, Mary-Lyn all dressed up like a dog's dinner, and a scarf tied over her hair Jackie-O-style. Jesus, where has the woman been the last forty years? But I tell myself this is my chance. If I'd had any doubts before, they've melted like a Carrioli's ice-cream cornet in a heatwave. Damn Ritchie – my first loyalty is to Nancy.

I lock up – as usual Ritchie's taken it for granted I'll do the necessary – get in my car and head for the Costello home.

Everything's pretty quiet this time of night, the malls deserted, no long queues of traffic at the traffic lights where the streets intersect. It's too late for shoppers, I figure, and too early for revellers. Not that we get many of those in Varna; it's a pretty staid town. The Residents' Council takes care of that. Do you know the beach is private? Only Varna folk allowed. And even they get black looks from the owners of the houses that back on to it, and whose garden gates open right on to the sand. And there's a neighbourhood jobsworth, voluntary, of course, stationed in a little shelter right by the way onto the beach to make damned sure their stupid law isn't violated. What the hell does that say about the place? Sometimes I wonder why I've put up with it so long, but hell, it's home.

I park on Nancy's driveway, walk round to the patio. I think I might find her there, sitting by the pool with a drink. But the patio's deserted. The garden door is ajar; I push it open, calling, but I can see Nancy's not in the kitchen either. I call again; still no response. I hesitate, undecided. It's not my way to enter someone else's house uninvited, but I'm feeling a little anxious. I want to be sure she's all right – she's eighty-four years old, for God's sake. I head for the living room, still calling, still getting no reply. My heart's in my mouth; I'm trying to prepare myself for what I might find. I push open the door, and see her.

She's in the big wing chair by the window, head turned sideways on and tucked into the nook between back and wing so that her neck is stretched and the loose crepey skin is drawn over elongated, high-definition sinews. Her hair's a bit muzzed, her eyes are closed. My heart comes into my mouth with a sick-making jolt. For a second, God help me, I think she's dead.

I'm holding on to the door for dear life. 'Nancy?' I say. I'm not calling out now – whispering more like.

And she starts suddenly and her eyes fly open. I don't know which of us is more startled.

'Monica?' she says, as if she thinks she's still asleep and dreaming.

'Gee, I'm sorry, Nancy.' I'm all confusion now. 'You had me real worried. I called and called and I couldn't make you hear. I thought you could be ill or something.'

'I was just having a nap. I often do, this time of an evening.'
Nancy's getting up now from the chair, straightening her overshirt,
tidying her hair. 'I wasn't expecting anyone.'

'You really oughta lock the door before you go falling asleep,'
I chide her. 'Anyone could just walk in and you'd never know. Jesus,
you could be robbed and murdered and nobody any the wiser.'

Nancy smiles, that lovely smile of hers that lights up her face
and makes her look years younger.

'Oh, I don't think so. This neighbourhood's as safe as Fort Knox.'

'Used to be, maybe. Times have changed, Nancy. Ritchie would
tell you the same.'

'Quit lecturing, Monica,' Nancy says, but good-natured enough.
'I never did like being lectured, and I'm not going to change at
my age. What can I do for you, anyway? Unless you came on
purpose to catch me napping.'

'You know darned well I didn't. I wanted to talk to you. There's
something I reckon you ought to know.'

'Aw, shucks, it's about Ritchie, I guess.' Nancy sighs. She looks
older again, weary, as if the weight of the world has descended
onto her shoulders. 'What's he done now?'

'This is awkward for me, Nancy.'

'Let's have a drink, then. There's a bottle of good Irish whiskey
in the bureau and soda and ice in the refrigerator.'

'OK, I'll get it.'

I mix the drinks. When I come back she's sitting in the wing
chair again. I put hers down on a little card table at her elbow,
take mine over to the chaise opposite and sip it even before I sit
down – I need it real bad. Nancy reaches for her glass, cups it
between those puffy hands, and levels her gaze with mine.

'Go on then, Monica. Spoil my day,' she says wryly.

I tell her how I've been worried for some time about Varna Aviation, and about the offer from Wings West, the outfit at Fort Myers. I tell her how Ritchie turned it down out of hand, and how he said he didn't want her worried with it.

'But I reckon you have a right to know,' I finish.

'I reckon so too.' Nancy's mouth is a tight line.

'You might want to turn it down anyway,' I say, 'but it just ain't right he shouldn't tell you about it.'

Nancy is silent for a good long while, thinking. But what those thoughts are I haven't a clue. Then her eyes meet with mine again.

'What's your take on it, Monica?'

'Mine?' I'm surprised. I've been with Varna Aviation a darned long time, but I'm not used to anyone asking my opinion. I offer it uncalled for, I admit, but that's not the same thing at all.

'You're on the spot,' Nancy says. 'If anyone knows the best way forward, it's you.'

'OK.' I take a long pull of my whiskey and soda. 'I reckon it's a pretty fair offer. Better to take it than go bust and have them snap up our assets for a song. I don't want to see the end of Varna Aviation, but I've got a nasty feeling it's coming one way or the other and we might as well go out with a flourish as have them walk all over us.'

She nods, deep in thought again. 'But Ritchie doesn't agree. Well, that figures, I guess. When did Ritchie ever take the sensible option?'

'He doesn't like the idea of working for someone else, and I can understand that,' I say, defending him instinctively.

'I dare say he'd like the idea of being on the Unemployment Compensation Programme even less,' Nancy responds tartly.

'He seems to think Varna Aviation can survive . . .' I hesitate. I don't want to go into the Dexter Connelly connection unless I have to. It's a breach of trust too far. The shit's going to hit the fan as it is, with me telling Nancy about the takeover offer. If I spill the beans about Connelly, Ritchie will never forgive me. And if Nancy should decide to go for selling out, hopefully the Connelly connection will die the death without her ever having to know. And if it doesn't, well, it won't be her problem any more.

'When he's not in the doldrums, he's a cock-eyed optimist,' Nancy says, and shakes her head. 'OK, Monica, thanks for filling me in. I'll talk to Ritchie. And I guess we shall all need to get together, have a good look at the books, and try to figure out a way forward.'

'I'm not gonna be flavour of the month,' I say ruefully.

'You are a jewel, Monica, and if Ritchie doesn't realise that he's an even bigger fool than I thought.' Nancy finishes her whiskey. 'Do you want another?'

All I really want is to get home and put my feet up in front of some mindless TV show. But I feel sorry for Nancy, left here alone again.

'OK,' I say. I refill the glasses. Search for another topic of conversation. 'Have you heard from Sarah lately?'

'I spoke with her yesterday. She's talking about coming back to see us soon.'

'Hey, that's great!'

But there's a guarded look in Nancy's eyes. I'd have thought she'd be over the moon at the prospect of having Sarah back visiting so soon, but for some reason, she's not. 'Isn't it?' she says, but her tone is guarded too. There's something she's not saying, and I feel awkward somehow, as if I'm treading on ground I shouldn't, and I sure as heck don't know why.

'She's not thinking of staying for good, is she?' I venture.

'I don't think so.' But she offers nothing more by way of explanation.

We chat for an hour or so, a gossipy catch-up that misses anything close to personal by a mile. If I wasn't feeling so damned tired, and so worried about everything that's going on, I'd say I enjoyed it. Nancy's still good company, just like she always was.

Ritchie's still not home by the time I leave. Nancy comes out with me to see me off.

'You be sure to lock this door behind me,' I warn her.

'Quit fussing.'

'You just do as I say.'

'OK, if it'll make you happy.' She touches my arm. 'Thanks, Monica. Come see me again sometime soon.'

'I will. Now, you get your cocoa and a good book and go to bed. Don't wait up till all hours for that no-good son of yours.'

'I quit waiting up for him when he was eighteen years old,' she says drily. But I have a feeling tonight she'll make an exception. She won't be able to sleep until she's had this out with him.

'Night, Nancy.' I turn back to wave. She's standing there, holding on to the doorpost, and if I didn't know her better, I'd have thought there were tears in her eyes. But she's a tough old bird, is Nancy. She might be old, she might be frail, but she's got a backbone that's pure steel. Nothing and nobody is going to get the better of Nancy. I don't envy Ritchie when he gets home and she starts in on him. And she will, I'm sure of it. Sure as I've ever been of anything.

Ritchie comes storming into the office and I know I was right. He fetches himself a coffee from the machine, bangs it down on my desk, and scowls at me.

352

'What the hell were you thinking, Monica?'

He doesn't have to explain; he knows that I know exactly what he's talking about.

'She had a right to know,' I say. 'You weren't going to tell her, so I did.'

'What goes on in this office is confidential. I ought to fire you.'

I fold my arms across my chest, glare back at him. 'Go right ahead.'

'You're a goddam fucking idiot. Why couldn't you leave well alone?'

'Because I know what's right. Because I've got your good at heart, if you want to know.'

'Oh, sure. I've heard that before. From my ex-wives.'

'How is Mary-Lyn?' I ask pointedly.

The colour rises in Ritchie's cheeks, but he doesn't answer me.

'You realise Nancy wants us all to sit down round the table with the books?'

'Best thing,' I say stubbornly. 'I have this feeling there's things there too you want to keep from her – or soon will be. Or aren't the accountants supposed to know about your trips for Mr Jack Pele?'

'Well, of course. Why shouldn't they?'

'You tell me. I didn't mention them to Nancy, by the way. And I didn't tell her you'd gotten mighty friendly with Dexter Connelly, either. And I'm hoping I won't ever need to.'

'For Chrissakes, Monica . . .' But he's looking shifty and he can't meet my eye.

'Don't take me for a fool, Ritchie,' I say. 'I know what you're up to – or at least, I can hazard a good guess. And I think you should call Mr Jack Pele or whatever his real name is, and cancel. You don't

353

want to be mixed up with stuff like this. Or people. They're dyna-
mite, and so's what you're doing.'

'I need the dough, Monica.'

'Then get it the honest way. Sell out to Wings West. Think about
it, Ritchie. Do you really want to end up in gaol?'

'Are you calling me a criminal, Monica?'

'If the shoe fits. And it's downright wrong, as well as illegal.
Where's your conscience, Ritchie?'

'A conscience is a luxury I can't afford just now.'

'Can't *not* afford, you mean. I tell you, Ritchie, if it don't stop,
I'm outa here. You won't need to fire me – I'll walk. Are you gonna
call Connelly and tell him it's off, or am I?'

'For Chrissakes, Monica!' Ritchie is sweating now. A fine sheen
of moisture is gathering on his forehead. 'Don't even think about
it.'

'Oh, I'm doing more than thinking.'

'You want to end up with a bullet between your eyes? You don't
cross Connelly and get away with it. This is between him and me.
I told you to keep your nose out. If he knows you know . . .'

His consternation is all the proof I need. 'So I was right. You're
an asshole, Ritchie. A greedy asshole.'

Ritchie is looking now like a rabbit caught in the headlights.
He's midway between panic and anger; it could go either way. But
he doesn't scare me. I've known him too long.

'Why the hell did you get mixed up with this?' I demand.

'You know why.'

'It's got to stop.'

Ritchie shrugs miserably, looking like a whipped puppy.

'The way out,' I say, 'is to sell Varna Aviation. It always was. You
can't make it pay legal and level, you know that. You've gotta take

the offer while it's still on the table. I think Nancy will, anyways. And that will get you shot of Connelly. He won't risk anyone else knowing about his lucrative little business, and they'd be bound to. You couldn't even keep it hidden from me, and you're the boss as things are. Call him, Ritchie. Tell him it's off.'

I can see Ritchie's thinking it over. His eyes are skittering, he's drumming his fingertips against his chin.

'I've got to do the trips we've planned, Monica. Like I said, Connelly doesn't take kindly to being crossed.'

'OK.' I don't like it, but I can see where he's coming from. Connelly is a powerful, dangerous man who thinks he's got himself a plane for his dodgy dealings tonight and again next week. There's careful planning involved here, and if it goes awry, heads will roll. Ritchie's more than likely. How the hell could he have been so stupid as to get himself mixed up in something like this with the likes of Connelly? But he has. Now it's about damage limitation.

At least it's out in the open between us now. And I might just be able to help him out of the mess he's gotten himself into. Just so long as he doesn't continue to get sucked in by the promise of what looks like easy money. That's the sticking point.

'OK, I can see it's probably prudent to keep tonight's arrangement. And before next week we'll get our heads together. If we can get Wings West on the scene, it'll make things easier. But for Chrissakes, be careful. This is just a regular booking as far as anyone knows. Let's keep it that way.'

'You bet.' I think Ritchie's actually relieved that we're talking about it, but I feel like I'm locked in a nightmare. My head's pounding and I can feel the muscles down the back of my neck tight and throbbing in time.

'Get me a coffee, Ritchie,' I say. 'And make it strong and sweet. I sure as heck need it.'

Tuesday comes, and Ritchie goes. Off on his clandestine trip that looks just like a regular booking. I've got this really bad feeling eating away at me. I'm depressed as well as worried, and that just ain't me. I don't do depressed. Today there's this great black cloud that's not just hanging on the horizon, it's gotten right inside of me. Not even an enquiry for a trial lesson and some tourist wanting to book a sightseeing trip over the Everglades has made me feel any better. All I can see is trouble with a capital T.

Ritchie's still not back by the time I pack up and head for home. I didn't expect he would be, but I couldn't keep from wishing, all the same. Troy calls, says he's gotten a promotion at work. That should cheer me up, but the mood I'm in, nothing can. I tell him great, I'm real proud of him, but my mind's elsewhere. I cook myself eggs, sunny side up, because I can't be bothered to make the spaghetti and meatballs I'd planned, watch the news on Fox, soak in a hot tub full of bubbles, and go to bed. I'm tossing and turning for what seems like hours, and I think I'm still awake. But I must have dozed off because when I realise the telephone's ringing, it's one hell of a shock. I catch the clock on the nightstand as I fumble for the handset – it's a quarter after twelve. A million fears chase through my head before I can get the phone to my ear. Nobody calls this time of night unless something's wrong.

'Monica?' It's Nancy. My heart stops beating. Oh my God, Ritchie. 'Nancy?'

Before I can ask what's happened, she says: 'I'm real sorry to call you so late. I wouldn't bother you, but . . .'

It's not just my heart that's stopped, it's the whole world too.

I'm shaking; the dread has made me go weak. I don't want to hear this, I really don't, but I have to. I have to know.

'What's happened, Nancy?'

'You're gonna be real cross with me . . .'

She's not making any sense. 'What?'

'I guess I left the garden door open again, fell asleep in the chair. Somebody's gotten in. They've ransacked the place and I never heard a thing. Slept right through. I've dialled 911, but the police haven't got here yet. I guess it's not an emergency. Maybe they won't come at all tonight. But Ritchie's not here, I'm on my own, and I don't feel so good . . .'

I'm still shaking, but the relief is washing over me in waves. It's not Ritchie, thank God. A burglary I can cope with.

'I'll be right over.'

'Oh, Monica, no! I just wanted . . . I needed to talk to someone, and you—'

'Quit arguing, Nancy. I'm on my way.'

All the lights are blazing out in Nancy's house and there's a squad car in her drive. I pull up at the kerb, taking care not to block it in. I don't want to get on the wrong side of the law.

I meet the officer in the hallway. I know him by sight. He's a big fella built like a boxer, and he has a boxer's nose too, like he's gotten in the way of a pretty solid punch some time or other. Vesty, his name is. Officer Vesty. He's worked Varna as long as I can remember, but I don't have much contact with law enforcement. Except once when Russell had a little too much to drink on a night out with his buddies. Officer Vesty found him lying in the carriageway and brought him home. He could have locked him in the cooler till he sobered up, but he didn't, he brought him home and rang the bell so I'd know he was on the doorstep, so I figure Officer Vesty is a pretty regular guy.

It seems he remembers me too. 'Mrs Rivers, isn't it?' he says.

'You've got it. I work for the Costellos up at the airfield. What's happened here? Nancy said she'd been burgled.'

'That's the way it looks.' Officer Vesty – I have a feeling his given name is Roy – jerks his head in the direction of the kitchen. 'Mrs Costello's in there. She's pretty shook up.'

'I'll go see her. I warned her only last night about making sure the place was secure before she went falling asleep.'

Roy Vesty doesn't budge out of my way. He's standing there, hands on hips, looking at me very straight.

'Looks like she took your advice. The window in the door's busted.'

I feel my eyes go wide. 'She slept through that?'

'She took tablets for her arthritis, she tells me. Like I say, she's groggy. Good thing you're here, if you ask me. Where's that son of hers?'

'Ritchie? He's flying a job for a client.' I don't go into detail, it doesn't seem wise, given what I know. 'He should be home soon.'

'Yeah. Well.' Roy Vesty shifts his bulk and I go into the kitchen.

First thing I notice, it's been turned over. All Nancy's storage jars are out of the cupboards, drawers pulled out, contents strewn over the floor, and the refrigerator door is open.

Second thing is Nancy. Roy Vesty wasn't kidding when he said she was shook up. She's white as a sheet and she's kinda shrunk into herself, so she looks real little. Nancy's never been big, never had a lot of meat on her, but right now she looks like you could brush her with a feather and blow her clean away.

'Monica, thanks for coming. You're a naughty girl, I told you not to. But I sure am glad you're here.' Her voice sounds shaky too.

The door's open. I can see the window in it was busted, just like Roy Vesty said. There's glass all over the floor, some big shards, some glinting like glitter dust in the spilled coffee, salt and dish-washer powder.

'What the hell happened here?' I ask.

Nancy sits down on one of the kitchen chairs. 'Something woke me up – the garden door banging, I think. And I saw stuff all over the floor – dresser drawers open, everything pulled out . . .'

'They'd been in the room where you were asleep?' I say, shocked.

'Must have been. I took a quick look in the kitchen, and found all this, though I didn't notice at first the window in the door was smashed. I can't understand how come I didn't wake up.'

'Thank the Lord you didn't!' I've gone cold, thinking what might have happened if Nancy had come to and found the intruders in her sitting room. 'You need a cup of tea, Nancy, and I could sure do with one too.'

I put the kettle on to boil, find cups and some tea bags that have been scattered all over the counter. This mess is going to take some clearing up, but for the moment it can wait. I guess the crime scene investigators are going to want it left as it is for the moment, in any case.

I make the tea for Nancy, myself, and a couple of extra cups for Roy Vesty and his partner. I'm just stirring in milk and sugar when I hear a car door slam and a second later Ritchie's in the kitchen.

'What the . . . ?'

I'm expecting the air to turn blue, but to my surprise and relief, Ritchie's first thought is for Nancy. He goes right over to her, and the concern on his face shows me that for all the antagonism he usually displays, deep down he thinks the world of her.

'Mom? Are you OK?'

'I'm fine, Ritchie. Don't worry about me.'

But for just a moment she leans, head bowed, against the arm he's offered her, and I catch a glimpse of the bond that's there between them, though it's all too often hidden by their constant chipping at one another. The bond between mother and son, stretched too tight for comfort sometimes, maybe, but strong as a strand of spun silk.

'What the hell's happened here?' Ritchie asks. But he's still being gentle with her.

I make an extra cup of tea and we fill him in on the situation.

'What have the bastards taken?' he asks.

'That's the funny thing,' Nancy says, sounding bewildered, 'I can't see that they've taken much at all. A few bits of silverware, maybe, but my jewellery seems to be all there, and your music system. I'd have thought they'd go for that, seeing what you paid for it.'

Roy Vesty is leaning against the counter, cup cradled between big hands.

'Seems to me,' he says thoughtfully, 'that they weren't so much thieving as looking for something.' He twists his head, looking straight at Ritchie. 'Any idea what that might be?'

Ritchie shakes his head, but there's a shifty look about him now. He's gone back to being the old, more familiar Ritchie, and all of a sudden I feel sick. I know that look. And I don't like what it tells me. All of a sudden, I don't want to be here. I don't want any part of this.

'Now you're home, Ritchie, I think I'll be getting off,' I say. 'I'll come over in the morning, Nancy, help you clear up. I reckon I'll be more use here than at the airfield.'

She thanks me again and I give her a hug. She feels very small, brittle almost. Like a broken bird. I'm real worried, leaving her with this mess, which I'm pretty sure is of Ritchie's making. But some things go beyond the call of duty.

Ritchie follows me out. 'Monica—'

'Don't say anything, Ritchie,' I warn him. 'I don't want to know. Just one thing: I think you should get the doctor to take a look at your mom. She's looking real sick, if you ask me, and a shock like she's just had . . . well, you can't be too careful.'

'I was thinking the same myself. I'll give him a call, get him to check her over. Thanks for everything, Monica.'

'No problem.'

I get in my car, start up the engine. I'm going home, to make the most of what's left of the night. I have a feeling I'm going to need my batteries recharged to deal with tomorrow. But when I get there, I know I'm not going to sleep. I've got too much on my mind. I don't want to think what I'm thinking, but I can't help it. I'm scared to death Ritchie's in this deeper than even I guessed. And I'm worried sick about what it's going to do to Nancy if I'm right.

I could kill Ritchie, honest to God I could. I'd like to get hold of him and shake him till his teeth rattle. And much good would it do. But I can't just do nothing.

I check the clock – it's a quarter after three. Do a quick calculation. It'll be morning in England. Before I go to bed, I'm going to ring Sarah.

I punch in the international code, followed by the number of her cellphone. It rings a long while and I'm just thinking she's not going to answer when I hear her voice on the other end of the line, half a world away.

'Sarah,' I say, 'it's me. Monica.'

'Monica?' I can hear the alarm in her voice.

'Don't worry, it's OK,' I say hastily. 'Well, not altogether, but I don't mean to frighten you. It's just that your grandma's been burgled tonight, and it shook her up. She said you were thinking of coming back, and I just wanted to say I think you should. I'm worried about her, Sarah. She needs you.'

SARAH

I can't believe I'm back in Florida again so soon. But when I got that early morning phone call from Monica, the decision was taken for me. I'd been wondering how on earth I was going to get more time off when I'd only just come back from my holiday; now I had a good reason. I applied for leave on compassionate grounds and got it. I went onto the internet and booked a flight. And before I could turn round I was back on a plane halfway across the Atlantic. I had hoped perhaps Mum would come with me. I'd already suggested it when I'd filled her in about my visit to Gloucestershire and told her what Chris Mackenzie had said. Her response, though, was less what I'd hoped than what I'd expected.

'What a cheek! Making out he knows more about our family than we do!'

'He could hardly know less,' I retorted. 'Are you sure, Mum, about John being Mac's son?'

'I'm not going into all that again,' Mum snapped. 'What you do is up to you, Sarah. You'll do as you please, I suppose, as you always

363

do. But I am certainly not running off to Florida just because the son of that man tells me to, even if you are.'

'I'm going because I want to, not because he told me to,' I said shortly. 'And I really think you ought to come too.' But I knew I was flogging a dead horse.

I did think that maybe she would have second thoughts, though, when I told her about what had happened, and that Monica was seriously worried about Nancy. Certainly, she didn't dismiss it out of hand this time. But she said there was no way she could just drop everything and go, she had too many commitments. If I could leave it a week or so, then maybe.

'No, Mum, I'm going as soon as I can. It's now Grandma needs support, not next week or next month.'

'Well, give her my love,' Mum said, and it sounded as if she meant it.

I landed in Miami and got a connecting flight to Fort Myers. Monica is waiting for me there, with Grandma's car.

'Oh Sarah, thank the Lord you're here,' she says as I slot myself into the passenger seat.

'How is Grandma?' I ask.

'Not so good. All this has taken a toll of her.'

All this . . . Monica is talking about the burglary, I imagine. But I know there's more to it than that. She's bound to be upset about Mac too. I'd been forced to abandon my plan to tell her face to face; to be honest I'd always known that was a pretty unrealistic option, and naturally enough the first thing she had asked when I phoned was if I'd had any luck with the task she'd set me. But my heart had sunk like a stone in a murky pool all the same.

'Well, yes and no. I've found his son.'

'His *son*.'

364

'Yes. He's a doctor. His name is Chris.'

'And Mac . . . ?' Into the pause, as I tried to find the right words, she said: 'He's dead, isn't he?'

'I'm afraid he is, Grandma.'

There was a little silence. I could imagine her getting herself together. Then she said, very matter-of-fact: 'I thought he might be. When . . . ?'

'A couple of years ago. Grandma, I'm going to try and come back and see you so that I can tell you all about it.'

'That would be nice, Sarah. Did you give him Mac's DFC?'

I didn't want to go into all that over the phone. 'I'll make the arrangements to come over to Florida. We can talk about it then.'

'Please do. And thank you, Sarah.' Her voice was flat. I knew then that she'd died a little inside. It might have been the news she was expecting but until this moment she'd been able to hope. Now that last little candle had been snuffed out, and I guessed it had hit her hard.

Monica knows nothing of that, of course – at least, I'm assuming she doesn't – and I'm not going to be the one to enlighten her.

There's a Beech Baron on the runway – a good bit newer than Grandma's, by the look of it. It's just taking off, and Monica is staring at it so hard she almost runs off the perimeter road.

'Wings West,' she mutters. 'That's a Wings West plane. White with a ruby flash. Smart, eh?'

'Wings West?' I'm puzzled by her interest.

'Something else that's going on. I'll leave Nancy to tell you.'

'Tell me what?'

'Oh – OK. They've made an offer for Varna Aviation. Nancy's talking to them, and Ritchie's pretty mad. He wanted to tell them to go to hell.'

Ritchie would. 'What do you think?' I ask.

'Best thing, under the circumstances. We're really struggling and Ritchie . . . least said about Ritchie the better.'

I'm surprised at that. Monica is usually so protective of Ritchie.

'I always thought you'd be there to sort him out, Monica.'

She snorts. 'Would you believe he and Mary-Lyn seem to be hooking up again? Anyway, I reckon I've come to the end of the line with Ritchie. There's only so much crap I'm prepared to take.'

'Him and Mary-Lyn, you mean?'

'Yeah, that too.' I get the feeling there's something else, something she's not saying. 'You have no idea what's been going on here since you went home,' she says.

I'm alarmed. 'What?'

But Monica shakes her head. 'No, I've already said more than I should. You just see Nancy's all right. Me – I can take care of myself.'

She swings out onto the freeway, southbound, and I know I'm not going to get anything out of her. She's loyal to a fault, is Monica. More fool Ritchie that he seems totally incapable of appreciating her.

'Tell you what, though,' she adds thoughtfully, 'if I did want somebody to take care of me, I did clap eyes the other day on a guy that I wouldn't mind handing the job over to. One of the cops who came out when Nancy got burgled. Ray Vesty, his name is. Good-looking fella, even if he has been round the block a few times; kinda solid. I made some enquiries and it seems he's single right now. If Roy was to come calling I don't think I'd turn him down. But I don't suppose he ever will. I don't get a whole lot of luck when it comes to fellas.'

'You never know, your luck might change,' I say. And I think that if anyone deserves a break when it comes to love, it's Monica.

* * *

It's not that long before we see the sign for Varna. The road from Fort Myers is a good one, and at this time of day, mid-afternoon, it's not as busy as it sometimes is. We swing over the long low bridge and the bold brightness of it all after the more muted shades of England hurts my eyes. Periwinkle sky above, water, an even more intense blue, beneath. Lush emerald green to either side. Gleaming white bridge superstructure. Tarmac shimmering silver. The air conditioning sucks in the smell of Florida and something happens to my heart. It's always the same when I cross the bridge to Varna. A flutter of excitement, a deep sense of satisfaction. Though I've never lived here I feel I'm coming home.

Monica pulls onto the driveway of Nancy's house. I look towards the door expectantly; Grandma usually comes out to greet me, as if she's been watching for me from the window. Not today. The door is firmly closed, the windows shuttered eyes. I hoist my bag out of the boot and when I turn to the house again, there she is. And for all that Monica had warned me, I'm shocked by the change in her. I'd noticed a deterioration the last time I was here, but it had been a year since the last time I saw her. Now, though it's only a couple of weeks since I was here, she's noticeably more frail, and vulnerable somehow. My heart sinks. Monica did right to call me. Whether it's Mac's death, or the trauma of the burglary, or the worry of a takeover bid and whatever else it is that Monica was hinting at, or all those things put together, she has gone downhill a lot in a very short time. There's not a lot I can do about any of it. But at least I can be here for her. And I am.

Monica stays for a while. She seems in no hurry to get back to the airfield, which is very unusual for her and underlines the fact that she's feeling fed up with Ritchie. It means that Nancy and I don't get to talk about personal matters, of course, though I know she must be itching to ask me about my visit to Gloucestershire. We do discuss the burglary, though, and it seems the whole thing is a complete mystery. Nothing of any value was taken, though the intruders had the run of the house, and were actually leaving before Nancy woke up. Police investigations don't seem to have turned up any solutions and for all that Monica is so taken with Officer Roy Vesty, he and his colleagues don't seem to have made any great effort to find the culprits. It's the same in England these days, of course. A burglary is treated as more or less routine, issued with a crime number and put on the back burner.

We talk about the takeover bid too.

'Are you really seriously considering it, Grandma?' I ask.

'Yes, Sarah, I am. Ritchie thinks I shouldn't, but to be honest, it's his good I'm thinking of. He's just not up to running a business and there's no one else now that I can't do it any more. His pride's hurt, I know, but at least he won't have the bills to worry about and he'll have money behind him if it's invested wisely, as well as a wage from Wings West.'

'Just as long as he doesn't do something stupid and get himself fired,' Monica puts in.

'Well, I can't wet-nurse him,' Nancy says wearily. 'I can only do what's in his best interests and leave the rest to him. I've been in contact with Wings West, told them I'm thinking it over, and that I'd insist on there being a job for Ritchie – and you too, Monica – as part of the deal. And I've arranged for my lawyer to come see me next week.' She grins at me ruefully. 'Could be this will be your last chance to fly a Varna Aviation aircraft, Sarah. Do it while the opportunity's still there. Though I might be able to get cheap rates for you written into the deal too,' she adds.

'That is the least of my worries right now,' I say. 'Just do whatever you think is best for you and Ritchie.'

'Ritchie,' she corrects me. 'None of this will make a dime's worth of difference to me soon.'

A shiver whispers over my skin. 'Don't talk such rot, Grandma.'

But I know, deep down, she's only speaking the truth.

It's evening before we get the chance to talk heart to heart. Ritchie came home, had a shower and grabbed a change of clothes, and went out again.

'Mary-Lyn, is it?' Nancy enquired drily.

'Mom, if we get back together it's one less lot of alimony I have to pay,' Ritchie said. And drove off. At last Nancy and I are alone.

'Let's go on the patio,' Nancy says. 'It's real nice out there in the evenings.'

We go out through the kitchen door. The glass has been repaired; apart from the new putty you'd never know it had been smashed a few days ago. We sit at the table by the pool. Just as we did when she first broached the subject of Mac. Back where it all started.

Nancy sits back in her chair, hands folded in her lap, head cocked a little to one side. She's looking at me very straight, waiting. All of a sudden I don't really know where to start. I've gone over it so often in my mind, but sitting here, with Nancy's eyes on my face, it's different from how I imagined it would be.

'Did you tell your mother what I'd asked you to do?' she says into the silence. I nod. 'And what did she say?'

'She wasn't very keen on the idea.' I'm not ready yet to go into details of what Mum actually said.

Nancy sighs. 'Oh, Ellen! So I've upset her again.'

'Grandma, you have every right to do what you want.'

'I know. But still . . . I do wish Ellen could see it like that.'

The fact that I know the reason behind Mum's antagonism weighs heavily on me. And it also strikes me how important her reaction is to Nancy. So important she raised it first, before asking me a single thing about Mac. I make up my mind to have another go at trying to persuade Mum to come over and make her peace with her mother while she still can. It would mean so much to Nancy, and I feel sure Mum will live to regret it if they are still in a state of estrangement when the end comes.

Grandma sits up a little straighter. I can feel her mentally preparing herself.

'So – Mac. Tell me what you were able to find out.'

I tell her. About how my investigations led me to Chris, and what he told me about his father's life after the war, and his death. I tell her how much I liked Chris, that if he's anything like his father I can understand why she's never forgotten him. And how Chris told me that Mac had never forgotten her either. She smiles sadly.

'What we went through together . . . well, there are some things you never can forget. And some people.'

A silence. I know she's remembering. Then she says thoughtfully: 'I'm glad he had a son.'

The blood begins to tingle in my veins. I hadn't known how to get around to the really awkward part of this conversation; suddenly the opening is there before me, handed to me on a plate. If I have the courage to take it.

I take a deep breath. Look Nancy straight in the eye. And go for it.

'*Another* son,' I say. And when she looks back at me blankly, incredulously, as if she can't believe what she is hearing, I add: 'It's

OK, Grandma. I know about John. I know he was Mac's, and Grandpa Joe brought him up as his own. You don't have to pretend any more.'

'Oh, Sarah,' she says. I have the awful feeling she's going to cry. I suppose it's weighed heavily on her all these years, that secret.

But it's out in the open now. She can talk about it if she wants to. Certainly I want to hear what she has to say.

RITCHIE

Things are not looking good. I'm in one hell of a mess and I know it. Monica was right – ain't she always, damn her? I should never have gotten myself mixed up with Dexter Connelly. I guess I knew it myself all along, but it didn't seem like I had any choice. I needed the money, and I needed the business, legal or not.

And heck, it seemed to be working out. All I had to do was fly the plane, the one thing which, if I say so myself, I'm good at. I could leave all the rest to Connelly's organisation and pocket my share of the profit.

Trouble was, for the risks I was taking it didn't seem like a very generous share. Fool that I am I thought he'd never miss it if I helped myself to just a little bit of that illicit cargo. I should've known better. A businessman like Connelly didn't get where he is through being asleep at the wheel. Just a couple of little bags out of a haul worth thousands of dollars, but he knew. Or suspected, anyway. And he sent his goons over to my place looking for it. Had them break in, and scared Mom half to death.

They never found anything, of course. I'd long since got rid of it. We'd snorted it, Mary-Lyn and me – just a couple of lines – one crazy night at her place, the place that used to be mine as well. Like I say, it was only the smallest amount. Just a little bonus, I figured. Who'd have thought Connelly would have gone to such lengths as to break into my house looking for it? But then I guess he'd say it was a matter of principle.

Or maybe not so much principle as a warning to me what would happen if I didn't toe the line. As if I needed a warning! I know Connelly's not a man to cross.

Whatever, you just can't do that, scaring an old lady like that. And what if she hadn't been asleep at the time – what if she'd challenged them? My blood runs cold when I think about it. I might be an asshole, I might be working for drugs smugglers, but when thugs like Connelly start involving my mom, it makes my blood boil.

But what the hell am I gonna do about it? Seems like I'm damned if I keep on working for Connelly and damned if I don't.

I guess, like Monica says, it could all get solved if Mom decides to sell out to Wings West. But selling out ain't something I want to do. And I sure as hell don't have a choice about doing the jobs I've already agreed to with Connelly. He wouldn't take kindly to me backing out now, and it gives me the creeps when I think of what he might do to show his displeasure. Arson wouldn't be beyond him, I'm thinking. Bad enough if he decided to make an example of me by setting a fire at the airfield, destroying one of the planes or the office even, but what if he should take it into his thick head to do the house instead? Mom would be a sitting duck. No, I gotta do these jobs for him. I just can't take the risk of getting on his bad side, especially with Mom so vulnerable.

At least there's one good thing come out of it all, though. When I had some money to spend again, Mary-Lyn was there like a sniffer dog on the trail of some of Connelly's dope. Now I know that's not the soundest basis for a relationship, especially when the cash might run out again any time, but the funny thing is we've been hitting it off real well, like the money doesn't come into it at all. We've been having real good times, like we used to in the beginning.

You know what she said the other night? 'I've never enjoyed being with anyone as much as I enjoy being with you, Ritchie. I've missed you, you know that?'

'You've missed me spoiling you, you mean,' I said.

And: 'Well, that too,' she said, 'but I'm coming to realise money isn't everything. Maybe it's just that I'm getting old and going soft.'

'You mean you'd still love me if I was broke?'

'And aren't you?'

'I might be soon.'

She sighed. 'Ah well, the big question is, will you still love me when I'm old and fat?'

I gave her a straight look. 'Well – aren't you?'

She glared, then burst out laughing. We laughed together for quite a while.

I guess that's what we've got, Mary-Lyn and me. Even if we didn't make it work last time, we're good together. We make each other laugh. I guess I love her, and I guess she loves me. And that's about as good as it gets.

So maybe some good has come out of this whole mess. But it ain't over yet. And I can't help but admit I'm pretty damn worried as to how it's going to end.

NANCY

I knew, of course, when I asked Sarah to try to find Mac that there was a pretty good chance the truth would come out. I think that in my heart of hearts I wanted it to. I'm tired of the secrecy. It's burdened me down for most of my life and I want to be free of it.

Perhaps I should have told Sarah the whole story, but the fact is I didn't know how. And much as I love her, it didn't seem right that I should enlighten her when Ellen and Ritchie are in the dark. I need to talk to them first. They are the ones who truly deserve an explanation; they shouldn't hear it at second-hand. And I figured too that there would still be time for me to set the record straight. There was a pretty good chance Sarah would be unable to find Mac or his family. And if she did . . . knowing Mac as I did, I couldn't imagine he would leap in with both feet and spill the beans if he were alive, and if he wasn't, well, I didn't suppose his family would either. If they knew. Which, given the circumstances, seemed pretty unlikely.

It seems I was wrong. But I'm startled, all the same, by what Sarah has just said, and not only because I really wasn't expecting

377

her to come out with what she's learned so straight. No, it's because she's somehow got it all wrong. My mind is racing; where the hell do I go from here?

'Did Chris tell you this?' I ask, floundering.

'No. Mum told me.'

I can't believe what I'm hearing. 'Your mom told you?'

'Yes. A long time ago, when she was in her early teens, she found a letter Mac wrote to you. Actually . . .' She bites her lip, takes a deep breath, and goes on: 'Actually, I think it might be the root of the trouble between you. She never said anything to you about it, and I think she should have. If it had all come out into the open she might have been able to deal with it better.'

Oh, Ellen. My mind is racing. I should never have kept Mac's letters. I always knew it was too darned dangerous. But tearing them into shreds had been like tearing out my heart; dumping them in the trash can was dumping a big part of my life. It was something I'd put off doing for as long as I dared. But I'd left it too long. Ellen had found the letters, and maybe the DFC too.

I know, right off, when that happened. The High School Hop when she'd borrowed my camisole. Across the years I can still remember clearly the way my heart stopped when she said she'd been to my underwear drawer. But I'd checked the first chance I got, and the letters and the DFC were still there, buried beneath stockings and panties. I thought I'd gotten away with it this time, but I'd known I couldn't risk leaving the letters lying about any longer. I'd disposed of them right away, and found a safer place to conceal the DFC, never realising I'd already left it too late.

Ellen never said a word. She always was a secretive girl; I guess she gets that from me. But there's no doubt that from that moment on she changed. I never put two and two together; I put it down to her starting that difficult stage most teenagers go through. Except that she never did grow out of it. That barrier came up between us and never went down again. Now I know the reason, and it makes me sick with guilt and regret. I thought I was protecting her, protecting my family. Instead I'd destroyed our relationship.

I can see too how she came to make assumptions that were all wrong. They were pretty ambiguous, those letters (I can still remember word for word what they said). What Ellen had thought they meant would have made perfect sense. Except that that is not the way it was.

Well, there's nothing for it now but for me to tell Ellen and Ritchie the truth while there's still time. It's going to be one hell of a shock for them. They are going to feel betrayed and cheated, and I doubt they'll ever forgive me. Over the years I've compounded my sins by trying to hide them. And I guess I've deceived myself too. I've pretended what I was doing was to save them hurt, when in reality I guess I was just being one hell of a coward. How do you tell your kids something like this? But there's no way I can go on running away from it. I have to set the record straight. That much I owe them.

Sarah is looking at me expectantly.

'Sarah, honey,' I say, 'I know you want answers. But I can't give them to you right now. I need to talk to your Mom and Ritchie, and I need to talk to them together.'

Sarah chews her lip. 'Mum did say she'd come over to see you. Do you want me to ring her?'

This is something I have to do myself. 'No, I will. And then, if you don't mind, Sarah, I am going to bed. I'm real tired.'

But I know however tired I might be, I won't sleep. I shall lie awake, seeing faces from the past in the shadows, and remembering.

Part Six

The Past

I

Once, when she had first been accepted as a ferry pilot with the ATA, Nancy had pondered the enigma of time, and how it was possible that minutes could sometimes seem like hours whilst on other occasions a whole day could disappear in the blinking of an eye. Now it seemed that time was managing to do both simultaneously. She could scarcely believe it was little more than a year since she had come to England; Florida seemed not just half a world away, but a lifetime ago too. The days were oddly elastic, flashing past in a busy blur, every moment filled, yet dragging endlessly towards some distant future when she might see Mac again.

Her appetite for the war had gone now, buried beneath an avalanche of anxiety and frustration. She worried constantly about Mac and Joe, the one leading a squadron of fighters nightly, the other flying a bomber. And overlaying everything was the ache of longing for Mac. They had had their stolen interlude; far from being enough, it had given Nancy a glimpse of the way things could be and ignited a fever that burned in her bright and fierce as a forest fire.

She didn't know when they would be together again or even if they ever would be, and the poignancy of it, razor-edged and haunting, lent an aura to her emotions that was bittersweet to the point of unbearable. She loved him and he loved her. Yet the barriers that kept them apart were insurmountable.

Nancy flew Blenheims and Wellingtons and Ansons, working anything up to a twelve-hour day. And all the while Mac was with her, in her thoughts and in her heart.

September 1943: brilliant blue skies and sunshine so sharp and clear it hurt the eyes. Blackberries ripening in the hedgerows, and early mornings and late evenings that bore the scent and the touch of autumn. September: the month in which Nancy had been born.

As far as she was aware only one person at White Waltham knew the date of her birthday – Krystyna Rabouwski, a Polish girl who had escaped from her homeland and had been flying with the ATA since the beginning of 1941. She and Nancy had struck up a friendship, and Nancy had let slip the information during one of their chats.

'You must try and arrange to have a day off then,' Krystyna said imperiously.

'No way.' Nancy didn't feel like celebrating and she didn't want anyone else to force her into it. 'And don't you go spreading it around either. I don't want everyone knowing.'

'Why not? For you, a birthday comes only once a year. You do not have a name day to celebrate as we in Poland do. That makes it special. You have to make sure that it is so.'

'My birthday will be just like any other day,' Nancy said firmly. 'It always has been and it always will be.'

'Did your parents not make birthdays special when you were a little girl?'

Nancy shrugged carelessly. 'We didn't have that kind of life. Never settled anywhere long enough for me to make friends I could ask to a party, and no home to invite them to if I had. My best birthday treat was being allowed to sit on Daddy's knee while he flew his aeroplane and when I turned sixteen I got to wing walk for the first time. Mostly, though, I think my mom and daddy had a hard time even remembering it was my birthday.'

Krystyna looked shocked. 'That is just not right. Me – I always had a round cream cake – a torte – with candles, one for each year, because my parents liked to celebrate my birthday as well as my name day.'

'What is a name day?' Nancy was anxious to get off the subject of birthdays.

'The name day – the Imieniny – is the day of the patron. We are a Catholic country, remember? My name day is on March the thirteenth. Krystyna – you see, like St Krystyna? In Poland everyone celebrates their name day. Each of us is named for a saint with at least one of our names. You . . . there is no St Nancy, I think.'

'Nor likely to be.' Nancy grinned mischievously.

'All the more reason, then, to celebrate your birthday. At the very least I shall sing to you.' She struck a pose and burst into song.

> 'Sto lat, sto lat, niech zyje, zyje nam!
> Jeszcze raz, jeszcze raz, niech zyje, zyje, zyje nam.'

'What the hell does that mean?' Nancy asked.

> 'For a hundred years, for a hundred years,
> May she live for us.'

'Amen to that! But I'm telling you, Krystyna, if you start singing that in the mess, you'll be lucky to live five minutes, never mind a hundred years. Whatever you might say, my birthday is best forgotten,' Nancy said.

And had no way of knowing that this particular birthday was one she would remember all her life.

The news Nancy had hoped she would never have to hear came just a week before that birthday, broken to her by the station commander himself.

Nancy was puzzled but not unduly alarmed when she was summoned to his office on her return from a day's ferrying; the hierarchy here was more relaxed than at some stations, the CO friendly and approachable. The moment she entered his office, though, a cold dread began in the pit of her stomach and seeped into her veins. There was something about the stiffness of the CO's shoulders and the way his eyes narrowed when he looked at her that told her this was no run-of-the-mill operational briefing.

'Nancy.'

'Sir.' She could hear the apprehension in her own voice, and if the CO heard it too, he did nothing to dispel it.

'We had some bad news today. I know James Mackenzie was a good friend of yours, and I wanted to tell you myself before you hear it from gossip in the briefing room or the mess.'

Nancy had heard of knees turning weak; she had never before experienced it. The strength seemed, quite literally, to drain out of her legs; she felt them buckling beneath her and grasped the back of the upright chair on her side of the CO's desk for support.

The CO looked concerned. 'Do you want to sit down?'

'No, I'm fine, thank you, sir.'

Fine. Dear Lord! Nancy wanted to scream at him that she was not fine at all, and if something had happened to Mac she never would be again. But prudence demanded she did not admit to just how shaken she was.

'What's happened, sir?' she asked as matter-of-factly as she could manage.

The CO rolled his pen between the index finger and thumb of each hand, twirling it back and forth like a baton. 'It seems he didn't return from a sortie last night. There was a dogfight over occupied territory and according to his wing man, Squadron Leader Mackenzie was hit. Officially he's listed as "missing", but I'm afraid it doesn't look good, Nancy.' He paused, looking at her. 'I wanted to put you in the picture since you were a friend of his rather than have you hear half a story, or some distorted version of it.'

'Thank you, sir. You will . . . ?'

'Let you know if I hear anything else? Of course. But to be truthful, I rather doubt that I will.'

Nancy nodded, mechanical as a wind-up clockwork toy. Later, she had no recollection of leaving the room, collecting her belongings and making her way home. Only when she was alone in the flat Mac had found for her did she allow herself to think about what the CO had told her. Holed up like a wounded animal, Nancy gave way to the emotions that were bubbling in her like a geyser about to erupt. She cried herself empty and when the tears stopped there was nothing left but the hollow blackness of the most utter despair she had ever experienced.

Busy. Keep busy. It was the only way to retain her sanity. At least keeping busy was something she had to make no effort to do; it was thrust upon her on a daily basis. Ferrying planes from morning

387

till night had become a way of life and it demanded total concentration. But there was a blackness behind her eyes and filling her head, and a knot of wretchedness had settled deep inside her like a cancerous growth. Sometimes a wild, almost euphoric sunburst of optimism would envelop her; Mac could have crash-landed somewhere behind enemy lines and was either in hiding or taken as a prisoner of war – not a pleasant prospect, but infinitely preferable to thinking of him dying in a burning Spitfire. But the release never lasted long, and the horrific imaginings and the dark despair that inevitably rushed in to fill the void were all the more unbearable by contrast, worse even, it seemed, than they had been before.

The days dragged by relentlessly with no news. Nancy talked to no one about what had happened. She couldn't trust herself to do so without betraying her true feelings. They had been so careful, she and Mac, to conceal the true nature of their relationship and Nancy did not want to be the one to put it in the public arena now. She didn't want it gossiped about and pawed over; Mac was a married man and others would see what they had shared not as a love beyond the control of either of them, but as a grubby little affair. She couldn't bear to have it cheapened in that way, and strangely Mac's reputation seemed even more important now than it had before. If he was dead, he should be remembered as the fine man he had been, not as an adulterer who cheated on a sick wife.

It could be, of course, that others suspected she and Mac had been more than 'good friends' as the CO had put it. Perhaps the CO himself suspected it and that was the reason he had called her into his office to break the news. She couldn't do anything about that, but she could avoid doing or saying anything that would put flesh on the bones of these suspicions. Nancy gritted her teeth, held her head high – at least in public – and hid the fact that her heart was breaking.

Sharing her pain would not lessen it by one jot. Mac had been lost in a plane over France and nothing that anyone could say could change that. Nancy, independent as she had always been, suffered silently and alone.

The day of her birthday. Nancy gave it scarcely a thought beyond hoping that Krystyna had not arranged some surprise party for her. She really couldn't cope with that. If a load of people burst in singing 'Happy Birthday' or that inane Polish song, she thought she would crack completely. But it seemed Krystyna had taken notice of what she'd said. No one mentioned it and the day passed off like any other. Nancy took off from White Waltham in a taxi Anson at around nine thirty in the morning and by the time she returned at five thirty in the evening she had moved two Spitfires and a Beaufighter, and done three Fairchild taxi trips. Utterly exhausted, she headed for the mess and had just settled herself at one of the small square tables with a cup of tea when the Tannoy crackled into life.

'Pilot Kelly to Operations, please.'

Nancy's heart sank. It was one thing to like to be kept busy, quite another to have to turn out again when she was dropping with exhaustion, and without a doubt that was what this summons meant. Some priority plane had come onto the books and there was no one but her available to move it. Useless to plead she would be in danger of falling asleep at the controls. The ops officer would know better. Adrenalin would keep her awake as long as she was in the air, and he would promise to get her home again as soon as she landed.

Nancy stuffed the cigarette she'd not yet had time to light back into the pack and stowed it in her purse. *Go, girl. You wanted to have no time to think; you got your wish.* She dragged her tired legs in the direction of the ops room, wondering what was waiting for her, and having no inkling of the truth. She pushed open the door and drew in a sharp breath of surprise.

A big bear-like figure in the uniform of the USAAF was standing by the window, smiling at her. 'Hi, Nancy. Surprise!'

'My God. Joe!'

'Yep. Come in person to wish you a happy birthday.'

'Joe – you shouldn't have!'

'Why not? Ain't you pleased to see me?'

'Well . . . yes . . .' Nancy was at a loss for words.

'Don't mind me.' Whitey, the ops officer, was grinning broadly. 'I'll leave you two alone for a bit. If the telephone rings, I'll be just next door, in the CO's office.' He winked at Joe, gathered together a sheaf of papers, and went out.

'Great guy,' Joe commented.

'Sneaky.' They'd connived, Joe and Whitey, to get her to the ops room on false pretences. Could be it went back further than that. It had to be planned, Joe turning up here. Maybe Krystyna was in on it too. Nancy could almost hear the phone lines buzzing. Joe: 'I'm Nancy's fiancé. I've fixed it up so I can come see her on her birthday. I wanna surprise her. Can you help me out here?' Whitey: 'Leave it with me. I'll see what I can do.' Had he played along because he didn't know about her and Mac? Or because he did? Maybe this was his way of trying to nudge her back to the guy she belonged with, make her forget about a crazy affair with a married man that had always been an impossible dream even before Mac was reported as missing. Nancy didn't know whether to be angry or touched by Whitey's well-meaning interference. She only knew it wasn't going to work. Nothing and nobody could make her forget Mac; nothing and nobody ease her pain at his loss.

'Come here, honey.' Joe was close, too close, invading her space, the space she needed around her raw and battered spirit. She took a step backwards, glancing over her shoulder, jumpy, defensive.

'Not here, Joe.'

His arms dropped to his sides, his forehead furrowed into a frown, some of the light went out of his eyes. She'd hurt him, she knew, and felt a flash of the old familiar guilt. He didn't deserve to be hurt, and he didn't deserve to be deceived either.

'Anyone could come in,' she said lamely.

'I was only gonna give you a hug.'

'I know, but—'

The telephone shrilled, saving her. She grabbed it up. 'Hello?'

'Hello? Who's that? I wanted your ops officer . . .'

'I'll get him for you.' She had the door open, calling for Whitey. Turned to Joe with an urgent jerk of her head. 'Come on, let's get out of here. If that's an urgent Spit coming on line . . .'

'They wouldn't send you, surely? Not after I've come all this way to see you.'

'If there's nobody else . . .'

Ten minutes ago, she'd dreaded the thought of flying again today. Right now it would have provided an escape. But she couldn't do it to him. Like he said, Joe had come a hell of a long way to see her, and besides . . . there were things they had to talk about. She couldn't let this go on. Couldn't keep deceiving him. She should have told him about Mac a long time ago; hell, she should have put him straight long before that, back home in Florida when he'd asked her to marry him. This mess was of her own making; she'd pretended to herself she didn't want to hurt Joe but in reality she had been taking the coward's way out. All she was doing was hurting him more, by keeping him hanging on. She had to tell him the truth, and she had to do it now, before things dragged on again. It wasn't fair on him, and she no longer had the stomach for keeping up the pretence.

'Do you know a good place to eat?' Joe asked. They were out in the balmy September evening now, walking the length of the office block.

'A few . . .' She hesitated. What she had to say to him needed to be said in privacy. 'Let's go back to my place,' she suggested.

'On your birthday? I was thinking of something a bit special.'

'Spam fritters and fries from the chip shop. They're about as special as you can get.'

'OK, if you say so.' He sighed, but he didn't look displeased. No doubt he thought her desire for privacy was for quite another purpose. A nerve jumped in her throat. She wasn't looking forward to disillusioning him.

'You were right as usual. Those Spam fritters sure were a feast.' Joe pushed back his chair, patted his stomach and reached across to take Nancy's hand. 'Time for dessert now, wouldn't you say?'

Her heart jarred. She knew what he meant. So far she'd managed to avoid any intimacy, using the excuse that the food needed to be eaten before it got cold. They'd brought it back to the flat in newspaper-wrapped parcels, which they'd spread out on the table, not bothering with plates, and eaten it with their fingers, which Nancy said was an English custom, washing it down with bottles of beer that Nancy still had in the cupboard from the days when Mac had come visiting, and a tipple or two from a bottle of bourbon

Joe had brought in his kitbag. The conversation, too, had been relatively impersonal, a catching-up on the operations Joe had flown, the planes Nancy had ferried, and the war in general.

'Reckon it won't be too much longer now,' Joe had said. 'We've got them on the run everywhere you look. The Nazis are having to build fighters to defend themselves now instead of bombers to knock the hell out of British cities. The US Eighth have made a real difference, taking the war to them.'

Nancy swallowed hard. The war in the air had been taken across the Channel and Mac had gone with it. And failed to return.

'Our boys have done wonders in the Pacific too,' Joe went on. 'The Japs aren't having it all their own way any longer, and Australia and New Zealand can thank us that they won't get invaded now. Yep, all in all, I reckon we're doing a pretty fine job. If you want something done, send for the Yanks.'

That stuck in Nancy's throat too. She was proud, of course, of the exploits of her countrymen, but she couldn't help a stab of irritation on behalf of Mac and the Englishmen like him who had picked up the gauntlet and run with it for three long years before the US had joined the fight. There was something of the Don Quixote about them, she thought; valour and determination in the face of overwhelming odds. She'd changed the topic of conversation then, asking Joe if he'd heard from home lately, and he regaled her with the news he'd got in letters from Aunt Dorothy, though Nancy scarcely listened to what he was saying. Dorothy and her moans and triumphs were a world away, and it seemed unreal somehow, like the echo of a distant dream that merely lingers on the periphery of consciousness. Reality now, to Nancy, was England. And Mac.

Now she looked across the table at Joe, sitting where Mac had

393

once sat, and expecting from her something she was quite incapable of giving, and knew the moment had come; she could put
it off no longer.

'Joe,' she said. 'We have to talk.'

And to her surprise, Joe replied with resignation: 'I know, honey.
I was afraid you were gonna get around to that. There's somebody
else, isn't there?'

For all that he was trying his best to hide it, a sick dread was gripping Joe's stomach. Nancy was staring at him, startled, and he
grinned ruefully. Did she really think he didn't know? Hell, she'd
never been demonstrative, never reacted to him in the way he
wanted her to. But he'd fooled himself into believing that if he
was patient he could win her over. He'd never felt about anyone
the way he felt about Nancy, and he'd been prepared to go doggedly
on, waiting for her, because the alternative – losing her altogether
– was something he didn't dare risk. He had hoped that when
she'd tasted freedom and found it wanting she would turn back
to him; she might never love him the way he loved her, but he
could live with that. Just as long as he had her. Just as long as he
could look at her lovely, impish face and her irrepressible curly
hair, hear her laugh, have her around in his world. All he wanted
was for her to be happy – just as long as he was part of it.

He remembered the way he had felt when he'd asked her to
marry him and he'd thought she was going to turn him down flat.
The heaviness in his chest that felt like a load of concrete setting.
The bleakness in his heart at the prospect of living the rest of his
life without her. But she hadn't turned him down. She'd given him
a 'maybe' and the hope she'd offered had kept him going.

But he'd felt her slipping away from him almost from that

moment on. He had tried to tell himself he was wrong. It was just this damned war, and being apart. But today, her face when she'd come into the ops room and seen him standing there had told him without a single word what he'd known for months now and refused to acknowledge. She hadn't been pleased to see him, just as she hadn't been pleased to see him when he'd visited her in the hospital after her flying accident. She'd been surprised, shocked, maybe even dismayed. And guilty. It had been written all over her. Guilt, and not just for not feeling the way he wanted her to feel. She'd been cheating on him. He knew it as surely as he'd ever known anything. There was somebody else.

He'd known it, truth to tell, from what the ops officer – Whitey, as they called him – had said when Joe arrived. Well, not exactly from what he'd said, maybe, more from what he hadn't said.

'Just what she needs, old boy.' And: 'Good luck.'

Now there was no room left for doubt. Or for hope either. Nancy had never got around to writing him a Dear John. Now she was going to deliver it in person.

'There's somebody else, isn't there?' he said.

'You know?' Nancy looked shocked. 'Who told you?'

Joe grinned crookedly. 'Nobody told me. They didn't need to. I'm not a complete fool, even if I look like one.'

'Oh, Joe . . . I am so sorry . . .'

'Who is he?' His voice was flat, conversational.

'A British pilot, a squadron leader. Joe, it's not what you think . . .'

'No?'

'No. Joe, I'm real fond of you, truly I am. I didn't mean for it to happen. It shouldn't have happened, but . . .'

'It did anyway.'

'Yes.' She broke off. He saw her eyes filling with tears. She bit her lip hard, closed her eyes and still those tears spilled out, coursing down her cheeks.

'Honey, don't cry.' He wanted to cry himself, but he wasn't going to. Not here. Not now. 'It's OK.'

Nancy shook her head wordlessly, pressed the back of her hand against her nose and mouth, swallowing hard.

'It's not OK. It's not OK at all.'

'You've met someone else. End of story.'

'No. Not end of story. Oh, Joe . . .' She gulped and began crying in earnest.

'Nancy, for Chrissakes . . .' He poured bourbon into her glass, pushed it across the table towards her. 'Come on, drink this. We're all adults here.'

She picked up the glass, draining it in one quick gulp. It didn't seem to help much. Joe felt overwhelmed with helplessness. Most things he could stand, but seeing Nancy crying like this was not one of them.

'Come on, honey, it's not so bad, surely.' He crouched down beside her, putting his arm around her shoulders, frustrated and a little angry even. Surely she was the one who should be comforting him, not the other way around.

'Oh, Joe.' She turned her head into his chest, burrowing into him as if she were a child. Her hair was silky soft against his cheek. It smelled of the soap she cut off a bar into shavings and mixed with water to make a kind of shampoo, and also, faintly, of aero fuel. It was almost more than he could stand, having her so close and knowing that he'd lost her. He steeled himself, stroking her back, holding her, until she had cried herself out. She sat back, scrubbing at her swollen, fluid pink eyes with the handkerchief he fished out of his pocket for her, gulping, blowing her nose.

'Oh Joe, I am so, so sorry.'

'I'll survive,' he said roughly.

For some reason that set her off again, except that this time she buried her face in her arms, which were resting in the middle of the newspaper which had wrapped the Spam fritters and chips and was still spread out on the table. Then, after a moment, she got up, pushing back the chair with such violence it almost toppled over, and paced the room like a caged animal, still crying bitterly.

'Nancy, for Chrissakes, stop this!' He was alarmed and puzzled now, at a loss to know what to do. He'd never seen her like this before and he was beginning to realise there was more to this than remorse. 'Come on, tell me what's wrong. Is he treating you bad, is that it? Jesus, he hasn't knocked you up and walked out on you, has he? If he's done something to hurt you, honey, I'll kill him with my bare hands.'

She shook her head, eyes still brimming. 'He's dead, Joe.'

His heart lurched. God help him, he could feel nothing but elation surging through his veins. Afterwards, when he remembered that moment, he cringed at his reaction and wondered what sort of man he was, but there, then, all he could feel was relief and that spark of hope reigniting deep inside him, a smouldering taper that refused to die and that her words had fanned back to life.

'Dead?' he repeated.

'I think so. His wing man saw him take a hit, but he didn't bail out. They've listed him as missing, but we all know what that means. Missing presumed dead.' She was calmer now, still sniffing, but calmer.

'When?' Joe asked.

'A week ago. Well, a week since I heard, anyway. It's just awful, waiting, not knowing for sure, though really there's not much hope, is there? And I haven't been able to talk to anyone about it, not really. I can't let it show just how I feel. I have to pretend . . . He was assistant station commander here before they drafted him back to his squadron, so everyone's upset about it, naturally. But not like I am. I couldn't let them see, or they'd know . . .'

'You mean they didn't?'

'No. Well, I don't think so. We tried to be discreet.'

'I guess . . . the assistant station commander and an American girl ferry pilot.' He couldn't contain the bitterness.

'Not just that. He has a wife.' She saw the censure that flared in Joe's eyes, and hurried on: 'She's real sick. In a coma, and has been for years. She was in an automobile accident at the beginning of the war, knocked off her bicycle by a car with blacked-out lights.' Her lip trembled again. 'What will happen to her? Judy? Mac paid for her to have special care. He'd want to know she's being looked after OK.'

'Let's not worry about that,' Joe said. 'She's got family to take care of all that, I shouldn't wonder.' He didn't add that this Mac hadn't worried much about his wife when he was alive, not enough to keep him from having an affair with Nancy, anyway. 'I reckon,' he said, 'that we could both do with another drink.'

He filled their glasses, put them and the bottle on an occasional table within easy reach of the overstuffed sofa, and sat down. Nancy came and sat beside him, cupping the glass between her hands and sipping frequently as she talked about Mac.

Joe didn't especially want to hear. In fact he did not want to hear at all. The sharp edge of jealousy was raw inside him; this unknown man had aroused feelings in Nancy that he would have given his right arm to arouse. He wondered if she would have been so distraught if it was his plane that had failed to come home, and ruefully concluded she would not. But then again, when something was snatched away from you it always made it the more desirable. If this Mac hadn't gone missing, presumed dead, then very likely the affair would just have run its course and petered out. He was *married*, after all, and the story about a sick wife sounded to Joe like a variation on 'my wife doesn't understand me'. Just an excuse to get his hands on a pretty girl who was a long way from home. Joe was beginning to feel indignant now, and impatient. But there was no doubt Nancy was in one hell of a state over it and needed to let it out. She was in the position of mistresses all over the world, sidelined when it came to the crunch, forced into secrecy and silence because some men just couldn't resist a piece of skirt on the side. So he gritted his teeth and let her talk, keeping her glass well topped up, battening down his anger, and retreating into his own thoughts.

'I should have told you, I know I should,' Nancy said. 'But I didn't know how. I knew you'd be so hurt, and I didn't want to hurt you. Hurting you is the last thing I want.'

Another nugget of hope. Did he have no pride? But it cheered him all the same. Nancy had thought it was a fleeting fancy too. She had been going to come back to him. It didn't stop it hurting. It didn't stop him from feeling a stupid idiot. If he was any sort of man he'd tell her to go to hell. But he couldn't. It was Nancy and he loved her, for better or for worse. To hell and back. And right now he was all she had.

Tenderness came flooding in, and he made up his mind. He wasn't going to go off back to his base and leave her like this if he could help it. She might not want him to stay, and if she didn't there was nothing he could do about it. But the thought of her here, alone and hurting, was more than he could stand.

'Look, honey, I'm due a couple of days' leave. If I can fix it, would you like me to stick around? No pressures, nothing like that. Just so there's someone here for you who knows what you're going through.'

She looked up at him with those tear-filled eyes.

'Oh, Joe, that is so kind. But I can't expect you to do that. Not now.'

'Honey, you need a friend. I'm offering. How about it now?'

She chewed on her lip, indecision written all over her face. Then she crumpled again, nodding almost imperceptibly.

'I would like that, yes.'

It was all he needed to hear.

Until she had Joe there to lean on, Nancy had not realised just how close to breaking point she had been.

She had forgotten too just what a rock he could be in times of trouble, forgotten his capacity for kindness and calm, forgotten how safe he made her feel. When she had first met him he had given her a sense of security that had been lacking in her transitory life, and she had grown to love him, she realised now, though her restlessness and thirst for life had made her struggle against the bars of the cage that love had imposed on her. More her own doing than Joe's, she realised. He had never sought to imprison her. Never tried to tie her down. And he wasn't now.

The love she felt for him wasn't the love she felt for Mac, of course. That had been a bright shooting star, a comet blazing so brightly from horizon to horizon it dimmed everything in its path. The love she felt for Joe was gentler, more comfortable, perhaps. A tenderness, a caring for his feelings that had kept her from telling him about Mac for so long, and a deep sense of gratitude.

In many ways, she realised, it was more like the love for a father, or the brother she had never had, whilst her love for Mac was sheer blinding passion. Joe was reality; Mac, even before his loss, had been a dream. Joe was solid and accepting; she needed him with every bit of her failing spirit and broken heart.

'I wish I didn't have to go, Nancy,' Joe said.

It was the last night of his hastily arranged leave; they were in Nancy's flat, where they had shared a vegetable cobbler that she had made.

'I wish you didn't have to,' she said, and meant it.

'Come here.'

He took her in his arms, stroking her hair, kissing her face tenderly, and she clung to him, dreading the abyss she knew she would plunge into once more when he was gone.

Just how it came to happen, neither of them was sure afterwards. Certainly neither of them intended it. But somewhere along the line their respective needs collided and fused. Joe's overwhelming love for Nancy, Nancy's desire for oblivion. They made love there on Nancy's narrow bed, and it was at once both blessed relief and anaesthetising balm. But afterwards, when Joe had gone, Nancy was overwhelmed by guilt. She had, she felt, betrayed both the men in her life. But most of all she had betrayed herself.

II

Even before she missed her first period Nancy knew she was pregnant. However much she tried to tell herself that the nausea she was experiencing was a result of her churning emotions and the niggling ache in the pit of her stomach the product of knotted nerves, she knew, with an undeniable certainty. She recognised the signs and trembled.

It wasn't the first time she had felt like this. She'd known then too that the peculiar twinges and the general malaise were the product of earth-shaking change in her body. The denial then had been all the greater, though. She had been seventeen years old and alone in the world, with no way of supporting a baby.

The father had been the boss of the air circus she was travelling with. William Eagle was the name he went by, though it was not the one he had been born with. He was forty-two years old and as ruthless as he was charismatic. When he had forced himself on her in the dark shadows of the barn where they'd stowed their gear for the night she had been too ashamed and frightened to tell anyone what he had done. He'd warned her what would happen if she complained: she'd be out of a job before her feet could touch the ground. Nancy knew it was no idle threat. The days of air circuses were almost over, there were scarcely any jobs any more in the world that was the only life she knew. The outfit was her home too, and her only family since the loss of her parents. She was terrified of losing it, and she didn't think William would try anything like that again. He'd been drunk at the time and she sure as heck hadn't made it fun for him, kicking and biting and screaming so that he'd had to press his hand over her mouth to keep her quiet. There were always girls in the venues they played ready to throw themselves at the good-looking daredevil stunt pilot; he wouldn't want a repeat of that fiasco.

She was right; though he was surly and unpleasant towards her, he never tried to touch her again. Trouble was, once had been enough. With a sick certainty that grew with the passing weeks, Nancy knew she was pregnant.

When she could keep it to herself no longer, she went to William to confront him with the consequences of what he had done. And predictably, William responded with what was, to him, the only solution. He snarled at Nancy that she would have to get rid of it, and made the arrangements for her to visit a backstreet abortionist in one of the towns they played.

When it was all over, Nancy had managed to put out of her mind the turmoil of those months when she had lived in a vacuum of dread and despair, and even managed to blot out the degradation and terrible pain of the abortion. What she had been unable to forget was that she had killed her baby. Maybe it had been conceived as a result of what was no more nor less than rape; maybe the despicable William Eagle was the father. But the baby had been hers too. She should have protected it. Instead she had colluded in allowing it to be murdered. The guilt and the grief had overwhelmed her; she felt utterly worthless.

Joe and the job he had offered her at Varna Aviation had been her salvation. Gradually the negative emotions had faded, though they had never completely gone away. She still ached sometimes for the baby she had allowed to be torn from her; still felt herself unworthy of love. But her natural resilience had sustained her so that she thought about it less and less often; it was almost as if the nightmare had happened to someone else. Flying had sustained her and gradually she regained some of her self-esteem. Her restlessness had reasserted itself; new experiences had filled the empty places inside her. But in the dark reaches of the night she still remembered sometimes, and wept.

And now the wheel had turned full circle. Once again a new life was growing inside her. Once again she had nothing to offer it. But Nancy knew there was no way on earth she would even contemplate taking the same escape route as she had allowed herself to be pushed into before. She couldn't save the baby she had lost on the filthy table in the abortionist's hellhole, but she could not, would not, reprise the solution that was no solution at all.

Lying awake night after night, Nancy wondered what she was going to do. She was fairly certain that once he knew about the baby, Joe would be anxious for her to marry him. He was no William Eagle; he was the kind of guy who believed that if you knocked up a girl, you married her, even if you didn't love her. And Nancy was as sure as she could be that Joe did still love her, in spite of everything.

The trouble was, she wasn't sure that they ought to go down that road. The prospect of committing to a lifetime's relationship still frightened her, and it seemed more wrong than ever, feeling the way she did about Mac. Fond of Joe as she was, she had glimpsed the strength of feeling that was possible between a man and a woman, what it was like to be drawn together, body and soul. Supposing by some miracle Mac should come back from the dead? She'd betray Joe in the blinking of an eye, she knew. It just wasn't fair on him to marry him without being totally, absolutely sure that she could make him happy.

The alternative was equally daunting. She couldn't imagine how she could manage to raise a child on her own. She'd have to go back to America, of course, but what then? She had a vision of a godforsaken trailer park, or an apartment in a seedy part of a seedy town, the only kind of accommodation she would be able to afford. It was no place to bring up a child. But somehow, she'd manage. She'd have to. Somehow she'd pull herself up by her boot strings. It seemed to Nancy it was the only way.

Joe had to be told, though. She owed him that.

She thought about writing, but dismissed it as too impersonal. This was something that she should tell him to his face. She managed to arrange to get down to his south coast base, and then, standing outside a pub, with the raucous laughter of the American aircrews who were relaxing there billowing out through an open window, she broke the news to him that he was to be a father.

'Oh my God!' he said. She looked at him, saw the blank astonishment on his face. 'Oh my God – are you sure?'

'Yes, sure,' she said.

'You mean – that night . . . ? Nancy, honey, I am so sorry.'

'My fault too. The thing is, I have to decide what to do.'

'Well, we'll get married, of course.' Exactly the reaction she'd expected.

'Joe, I've been thinking about that. I'm not sure it's a good idea.'

His eyes narrowed in an expression of consternation. 'What d'you mean, honey?'

'Joe, you know very well what I mean. When you asked me to marry you before I couldn't say yes because I just wasn't sure. And now, with – well, you know . . .' she couldn't bring herself to mention Mac's name, '. . . all the other stuff . . . I just don't think it would be right.'

'Not right to give our baby a proper home?'

'Well, yes, but—'

'You weren't thinking of getting rid of it, were you?' he asked, sounding worried.

'No, of course not. Absolutely not. I was just thinking that maybe it would be more honest for me to bring it up by myself. Fairer on you. It wouldn't be easy, I know that, but I could manage. Especially if you were to give me a little help. Financially, you know.'

'Well, of course! You don't think I'd see you go short, do you? What the hell do you think I am? But, Nancy, it's not good enough. A child needs a family. A father as well as a mother. A proper home. Are you telling me you'd really rather struggle on alone?'

She was silent, and he went on, fighting now for the girl who had been his life from the moment she walked in his door, fighting for her, whether she loved him or not. He could put up with that. He couldn't stand to lose her again. Her and their unborn child.

'Honey,' he said more gently, 'I know the way you feel right now. I know I ain't that Mac. But give us a chance, huh? We're good together. I know damned well there'll never be anyone but you for me, and I truly think that in time you'll come to feel the same. See that it was meant to be. Please, honey, don't make it

407

harder for all of us. Let's get married. I'll look after you and I'll look after our baby, and I promise I'll do everything I can to make you happy. Come on now, what do you say?'

There were tears sparkling in her eyes, but in the half-light he did not see them. What choice did she have? Nancy was wondering. When it came down to it, what choice? Joe was a really good man. He'd make a wonderful husband and father. And she wasn't deceiving him any more. He knew the score and still wanted her.

'Maybe you're right,' she said. 'Maybe it would be for the best.'

'You're saying yes?'

She nodded. He let out a whoop that caused a courting couple who were canoodling on the far side of the yard to break off and stare in astonishment, then pulled her into his arms.

'I promise you won't regret it, Nancy.'

She forced a smile, making up her mind that she would do the best she could to make theirs a happy marriage.

They were married on a crisp clear day in mid-October in a simple civil ceremony at the register office in Maidenhead. Kay Butler, Nancy's friend since they had come to England together at the very start of their service with the ATA, and Red Flaherty, a USAAF pal of Joe's, were the witnesses, and apart from them no one knew the reason behind the hastily arranged marriage even if they guessed at it. Nancy had not even intended to tell Kay, but the night before the wedding the two girls were sharing a bottle of champagne Kay had brought with her, courtesy, she said, of Jackie Cochran, and it had all come pouring out.

'He's a great guy, honey,' Kay said. She had met Joe earlier when they'd all had supper together at Skindles Hotel where Joe and Red Flaherty were staying. 'I remember you telling me about him way

408

back when we were on our way to England in that damned troop ship. I thought then he sounded pretty nice, and I was right.'

Nancy bit her lip, stared down at her glass where Jackie Cochran's champagne still bubbled lazily.

'He is nice.'

'Nancy,' Kay said perceptively, 'you aren't still carrying a candle for Mac, are you?' Nancy's silence gave her her answer. 'Then why the heck are you marrying Joe?' she asked in exasperation.

Nancy shrugged miserably. 'I don't have any choice.'

'Oh shucks, Nancy, you don't mean . . . ?'

'Yep. I'm pregnant.'

'Oh, you poor kid!'

'Don't pity me.' Nancy's voice was hard, brittle suddenly. 'Whatever you do, don't say a word. Because if you do, I am gonna crack up, and that is not gonna happen tonight. Or ever again, come to that. I've done enough cracking up to last me a lifetime. What's done is done. I'm gonna marry Joe, and I'm gonna be a real good wife to him – well, as good as I know how, which, to tell the truth, isn't very. But I'm sure as heck gonna do my best. He deserves that. It's not gonna be easy, forgetting Mac. I guess I won't. Ever. But that's something I'll be keeping to myself. From tomorrow I'll be Joe's wife, and in a few months or so I'll be a mother too. And I'm gonna give it my best shot, Kay. I won't be wasting time feeling sorry for myself. Joe deserves better than that. I'll be working at building something real good for him to come back to when the war's over.'

'You're going to have to leave the ATA . . . go home . . .' The thought had only just struck Kay.

''Fraid so,' Nancy said ruefully. 'I was looking forward to flying bombers too. I'll stay on as long as I can – if Joe'll let me. After tomorrow I guess it's up to him to call the shots. But I can't let them go to the trouble and expense of training me on the Halifax when I know I'm never gonna make first officer.'

'At least you'll be first officer in your own home,' Kay said, consoling.

Nancy had a fleeting – and sobering – image of Aunt Dorothy muscling in, trying to run the show.

'You can count on it,' she said grimly.

It wasn't so easy. It wasn't easy at all. Dorothy Costello had always been a martinet; now she had more excuse than ever, in her view, to keep an eye on Nancy. She was, after all, Joe's wife now, pregnant with his child. Nancy had no choice but to move into the house under Dorothy's wing; until Joe got home there was no way she could go about finding a home of their own, and Dorothy flatly refused to allow her back into the trailer she had occupied before going to England, insisting it just wasn't suitable for someone in her condition. Nancy lacked the will to argue with her; a sort of fatalistic lethargy had descended on her, smothering her usual vitality. It was almost as if nothing mattered any more. Except, of course, that it did. Dorothy's constant company was soon driving her mad, and this time round there was no escaping it. She was trapped, totally trapped, with a woman who thought she knew best about everything and imposed her opinions with the sanctimonious certainty that everything she did, she did for the good of her victim.

Though she had never had a child of her own, Dorothy suddenly became a world expert on impending motherhood. She bought some kind of revolting unction that she insisted Nancy should massage into her stomach and breasts, she prepared food for which Nancy had no appetite and practically stood over her while she ate it because, she said, Nancy had lacked proper nutrients in England, and needed feeding up. She bought a bottle of syrup of figs and presented it to Nancy each morning with her breakfast because it was important, she insisted, that Nancy 'keep regular'. She banished Nancy to her room for an hour every afternoon to rest; she carped about her footwear; she went out herself and bought two new, and vast, smocks, because in her opinion the dresses Nancy was still wearing were too revealing of her fast-increasing girth to be 'decent'. Nancy was a virtual prisoner and the days dragged endlessly, a penance to be served.

The last month of her pregnancy seemed the longest of all. Nancy loathed her huge inflated belly and swollen breasts; she thought she looked like one of the barrage balloons that she'd had to fly around at strategic sites back in England. And her time there had accustomed her to a cooler climate; the heat back here at home in Florida in June was unbearable to her. Her ankles swelled, her back ached, she was in permanent discomfort. And always, however hard she tried to suppress it, there was the raw grief for Mac and the deep-seated regret that somehow she had managed to get herself into this situation. How the hell could she have been so stupid? But it was too late now for regrets. She'd made her bed, as they said in England, now she had to lie on it. The present was unmitigated purgatory, the future an uninviting country she must plough through like Pilgrim's Slough of Despond.

Then, just when she thought it would never end, it did, and from the moment her baby was placed in her arms, everything was totally, utterly different.

It had been a long and difficult birth. The twinges in her lower back, not unlike period pains, began some time during the morning; by bedtime Nancy was thoroughly uncomfortable but still unsure

411

as to whether it was the onset of labour or just another ghastly stage to be lived through. She went to bed without mentioning it to Dorothy; the last thing she wanted was the infuriating woman fussing around her. She couldn't sleep, though. The pains were definitely getting worse, gripping cramps that made her squirm and wriggle and groan quietly to herself. She put up with them until the first light began to soften the sky, unwilling to disturb Dorothy, but beginning to become a little alarmed. She was up and pacing the bedroom when the door opened and Dorothy looked in – she had woken and heard Nancy moving about.

'You've started,' she said. Her mouth was pinched, disapproving, as if somehow it was Nancy's fault, not nature working, but her chins quivered with suppressed excitement and her plump, night-gown-clad body exuded importance.

Nancy nodded, fighting the onset of another contraction.

'Just let me get some clothes on, and we'll call a cab and go to the hospital.'

'There's no need for you to come with me,' Nancy protested. 'I'll be OK.'

'As if I'd let you go all alone! Joe would never forgive me.'

At that moment, Nancy was hating Joe with a vengeance.

'This isn't about Joe. It's about me.'

'And suppose you deliver the baby right there in the cab? Oh, no, I'm coming with you, that's for sure.'

Fleetingly, it occurred to Nancy to wonder how much use Dorothy would be if such a thing should happen. But in the event it was not put to the test. Though when the cab deposited her at the clinic and the doctor was able to examine her he told Nancy the baby would likely be born within a few hours, morning became afternoon and afternoon evening and still the baby had not arrived.

Sweating profusely, dazy with drugs, Nancy heard them saying something about the baby being 'the wrong way round'. She hadn't a clue what that meant; nobody had discussed such a possibility with her, and frankly she really didn't care. She just wanted this torture to end. The doctor and midwives examined her frequently, pushing and prodding her and listening to the baby's heartbeat, but Nancy was too lost in a sea of pain to take much notice. The mounting concern was quite lost on her. Even when she heard the words 'Caesarean section' they barely registered. But perhaps her body understood and rebelled. Suddenly, miraculously, the baby was coming and she heard the joyous words of an ecstatic nurse: 'Hey, Mrs Costello, you've got a lovely baby boy.'

Half an hour later, utterly spent, Nancy was straddled into stirrups, being stitched. She ran her hands over her stomach, flabby now, like a Jello, and squinted at the nurse beside her bed.

'My baby! Where's my baby?'

'He's right here, Mrs Costello.'

Nancy couldn't see him. All she could see was a crib that looked like a plastic box and another nurse bending over it, doing Nancy knew not what. Panic flooded her; she struggled against the constraints of the stirrups.

'Is he OK? Oh, please tell me he's OK!'

'He's fine, Mrs Costello. Just lie still now . . .'

Nancy was filled with the panicking conviction they were keeping something from her. The birth had taken too long, and what the hell was that nurse doing to her baby? The long labour was forgotten now; all her heartache and doubts, her grief for Mac, her pessimism for the future, had disappeared. Nothing mattered but the scrap of new life that she had carried inside her for nine long months. Nancy was back in another room in another life where a gelatinous mass and a foetus that would never draw breath lay like so much garbage in a tin bowl.

'My baby!' she screamed. 'I want my baby!'

'It's OK, Mrs Costello.' The nurse by the crib moved aside and Nancy caught her first glimpse of him, slippery with blood and mucus, resting on a gauze. The nurse placed him on a set of scales, noted his weight – seven pounds three ounces – wrapped him in a blue blanket and approached the bed.

'Here you go, Mrs Costello. Your son. Do you have a name for him?'

'John,' Nancy said. They'd agreed it in the letters they exchanged, she and Joe. 'We're gonna call him John.'

She opened her arms, and the nurse placed the small firm bundle in them. She cradled him to her breast, looking down in wonder at the glistening black cap of hair covering a head that had squashed into a pointy shape in the long time he had taken to be born, at a button nose, a small pursed mouth, and ears squashed flat against his skull, and fell in love. Her baby. The most perfect thing in the whole universe.

At that moment, as the love welled in her, Nancy knew that nothing in the rest of her life would ever be the same, and she didn't want it to be. She'd go through hell and high water for this child. Whatever she had lost, whatever she would miss, he was worth it. Her baby. Not her first born, but all the more precious for that. A miracle she didn't deserve.

For the first time in her entire life, Nancy knew pure, unadulterated bliss.

Dorothy, naturally, tried to take over the baby as she had tried to take over Nancy. She was now the world's number one expert on breast-feeding and swaddling, fresh air and sleep patterns. With a return of her old confidence, Nancy ignored her and did things in the way she felt instinctively to be right. There were moments of terror, when she was overwhelmed by the responsibility of caring for this tiny, needy human being, but mostly she felt serene and empowered in a way she would never have believed possible.

And John was the easiest of babies. He cried when he was hungry, fed efficiently, and fell asleep again on her breast. He grew at the rate he was supposed to, he kicked happily when she bathed him or changed his diaper. It was Dorothy he sprayed once like a miniature fountain when she was attending to him; thereafter Dorothy left the messy business to Nancy, standing at a safe distance whilst still offering nuggets of advice.

She didn't like being disturbed in the night, either. When John woke in the wee small hours demanding to be fed, Nancy would take him out onto the porch and sit with him at her breast in the big old rocking chair, gazing at the stars and feeling at one with the universe. The peace was profound; hard to believe that this was a world at war. That on the other side of the Atlantic, guns were blazing, shells splintering the sky, bombers. Joe's maybe, unleashing their deadly cargoes. Well, not at this minute, maybe, given the time difference. But the aftermath would be there, death and destruction. Here, everything was as it always had been, the buildings still standing, the landscape unspoiled. There was only the occasional roar of an aircraft flying out of the base at Tampa to break the silence of the night.

Nancy breathed in the perfume of hibiscus along with the sweet baby smell of her beloved son and counted her blessings. This was her special time, a prison no longer, rather a sanctuary in her turbulent life. She wished it could last for ever.

* * *

During the spring and early summer of 1944 the war in Europe moved inexorably towards its climax. In April a victorious Red Army had powered through the Crimea; in May the resistance of the Axis powers was broken in Italy. And in England, preparations were underway for the D-day landings in Normandy, France.

Nancy, of course, knew nothing of what was going on at the time, but when they met up years later Kay was able to tell her of the heightened sense of excitement that had prevailed at the ATA ferry pools. Everyone was aware something big was afoot, though at the time the date of the landings was a matter of utmost secrecy. The girls only knew that the skies were full of wave upon wave of bombers on their way to their pre-invasion targets, the railroads and marshalling yards in France, and a large part of their work was delivering Stirlings to the new airfields of Keevil and Fairford. There, and in the skies, they noticed that gliders were multiplying like greenfly on the roses on a humid summer's day. Some of these were being painted with black and white 'invasion' stripes, or so one of the women pilots reported when she returned from delivering a Mosquito to Hullavington. But exactly what was planned could only be speculated upon. Only the chosen few knew the truth, that troop ships were being mustered as far away as the Clyde in Scotland and Scapa Flow, and that meteorological reports had been pored over to decide when flying conditions to provide air cover would be likely to coincide with the moon and tides that would give the best possible chance of a successful invasion. In fact, the best-laid plans had almost gone awry when a spell of hot fine weather suddenly gave way to a series of depressions, but by then it was too late to call off the operation. In the early hours of Monday, 5 June, the order to go ahead was finally given; late that night the first aircraft left Harwell crammed with airborne troops bound for Normandy. D-day had begun.

Like millions of others the world over, Nancy followed the news of the invasion. First the tricolour was fluttering over Cherbourg, then the Nazi armies were being driven from Normandy, and at last, in August, came the news that Paris had been liberated. Nancy could only guess at the role the ATA were playing, ferrying now into and out of Europe as well as the relatively local 'hops' she had made, but it all seemed a lifetime as well as half a world away. Her life now was here in Florida, mother to John and wife to Joe. Please God he would return safely.

Her prayer was answered sooner than she expected. With the focus of the conflict turning towards Japan and the east, Joe was posted back to the US, to MacDill, the South-East Air Base at Tampa, just a short hop up the coast from Varna. He might still be a USAAF pilot, his war might not be over, but Joe was coming home.

III

Once Joe was back on American soil it was all he could do to keep from going AWOL to be with Nancy and John. He was a homebody at heart, and almost from the first moment he had met Nancy he had wanted nothing more than to settle down with her. Now he yearned not only for her but for his son too.

John was six months old when Joe first saw him, and instantly he was filled with wonder that this beautiful, robust child could really be his. He stared in awe at the plump, fair-haired baby in Nancy's arms, afraid for a moment to touch either of them in case they were just some figment of his imagination and they both disappeared like a fading dream.

'Gee,' he said softly.

Nancy was smiling, whether from pride in her son or pleasure at seeing him, Joe neither knew nor cared. She was wearing a floral cotton dress, her hair freshly washed, curling round her lovely, impish face, her lips reddened with a touch of rouge. The baby, John, was all in white, a silk smocked romper suit that buttoned onto little shorts from which dimpled legs protruded. His eyes were wide and blue, patches of red colour high in his cheeks because he was teething.

'Gee,' he said again.

'Well, aren't you gonna give us a hug?' Nancy said.

He shook his head, laughing at his own ineptitude, and put his arms round both of them, very carefully, so as not to squash the baby. Over his head, he kissed Nancy, and John lay between them, not an obstruction but a bond.

'Hey, you take him,' Nancy said.

'Can I?'

'Well, of course you can! It's high time he got to know his pa.'

She placed John in his arms and though the baby turned his head anxiously so as not to lose sight of his mother he did not wail or even whimper, as Joe half expected him to. Joe was surprised at the weight of him and how solid his round little body felt; surprised too at the way his heart contracted. Like most men, he'd never given much thought to babies. He'd had his dreams of how it would be with his son, of course, a little boy growing up into a bigger boy that he could do man things with, but babies . . . well, it was women who cooed and liked to make a fuss of them when all they did was cry and puke and mess their diapers. In that moment he realised he had been wrong. There was no mistaking that this was a small person. He was looking at Joe now, those wide blue eyes trained in fierce concentration on Joe's face, and his chubby fingers plucked at a button on Joe's uniform jacket.

'Well hello, son,' he said.

Somehow he managed to juggle John into the crook of one arm without dropping him, then slid the other round Nancy. His throat was full; he had to blink because he could feel moisture gathering in his eyes.

It seemed to Joe that he held the world in his arms.

'Did you hear Glenn Miller is missing?' Nancy said.

'No way!'

'He is too. He was flying to France to play for the troops, but he never made it. They never got a distress call from him or anything, and there's no sign of the wreckage. Looks like he's had it.'

'Gee, that's a shame. I like Glenn Miller.'

'Me too. Especially "Moonlight Serenade".'

'And "In the Mood".'

Nancy and Joe were out on the porch in the cool of the evening. John was asleep upstairs in his crib and Dorothy had tactfully taken herself off to visit a friend who lived just down the street. The heat of the day still hung in the air, capturing the scent of the hibiscus, and crickets chirped their endless symphony. Nancy and Joe sat side by side on the hammock, smoking, comfortable and easy in one another's company as if the time they'd been apart and all that had happened since they had last shared a cigarette on Dorothy's porch had never been.

'Well, if this isn't just like old times,' Joe said after a moment.

'Except that now we've got a baby.' John was never far from Nancy's thoughts.

'Yep.' Joe tossed his cigarette butt onto the driveway where it glowed briefly like a firefly in the gathering dusk. 'I've got something for you, though, Nancy, from way back then.' He fished into his pocket, pulled out a small square box she recognised. 'It's a bit late, I reckon, but better late than never. I could have told you where to find it, but I wanted to give it to you myself.'

He opened the box, took out the ring he'd bought for her before he'd left to join the USAAF. 'This has been waiting for you, honey. It's a real good job you didn't make me take it back to the jewellery store.'

He took her hand and slid the ring onto her finger so that it sat above her plain gold wedding band. It was a little tight; her knuckles had swelled a bit along with her ankles when she was pregnant and never quite gone back to the size they had been before. Her throat closed.

'Oh, Joe . . .'

'You don't know how proud that makes me, honey, seeing my rings on your finger. And knowing you and our son are gonna be here waiting for me next time I get home. Reckon I'm the luckiest man alive.'

'I'm the lucky one, Joe. I don't deserve—'

He put a finger on her lips. 'Don't say a word, honey. What's past is past. We've got the future to look forward to now.' For Joe, it was quite a speech. He pulled her close, kissed her, and a wave of tenderness enveloped Nancy.

'I do love you, Joe,' she said softly, and knew it was nothing less than the truth.

He wasn't Mac. He didn't stir in her the volcanic emotions she felt for Mac and never could. But there were many kinds of love, she knew that now, and none of them detracted from the others. There was room in your heart for all of them; the all-consuming love she felt for John had shown her that. The love she felt for Joe was gentler and sweeter than the painful, demanding passion she had experienced with Mac, and which had consumed her like a forest fire. But it was the enduring kind, growing slowly like a seedling, unfurling its leaves and sending out shoots to twine around her heart instead of bursting like a star shell in the night sky. And whilst it might not reach the heights, it did not have the power to send her plummeting to the depths either. Loving Joe was not an adventure but a safe haven.

A part of her still mourned Mac, still yearned for him, and always would. But Nancy was weary of turbulent emotions that tossed her like a leaf caught in a tornado. She loved Joe for his patience and his steadfastness, and for loving her. As she had begun to say before he stopped her, she had been luckier than she deserved.

Nancy made a vow that she would never again hurt Joe. She took his hand, smiled up at him.

'Let's go to bed,' she said.

The Germans were struggling. France had been liberated and the Allies were closing in on Berlin. It could only be a matter of weeks now, everyone said, before the war in Europe was over, though it would probably take a bit longer to break the Japs. Nancy hoped wholeheartedly that they were right. Too many lives had been lost already; now she could reflect on it from a distance it sickened her. Please God the warmongers had learned their lesson here. She didn't want John growing up in a world where life was held so cheaply. And she prayed that he would never be called on to put his life on the line in the name of liberty.

But there was no doubt about it, it had had to be done. If ever she had had any doubts about that the concentration camps the Allies were liberating were proof of the evil the Nazis were capable of. She and Dorothy had pored in horror over the newspaper reports of what the Red Army had discovered at Auschwitz where Jews from all over Europe had been sent to be slaughtered, starved or worked to death.

'You just can't believe the wickedness of it,' Dorothy said, shaking her head so that her triple chins wobbled. 'It says here they found mounds of corpses, all just skin and bone. Will you look – just look! It's terrible.'

'Don't let's talk about it,' Nancy said. Although she knew Dorothy was as shocked as any other decent, right-minded person, Nancy could not help but feel her interest bordered on the ghoulish. And in any case, the reports of the concentration camps upset her for quite another reason. She still wondered sometimes if Mac might have survived whatever had happened to his plane and been captured by the enemy; if this was what the Nazis had done to millions of innocent civilians, then the chances were they wouldn't treat their prisoners of war any better. She couldn't bear to think of Mac starved to a skeleton; it was almost preferable to think of him as having died. At least that way his suffering would have been short-lived and his dignity preserved.

Mostly, however, she tried not to think about Mac. That way led to madness. Her days were full caring for John and helping Dorothy keep house, which was becoming more and more demanding by the day. Dorothy wasn't well; she seemed to be finding everything a dreadful effort, though she still issued instructions from the depths of her armchair and had enough energy to criticise and pontificate – more, in fact, since she now expended it on little else. Though she too doted on John, Nancy wondered if having a baby in the house was too tiring for her, but when Nancy suggested they should look for a home of their own, Dorothy would have none of it.

'Joe wouldn't want that. This is his home. Where's the sense in me rattling round here all alone and you doing the same some-place else? I never heard such a silly idea in all my life!'

Nancy sighed and resigned herself to the inevitable. At least Joe was not flying operations any more. He was now training new pilots at MacDill, Tampa, which undoubtedly he was very good at. His experience, coupled with his patience, made him the ideal instructor. And his new role meant he could get home often. Life settled into a pattern, and though the old restlessness stirred from time to time, Nancy was content.

Early May 1945, and all the wireless channels were buzzing with the news that Germany had surrendered. The war in Europe, at least, was over.

Nancy was in the laundry room, struggling through a pile of ironing, when she heard it, an interruption to the music programme she'd had on to pass the time. Excited, she scooped up John, who was amusing himself with a 'treasure bag' she'd prepared to keep him occupied – a variety of kitchen implements stuffed into a cloth sack – and rushed into the living room to share the news with Dorothy.

'Hey, what d'think . . . ?' She stopped short in the doorway. Dorothy was no longer in the wing chair where Nancy had left her reading one of her favourite romantic novels. She was lying on the floor, face down, spread-eagled like a beached whale.

'Oh my God.' Nancy went cold with panic. She dumped John in the playpen in the corner of the room. He wailed in protest; he wasn't used to being confined by a wooden cage, even if it did have rows of beads, which were supposed to amuse him, structured into it. For once, Nancy ignored him. 'Mrs Costello! Mrs Costello, are you OK?'

A stupid question, since she clearly was not OK. Nancy took her by the shoulder, heaving, but Dorothy's bulk was too much for her.

'Oh my God,' Nancy said again. In that moment she was convinced Dorothy was dead. Then she caught the sound of laboured breathing, and Dorothy groaned. Nancy grabbed up a cushion from the sofa, placed it under Dorothy's head, and dropped to her knees beside Joe's aunt.

'Can you hear me, Mrs Costello? What is it? What's wrong?'

'Pain . . . in my chest. Oh Nancy, Nancy . . .'

A heart attack. Dorothy was having a heart attack. 'Hold on, I'll get help.' Nancy ran for the telephone and dialled. Her own heart was pounding, her mouth was dry. John was yelling loudly now, indignant and frightened too. His cries almost drowned her out as the operator answered and she gasped: 'Ambulance, please. I need an ambulance, right now. Oh, please, come quickly!'

They were, thank goodness, very quick. Nancy, with John in her arms, went with Dorothy in the ambulance to the hospital, where she was whisked away by medical staff. Nancy could do nothing but wait.

It was more than an hour before a doctor came to find her and told her that Dorothy had indeed suffered a heart attack and would have to be admitted.

'Is she going to be OK?' Nancy asked.

The doctor looked old, tired and tetchy. The younger medical staff had gone off to join the military, Nancy assumed, and he had been pulled out of a comfortable retirement that involved a good deal of golf and sailing to cover for them.

'Too early to say,' he growled. 'At her size and weight she sure hasn't done herself any favours.'

'So . . . what happens now?'

'We'll do our best to stabilise her, that's all I can say. She does have medical insurance, I take it?'

426

'I don't know . . .'

'Well, I sure hope so. If she does pull through, she's going to need a lot of nursing. Are you her daughter?'

'No, she's my husband's aunt, but we live with her. She hasn't got anyone else.' Nancy's mind was racing, and she was sick with anxiety. Besides this, she felt oddly guilty and responsible, somehow, for what had happened. 'Can I see her?'

John had begun to cry again; he was hungry and his diaper needed changing. The doctor scowled at him. 'A hospital room is no place for infants.'

Nancy, her nerves in tatters, snapped, 'You think I don't know that? You think I'd have brought him with me if I hadn't had to? I only want to see her for a minute, give her my love and tell her everything's gonna be fine.'

'I'll have a nurse pass on your message. And that you'll be back when you've arranged for child care.' He turned away, impatient to be gone, and Nancy was left fuming. Didn't he care that she was worried sick? Couldn't he see she was at her wits' end? If that was the way he treated his patients, she felt sorry for them. But there was nothing more she could do right now. And he was probably right about one thing: John's crying would be upsetting the other patients.

Nancy found a bench outside the hospital and tried to feed John, but he was practically weaned now and her milk almost dried up. She no longer had enough to satisfy him. He cried all the way home, and by the time they arrived, Nancy felt like crying too.

It might be Victory in Europe, but here in Varna, it felt as though World War Three had broken out.

*   *   *

427

Dorothy was still in the hospital two weeks later. Joe had managed to get home for a couple of days and he and Nancy had discussed a plan of action. Thank heavens she did have medical insurance, but that wouldn't cover her care when she was discharged, and the doctor had told them that she would be bedridden for the foreseeable future. The slightest exertion could bring on another attack.

'We're gonna have to bring her bed downstairs,' Nancy said. 'And . . .' she hesitated over the prospect, 'I guess we'll have to fix her up with a commode.'

Joe shook his head, looking worried. 'This is gonna be hard on you, honey.'

'I'm not looking forward to it, that's for sure,' Nancy said. 'But what's gotta be done has gotta be done.'

'You're a jewel, honey.' He went to put his arms round her; Nancy twisted away. She didn't feel like a jewel. She felt trapped and resentful, filled with dread at the thought of having to nurse a woman she'd never liked very much.

Nancy visited the hospital regularly. It wasn't easy getting across town with a baby, but she knew Dorothy looked forward to seeing them both, so most days she took the trolley, which set her down almost at the entrance to the hospital. The boarding stop was some distance from the house, though, so she walked that, carrying John on her shoulders, because getting the buggy onto the trolley caused too much disruption to the other passengers.

On the Thursday of the second week, Nancy made the trip as usual. It was a hot, humid day and when she came out of the hospital she saw that storm clouds had begun to gather, dark and threatening, over the sea. She swore softly to herself.

'Gee, John, I hope we get home before that lot strikes land. If not, we're gonna get a wetting.'

She watched the sky anxiously from the windows of the trolley. The sun was no longer visible, hidden in a luminescent haze, and slanting sometimes in bright rods through the heavy cloud. Nancy began to wish she'd given visiting a miss today. Dorothy hadn't even seemed that pleased to see them; she'd spent the entire hour they'd been there grumbling about one thing and another. She didn't like the food, the other patients were driving her crazy, she needed a new nightdress, her hair wanted cutting. It was a sure sign she was feeling better, Nancy thought, which had to be good. But it was tiresome to have to listen to her carping whilst trying to keep John amused and chasing after him as he scooted across the tiled floor every few minutes. He was crawling now, and when he chose, he could move like greased lightning, arms and legs working like pistons, romper-clad bottom raised high in the air.

When the trolley reached their stop Nancy got off, hoisted John up onto her shoulders and set off at as fast a pace as she could manage in the overbearing heat. Maybe they were going to make it after all before the storm broke.

As she turned into their street she thought it looked as if there was a car parked on the driveway of Dorothy's house. Couldn't be. Joe's was the only car in the family, and he wasn't due home. Besides, his car was grey and this one black. It must be on the drive next door, and this peculiar light was playing tricks with perception. Must be. But as she got closer, she could see she had not been mistaken. The car certainly was on their driveway.

Nancy's first thought was that someone must have come visiting Dorothy. She had family up in Daytona and though contact between them was minimal, Nancy had let them know Dorothy was ill. She could only imagine they had made the trip down to see her. Nancy hastened her step. If they'd come all this way and found no one home it was not much of a welcome.

She turned into the driveway, squinting at the car. Whoever it was was still sitting inside. As she approached, the driver's door opened and a man uncoiled himself and got out. Tall and lean, wearing a white shirt and tan-coloured trousers. Dark hair springing away from an angular face. Nancy stopped short, her heart seeming to stop beating and the world stopping with it.

This wasn't real; it couldn't be. She caught a quick gasping breath and it came out on a shocked sigh that sounded like a question.

'Mac?'

He smiled at her, that crooked grin that had always had a direct line to her heart.

'Hello, Nancy.'

In years to come when Nancy recalled that moment she saw it as a kaleidoscope of chaotic emotions. Disbelief, bewilderment, and something that might almost have been shyness. But most of all joy, overwhelming, ecstatic joy. She had thought he was dead, or at the very least a prisoner in one of those terrible POW camps. She'd never expected to see him again. But he was here, whole and alive, not maimed or disfigured like some of the returned soldiers she had seen at the hospital whilst visiting Dorothy. She wanted to touch him, to make sure he was real and not some figment of her imagination. She wanted to throw her arms around him, hold him, feel him holding her. But she couldn't move. She could only stand staring at him, open-mouthed, tears filling her eyes.

'Mac! Oh my God – Mac! What are you doing here? I thought . . . They said you were missing, presumed dead.'

'Takes more than Jerry to kill me.'

'But . . .' There were too many questions. She didn't know where to begin. And yet the answers were unimportant, mere details. Mac was alive. Nothing else really mattered.

The first heavy spots of rain began to fall. She felt them on her face, cool and refreshing. She rummaged in her bag for her keys, hoisted John from her shoulders and settled him instead on her hip.

'We'd better go inside.'

She unlocked the door, led the way into the house. The living room looked untidy. It was cluttered now with the dining table and chairs they'd moved in from the diner to make room for Dorothy's bed in readiness for her return home, a pile of laundry waiting to be ironed was stacked in a chair, the toys John had been playing with before they left for the hospital scattered about the floor. Ashamed, she dumped John in his playpen and put a few of the toys in with him. Immediately, he pulled himself up on the bars, trying to climb out.

'Oh . . .' She lifted John out again, set him down on the rug. Better to have him scooting round the floor than setting up a clamour of protest.

'Can I get you something to drink?' she asked Mac, for all the world as if he were an unexpected visitor, not the man she loved, come back from the dead. 'Iced tea? A highball? A beer?' And then burst out laughing. 'Oh, Mac, I don't believe it! What happened to you? I thought you were dead!'

'I'll tell you all about it in a minute. But first of all . . . come here.'

He pulled her to him, kissing her, holding her as if he'd never let her go. Nancy melted into him, her world reduced to the circle of his arms. She couldn't think straight, couldn't think of anything

431

but the overwhelming joy, his hunger and her own. Then John was tugging at the hem of her skirt, grunting the strange guttural sounds that would soon become his first words, and she eased away.

'It's OK, John. Play with your toys, there's a good boy.' She beamed up at Mac. 'I'll get you that drink. What was it you fancied?'

'You.'

She giggled again from sheer happiness. 'Behave! Beer, highball, iced tea. What's it to be?'

'OK, if you're not on the menu at the moment, I'll have beer.'

She practically skipped into the kitchen, found the beer in the ice box where it had been since Joe's last visit home. She poured one for Mac and another for herself. This was surreal. When she took them back into the living room, Mac was hunkered down beside John, pushing a toy car across the floor. He squinted up at her.

'This must have been a hell of a shock for you. It certainly was for me. But my goodness, he's a real corker.'

His words brought her up short and her throat closed as she realised what he meant. Mac thought John was his. It hadn't occurred to her before that he might, she had been too excited and happy to see him. Now . . . oh my God, Mac thought John was his. Nancy suddenly wanted to cry.

'Your beer.' She held it out to him. 'Mac, before we go any further, we have to talk. I want to know how come you're here in one piece, and . . . well, I've got a few things to tell you . . .'

'OK.' He took the glass from her. 'You go first, while I get some of this down me.'

She swallowed hard at the lump in her throat. She honestly did not know where to begin.

'No, you,' she said.

IV

God, but it was good to see her again. Mac looked at Nancy over the rim of his glass and drank her in along with the beer. There hadn't been a day they'd been apart that he hadn't thought of her. He'd pictured her face, her impish grin, the way she puckered her lip with her teeth when she was perplexed, and even in his darkest moments it had made him smile. Now he was looking at her in the flesh and she was even lovelier than he remembered her, rounder, somehow, softer. Motherhood had done that to her, he supposed.

How the hell it had happened he didn't know. He'd thought he'd been careful. Obviously not careful enough! Just as well he hadn't known when he was stuck in France and Switzerland. He'd have gone crazy if he had. As it was, he hadn't known a thing about it until he got back to England and learned that she had married Joe and gone back to America – one hell of a shock, which had got him where it really hurt. The consensus of opinion among the people at White Waltham was that she was pregnant by Joe. But Mac knew better. He imagined the way it had been – Nancy alone and frightened, thinking he had been killed in action, taking the only way out she knew, and it wrenched his gut. But there was nothing he could do about it. He was married, she was married now too, and in any case, he was back on active service almost immediately.

But circumstances had changed now. He was here, with her and their son. And Mac knew that he wasn't going to leave, if he could help it, without them.

When he had taken off with his squadron that night back in September 1943, Mac had never for one moment thought that it would be almost a year before he set foot once again on English soil. There was always the possibility that you would not come back at all; that was something every flyer lived with, fighter and bomber boys alike. But it didn't do to think about it too much, and when you did, it was more in terms of which of your friends would not be coming back. You never considered that the blank space on the ops room blackboard that never got filled in with the magic words 'time landed' might be the one beside your own name. That way led to madness.

Since returning to active service, Mac had been flying Beaufighters and they were a totally different proposition from the Spitfires and Hurricanes he'd flown before. Some pilots loved them, singing the praises of the excellent forward vision and the sense of security that came from being sandwiched between two massive Hercules engines that would stop shrapnel, shells and bullets that might come from the side or the two front quarters, and enthused by the fire power – four cannons and six Browning guns. But the vast majority disliked the Beaufighter. There was no nose to line up with the end of the runway on takeoff, the engines were none too reliable, and the sheer weight of the plane made handling difficult, especially in tight turns.

Mac had been amused by one of the stories that was told. Way back at the beginning of the war a certain squadron had dubbed the Beaufighter 'the suicide ship' and been on the point of refusing to fly it. One foggy day when no flying was possible they had been sitting around discussing this rogue of a plane when one whistled in over their heads, pulled up in a stall turn, dropped its wheels and flaps and made a perfect landing on the runway. The men had assumed the Beau was being flown by a crack test pilot, come to show them how it should be done. As they clustered round the plane, eager for all the gen, a white flying suit emerged, topped by a mane of blonde hair, and jaws dropped as the men realised this was no test pilot, but one of the ATA girls delivering a plane. The squadron, it was said, never complained about the awkwardness of Beaus again.

Mac wasn't surprised by this story. From his own experience, a good girl pilot was very, very good, and the ATA had the best. He thought again of Nancy, with her light touch and aerobatic skills, and was proud. He had no problems with the Beau himself. The only thing that took some getting used to as far as he was concerned was that he was no longer flying solo, but carrying a radio operator/observer as a passenger. The Beau was equipped with Serrate, a home receiver that picked up on enemy radar impulses, and it was up to the observer to operate the equipment and give the pilot directions that would bring him to within a few hundred yards of the German bomber so that he could take a shot at it.

Mac was feeling a bit jaded, though, that night in September 1943. He should have been daisy fresh – the night before had been a 'night off'. But there had been a party in the officers' mess with a famous striptease artiste billed to appear. Parties at the station were legendary; there was always someone who had contacts in the world of show business. Unsurprisingly, the turnout for the stripper was even greater than usual, and with drink flowing freely, it had been three in the morning before Mac left.

'Good night last night, wasn't it?' 'Dai' Renshaw, his partner, commented as they kitted up for the tour of duty. 'What that girl couldn't do with a tassel and a feather . . . Phwah!'

Mac's head was throbbing. 'D'you have to shout, Dai? Put a sock in it, can't you?'

'What's up, Mac? Having trouble keeping pace with us young 'uns?'

Dai was a sergeant, nineteen years old, fresh-faced and as full of enthusiasm as a young puppy. He made Mac feel old as Methuselah. But he was a good lad, and a whiz on the Serrate – when he could be persuaded to forget about the women who flocked around the fighter boys, and enticed away from the WAAF 'glamour girls' who worked in the ops room.

The night's work had begun much like any other. Whilst many of the Beaufighter squadrons were employed hunting down the mine-layers who were such a hazard to shipping, and others were flying night-time ranger patrols over France, Belgium and Holland to attack any enemy surface transport they could set their sights on, the one Mac was serving with gave support to the bombers operating over Germany and occupied Europe. The target that night was a cluster of factories close to the French/German border that manufactured, amongst other things, ball bearings that were vital to the German war effort. The squadrons that were to escort the bombers had already left; Mac's squadron of Beaus was the target-withdrawal wing; their job was to arrive in the target area as the bombers turned for home, assist in any scraps, and mop up any stragglers.

They flew in over the French coast, dodging the flak that splintered in bright shards around them and looked for all the world like the sparks from a giant Golden Rain firework on 5 November. Though he had Dai with him as observer, Mac kept a sharp lookout for German fighters; after his years flying solo it was second nature. But he saw nothing.

The open fields beneath them began to give way to a sprawl of heavy industrial buildings, and now Mac saw the glow of a huge fire burning out of control on the horizon. The bombers had hit their target by the look of it and would be turning for home. But the night sky was crisscrossed with bright streaks of gunfire and Mac knew the Luftwaffe had no intention of letting them get away unscathed.

Mac issued an instruction to his flight and they went in, a neat formation that would soon be divided into its separate parts. The P47s escorting the bombers had bounced two Me109s; they broke away and Mac followed one, lowering his nose to gain speed. The Beau began to whistle, the eerie sound that had gained the plane the nickname of 'Whispering Death', but Mac scarcely noticed. His whole being was concentrated on squinting through the ring sight and flexing his fingers against the twister-ring on the firing button. Almost right; another ring deflection, maybe, and . . . now! The air was suddenly torn apart by an ear-splitting explosion and lit as if by a searchlight as his four cannons and six machine guns blazed into the night. The canopy flew off the Me109 and the plane dropped like a stone, a mass of orange flame.

Flying through the debris, Mac turned again and saw Lieutenant Dodds, his wing man, firing doggedly at another Messerschmitt until it fell in flames. But another group of Me109s was closing in, their guns spitting fire. One shot caught the canopy of Mac's Beau, shattering the Perspex so that razor-sharp shards grazed his face; a cannon shell punched through the fuselage to the rear. He heard Dai scream, a thin, unearthly sound, and knew he had been hit.

Suddenly Mac's veins were pumping not just adrenalin, but fury. He kicked hard on the rudder bar and turned on the attackers, stabbed at the firing button, scarcely bothering to line up the ring sight. He hit the bastard with a volley of shot, saw the Me109 turn over, recover, and dive steeply. Mac followed him, opening fire again at close range, and the Luftwaffe plane spiralled down, trailing flame and thick black smoke in its wake.

His satisfaction was short-lived. Two more Me109s were coming for him. At once he took evasive action, somehow positioning himself to come down on them from five o'clock high. They broke in opposite directions; he followed one, opened fire and with less than a hundred yards separating them, managed to blow the tail off the 109. He saw the pilot bail out, and the German fighter plane nose-dived earthwards.

As he turned again to rejoin his flight Mac realised the second of the two 109s had come around on to his tail. Again he began evasive action, swooping, circling, turning, but the Beau was not responding as it should. Mac swore and gritted his teeth. The bastard was going to get him and there wasn't a damned thing he could do about it.

In that moment he felt close to resignation, but the anger was still hot in his blood. If he was going to die he was determined to take the German with him. His finger hovered over the button for one last burst the moment he was angled right. And stared wide-eyed as the Me109 exploded before his startled eyes. For a split second he simply did not know what had happened to it; he hadn't yet fired his guns. Then he saw two dark shapes zoom past him, and understood. Dodds and Lieutenant Green, another pilot in his flight, had seen what was happening and taken out the Me109. Which of them had got it, he didn't know – both of them, from the look of it. Or a cannon shell had got the fuel tanks. At that moment Mac neither knew nor cared. They'd given him another chance.

His fight was over, though. His plane was badly damaged, he knew, making him a sitting duck. He doubted whether he could make it back across the Channel the way it was handling. It was as if the Beau were a living entity, which had somehow summoned its dying strength for a last superhuman effort, then subsided, utterly spent. There was nothing for it; he was going to have to put down somewhere if he could manage it. If things got worse, they'd have to bail out. Abandoning a plane went against the grain, but there might be no option.

Problem was, they were over occupied France – might even have strayed into Germany.

'Dai? Are you OK?' He feared there might be no reply from the rear of the Beau, but to his relief, Dai answered.

'Just about. They got me in the leg, though.' His voice sounded shaky, though he was attempting his habitual chirpiness.

'I'm going to try for a forced landing. But if things get worse, I'll give the order to bail out.'

There was a silence, then Dai said: 'I don't know if I can, Mac.'

Mac swore to himself. He'd just have to do his best to get the plane down in one piece. If Dai couldn't bail out there was no way he could leave him. 'Can you give me a fix on where we are?' he asked.

'Christ knows.' Dai was beginning to sound woozy.

The Beau had lost a lot of height. Mac put the nose down to gain some speed and levelled out, trying to get his bearings.

'Hang in there, son.' He pressed the radio button, hoping one of his flight could hear him as he passed the message: Damaged, heading for Switzerland. His concentration now was centred on nursing the maimed Beau; the closer he could get to neutral territory the better their chance of evading capture. But it was a balancing act. Push her too far and she might give up the ghost altogether. One of the engines was already banging. Mac throttled it back, but he didn't care for the sound of the other.

There was open countryside beneath them again now; by the light of the moon Mac could clearly see good-sized fields interspersed with clumps of trees, and he decided this was about as good as it was going to get. There was nothing visual to give him an indication of the wind direction or speed, but he knew that earlier it had been a westerly. Mac nursed the plane into a turn and headed into it, reducing height until he was just a few hundred feet above the ground. Both engines were banging now; Mac took off all power, gliding down and hoping they'd resurrect for one last burst if he should need it. But the field looked good.

'Hold tight, Dai.'

He could feel the wind lifting one wing now; it had swung around somewhat to the south, and he didn't think his flaps were operating properly. Too bad. At least the undercarriage was down and locked. With the ground rushing by beneath him, Mac stood on the rudder bar and crabbed in. The wheels hit the grass and bounced once, twice, and Mac struggled to keep control. Then the hummocky ground did what the useless flaps had failed to do; the

Beau pitched forward and slowed, coming to a sudden jolting stop just a few feet short of a boundary hedge.

Beads of sweat rolled down into Mac's eyes and he wiped his forehead with his silk scarf. In the rear, Dai was moaning; the bumpy landing had exacerbated his injury, Mac guessed.

'Sorry, pal, best I could do.' He looked round. Dai's head was thrown back on his shoulders, eyes closed, mouth open in a contortion of agony. Mac wondered how the hell he was going to get him out of the plane, but he had to, somehow. If there were Germans in the vicinity they might strafe the stricken Beau, and in any case he needed to destroy it, and quickly. He was fairly sure they were still in enemy-occupied territory; a burning plane would be of no use to German intelligence, and if anyone had seen it come down and a fire followed almost immediately there was always the chance they would assume the crew had died in the flames and not bother looking for them.

'Come on, Dai, old son, we've got to get you out of here,' Mac said, and crawled back to his wounded partner.

It is sometimes said that in moments of necessity we find a strength we never knew we possessed. So it was with Mac that night. Looking back, Mac had no recollection of forcing twisted metal to free Dai or somehow extricating him, a dead weight, from the Beau – Dai had passed out from the pain. When it was done he hoisted him onto his back, carried him a safe distance from the stricken plane, and went back to set it on fire. As the blaze took hold he ran back to where he had left Dai, diving to the deck as an explosion sent up a roar of flame and a shower of burning debris, then scrambling to his feet and running on again.

Dai was still unconscious; Mac examined his leg by the light of the moon and gritted his teeth at the mess of torn flesh and splintered bone. Mac hoisted him onto his back again and set off across the fields, staggering now beneath the weight of him. He had noticed what looked like a farmhouse as he came in to land; now he headed in that direction, hoping desperately that the occupants were sympathetic, and not collaborators.

A hedge ran a long dark shadow across the moonlit fields. Mac aimed for a gap in it that looked like a gateway. He staggered through, stumbling in the uneven rough mud that had been churned up by the traffic of feet or farm implements through it, and was totally shocked when two figures disengaged from the shadows on the far side, appearing suddenly on the edge of his field of vision and shouting something in French. Startled into a moment's blank incomprehension, Mac had no idea what they were saying, but there was no ambiguity about the shotgun that was levelled at him, the barrel wavering little more than a foot from his forehead. He stopped short.

'*Anglais*,' he said, not sure whether that made things better or worse.

To his relief, the shotgun lowered a fraction and one of the men said in heavily accented English: 'What is your name?'

'Squadron Leader James Mackenzie. And Sergeant David Renshaw.' Dai was slipping down his back; he bent double and hoisted him up again, half expecting the movement to precipitate a further jab of the gun. But the man merely regarded him with narrow suspicion.

'What are you doing here?'

'Trying to free your country from the bloody Hun,' Mac snapped. 'We've had to crash-land. My sergeant is badly hurt. I don't think I can carry him much further.'

442

At last the shotgun lowered. The two men circled Mac, peering at Dai, examining his shattered leg.

'You wait here,' the younger one said. He spoke in rapid French to his companion, then set off across the fields at a trot. Mac waited, still supporting Dai, and looking at the older man, who had raised his shotgun again, worried obviously at being left alone with two foreigners, even if they purported to be English. He was wearing a rough cloth jacket, Mac noticed, over what appeared to be a flannel nightshirt. The hem of it hung down over his trousers. His lined and weather-beaten face and shaggy appearance suggested to Mac that he was the farmer on whose land he had come down. He'd seen the plane circling, no doubt, or been wakened by those rattling engines, alerted some other member of the household, grabbed his shotgun and come out to investigate. Again, Mac hoped fervently that they were not collaborators. If they were, the younger man was probably putting in a call to the local commander of the Nazi occupying force at this very moment.

His anxiety was allayed somewhat when the younger man returned a few minutes later with what looked like a section of a cattle pen. He put it down on the ground and indicated that Mac should lay Dai on it.

'We take him to the house,' he said.

Mac had never heard more welcome words. But he knew that, though for the moment it appeared they were amongst friends, they were far from being out of danger.

Looking back afterwards, Mac thought that night had all the quality of a bad dream. He and Dai were taken first to a barn where they were hidden in a hollowed-out section in a stack of hay bales that almost seemed to be waiting for them. And perhaps it was; perhaps the farmer had prepared for just such an eventuality, perhaps it had been used for others before them. The younger man, whose name was Yves, explained in reasonably good English that it was not safe yet to take them into the house. The area was still under Nazi occupation and if an observer had seen the plane landing – as they almost certainly would have, unless they were asleep at their posts – they would be combing the surrounding countryside looking for survivors.

Mac nodded that he understood; if he and Dai were discovered here the farmer and his family would most likely be shot. But it wasn't a pleasant experience, squatting beside the unconscious Dai in the cramped hollow whilst the bales of hay were replaced, one by one.

'When it is safe, we will come back with food and water and a doctor for your friend,' Yves whispered before slotting the final bale into place. And then the darkness was complete and all sound muffled. It was, Mac thought, like being in a coffin of straw.

Dai was drifting in and out of consciousness now, muttering and threshing, and Mac thought he had lost a good deal of blood. Perhaps he should have left him with the plane; if the Nazis had come looking and found him there, he might have been in captivity but at least he would have been given medical attention. As it was, Mac guessed it would be hours at the very earliest before Yves and his father were able to get a doctor to him, and even then there would be a limit to what the doctor could do. He thought Dai probably needed an operation and should be in hospital, not lying in a straw cell. But there was nothing he could do for him now, except make the boy as comfortable as possible and rely on the farmer to bring help as soon as he safely could. For the moment, at least they were both alive.

Mac eased himself down into a prone position, pillowed his head on his arms and tried to get some sleep.

Mac spent two days and two nights in the barn before Jacques, the farmer, deemed it safe for the two men to leave their hiding place, though he did emerge for short periods to stretch his legs and breathe in clean, fresh air whilst the farmer and his family kept lookout from vantage points at each end of the yard. They brought fresh food too, hunks of bread and cheese, water, strong coffee and even a jug of rough wine. They were understandably nervous; the boldest member of the family was Jacques's daughter, Anne-Louise, a pretty, fresh-faced girl who was fearless in her condemnation of the Germans.

'Paw! I will not let them frighten me!' she declared when Mac expressed his concern as to what would happen to the family if they were found to be sheltering Allied airmen. 'I will be true to myself and to France. You are fighting for us – we will look after you until we can find a way for you to go home.'

Mac was filled with admiration for her courage, but concerned about her foolhardy bravado.

He was becoming increasingly concerned too for Dai. A doctor from the village, by the name of René Sambussi, had been smuggled in to tend to him, but as Mac had feared, there was little he could do within the confines of the barn beyond dressing the wound and administering painkillers. Mac's French was far from fluent, but from what he understood of the doctor's jabbering, he gathered that it could well be that the leg would need to be amputated, and Anne-Louise confirmed this.

'He is worried it will turn bad,' she said. 'If it does . . .'

'Gangrene,' Mac said heavily.

445

They were in the yard outside the barn; warm September sunshine had baked the bare earth underfoot to a cracked desert, but to Mac it was heaven on earth after the fetid air in the barn, where every breath was foul and the dust from the hay an irritant to his eyes, nose and throat.

'Papa thinks the Germans have given up searching especially for you,' Anne-Louise said. 'Tonight when it is dark we will take you into the house, I think. But still we must be careful. The Germans, they always search. Search, search . . .' Her tone was bitter; her small round face portrayed her disgust for the enemy.

Mac stared into the sun and ground his jaw. He hated endangering these good people by remaining here. He could imagine the Germans combed the countryside and carried out snap searches of lonely farms in the hope of mopping up a pilot or the crew of a stricken bomber who had ejected and were trying to escape. By nature, he was a self-reliant loner. All his instincts were to try to make it home. But there was Dai to think of. Mac felt strongly that the boy was his responsibility, and Dai was not in any condition to be moved, whatever the danger to his rescuers. Though he was itching to strike out on his own, Mac felt it his duty to remain with Dai and hope that, with the help of the Resistance, he could get him out by one of the escape lines. Planes came in under cover of darkness to pick up stranded British flyers, he knew, and this was, as far as he could see, an ideal location for such an operation. As yet he had been unable to ascertain whether there was a Resistance cell nearby who would be in radio contact with London, but for the moment it was his only hope.

That night Jacques and Yves came for them, and between the three of them, they managed to get Dai into the farmhouse and upstairs into a tiny attic room that was reached by way of a ladder.

A couple of makeshift beds had been made up on the floor. Dai, barely conscious again, was lowered onto one of them and for the first time Mac went downstairs to have supper with the family. But although it was a good hearty stew, he had little appetite. He was too edgy, sharply alert at every sound, and with anxiety for the boy upstairs weighing heavily in his stomach.

I wish that bloody Messerschmitt had done the job properly and finished me off, he thought. It was the first time such a thing had even crossed his mind, and it would be the last. But at that moment it seemed to him it would have been better for all of them if the Beau had crashed in flames. At least that way Dai wouldn't have been put through this torment and faced the prospect of being crippled – if, by some miracle, he survived. At least this decent French family would not be in danger of being tortured and shot for giving them shelter. And at least he would not be struggling with this God-awful dilemma of whether he should go or stay.

For that one night at least in the low-roofed, sparsely furnished kitchen of a French farmhouse, lit by a single oil lamp and redolent with the aroma of meat stewed with herbs, Mac wished that it was all over. For he could see no solution, no way out, that would not end in disaster for all of them.

Dai was worse. He had become delirious, rambling and crying out, and Mac was fearful that the noise he was making would give them away should a German come calling. Thankfully, none did. Dr Sambussi came, however, shaking his head and tutting. He was as worried as Mac by the responsibility that had been forced on him, Mac knew.

It was not to last. On the third day, weakened by loss of blood and ravaged by fever, Dai died. When it was over Mac stood at the side of the makeshift bed, looking down at the pitifully young face, peaceful now in death, and wept. This was his doing. If he had been skilful enough to evade the Me109 that had got him, if he'd managed to nurse the Beau to Switzerland, if he'd given Dai up to the Germans, he wouldn't have died. He'd failed him. The sense of guilt and the agony at the loss of this young, vibrant life was crucifying him. He had seen many men die and accepted it as the price to be paid in the pursuit of freedom. This was different. He could have made a difference to the fate of one young man, and he hadn't. Mac thought he would never forgive himself.

But at least there was no longer any need for him to continue to impose his dangerous presence on Jacques and his family. Mac made up his mind he would leave at the first opportunity.

When Mac first told Jacques and his family of his plans to make for Switzerland, the farmer seemed relieved, but both Yves and Anne-Louise did their best to dissuade him. Anne-Louise in particular was adamant that he should stay. Mac put it down to her liking for playing with danger; the truth, that she had taken more than a passing fancy to him, never occurred to him for a moment.

'You will be caught,' she warned. 'You can never pass for a Frenchman. You do not speak the language well.'

'I should have paid more attention at school,' Mac said ruefully, remembering lessons when he had done nothing but stare out of the window and count the minutes until he could get out onto the sports field for a game of cricket.

'Oui, you should. Me – I worked hard at my English lessons. They have served me well.'

'Your English is excellent,' Mac agreed, and failed to notice the pleased flush that coloured her cheeks. 'You put me to shame. But

I have to try to get home, and I can't put you and your family in danger any longer.'

'Soon we will make contact with London once more. Wait for that.'

'I can't. And besides, it's not safe for them just now. They need to keep their heads down.'

The local group of Resistance fighters had suffered a serious setback a few months earlier, she had told him. The Germans had traced radio transmissions to an isolated hut where their equipment was hidden, and the man on whose land it stood had been arrested and taken away. The rest of the cell were lying low, and praying that he would not reveal more names under torture, and as yet they had been unable to replace the confiscated radio.

'Well, if your mind is made up . . .' Anne-Louise said, resigned. 'You will need better clothes. The ones you have are not good.'

'They're fine.'

'No, no, they are . . . oh, you know!'

When they had first taken him into the house, the family had found a shirt and trousers for him and burned his uniform in a bonfire in the fields. But both Jacques and Yves were shorter and stouter than Mac; whilst the shirt was a passable fit, the trousers gapped badly at the waist and bagged over his behind, whilst the turn-ups sat several inches above his ankles, revealing his flying boots. He was reluctant to part with the boots, especially since the shoes Yves brought for him to try on were all a size or more too small. If he was going to set out for Switzerland on foot, at least he wanted to be sure he was wearing shoes that fitted.

They fetched a tape and measured him, chattering all the while in rapid French, and next day a pair of heavy duty cotton trousers materialised. When he tried them on, Mac was relieved to find that

449

he could let his braces down to their usual length. With an old jacket belonging to Jacques and a black beret Mac could, at a fleeting glance, pass for a Frenchman.

The next step was to work out the route he should take. Yves and Anne-Louise pored over maps, both their own, torn from telephone directories, and Mac's escape map from his survival kit, and made a list of the villages Mac would pass through. From the back of a cupboard, Yves unearthed a rucksack that did not look like military issue. Into it, Mac packed a plastic bottle filled with water, his pouch and survival kit, and a mound of bread, cheese and meat wrapped in greaseproof paper, which Anne-Louise had prepared for him. Then there was nothing more to be done but wait until it was dark enough for him to leave safely.

The whole family came out to see him off, saying their goodbyes on the steps of the farmhouse.

'I shall never be able to repay you for what you've done,' Mac said, and though they might not have understood every word, the sentiment was clear enough. Yves shrugged, a typically Gallic gesture.

'We do what we can for our friends.'

The night air was suddenly throbbing with the sound of heavy aero engines. Mac squinted up at the sky; there were no stars tonight, but a sliver of moonlight radiated from behind a thick bank of cloud. By it he could make out the dark shape of a formation of bombers and the fighters that flanked it. He wondered what the target was tonight, where they were headed, and hoped fervently that if the Luftwaffe came after them they wouldn't clash in a battle overhead. Another plane down, a flurry of parachute silk catching the fitful light of the moon, and the area would be crawling with Germans.

'I'd better go.' He hoisted the rucksack onto his shoulder.

'*Bon chance.*' Yves embraced him roughly, kissing him on both cheeks, and the others followed suit. Mac, unused to such tactile gestures, shrank inwardly but managed to hide his reticence, patting them on the shoulders and back. The last thing he wanted was to offend this family of good, honest folk who had saved his life.

He walked the breadth of the farmyard, turned and looked back. They were all still there, waving, but Mac was thinking now of Dai, who should have been leaving with him but who would never go home. Someone would have to break the news to his family; Mac felt that it should be him.

Some lines of Rupert Brooke's poem, learned long ago in school, came into his head.

> If I should die, think only this of me:
> That there's some corner of a foreign field
> That is for ever England.

It may have been written in the First World War – but it was just as relevant now.

His throat closed, his eyes burned. *Goodbye, Dai . . .*

The bomber squadron and its escort was directly overhead now. It couldn't be long before the Luftwaffe turned out in force to engage them. Mac wondered how many other young men who had climbed boisterously into those planes tonight would not be going home. Reluctantly he averted his gaze and headed for Switzerland.

What had seemed on the map to be not so far was, in reality, a marathon, and it was more than a week before Mac was within striking distance of the Swiss border. That first night and most of the next day he walked without stopping, fourteen hours of back roads and lanes, sustained by the Benzedrine tablets from his survival kit and his own dogged determination. He stopped from time to time to check his course on the maps he'd folded into his pocket and a compass Anne-Louise had sewn into the lapel of her father's old jacket. He had another compass too, two fly buttons which could be superimposed one over the other and which he had salvaged from his uniform before Jacques threw it on the bonfire, but the other was easier to use, especially when his eyes were aching from tiredness and blinded by the sun.

The first night of his long trek he spent under a hedge, the second in a haystack. By now, not only his legs, but his whole body ached relentlessly, and his feet felt as if they were on fire. When he tried to get up from the haystack he could barely move; his muscles seemed to have seized up completely. He massaged his legs, but did not dare take off his boots to tend to the blisters that he knew were raw and bleeding. He was too afraid he would not be able to get them back on again.

Gradually, as he walked, slowly at first, every step a conscious effort, his legs began to work again. The pain in his calves and thighs was excruciating, but at least he could put one foot in front of the other. A stream ran alongside the road; Mac splashed water over his face, dusty and burning from exposure to the sun, rasping several days of bristle, and refilled his bottle. He'd have to be careful, he knew, about filling it from a village pump. Nothing would give him away faster as an Englishman; the French used water solely for washing. They drank only wine.

In the heat of the afternoon he came across an isolated cottage. A few cows were chewing the cud lazily in the nearby fields in what shade they could find; some hens clucked in the dust around the house. Mac decided to risk knocking on the door. He needed a place to rest and something to eat. He doubted he could keep going for much longer unless he got it.

His luck was in. The occupants of the house – two elderly women – were as opposed to the occupying force as Anne-Louise had been. They took him in, fed him, heated water for him to wash, and brought a bottle of pure alcohol for him to rub into his aching legs. For the first time since he had set out, Mac dared to take off his boots and tend to his bleeding feet.

It was three days before he left that secluded refuge. Communication hadn't been easy as the women spoke no English whatsoever, but little was needed. They managed to make him understand the route he needed to take, and he set off again, rested and more optimistic about the loyalties of the local people in this part of France. The next village he came to, he confided in a fat elderly woman dressed all in black, who was sitting in front of her house snoozing in the warm afternoon sun. She pointed him in the direction of the village curé, a wiry little man and a staunch patriot. He welcomed Mac into his house, fed him good wine and wholesome food, and allowed him to stay in one of his many spare rooms for a few days.

Mac was beginning to feel more confident now. The bombers no longer passed overhead at night; there were fewer German patrols on the lookout for fallen airmen. Just a few days' more effort, and he should be in Switzerland. But he remained cautious. As he progressed, he tore off the names of the villages he had passed through from the scrap of paper bearing the details of his route. He didn't want to bring down German wrath on the heads of those who had helped him along the way should he be captured.

It was not until the last stage of his journey that Mac

encountered the enemy. With the border in sight, he was about to cross a shallow valley when he saw two German guards between him and safety. Instantly, he was on high alert, every nerve taut and singing. He looked around for cover; there was none, and he realised the guards had seen him. Mac ducked into a wheat field and began to run a zigzag course through the stubble, blood pounding in his head, legs feeling like rubber. Ahead of him, perhaps four hundred yards distant, he could see what looked like Swiss guards, straddling the road. They were staring in his direction, mesmerised. So near – so damned near! But the Germans must be gaining on him, he knew. They hadn't spent the last ten days walking from dawn till dusk, their feet were not lacerated with great bleeding blisters where their boots had rubbed the skin raw. As he emerged on the far side of the wheat field, Mac risked a glance over his shoulder. One of the Germans was rolling a little, but the other, a few feet ahead, was running with the dogged single-mindedness of an athlete entering the home straight.

Three hundred yards now between him and freedom. Gasping for breath, oblivious to the fiery pain in his feet and the sharp stitch below his ribs, Mac summoned every last bit of his strength and ran on. Ahead of him he could see a farmhouse, home, no doubt, to the farmer who owned the wheat field he had just raced through. Mac leaped a ditch, crashed through a hedge. Twigs slashed his face and hands, drawing blood, though he scarcely noticed. His whole being was concentrated on that farmhouse and reaching it before the Germans caught up with him.

A bullet whistled past his ear. It was only afterwards that it occurred to him; the Germans could easily have shot him in the back if they had wanted to. Maybe there were some of the enemy who couldn't bring themselves to kill an unarmed man in cold blood, a fellow soldier, even if he was on the other side. Maybe the shot had been a warning, trading on any man's natural instinct to hit the deck in such a situation. Maybe they simply wanted to have some evidence that they had done their duty when they were called to account by their commanding officer. If so, the ploy failed, and Mac was eternally grateful to them.

There was a man outside the farmhouse, cleaning some agricultural contraption. He looked up, startled, as Mac raced towards him, shading his eyes with his hand against the glare of the sun, and scarcely able to believe what he was seeing. Panting, Mac raced up to him.

'Switzerland?'

The man nodded, his leathery face bemused.

Relief was a tide that enveloped Mac; as it flooded through his veins and his bones it seemed to take the last of his strength with it. His legs were buckling beneath him, his spine sagging. The effort of turning his head to see what his pursuers were doing was enormous and the blood pounding behind his eyes distorted his vision with throbbing black streaks, so that a black veil seemed to hang over the sun-bright countryside. The Germans had stopped just short of the border, a few hundred yards behind him, one bent double to recover his breath, the other hands on hips, simply watching him. Mac raised a shaking hand; the Germans reciprocated. It was almost as if they were waving to one another across the border. Then Mac's knees gave way and he crumpled down, utterly spent. He had made it. He was in Switzerland.

It was almost a year before Mac was able to leave Switzerland. After interrogation by the neutral Swiss, he was informed that since he had been wearing civilian clothes when he crossed the border, he would be classed as an 'evade' rather than an 'internee'. This meant that instead of being sent to one of the dreaded prison camps, he was to be given accommodation in a ski resort hotel high above Lake Geneva. Life there was a relaxed and not unpleasant regime – Mac was allowed the freedom to swim, sail, and even learn to ski. The food was good, and supplemented by Red Cross parcels, which arrived from time to time. His room was comfortable. But he couldn't leave Switzerland and he chafed against his enforced stay there.

Some of the evades left, 'swapped' by the Swiss authorities for German pilots – the Swiss were eager to get rid of some of their unwanted guests – but Mac was not among them, though he did ask them to pass on messages for him to Nancy and his family when they got back to England.

It was only when the Franco-Swiss border was liberated by the US Fifth Army, and he was considering trying to make a run for it and jump the border himself, that he learned that his name was on a list of personnel to be repatriated. Just as well, he thought afterwards; had he gone for it alone and been captured he would almost certainly have found himself in one of the prison camps and even if he had made it home, could have faced court martial for breaking international law. As it was, Mac found himself back in London, facing yet more interrogation, taking a short, enforced leave, and being returned to active service.

The Germans had begun targeting London with flying bombs and Mac found himself back in a fighter plane doing his best to shoot them down before they wreaked their terrible destruction on a vulnerable civilian population.

His enforced sojourn was over and he was glad of it. But there was no way he could escape the news that awaited him on his return.

Nancy had married Joe and gone home to America. Rumour had it that she was pregnant. Mac's stomach kicked when the CO mentioned it, oh so casually. Dear God, he couldn't have been as careful as he'd thought. And when she'd needed him he had not been here for her. Frightened and alone, she'd turned to that damned American boyfriend of hers. The baby would have been born by now, be – what? – six months old. And there wasn't a damned thing he could do about it.

Despair descended over Mac like a clammy grey London fog. He immersed himself in flying and tried to forget.

V

Nancy was staring at him, wide-eyed.

'Oh my God, Mac! This just beggars belief . . .' She broke off, shaking her head.

He reached for her hand, holding it between his. 'I am so sorry, Nancy, that I wasn't there for you when you needed me.'

She shrugged, a small resigned movement of her shoulders and a tight little grimace. 'You couldn't help it. And in any case, there would have been nothing you could do.'

'But I should have been there.'

Another shrug. 'If you had been, it wouldn't have happened.'

'What?' His brow creased; as he stared at her, puzzled, he saw that her eyes were filling with tears.

'Mac, I am so sorry . . . I was in such a state, thinking you were dead . . .'

There was a hard nugget suddenly in his gut that he couldn't – didn't want to – identify. 'I know you were in a fix,' he said, grasping at the only acceptable explanation, the assumption he'd made when he'd learned she had married Joe. 'Pregnant, alone in a foreign country . . . I'm the one who should be sorry, Nancy. I should have been more damn careful.'

He heard the quick intake of her breath, saw a tear escape and run down her face before she turned her head away as if she couldn't bear to look him in the eye.

'Nancy, it's OK,' he said. 'I'm here now. I want you to come back to England with me.'

Her head snapped back as if she were a marionette and someone had pulled the string.

'Judy . . . ?'

'Judy . . . she's gone.' He still couldn't bring himself to use the word 'died', he, who had seen so much death and talked about it dispassionately even as the waste of life bruised his soul. He even found it difficult to accept that Judy was dead; that finally she had succumbed to pneumonia and slipped away. He had been by her bedside at the last, and he was grateful for that. If she had died whilst he was in Switzerland he would have felt that he had failed her yet again. He had held her hand and listened to her painful, rasping breaths, knowing that it was inevitable now, that her weakened, inert body could not withstand the onslaught on her heart. He had whispered comfort that he knew she could not hear, and witnessed her last tortured moments and the peace that followed; he had walked behind her coffin, and still he could not believe it. He had lost her so long ago, it seemed to him that she was still lying there asleep as she still lay in his heart, a beautiful woman who would be always young, simply existing in an altered state, on a different plane. But however unreal it might seem, the fact was that Judy was no more. And Mac, the least fanciful of men, had found himself wondering in the dead of night, when the shadows in our minds take on shapes and meaning that vanish with the harsh light of day, whether the essence of Judy that had lived in that sleeping body had decided that the time had come to set him free. For his sake, and for the sake of the woman he loved, and their child.

The irony of it was that now Nancy was married to someone else.

'I know this is all wrong,' he said now. 'And the way it's turned out, it seems as if it wasn't meant to be. But I'm here because I can't think of anything but that I want to be with you. It won't be easy on anybody, I know. But I can't just walk away from you.' His glance strayed to John, who was deeply immersed in turning out the contents of his mother's purse. 'I can't walk away from him. Can't we at least try to work something out?'

Nancy couldn't speak; the tears were constricting her throat, the hopelessness of it all and the enormity of what she had to tell him choking her. And as so often happened when emotion overwhelmed her, her defensive reaction was to flare angrily.

'You've got a nerve, Mac. You wouldn't leave Judy for me, yet you expect me to walk out on Joe. Just because you're free now.'

'Nancy . . .' He broke off, all too aware suddenly of how selfish he must appear. Heck, he *was* being selfish. Joe was a good bloke; he loved Nancy, he had taken care of her when Mac couldn't. He'd been prepared to marry her, even though . . . What the hell was he doing, expecting her to leave Joe and break his heart? How could he lay that on her? It went against everything in his nature. And yet . . .

And yet he couldn't give up on her. He loved her too much. She was a part of him, every breath that he breathed. He couldn't get her out of his head or his heart. If he had thought she felt differently he would have walked away. But deep inside he knew that she felt just the same way. She was his soul mate, and the child playing on the floor was his son. The strength of his feelings overrode all his natural sense of fair play, of right and wrong. And he was ready to fight for her, whatever the cost, whatever the consequences.

'Nancy . . . it's not easy, I know. But—'

'I couldn't do that to Joe,' Nancy said, shaking her head in distress. 'God, Mac, you know how I feel about you. But that doesn't mean I don't love Joe. It doesn't work like that. He's a wonderful man. I couldn't hurt him like that. I just couldn't.'

Mac glanced again at John. 'And our child? Don't you think he should have the chance to grow up with his own father?'

Nancy gasped. Her face crumpled and she pressed both hands to her mouth.

'What?' he said, unsure of himself suddenly. He gripped her arms. 'What?'

'He isn't yours.' The words, torn from her, grated into the space between them.

Mac was very still suddenly, every sinew in his body tensing as the kernel of unease exploded like shell shot in the night sky, blinding bright, mercilessly illuminating what he had not wanted to see. His eyes narrowed, his arms dropped to his sides. The shell shot flashed again, died, leaving only the darkness closing in around him.

'He isn't yours,' she said again, more softly, her voice shaking. 'He's Joe's. I thought you were dead, Mac. Joe came to see me, and I . . . we . . .'

Anger. Suddenly the numbing pain was anger.

'You didn't waste much time.' He turned away from her, unable now to look at her.

'Oh, Mac, please . . .' She grabbed at his arm. 'Please understand! I was beside myself . . . I didn't know what I was doing . . .'

'Don't give me that! Of course you bloody knew! He didn't rape you, did he?'

'No.'

'If he did, I'll smash his fucking head in.'

'He didn't rape me. But I—' She broke off, unable to find the words to explain the madness of grief, the safe haven Joe had offered her, albeit briefly. Life instead of death. Comfort and love, balm for her tortured spirit. 'He was good to me,' she whispered. 'He's always been good to me. I needed that. I needed it so badly.'

'Well, in that case you'd better stick with what you need, hadn't you?' He swung round. 'I hope it bloody satisfies you.'

John, alarmed by the raised voices, had abandoned Nancy's purse and was scooting across the floor towards her, clutching at her skirt and crying, an insistent gulping wail that might almost have been 'Ma-ma.' For the first and only time in her life, Nancy ignored him.

'Mac, don't be like this, please!'

He huffed, an angry explosion. 'How the hell do you expect me to be? And for Christ's sake, shut that child up!'

Suddenly she too was angry. 'Oh, he's "that child" now, is he? Don't blame him, Mac. It's not his fault.'

'I never said it was.'

'Then stop shouting, please. You're frightening him.'

'Don't worry, I won't be frightening him much longer.' He started towards the door, fishing car keys on the hire company's fob from his pocket. 'I'll leave you to it.'

Nancy ran after him. 'Mac – don't go like this. Please don't go like this!'

He stopped, turned. 'Nancy, you are married to someone else. You have his child.' He jerked his head toward John angrily, as if he hated him, and turned away again.

'But I didn't mean it to be this way. You're all I've ever wanted.'

John was clutching at her skirts; she was denying him. She hated herself for it, but she couldn't help it. If he walked out the door now . . . *Oh God, don't let him walk out the door!* 'I love you!' she cried.

She saw him hesitate, just the smallest indecision in his resolute posture.

'Mac, please. I know you're hurt. I know . . . it can't be. Only don't go like this.' His back was still towards her. His shoulders slumped as the breath came out of him on a long, agonised sigh. 'Stay, just for a little while. Let me explain.'

'What's to explain?' He sounded defeated now, resigned rather than angry.

She had no words left. She put her arms around his waist, laid her cheek against his back, breathing in the smell of him along with her tears, feeling the solid wall of his chest and the beat of his heart beneath her hands. The whole of her being was crying out at the unfairness of it, weeping for what might have been. There was nothing for them, she knew that without even thinking about it, and the bleak acknowledgement was a dull ache in every bone and muscle. There was a desperate sadness in her heart that was quite different from the one that had been there before, thinking he was dead, and worse, really, because when she had thought he was dead, there had been nothing to be done but try to come to terms with it, accept it. But this . . . this was sheer purgatory. To know that but for her own weakness they could be together now. To have her arms around him again, knowing he was going to walk away and she must let him.

Only not like this, please. Not in anger. She couldn't bear that. And not so soon. Just a little while with him – was that so much to ask? It was more than she deserved. But if her last memory of him was of his bitter, unyielding back, the icy tide of his anger at her betrayal . . . Nancy shrank inwardly, her pain now too deep for tears.

'Oh, Nancy.' Her name was wrung from him.

He should walk away from her, here and now. His innate sense of right and wrong told him that; the revulsion he felt thinking of her with another man told him that; the perception that he would only be making things worse if he stayed told him that. He should walk away without a backward glance, without looking back for a second at her temptress face. He should let the singing of the blood in his ears deafen him to her siren voice. She'd betrayed him and if he stayed she would betray her husband, if he had anything to do with it. He should hate her for the power she had over him, but he couldn't hate her. He hated himself instead for allowing it. And he couldn't walk away either. God help him, he couldn't walk away.

'Oh Christ, Nancy,' he said, despairing.

He turned, putting his arms around her. For a moment she buried her face in his chest, overcome by the emotions that were pulsing through her and the sheer joy of feeling him close to her once more when she had never expected to see him again. Then, as the electricity that was always there between them sparked like the crossing of two bare wires, a sort of guilty horror enveloped her, and she knew exactly how Mac had felt that long ago evening when he had walked out on her in her flat because he could not bring himself to cross the Rubicon and betray Judy. She was Joe's wife now; she couldn't do this. And especially not with Joe's son present.

465

She jerked away, the uncertainty of a heart and conscience being ripped in two written all over her face.

'Mac . . . we mustn't. I can't.'

'OK,' he said roughly.

'But don't go. Please. Not yet.'

Even as she said it she knew that it was folly. She couldn't remain strong for ever. Whatever it cost her she should tell him to walk out the door. But she couldn't do that either.

Just a little longer. Just a little longer and then she would say goodbye to him for good. She would, she really would . . .

It was, of course, a promise she was quite unable to keep.

She had given John his tea, meat and vegetables puréed the way he still liked them, followed by a ripe banana. She had changed his diaper and buttoned him into his sleep suit, but still delayed putting him to bed. Now, however, he had fallen asleep on the sofa, arms wound around the teddy bear Dorothy had knitted for him, and he barely stirred when Nancy picked him up, holding him to her with the teddy bear squashed between them.

'He's tired out.'

Mac was looking at her with his heart in his eyes. Her stomach wrenched. She took John to the bedroom, gently laid him in his cot and covered him with a light blanket. She touched her fingers to her lips and then to his forehead. 'Sleep well, little one.'

When she returned to the living room, Mac was waiting for her. Without a single word, he pulled her into his arms. 'Come here, Nancy.'

Breath caught in her throat, the guilt edging at her again. But the ache of longing and the fiery desire that was a madness in her blood was too strong. Like an avalanche it enveloped her, sweeping her along, tumbling her over and over, confusing her senses, making it hard for her to breathe. And she sensed it was the same for Mac. His scruples, like her resolution to remain faithful to Joe, counted for nothing now. All good intentions fell by the wayside, made feeble and hollow by their desperate need for one another.

They kissed, clung together, soared together in a world where there was nothing but the two of them and the overwhelming love they shared.

Was it their destiny never to be together but for a brief, stolen interlude when glorious love and swingeing guilt went hand in hand? When the prospect of imminent parting was like incense in the air, swirling around them, nebulous and potent, evoking layers of emotion that lay in some spiritual sphere that could not be reached or touched or fully understood, but which were ever present, all the same? When a sense of unreality, of inhabiting a land that was a distorted mirror image of what might have been, made everything crazy and dreamlike?

Mac knew, just as Nancy did, that for the present, at least, this could not be. He would willingly have taken John, as well as Nancy, back to England with him. He would have brought him up and loved him as if he were his own – the child was Nancy's, and that was good enough for him. But Nancy had made it clear she would never do that to Joe, and he knew too she would never go alone with him and leave John behind. He wasn't even sure he would want her to. If she could do that, she wouldn't be the woman he thought she was.

Mac was overwhelmed with utter despair. Even in his darkest days when he had been holed up in France he had not felt as bad as he did now. There was no way out for them. No way at all.

* * *

Evening. They were lying entwined on the sofa that Nancy had made up into a bed for Mac. They had agreed that he should stay this one night and no longer in case the neighbours should grow curious about the car on the driveway. Nancy already knew in her heart that she would confess to Joe that Mac had been here; there was no way she would be able to live with keeping it from him. But she wanted to be able to tell him in her own good time, not be bounced into it through Tilly Jacobson making some snide remark. And though there was no one else in the house, Nancy hadn't felt it right to let Mac use Dorothy's bed, and there was no way she would have allowed him into the one she shared with Joe. That was one step way too far.

His fingers tangled now in her hair, feeling the texture, committing it to memory. As if he needed to. Everything about her was in his soul and his heart.

'So I suppose I have to go tomorrow,' he said.

Pain, razor sharp, twisted her gut. 'Don't talk about it. Not yet.'

'Are you sure you won't come with me?' He hated himself for asking but it was out before he could stop himself.

'Mac, you know I can't.' He could hear the tears in her voice. 'It just isn't an option. Maybe one day . . .' She had to say that, had to believe that there was a chance that sometime in the future things would be different and they could be together. Otherwise she didn't think she could find the strength to stay. 'You know I'll always love you.'

'You will?'

'You know it! Will you always love me?'

'Yep.'

'Say it. Please, Mac, say it. For me.'

'I'll always love you. Come here.'

Lips and hands and bodies. Close. Close. But never close enough, oh, never that. Hearts touching. Souls touching. How to say 'I love you' with every pulse beat, every inch of sensitised flesh. Not enough. Never enough.

'I can't say goodbye to you, Mac. I just can't do it.'

'So come with me.'

'I can't do that either.' Silence, heavy with longing and despair. 'Oh, why did you have to fly that night? Why did you let that damned German get you?'

'I didn't do it on purpose, I promise you.'

Another silence.

'I am so damned mixed up!' Close to tears again.

'Don't cry, Nancy. Don't dare cry tonight.'

'I can't help it.'

'You can. And you know I'll be there for you, any time you change your mind.'

'I know.' Gulping. Kissing. Caressing.

'I really can't say goodbye. I have to go to the hospital tomorrow to see Dorothy. She'll be wondering what's become of me. Mac . . .' breaking voice, fighting the tears, 'just don't be here when I get back, OK?'

'If that's the way you want it.'

'It's not what I want at all. But there's no choice. You have to go. I have to stay. And I can't say goodbye.'

'OK, that's how we'll do it.'

One precious night. Nancy slept on the sofa curled in Mac's arms. When John woke at five a.m. she went to him, pulling a cover up over Mac. Fed John watching Mac sleep. Made him breakfast, pancakes and maple syrup. Mechanical, mechanical. The only way she could get through this.

At ten thirty she and John were ready to go to the hospital. She kissed Mac one last time and left. Her heart was a searing pain. Her throat ached with unshed tears. *I love you. I'll always love you. I'll never forget. Never.*

The trolley. The hospital. Dorothy talking and complaining. Everything happening behind a darkened veil, in a thick fog of pain and misery. When she returned there was no car on the driveway; the house was empty, Mac had gone.

A few weeks later, Nancy realised she was pregnant. Nine months later, Ellen was born.

Part Seven

The Present

I

The Costellos are all together for the first time in more years than Nancy cares to count. All together around the dining table in her home, their home. Her children, Ellen and Ritchie, her beloved granddaughter Sarah. Belinda, Ellen's elder daughter, is the only one missing, but Belinda is almost a stranger to Nancy, a face in a photograph on the dresser, a name on a Christmas or birthday card. She's close to Ellen, Nancy knows; perhaps that is why she has never spent as much time in Florida, or bonded with Nancy as Sarah has. She's taken her lead from her mother. Nancy regrets that she has never had the chance to really get to know Belinda, but that is the way it is. The ones who are close to her are all gathered.

It should be a cause for celebration, Nancy thinks. She should be proud and content. Instead her overwhelming emotion is apprehension. She can think of nothing but the need to tell them the truth, set the record straight whilst she still can, and time is shorter than she thought. She owes it to them, especially to Ellen. But how the hell will Ellen take it, discovering that the whole of her life has been based on a lie? That her father was not Joe, whom she

473

had adored, but a stranger? That she is not the person she has always believed herself to be? The foundations of her world will shift and she will have to put herself back together, piece by piece.

Nancy knows it is quite possible Ellen will turn against her entirely. If believing that John had been conceived as a result of an illicit relationship and foisted off on her and Ritchie as their brother had been enough to alienate her, then this will surely be beyond her understanding or forgiveness. Nancy suspects that Ellen would be censorious of any infidelity and any deception; that is her way. She sees everything in stark black and white; for her there are no shades of grey. How much more strongly will she feel when she learns the truth?

Nancy's consolation is that the same certainty that makes Ellen so entrenched on moral issues also gives her a strong sense of self. Ellen is by nature independent, grounded, self-confident. Nancy prays that it will be enough to help her come to terms with the truth, yet still cringes inwardly each time she anticipates Ellen's shock and distress. There is a vulnerable streak in Ellen too, though she is good at keeping it hidden.

But Nancy knows there can be no turning back now, hasn't been ever since she called Ellen and asked her to come to Florida. And perhaps the point of no return had been reached even before that, when she had enlisted Sarah's help to try to find Mac. The time has come for the truth to be told; she is weary of deception and half-truths, and there is not much time left. But she is not looking forward to it. Oh, she is not looking forward to it at all.

After talking with Sarah, Nancy called Ellen herself, apologetic but firm.

'I really have to talk to you, Ellen. I know it's a lot to ask and

I'd come to you if I could, but I can't, and in any case I want to speak to you and Ritchie together. If you can only find the time, I'll happily pay for your flight.'

'There's no need for that, Mom.' Ellen sounded faintly offended, the last thing Nancy wanted.

'I'd like to,' she said.

'You'll do no such thing.'

'But you will come?'

'Let me talk with Bob. I'll call you right back.'

'This is very important, Ellen.'

'I'll call you right back, I promise.'

'OK.' Nancy returned the receiver to its cradle. Her hand was shaking a little, and not just from the arthritis. She stared at it for a moment, sighed deeply, turned to Sarah.

'She's gonna talk with your dad and call me back.'

Sarah smiled faintly. When did Mum ever consult Dad? She made up her own mind and put her decisions to him as a *fait accompli* for his nominal approval.

'You think she'll come?' Nancy asked anxiously.

Sarah nodded with more confidence than she felt.

'I think she'll come, Grandma.'

Ellen found Bob in the den leafing through his golfing magazines. He glanced up as she came in.

'Who was that on the phone?'

'Mom.' She perched on the chair opposite him, legs drawn up neatly beneath her, hands clasped together resting on her knees. 'She wants me to go to Florida.'

'I think you should. It's such a long time since you saw her, and she's getting older, Ellen.'

'I know.' She stared down at her knuckles, pushing her wedding ring up and down her finger. 'I should, I know I should. I just don't know if I can face it.'

'Oh, Ellen.' He sounded faintly tetchy, the way he always did when faced with something he didn't know how to deal with. Ellen didn't need to explain why she didn't want to go home – she'd told him everything long ago in the days when they'd shared everything. Back then she had often sunk into black depressions that could be triggered by the strangest things, seemingly unconnected to anything that had happened – a wrong word, a rock 'n' roll tune on the radio, a shared joke that suddenly triggered another, darker emotion. Her face would change as if a light inside her had gone off and she would be struggling with her inner demons. Bob had understood that she was hurting about her brother's death, tormenting herself at the part she believed she, Ritchie and her mother had played in it. But that hadn't made it any easier. He'd never known what to say to comfort her; his clumsy advice to her to 'try and forget about it' had only seemed to make things worse.

Thankfully, over the years the moods had come less and less often, the times when he'd heard her sobbing behind the locked bathroom door became a memory. But he'd seen her wavering back in that direction ever since Sarah had told her that Nancy wanted to find this man Mac. He'd heard it in the brittle edge of her voice, noticed her brooding, closing in on herself, sensed her heightened impatience with him and the world in general, seen the tears come into her eyes for no apparent reason. She hadn't actually broken down, to his knowledge anyway, but he had seen her fighting to get a grip on herself, which usually culminated in her finding something to busy herself with where she would be alone, such as changing the bed or going into the garden to prune the roses, and he had cursed Sarah, and Nancy, for resurrecting her demons, and himself for his inability to know how to help her.

'Take things a bit easier, love,' he had said ineffectually. 'You push yourself too hard.'

And Ellen, being Ellen, had shrugged impatiently, said she was fine, and carried on exactly as before. The Ellen the outside world saw was tough, efficient, a perfectionist, someone who took everything in her stride. Only he knew the other Ellen, the one with a raw place inside she never allowed others to see, and which she had spent years trying to deny to herself. He knew that however hard she tried to pretend otherwise, inside that hard outer shell lingered the ghost of a girl whose world had broken apart, a girl who had lost her entire family, not just a beloved brother. That although she would deny it to the death, Ellen was vulnerable. He looked at her now, tight as a bow string, playing with her wedding ring as she struggled with her demons and her conscience, and felt utterly helpless.

'I suppose she wants to talk about John,' she said without looking up. 'I would have thought Sarah would have told her by now that I know this Mac was his father.'

Bob shuffled his feet into his slippers.

'Perhaps she wants to explain.'

'I suppose she does.' Ellen snorted. 'I'm not sure that I want to hear.'

'But if it's so important to her . . . don't you think you should perhaps let her? I know it's not easy for you, love, but she is your mother. I honestly think you should humour her, let her make her peace with you as she sees it. If you don't, when something happens to her, I think you'll regret it.'

When something happens to her. Not if. A muscle clenched in

Ellen's stomach. Whatever Nancy had done or not done, she *was* her mother, and she'd been a good mother too. There were plenty of happy memories if she cared to think about them, it was just that they were overshadowed by what had happened. Just because Nancy had favoured John – and Ellen could never get it out of her head that she had – didn't mean she didn't love Ellen and Ritchie too.

Yes, she would like to see Nancy. But Ritchie was another matter. She had never been able to forgive him for, as she saw it, being responsible for John's death, never been able to forget the terrible things he had said the night before John died.

'I think I could just about bring myself to go if I didn't have to see Ritchie,' she said.

Again, Bob had no need to ask her what she meant. 'Perhaps you don't need to,' he offered.

Ellen tutted. 'How can I go to Varna and not see Ritchie? He's been living with Mom since he and Mary-Lyn broke up. He runs the business.'

'Oh, Ellen, I don't know what to say . . .' Bob sighed helplessly.

'In any case, Ritchie will certainly be there because she wants to talk to us both together.'

Bob said nothing for a moment. In the silence he could hear Ellen hyperventilating a little.

'Maybe that's not what she wants to talk to you about at all,' he said thoughtfully. 'Maybe it's something else entirely.'

'What else could it be?'

'I don't know, Ellen. But I do think you ought to go.'

She was silent, chewing on her lip, twisting her gold bangle round and round her wrist.

'Would it help if I was to come with you?' Bob asked.

478

For a moment he thought she was going to refuse his offer, that her pride in her own independence was too strong. Then he saw her lip tremble.

'Oh, Bob – would you?'

'Well, of course I would. If you want me to.'

She was twenty-one again, her world in tatters; with his face in shadow the toll of almost seventy summers was hidden from view, full on there was no hint of a paunch over the waistband of his bagged-at-the-knee jeans. He was young again to her, handsome in a crisp shirt and cavalry twills, the knight in shining armour into whose shoulder she had cried, who had rescued her from the nightmare that her life in Florida had become, brought her to England, given her a fresh start and two lovely daughters, stuck by her, for all her faults. Ellen experienced a moment of overwhelming love.

'Oh, Bob, thank you,' she said.

Ellen returned her mother's call whilst Bob went on-line to check flights. She took the walkabout phone into the study, watching the computer screen over his shoulder.

'There's one leaving Heathrow early on Friday,' Bob said.

'Did you hear that, Mom? Friday?'

'Sounds fine to me.'

'OK, we'll book onto that. I'll call you back to confirm.'

We.

'Bob's coming with you?' Nancy asked, surprised.

'Yes. He's a gentleman of leisure now. Is that OK with you?'

'Sure. It'll be good to see him.' Someone else to hear her confession, Nancy thought. But support for Ellen. She would need that. 'If you fix a connecting flight to Fort Myers, we'll pick you up from there. Or if Ritchie's not busy, perhaps he could hop over to Miami to pick you up.'

Ellen's stomach clenched.

'No. Don't complicate matters. We'll get ourselves to Fort Myers.'

'OK, we'll see you on Friday.' A tiny pause. 'Thank you, Ellen.'

'Oh, Mom, don't be silly.'

Keeping busy, Nancy found, was the best way to combat nerves, and certainly there was plenty to do. Sarah had been using her mother's old room; now she volunteered to move into the small guest room, so there were two lots of bedding to be changed, two rooms to be cleaned and put in order. Nini, the Filipino maid who came in for a few hours twice a week, did most of it, but Nancy felt the need to supervise her more thoroughly than usual. She wanted to be sure everything was perfect for Ellen's first visit in years.

Then there was the proposed takeover of the business to think about. Sarah had driven her up to Fort Myers where she'd met with Roscoe Feldman, boss of Wings West, and then to her lawyers in Varna. Matthew Pitt had handled all her affairs for years and was a friend as well as her legal adviser; she trusted him implicitly and knew she could safely leave matters in his hands. But this was too important to her to delegate entirely. She wanted to meet personally with the man to whom she was proposing to hand over the business that she and Joe had built up together, and she wanted to be sure that if she went ahead with it, Ritchie's future would be secured. A nice lump sum invested, and a steady salary that would take him comfortably into his retirement. She would settle for nothing less.

It hadn't been easy, though.

'You know that if I was to sit tight, I reckon there's a good chance Varna Aviation would go bust and I could pick it up for a song and there'd be no strings either?' Feldman had said when she set out her terms.

'So why don't you?' Nancy returned acidly, determined not to be bullied.

'Reckon it suits me to take it over as a going concern. But your son . . . well, I'm not so sure about that.'

Nancy held his gaze steadily. 'I'd have thought an experienced pilot like Ritchie would be an asset, particularly when he's totally familiar with how things work at Varna.'

'Not when he's reached the age when he expects to be paid full whack. And not when he brings with him the kind of reputation your son has, if you'll forgive me for saying so.'

Nancy bristled. 'Ritchie has been flying ever since he was old enough to hold a licence, without a single mishap.'

Roscoe unwrapped a strip of gum, put it in his mouth and chewed, his narrowed eyes meeting hers directly.

'It's his judgement I'm questioning, not his ability as a pilot. Varna Aviation has gone downhill since he's been in charge, from what I can make out. It was a good, profitable concern in your husband's day.'

'Times change,' Nancy said shortly. 'It's not so easy now for small independent outfits. You need capital behind you to expand. You grow, or you die. Well, I don't have to tell you that, Mr Feldman.'

He smirked. This was not one sweet little old lady, this was a woman with an eye for business and a steely determination not to be done down.

'I'm not sure I'm keen on the company he keeps either,' he said, watching her speculatively.

'And what the hell business is that of yours?' she demanded. 'If Ritchie does a good job I can't see that his personal life comes into it.' She began gathering her things together. 'It's been nice to meet you, Mr Feldman, but I reckon we've both been wasting our time.'

'Hang on now, hang on!' Feldman transferred the chewing gum to his cheek where it bulged like stored food in a hamster's pouch. 'I didn't say I wouldn't keep your son on. Means a lot to you, I can tell.'

'It means a lot to Ritchie. Varna Aviation has been his life. I won't see him cut adrift from it now.'

'OK.' His jaws moved rhythmically on the gum again. 'I can see you're not gonna budge on this one. If I keep Ritchie on, you'll consider my offer, right?'

'And Monica Rivers.'

'You've got it. She is an asset, from what I hear.' Clearly he'd been doing his homework; Nancy would have expected nothing less. But she liked the man; she thought he was straight. 'And Ritchie?' she pressed him.

'You drive a hard bargain, Mrs Costello.' He sighed. 'Just one proviso, though. If Ritchie steps out of line, he's out the door. Deal?'

Nancy hesitated. Once she'd given her word, that was it as far as she was concerned. The legal papers might not be drawn up yet, but that was just a formality. If she agreed now she would, in her own mind, have crossed the Rubicon. It would be the end of an era. The business she'd seen Joe build up from one little crop-sprayer to a fleet of single- and twin-engined planes with their own livery, gone. Swallowed up by Wings West. Though she knew it was the right way, the only way, still it tore at her gut to do it.

I'm sorting out all the loose ends of my life, Nancy thought. Tidying up before I leave. And, if what the doctor told me last week is right, if the tests they ran were mine and not mixed up with somebody else's, then I'm not doing it a moment too soon.

She held out her hand, a little puffed, a little gnarled, across the desk.

'Deal.'

'Nice doing business with you, Mrs Costello.'

'And you, Mr Feldman. My lawyer will be in touch.'

Sarah was waiting for her in the car. She glanced at her grandmother expectantly.

'Well, honey, I did it,' Nancy said, and sighed.

'You're sure it's the right thing?'

'Sure. Like I said to Mr Feldman, there's no room for the little man any more. And Ritchie's just not up to stretching his horizons. Maybe if John had lived it would be Varna Aviation taking over Wings West, but as things are . . . well, you just gotta face facts.'

'Ritchie is going to be pretty upset.'

'Don't I know it! But he has to count himself lucky he's not going to end up on the Unemployment Compensation Programme. This is a pretty good deal, all things considered. I think that Roscoe Feldman wants Varna Aviation pretty bad. And he wants it now. He admitted as much. If he'd hung on and waited, he could well have picked it up for a whole lot less, the way things are going. But for some reason he can't wait.' She hesitated. 'And neither can I.'

'Oh, Grandma, don't start that again! You have years and years left yet.'

Nancy glanced through her lashes at Sarah. Something else she should tell her. But she didn't want to, not yet. She wanted to come to terms herself first with the certain knowledge that time was much shorter than she had thought, and that it was going to be all downhill from here on in.

'Come on, Sarah,' she said instead. 'Let's get back to Varna.'

She was struggling to fix her seat belt; Sarah leaned across and did it for her.

'Where to, Grandma? Home, or your solicitor's?'

There was a determined set to Nancy's chin. 'My solicitor, as you call him. Let's get this sorted out before Ritchie has the chance to rock the boat.' She smiled thinly. 'Unless he's done that already, and that's why he's gone so quiet.'

When Nancy told Ritchie what she had done, however, she was surprised by, if grateful for, his reaction.

'That's it, then.' He sounded resigned, relieved almost.

'I've made sure you've got a job there, Ritchie, as long as you want one. And that needn't be long at all if we invest the capital wisely. And you don't think of getting married again.'

He threw her a look.

'I know . . . you're getting it together with Mary-Lyn. Monica told me. She's an expensive item, though, Ritchie.'

'Don't I know it! But so is her alimony.'

'That's not a good reason for hooking up with her again.'

'Give me credit for some sense, Mom.'

'So?'

'Truth to tell, we're good together.'

'So why did you split up?'

'Hell, I don't know. I was too busy working, I guess. Mary-Lyn doesn't take kindly to being a grass widow.'

'And now you'll have more time to spend with her if you want it.'

484

'Yeah. Sure.'

Nancy was greatly relieved there was to be no big bust-up but still a little puzzled by his change of heart. Maybe it was as she'd thought, he'd decided there was more to life than trying to hold a failing outfit together. But there was something not quite right, and she wasn't sure what it was. He'd always been so damned determined to prove himself; giving in so easily just wasn't in his nature.

She was imagining things, she told herself. Just be grateful you've one less thing to worry about. Because with Ellen and Bob arriving on Friday, she surely had plenty else.

Sarah met her mother and father at Fort Myers as planned; just as well, Ritchie had a keen new pupil who was anxious to fly every day when he finished work in the Municipal Offices so as to get his licence as soon as possible.

As she waited for them Sarah puzzled over what it could be that Nancy wanted to say to Ellen, and why she had been so insistent she should speak to her and Ritchie together. It was connected somehow with what Chris had hinted at, it had to be, but Nancy had refused to explain. 'Your mother and Ritchie have to be the first to know,' was all she would say. And: 'I just hope she doesn't take it too hard.'

Sarah hoped so too, wholeheartedly. She was desperately anxious that this visit would go some way to healing the rift between her mother and grandmother. But Nancy was worried, she could tell. She was a little withdrawn, a little preoccupied, and more edgy than Sarah could ever remember her being. It didn't bode well. But though she turned the various possibilities over in her mind none of them made any sense, especially given that Sarah had told Nancy that Ellen knew that John was Mac's son, had done for years. And it couldn't be any other way . . . could it? On a timeline of Nancy's life, nothing else worked.

But there was something, and Chris Mackenzie knew what it was. Sarah struggled to remember exactly what he'd said, and failed.

She could see him clearly in her mind's eye, though; tall, good-looking, dark hair flecked through with silver and fallen rose petals. He'd made quite an impression on her, she conceded. More than any man in a long time. It was just a pity she wasn't likely to see him again. Gloucestershire wasn't a million miles from Bristol, just up the road, in fact. But their paths were highly unlikely to cross unless one or the other of them made the effort, and she could hardly turn up on his doorstep again.

There was always the gliding club, though. 'May see you there sometime,' he'd said. Had it been a hint, an oblique invitation? Sarah grinned wryly, laughing at herself. *You're getting desperate, missus.* But this wasn't about her other obsession, the longing for a child. This was about Chris, as a man. Though she certainly wouldn't object to him fathering her child either, come to think of it . . .

Stop it, Sarah. Stop it right here.

There was always the DFC. He'd said he'd be proud to take care of it if that was what Nancy wanted. Now that *was* the perfect excuse to see him again – to take him his father's DFC. Sarah brightened at the ray of hope on the horizon. And felt the curiosity tugging at her again as the train of her thoughts ran full circle.

A plane was downwind, turning on to base leg. Sarah checked her watch. That could very well be Mum's plane. She watched it bank another turn on to finals, slowly sinking as it lined up with the runway. Sarah watched it, mesmerised. God, how she loved planes! The nose was raising slightly now as the pilot flared, and the aeroplane hung for a moment like a hovering bird, then sank again, down, down, until wheels kissed the runway with no more than the tiniest bounce, just a hiccup really. Sarah let out her breath on a long sigh, realising she'd lived every moment of that descent and landing along with the pilot.

Sun glinted on slow whirring propellers as the plane turned to taxi back towards the airport buildings, wheels of shimmering silver. Yep, her mother's plane all right, she thought as she clocked the American Airlines logo and livery.

She closed the windows of the car, locked it, and set off towards the arrivals lounge to meet her parents.

II

Home. She was home. The place where she had been born and raised, spent the first twenty-one years of her life. Yet Ellen felt oddly displaced. So much was as she remembered it, and yet everything was subtly altered, as if she was seeing it through a prism. The streets, intersecting at right angles to form a grid, sunlight slanting through the trees that lined them, stark shadows on sidewalks, avenues of shops and cafés with parasol-shaded tables outside them, the drug store, the bowling alley, a host of memories attached to each one, yet seeming to belong to someone else entirely. Another person in another life.

Mom's house, the door painted blue. *Blue?* It had always been white. Mom, standing in the doorway, smiling, wearing cream linen trousers and a gaily patterned overshirt. Nancy had always loved her overshirts, must have had a closet full of them, all made out of silk. Ellen could remember opening the door and burying her face in them, smelled again the perfume Nancy had used that clung to them ever so faintly. Coco. Did she still use Coco, or had she moved on to something flowery, something that smelled of lavender or rosewater? Unlikely. Nancy would never conform to the stereotypes associated with an old woman. Hell, she probably didn't even admit to herself that she was old.

But oh my God, she is so small! Was she always that small? As she embraced her mother, Ellen was shocked by how fragile her frame felt, her bones like bird bones, the flesh on her arms had withered into goose-flesh, and she seemed to have no breasts at all. 'Mom . . .' Ellen's voice cracked, guilt suffused her. She shouldn't have left it so long. However difficult it was for her, she should have come before now.

'Oh, Ellen, it is so good to see you.'

Nancy's voice hadn't changed, but then Ellen already knew that. When she spoke to her mother on the telephone it was easy to assume that because Nancy sounded exactly as she always had, nothing else had changed either. But it had. Oh, it had.

'And Bob too.' Nancy kissed her son-in-law on the cheek and Ellen noticed her hands, little puffy claws, resting on his arms as he bent towards her.

'Come in. You want a cup of tea, or something stronger? And you must be dying to freshen up. Whichever comes first, just say. I've put you in your old room, honey. Sarah was using it but she's moved out into the little guest room.'

They settled on the tea and slices of carrot cake Nancy had baked, though Sarah had offered to do it. 'I'm not so old I can't rustle up a carrot cake,' Nancy had said.

To Ellen, the living room had the same unreal quality as the streets of Varna had, familiar yet seeming smaller, a subtly different shape. And the odd feeling persisted when she went up to the bedroom. Bob had already carried up the suitcases and gone back downstairs for another cup of tea; Ellen was anxious to change out of her travelweary shirtdress into something cooler and fresh, and needed a few moments alone to compose herself too. She didn't know what she'd expected when she'd entered her old room – something of Sarah, maybe, since she had been using it for years, presumably. But stepping inside was like stepping back in time. Same drapes at the window, though faded now in narrow stripes where the suns of forty summers had slanted in through the blinds; same blue patchwork quilt that Nancy had let Ellen choose herself when it was time for the bright bubble-patterned throw she had loved as a child to be replaced by something more grown-up. Same family of china rabbits lined up on the dressing chest, the third-place rosette she'd won in that long-ago Pony Club event still hanging above it. Some of her books were still lined up on the shelf beside the bed though they were held in place by a stack of more modern paperbacks that Ellen presumed Sarah had left there – a couple of Philippa Gregorys, *Captain Corelli's Mandolin*; *Birdsong*. Ellen selected one of her own old volumes, *A Summer Place*, and as she leafed through it a picture of James Dean, cut from a magazine, fluttered out.

Bizarre. It was quite bizarre. It was as if she had been transported back through time to another life that she couldn't quite believe had been her own.

Ellen looked at the bed, same headboard, different mattress – she hoped! Even in those days it had been a bit lumpy, though she had been too young and supple then to care much about such things, and she had loved the fact that it was a double bed, not the singles her brothers had been given when they outgrew their bunk beds. She remembered lying in on Sunday mornings, reading *Little Women* and crying because Jo didn't finish up with Laurie but with that ugly old professor. Hoping that her mother might bring her half a grapefruit, soaked overnight with a spoonful of sugar and topped with a dollop of cream, as she sometimes did. Oh, the flavour of those grapefruit! She could taste it now, tingling on her tongue. And that bed had seen her in so many moods, praying last thing at night that she would be pretty and *popular* – 'Oh, please, God, let me be pretty and *popular*'; agonising whether any boy would ever ask her out – 'Please, God, let *someone* ask me for a date. *Anyone*, just so I won't be the only one in class who hasn't been asked out. Except perhaps Fatty Lennox, with his terrible acne'; exulting when Ken Kelsey had asked her to the Spring Hop . . . oh no, don't go there.

Ellen crossed to the window, travelled further back in time as she looked out at the tree outside her window, still there, still shady and mysterious, allowing very little light to filter through its branches. When she was small she had used to weave all kinds of fantasies around that tree. Sometimes it was a ship, sailing right across the ocean, and she was all alone in the rigging. Or in the crow's nest. A crow's nest seemed exactly the right thing to find in a tree. Or she would imagine that if you climbed right to the top, through the canopy of branches, you'd be in another land, not a Jack-and-the-Beanstalk land, but another Narnia. She'd find it and she would take John and Ritchie there and they'd be Prince John and Prince Ritchie and she would be Princess Ellen.

Sadness overwhelmed her suddenly, sadness for those lost children. John dead. Herself grown old and bitter. Ritchie . . .

Ellen hardened her heart. She had to get through this somehow, and remembering the happy times wasn't helping. Because seen in retrospect, knowing how things had turned out, was just too darned sad.

Ellen sloughed off her crumpled shirtdress, tossed it in the linen basket. Wearing only her bra and panties she unpacked a few of the things she'd brought with her and hung them in a neat row in the closet, stacked underwear in a drawer, arranged toiletries on the dressing chest. She laid her nightdress – T-shirt-style cotton jersey – on one pillow, Bob's pyjamas on the other. Lined up shoes in pairs in a corner against the wall. Reverting to type, to efficient, organised Ellen, made her feel better. She'd have liked a shower, but Mom would be wondering what was taking her so long already. The shower would have to wait for later. Ellen slipped on a cotton T-shirt and a pair of walking shorts, slid her feet into mules, brushed her hair and slicked on a touch of lip gloss. Then she went back downstairs ready, she thought, for almost anything.

Monica looked up as a shadow fell across her desk.

'Officer Vesty!'

'Roy. Call me Roy.'

'Roy.' Foolishly she felt a blush beginning at the base of her neck, spreading upwards. 'What brings you here? Did you find out who broke into Nancy Costello's house?'

'Nope. Reckon we'll be lucky to track that varmint down.' He was fiddling with his gun holster, settling it more comfortably on his hip.

'Well, if you do catch up with him, I hope you give him a real hard time,' Monica said. 'It's a pretty sad thing when a woman Nancy's age can't be safe in her own home.'

'Reckon so.' Roy Vesty's mind was clearly not on Nancy; he shifted his not inconsiderable bulk from foot to foot.

'Anyway, she's got her family with her right now,' Monica said, feeling the need to fill the silence. 'Sarah's been here the best part of a week, and her daughter and son-in-law flew in yesterday. Reckon that's just what she needs. Company.'

'Sure thing.'

'Well.' Monica scooted her chair back a bit from her desk to a spot where she could look at the police officer without craning her neck, realised with a rush of self-consciousness that her wide thighs, spreading over the seat of the chair, were now clearly on display beneath the rucked-up legs of her shorts, and hastily scooted the chair back in again.

'What can I do for you then, Officer Vesty?'

Roy. He'd told her to call him Roy. But old habits die hard, and he hadn't corrected her this time. Just stood there, looking uncomfortable. Goddamit, he was making her uncomfortable.

'Could you drink a coffee?' she suggested.

'A coffee would be good. If it's not too much trouble.'

'No trouble.'

She slid the chair back again, managing to lever herself out of it simultaneously. Her legs looked OK when she was standing up. Well, not so bad anyway, because her shorts covered the flab, more or less. God, she oughta go on a diet. She would. Not today, though. Not until she'd finished the pack of Krispy Kreme Doughnuts that she'd bought on her way to work this morning. There were two in the pack; maybe Officer Vesty would like one. He looked more like a steak-and-fries man, but nobody much said no to a Krispy Kreme Doughnut, and one wouldn't do as much damage to her hips as two . . .

'Do you fancy a doughnut?' she asked, coming back with the coffees.

'Thanks, but—'

'I'm having one,' she said before he could get the refusal out.

'Oh, well, in that case . . .'

She got the doughnuts out of her drawer, opened the pack, stood it on the desk between the computer and the telephone.

'Help yourself.' She fished one out, and loose sugar cascaded down the front of her red T-shirt. Quickly she brushed it away, wondering why she'd suggested this; how the hell she was going to eat a Krispy Kreme Doughnut without getting herself in a mess; and just why she was so flustered? Oh, well, too late now. Officer Vesty had already bitten into his. A custard one. There was a smear of custard in the corner of his mouth.

'This is a rare treat,' he said, chomping.

'Not so rare for me. As you can see.'

'My late wife wouldn't let me have Krispy Kreme Doughnuts. Reckoned they were bad for me. Said I'd be dead of a heart attack before I could draw my retirement pension. Funny thing, really. She's gone and I'm still here.'

'Yeah. You gotta live while you can.'

'Well,' he said, looking at her appreciatively, 'they don't seem to have done you much harm.'

Monica wasn't going to argue.

'What was it happened to your husband?' Officer Vesty asked. 'Was that a heart attack?'

'Brain haemorrhage, except they called it by some fancy name. But that's what it was. A brain haemorrhage.'

Officer Vesty shook his head. 'Damn shame.'

Monica laughed. 'Will you just listen to us? They say gin can make you maudlin, but I never heard Krispy Kreme Doughnuts could do the same.'

'I guess life's full of surprises.' He was grinning too. It was a nice grin, she thought, mischievous like a little boy's, which, given his boxer's face, with that nose that looked like it had been on the wrong end of someone's fist more than once, was very appealing.

'Roy . . .' she said, and this time it came naturally, but before she could go any further his personal radio crackled to life. He threw her an apologetic look and went to the door, talking with his back towards her. Monica felt a pang of regret. Chances were he was going to have to go. Just as she'd begun to enjoy herself.

Sure enough, a moment later when the police officer turned back to her, it was with a resigned expression.

'Duty calls, I'm afraid.'

'Something serious?' She couldn't help her natural curiosity.

'Not so as you'd notice. Some visitor's managed to wrap his car round Annie Obern's display stand, and Annie's hollering blue murder. Reckons he's ruined half her stock. I keep telling her that stand is obstructing the sidewalk, but will she listen?'

Annie Obern ran a gift shop on Varna's Main Street, and she kept a stand bearing fancy purses, sun hats and sandals outside where folks could easily see them. Monica knew, she'd careened into it once herself when she wasn't looking where she was going.

'I don't suppose he's done his car much good either,' Monica said. 'There goes the excess on his insurance premium.'

Officer Vesty swallowed the last of his coffee, turned for the door, turned back again.

'I was wondering if you'd fancy stepping out one night. A drink, maybe a bite to eat?' he said, all of a rush.

Though she'd guessed ten minutes ago the reason he'd stopped by, the invitation now caught Monica off balance. Suddenly she was flustered again.

'Oh . . . well . . .'

'Say no if you want to.' Officer Vesty was rubbing his neck beneath the collar of his uniform shirt, half turned to walk away.

'Gee, thanks,' Monica said. 'I'd like that.'

'You would?'

'Yeah, I would.'

'How about tonight then?'

'Tonight would be good.'

'OK, I'll pick you up, say . . . about seven thirty?'

'Fine.'

'See you then.'

He didn't ask where she lived. But then, of course he knew. Hadn't he brought Russell home all those years ago when Russell had had too much liquor?

Monica watched the big frame walk out the door, picked up the remains of her Krispy Kreme Doughnut, paused with it halfway to her mouth, made a snap decision and aimed it instead at the waste basket. It hit its target and bounced in out of sight, removing the last hint of temptation. As she pulled the computer keyboard towards her, Monica was smiling.

Nerves were beginning to get to Nancy. So far, everything had gone well. So far they'd skirted around so much as mentioning the reason she had asked Ellen to come to Florida. Nancy was surprised Ellen hadn't questioned her before now; she'd half expected her to come to the point the minute she arrived, and had been ready to explain, as she had to Sarah, that she needed to talk to her and Ritchie together, and it would be Saturday evening before that could happen. But Ellen hadn't said anything. It hung in the air, though, an awkwardness that was almost tangible, and Nancy guessed that Ellen was as uncomfortable about the imminent heart-to-heart as she was.

She glanced through the open patio doors as she sliced toma-toes for a salad. Sarah, Ellen and Bob were sitting around the table by the pool, sipping pre-lunch drinks. They'd offered to help her

– well, Ellen and Sarah had – but she'd shooed them out, telling them she'd do it.

Ellen looked tired, she thought. Long-haul flights weren't a lot of fun when you got older, she knew that from experience. And Ellen sure was older. Nancy had been shocked when they first arrived at how much older she looked. Stupid, really, but she'd got into the habit of picturing Ellen as she'd been, oh, around her middle thirties, perhaps. Seeing an unmistakably middle-aged woman with sprinkles of grey in her hair, a face etched with a network of tiny lines and little jowls forming beneath what had once been a firm, clean-cut jaw line, and knowing that this woman was her daughter, had given her quite a jolt. Impossible, surely! My baby? But my baby is almost sixty years old. The realisation had brought her own ageing home to Nancy more sharply than any of the frailties she coped with daily, or the face she had grown used to seeing in the mirror, or even the unwelcome news the doctor had given her just a few days ago. *My baby is growing old. What the hell does that make me?* But Ellen was looking good for all that. She had taken care of herself. And . . . maybe it's in the genes, Nancy thought, and smiled to herself before the thought pierced her armour, reminding her with a sick jolt of the conversation that lay ahead.

How the hell was she going to tell her? In quiet moments, Nancy had gone over and over it in her mind, trying out various openings, and none of them was right. Each time she quailed inwardly as she anticipated the moment when she would have to go beyond the point of no return and shatter the deceit on which Ellen's life was founded. A nerve twanged now deep within Nancy and she felt sick with apprehension. It was her own fault; there was no one to blame but herself. She could lay it partly on Joe, and the fact that he hadn't wanted Ellen to know, but she wouldn't, unless they expressly asked. The years of silence were a web of her own making, the decision to hide the truth was the sting of the spider paralysing its prey. And concealing the truth had only compounded the original wrong. She should have been brave enough to admit it years ago instead of pretending to herself that she was keeping silent for the sake of others. In fact, she had only made things worse.

Oh, Ellen. Nancy stacked one wrist on the other, stabbed at the tomato, and bled inwardly for the pain she knew she was about to inflict on her daughter. But Ellen was strong, wasn't she? She was Mac's daughter too. And she had Bob. Not for the first time, Nancy thanked God that Bob had come too. He was good for Ellen, always had been. They were so different, but their personalities complemented one another. There was a solid pragmatism about Bob that would bed Ellen's anchor if only she let it. Nancy had seen how Ellen had turned to him in the dark days after John's death; she had not wanted her daughter to fly off and make a life half a world away, especially so soon after the loss of her beloved son, but she had told herself it would be Ellen's salvation, and she had been right. And if Bob had sustained her then, how much more would he do so now, with the bond of forty years of marriage between them?

Strangely enough, Nancy wished with all her heart that she could tell Bob and let him tell Ellen. Easier to admit her folly and failings to someone who was not her own flesh and blood, and who was not so personally involved. He wouldn't judge her either, or at least she didn't think he would. He would simply accept the facts and move on. But she couldn't do that, couldn't take the easy way out.

And Sarah . . . would Sarah judge her? This affected her too. She was going to be equally shocked to learn that Joe was not her grandfather at all. Would she too withdraw, feeling cheated and deceived? She had been incredibly supportive so far, but would the whole truth be a step too far? Nancy prayed not. If Sarah turned against her too, she did not think she could bear it. But she was determined, all the same, that she would not plead for their understanding or forgiveness, nor try to excuse herself. She would simply tell them what happened and hope they could come to terms with it, for their own sakes.

A few more hours, that was all she had. Ritchie had promised to be home for dinner; tonight they would all be together. A few more hours and the Rubicon would be crossed. After all these years, the truth would be out. And there would be no going back.

III

They're all around the table, and though so far not a word has been spoken about the reason they're gathered, the tension in the air is palpable. Nancy can feel it prickling on her skin, pulsing in her veins. She can see it in the tight line of Ellen's lips and Ritchie's scowl. Even Sarah is tense, though she's making a heroic effort to be bright and cheerful. Only Bob is acting normally. He's enjoyed his meal – chicken and corn fritters followed by apple pie – and eaten everything on his plate, unlike the women, who have left a good deal. He's feeling a bit drowsy now, and not surprisingly. Two days ago, this was way past his bedtime.

He gets up from the table, stretches, goes to the window.

'Looks like there's a storm brewing out there.'

In here too, Nancy thinks. In here too.

'They're pretty spectacular, as I remember it.'

Even as he says it, the first lightning flashes, lighting up the room, which has grown darker without them really noticing, and a spat of heavy rain scuds against the window.

'Let's get these dishes cleared, Mom.' Ellen gets up too, goes to pick up some of the detritus of the meal, briskly efficient as always.

Nancy stays her with a hand on her arm. 'No – leave it, honey.'

Ellen ignores her, piling plates one on top of the other. 'Easier done now. I hate clutter.'

But Nancy has waited long enough. She can't face clearing the table, loading the dishwasher, rinsing the glasses separately in the sink as she knows Ellen will insist they do, knowing what she's got to say to them. She wants to get it over with. And if Ellen still wants to worry herself with dirty dishes when she's heard what Nancy has to say, then that is up to her.

'Please, Ellen, leave it. I have to talk to you. Let's go through into the sitting room.'

'Mom.' Ellen clatters a couple of forks down onto the top plate. 'Do we really have to have this conversation?' She lifts the pile of plates purposefully.

Thunder cracks, seeming to roll over the house from one side to the other.

'Yes, Ellen, I'm afraid we do.'

'Why? When we already know what you're going to say?'

For a moment Nancy is totally floored. 'You do?'

'Yes, Mom, we do.' She delivers what she thinks is her *coup de grâce*. 'I have known since I was thirteen years old that John wasn't Dad's. That he was illegitimate. And Ritchie knows too. So can we please leave it at that?'

Nancy feels very little, as if she's shrunk inside her skin. She can feel herself shaking. This is it, then. All her carefully rehearsed openings gone for nothing.

'The trouble is, Ellen,' she says, very quietly, but very firmly, 'you have got it all wrong.'

Ellen bangs the plates down on the table again so hard that a wineglass jumps.

'Wrong? How do you mean – we've got it wrong? Are you trying to tell me you didn't have a child with this man you wanted Sarah to try and find? Because I know you did. I saw a letter he wrote you, years ago. So it's no good you trying to deny it now.'

'I'm not denying it,' Nancy says with dignity. 'I am trying to set the record straight.'

'You're not denying John was this Mac's child. So what, pray, is the point of dredging all this up? Really, Mom, I don't want to know about your sordid affair. I'm sorry, but I don't. And trying to find him after all this time, involving Sarah . . . to be honest, Mom, I think you've taken leave of your senses.'

'Ellen, cool down . . .' Bob is looking uncomfortable, alarmed even. This is going to end in tears. Ellen's. More guilt, more remorse, and he will have to deal with the fallout.

'No, Bob, I won't cool down,' Ellen snaps at him. 'Could you be cool if it was your mother who'd hidden the fact that your brother was illegitimate all these years and then suddenly decided to unburden herself when it suits her? Could you?'

'Ellen, please . . .'

'Well, I can't. I'm sorry, but I can't. Nothing against John. I loved him to death, even when I knew he wasn't my full brother. I loved him so much! And he might still be alive today if Mom had come clean from the start, if she hadn't favoured him because he was her secret love child. It's true, Mom, isn't it? You favoured him because every time you looked at him you saw your lover.'

'No, Ellen, it's not true.' Nancy is totally, utterly shocked. 'How could you think such a thing?'

'You did! You looked at him and saw his father.'

'Ellen . . . Joe was John's father.'

'But . . . you said . . .' It's Ellen now who's brought up short in mid-sentence, her certainty rocked for the first time. 'You said you weren't denying you had an illegitimate child with this man. You didn't deny it.'

'Please, Ellen, sit down.'

'No, I don't want to sit down. I want to know what you're talking about.'

Another flash of sheet lightning illuminates the room. Ellen, taut with a fury that has boiled within her for most of her adult life, but puzzled too; Sarah, screwing up a napkin between her hands, wanting her mother to stop, for this to be over; Nancy, a small resolute figure, steeling herself to say the words that will dispel the illusion for ever.

'I did have a child with Mac, Ellen,' she says, very quietly, but very deliberately. 'But it wasn't John. As I told you, Joe was John's father.'

'Then who . . . ?' Ellen glances wildly at Ritchie, who has been silent throughout this whole dreadful scene.

And Nancy speaks the words she has dreaded speaking.

'It was you, Ellen. That's why I had to tell you. It wasn't John who was Mac's son. You are his daughter.'

All the colour has drained from Ellen's face. Though she wouldn't sit when Nancy told her to, she sits now, plopping down onto the chair as though her legs will no longer support her. There's absolute silence in the room, broken only by another rolling clap of thunder. Then Ritchie says: 'Christ!' Nobody takes the slightest notice of him. They are all too stunned. Bob goes to put his arm round Ellen, she shrugs him away. Her body language reflects the fact that her whole being is in denial.

'I never heard anything so ridiculous!' Her voice is shrill, hysterical almost.

'Honey, I am so sorry . . . I should have told you, I know. But we decided, your father and I—'

'My *father*? Him, do you mean? This *Mac*?' She spits the name with venom.

'No, honey. Joe.'

'He knew?'

'Of course he knew. You don't think I could have kept it from him, do you?'

'I don't see why not! You kept it from the rest of us. And he could live with it? That you'd . . . that I . . .' Ellen breaks off, unable to put words to her mother's infidelity, her betrayal.

'Yes,' Nancy says quietly, though to herself she admits it wasn't always so.

When she had first confessed it had almost broken him, almost finished them as a couple. She had never for a moment considered deceiving him, though she could well have done. Joe had been home often enough from his teaching post in Tampa to make it entirely possible for her to pretend that he was the father of the baby she was carrying. Shift the dates a little, pretend that Ellen had arrived a little early or a little late, and he need never have known. But Nancy couldn't bring herself to do that. She couldn't face living a life with him that was based on a lie. Even though she had been able to do the very same thing with Ellen.

But of course it wasn't the same thing. It wasn't the same thing at all. Joe was her husband and there shouldn't be secrets between husband and wife. But Ellen was her child, and a mother's primary instinct is to protect her child, to give it security, a safe, stable environment in which to live and grow. And Joe's wishes had to be considered too. She had hurt him so much, not only his heart but his pride too. He couldn't stand the fact that anyone should know that he wasn't enough for his wife, that he wasn't the father of her child. Children.

Right away, when she'd confessed, practically the first thing he'd asked her was if John was his.

'Joe, you know he is!' she'd said, shocked.

And the new, cold, angry Joe had snarled back: 'How can I be sure of that? How do I know you didn't just tell me that to get me to marry you when you thought this other bastard was dead?'

She'd pleaded, distraught. It was the most important thing in the world that he should know John was his; she couldn't snatch that away from him too. And in the end either she had convinced him or he had worked it out for himself; he had never again suggested John had any other father but him. Indeed, he had used it against her.

'I suppose you want me to kick you out so you can go off with your lover? Well, it ain't gonna happen, Nancy. Leastways, if you go, you go alone. If you wanna go to this fucking Mac, I can't stop you. But I'm telling you straight. He's not having my son.'

She'd known that. She knew it was not an option. And she was strangely relieved, because at least it was one decision she didn't have to make. For all the compelling passion she felt for Mac, she loved Joe too, loved their life together. She didn't feel able to choose between the two men, the two quite different loves she felt for them. And Joe's stubborn insistence that John would stay with him whatever meant that the decision was made for her.

But how could things ever be the same now between her and Joe? She'd known he'd be dreadfully hurt, dreadfully angry. That there was going to be the most terrible scene. But this was worse than anything she'd imagined. This was a Joe she'd never seen before, saying things she'd never dreamed would come out of his mouth.

'Best thing you can do is get rid of it,' he flung at her now.

'*What!*'

'Get rid of the baby.'

'Oh, no.' Nancy was distressed but determined. 'I got rid of one baby. I'm not getting rid of another.'

Joe threw her a disgusted look that spoke volumes. When she'd told him, long ago, about William Eagle, the rape and the backstreet abortion, he'd been kind, gentle, sympathetic. Now, however, he threw it right back in her face.

'Honey, when it comes right down to it, you're no better than a bitch on heat.'

She gasped at that, pressed a hand to her mouth, tears starting to her eyes.

'That isn't fair, Joe,' she said, but she knew it was. William Eagle hadn't been her fault, but she'd forfeited any right to Joe's understanding when she slept with Mac. Remembering their uninhibited lovemaking, she had wondered if they had both subconsciously wanted this, and pushed the thought away. It was too painful. It made her feel too guilty.

How had it come to this? She thought briefly of all the girls she'd known who'd slept around when war made a mockery of morality, and gotten away with it.

'I guess I'm just too damned fertile,' she said bitterly.

Joe snorted. 'That's one way of putting it, I guess.'

She squared her shoulders. 'But I am not getting rid of this baby, nor leaving John. And Joe . . .' she hesitated, her eyes filling with tears, '. . . I don't wanna leave you either. I know I've hurt you terribly, and what I did was real awful, but I do love you. Honestly I do.'

He said nothing and he was refusing to look at her. She laid a tentative hand on his arm. 'So what are we gonna do?' she asked in desperation.

He shrugged her away with a cold disdain. 'What you do, honey, is up to you. I'm not your keeper. But I can sure as hell tell you what I'm gonna do. When I'm home, which won't be so often, except to see John, I'll be living out in the trailer.'

Nancy was aghast. When Dorothy had been discharged from the hospital she had gone to stay with her relatives up-state to recuperate, so Nancy and Joe were alone in the house. Had Dorothy been there, Nancy didn't think Joe would have suggested such a drastic step; he wouldn't have wanted Dorothy to know it had come to this. But then, if Dorothy had been there none of this would have happened.

'Oh, Joe, please . . .' she begged. She wanted this resolved as soon as possible, and how could that happen if they had no contact with one another?

But Joe refused to budge. He collected his things together and took them to the trailer and Nancy tried to tell herself it was probably for the best. Joe was hurting, real bad. He needed to hole up somewhere where he didn't have to see her. He needed time. Though she wasn't sure there was enough time in the whole of the universe for him to be able to forgive her. Or that she deserved his forgiveness.

Joe's antagonism lasted for the whole of Nancy's pregnancy; as her body swelled he could scarcely bring himself to look at her, let alone speak to her or touch her. He devoted all his attention to John, playing on the floor with him, holding his hand as he struggled to keep his balance and toddle, blowing bubbles for him from a clay pipe and bowl of soapy water. If Nancy attempted to join in he would simply pick up the boy and walk away, ignoring her. He didn't even glare at her now, it was simply as if she did not exist.

The change in his attitude, when it came, was so gradual it was almost imperceptible. There was no sudden conversion on the road to Damascus, no one event that triggered his change of heart. Perhaps it was the enormous effort Nancy made to show him how she cared for him, though over and over he rejected her, that made the first breach of the dam. Perhaps it was Ellen herself; the fact that she was a girl, no threat to John's supremacy, though she was a determined little character right from the start. Or perhaps it was simply that Joe loved Nancy too much to keep up the wall of silence and antagonism between them. Nancy would never know; she had not asked. She only knew that slowly Joe was softening in his attitude, embracing acceptance.

No one apart from themselves knew that Ellen was not Joe's child; no one, as far as she knew, suspected. The only other person who knew the truth was Mac – Nancy had felt it only right that she should write and apprise him of the situation – and he was in England. He had written back, pleading with Nancy to leave Joe, but she had told him her mind was made up and asked him to accept her decision. She didn't expect to hear from him again.

No one feels the need to whisper in a baby's ear that the man rocking the cradle or pushing the buggy is not really its father. Ellen heard John calling Joe 'Daddy', and when she began to learn to talk she followed suit. At that stage, Nancy and Joe never discussed whether or not she should be told, and later Joe made it clear he thought it would be in everyone's best interests that she should not. Though Nancy suspected it was partly his pride that ruled his reluctance to admit the truth, she did not argue with it. What Joe wanted was paramount; he'd been hurt enough. As Ellen grew up it did worry Nancy sometimes, but she tried to put it to the back of her mind. They were a unit, John, Ellen and, later, Ritchie; she didn't want Ellen to feel displaced, an outsider, and in any case, even if Joe had agreed to it, the time was never right. How could it be? When did you sit a child down and explain that the man she believed to be her daddy was not her father at all? That she belonged to a stranger she had never met? The years had passed; the deception was perpetuated, becoming ever more entrenched.

Only now does Nancy realise just how wrong she had been to go along with it. And wonders if perhaps she has got it wrong again, and if she should have taken the secret to her grave.

'Ellen, I am so sorry,' she says again. 'But please, honey, please try to understand the way it was. It wasn't just a one-night stand. Your father and I loved one another very much. I'd thought he was dead, and—'

'Stop it, Mom. I don't want to hear.' Ellen is on her feet again, rigid, trembling. 'To think I came all the way to Florida for this.' She rounds on Bob. 'Find me a flight, Bob. I'm going home.'

'Ellen—'

'I mean it. I don't want to see any of you ever again.'

'Mum, please, don't.' Sarah is as shocked as anyone, but as yet she hasn't had the opportunity to consider how this affects her, changes everything for her too. She just wants this terrible row to stop, and besides being distressed by her mother's reaction, she's worried for Nancy.

'That goes for you too, Sarah,' Ellen flings at her. 'You've colluded in this. How could you? I don't want to see you either.' She turns for the door, collides with it because although her head is held high, her eyes are full of tears. She yanks it open, goes through.

Sarah is on her feet too, making to follow her. Bob grasps her arm, halting her. He doesn't tell her in words not to go after her mother, just by a firm, decisive shake of his head.

'But, Dad, I have to—'

'Leave her to me.'

Then he's gone too, his heavy measured tread on the stairs following the scuttling clatter of Ellen's sandals. Helpless, Sarah stares after them.

Ritchie shifts. 'I need a drink.' He heads for the dresser, gets out the bottle of Jack Daniel's, pours three glasses. 'You want one too?' He holds out two of the glasses.

'Grandma?'

Nancy nods, but says nothing. She looks very little, as if Ellen's onslaught has physically diminished her. But her back is still ramrod straight, her chin determined. Sarah hands her the Jack Daniel's, she sips it, sits down.

'It had to be done, Sarah.'

Ritchie has drained his first drink, gone for a refill. Now he's patting his pockets for his cigarettes. 'I'm going out for a smoke.'

'Have it in here, Ritchie. It's pouring with rain.' Nancy's voice sounds surprisingly normal. How can she be so calm, so contained? Sarah wonders.

Ritchie crosses to the window, looking out. The storm is still circling, lightning flashing, thunder crashing and rolling, but the rain is no longer beating down.

'I think it's stopped now.' He goes out, glass in one hand, pack of cigarettes in the other.

Now it's just Nancy and Sarah.

'Oh, Grandma,' Sarah says despairingly.

Nancy levels her eyes with her granddaughter's.

'I am so sorry, Sarah, to spring this on you. But you can see why I had to tell your mother first.'

'I'm not sure it was such a good idea to tell her at all.'

'No, me neither. But it's done now. I just hope she'll accept it when she's had time to get used to the idea.'

'She shouldn't have said the things she said.'

'She was in shock. Still is. And you know your mother . . .'

'I do!'

Nancy lays her puffy hand over Sarah's where it's resting on the table, fingers curled around her glass. 'What about you, honey?'

'Well,' Sarah laughs shakily, 'I suppose I should be glad to be the product of such a grand amour. A pretty romantic background, really.' She pauses, then adds ruefully: 'Scuppered my chances with Chris Mackenzie, though, hasn't it?'

Nancy frowns, not understanding.

'I quite fancied him. Good thing I found out in time he's my uncle.' She chuckles again, but bitterly, regretfully.

'Oh, Sarah . . .' Quite suddenly, Nancy's control is slipping; she wants to weep. She'd thought she was ready for anything; that she should have broken any dreams Sarah was dreaming is a step too far. A tiny one, maybe, compared to the life-shattering truths she's revealed today, but somehow the one thing beyond being borne.

'I am so, so sorry . . .' How many times can she say it, and will it make the slightest difference? 'Can you ever forgive me?'

'Oh, Grandma!' Sarah relinquishes her hold on her glass, turns over her hand, clasping Nancy's. 'God knows, I've made my mistakes. We're all human. You too.' She smiles, a little wanly, but with all the love and tenderness that is in her heart for the extraordinary woman who is her grandmother. 'For goodness' sake, Grandma, you know me better than to think I'd blame you. I'm here for you, you know that. Just as long as you need me.'

'Oh, Sarah,' Nancy says with feeling. 'Thank God for you.'

Ellen checks the clock on the nightstand. One thirty a.m. She must have slept a little, she concedes, though she hadn't expected to. The bourbon Bob brought her earlier must have knocked her out, especially since she'd had so little to eat and rarely drinks alcohol. That and the exhaustion that follows a bout of good hard crying. But she is wide awake now, her thoughts chasing round her brain in endless circles, nerves twanging. And Bob is snoring. Not the awful farmyard noises he makes sometimes, but the kind of gentle rhythmic rattle that leaves you waiting for the next one. It reminds her of why they'd settled on separate bedrooms at home. He doesn't stir as Ellen pushes aside the covers and slides out of bed. How the hell can he sleep so soundly after all that's happened? But then, nothing much keeps Bob awake.

Ellen opens the bedroom door, listening. Not a sound from the house, and all the lights are out as far as she can see. She pulls the door closed behind her, pads downstairs barefoot. The dining table has been cleared, the remains of the meal taken as far as the kitchen, but the dirty plates are piled there on the counter and there are pans still on the hob. Ellen contemplates washing them up, decides against it. She unlocks the kitchen door, goes out into the yard.

The storm has passed over now. The night is still and warm, the air scented with the sweet freshness of the rain. It evokes unspecific memories, an aura, rather than pictures, of happier times. Ellen wants to cry again. She crosses the patio, passes the pool, heads for the grass beyond, wandering, just wandering, her arms wrapped around herself for comfort, not because she is cold, though she is only wearing her T-shirt nightdress. The grass, still wet from the rain, is cool beneath her bare feet. She reaches the picket fence and begins to cry. Not the excess of near hysterical weeping that had followed her angry outburst, but an ache in her throat, a trembling of her jaw, a gathering of tears in her eyes.

The first shock has passed now, leaving an unutterable sadness. It will probably hit her again sometime soon, but for the moment she is numb, washed out by anger and by tears. She feels bereaved rather than displaced, stripped of everything she has always taken for granted, the foundations on which her whole life was based. Joe was not her father. But he was, *he was*! She remembered his gentleness, his patience, his pride. It was Joe who had carried her on his shoulders when her little legs were tired, Joe who had wiped her tears away with his big handkerchief that smelled of tobacco and gasoline, Joe who had beamed with pride when he saw her up there on the podium on her graduation day. He wasn't her father, but he'd acted like he was. He'd known she was not his daughter, but somewhere along the line it had ceased to matter to him. Perhaps it didn't matter in the end. What mattered was that he'd been there for her, always there for her. There was no denying the bond between them; that had been real enough. She should count herself lucky. If he had rejected her it could have been so different. She'd have missed out on so much.

It was ironic. So damned ironic, that's what it was. She'd thought John was the odd one out and all the time it was herself.

'Ellen?'

She hasn't heard anyone come out of the house; hasn't realised she is no longer alone. She swings round to see Nancy standing there, a little diffident, a little uncertain, half expecting Ellen to rant at her again, no doubt. Ellen sighs. She's past that now.

'I saw you from the window. Honey, you've got nothing on your feet and that grass is so wet . . .'

'It's OK, Mom. I'm not ten years old any more.'

'No, that's true.' But I'm still your mom. Nancy doesn't say it, doesn't need to.

'I couldn't sleep,' Ellen says.

'Me neither.' Nancy is wearing a bright patterned silk kimono that Ellen remembers. Mom cooking pancakes for breakfast, wearing that kimono. Pretty. She had been so pretty. Now she looks tiny and fragile. And unsure of herself. So very unsure.

'Mom . . .' Ellen hesitates. 'I guess I said things I shouldn't have.'

'Not surprising. I know this has been one hell of a shock for you, honey. We should have told you years ago but somehow we got the idea there was no need for you to know. You loved Joe and he loved you, so much. He was so proud of you. I think in the end he forgot himself that his blood didn't run in your veins. You were his girl, and that was all that mattered. But when he was gone and couldn't be hurt any more . . . maybe I should have told you then.' She paused, considering. 'It would have seemed like a betrayal, though.'

'So why tell me now?'

'Because I realised I owed you the truth. Not just you, but Sarah too. And I guess this will have hit her just as hard. She adored Joe too. But she needs to know who she is, and so do you.'

They are silent for a long moment, two ghostly figures in the soft moonlight. Then Ellen asks: 'What was he like, my real father?'

Suddenly Nancy wants to weep, but with relief.

'He was a wonderful man, honey. You'd have been proud to

515

know him.' She hesitates, makes up her mind. 'Why don't we get something to drink, sit on the patio, and I'll tell you about him.'

To her relief, Ellen nods. 'You go sit down, Mom. I'll make the drinks.'

'OK,' Nancy agrees. She feels unutterably weary, but she's beginning to dare hope maybe this is going to work out after all. There's a long way to go yet, but at least they're taking the first steps.

'There's milk in the refrigerator and chocolate and malt in the dresser,' she says. 'And if you feel like adding a snifter, there's some Jack Daniel's left in that bottle – or was, if Ritchie hasn't decided to finish it. Though I don't think he will have. He's got a long trip tomorrow, and the day after to Houston, if I'm not much mistaken.'

But Ellen doesn't want to talk about Ritchie. 'I'll make those drinks, Mom,' she says, and disappears into the kitchen.

They talk for the best part of an hour, Nancy telling Ellen the things she has never told her before. England. The ATA. Mac. She starts out anxious; she wants to do Mac justice, make his daughter see the sort of man he really was. Brave, honourable, not a cad who'd taken advantage of her as she suspected Joe had always thought.

But soon she's losing herself in memories, even laughing as she recounts some of the things that happened – how she'd flipped over the plane the first time she met him, the good times they'd shared in the midst of constant danger.

'You should have told me, Mom,' Ellen says.

'I know it. You could have met him. You don't live so far from where he lived. But it's too late now. I only wish we'd had this conversation a couple of years ago. Maybe we would have done if I hadn't got too old to fly the Atlantic, and you . . . well, you never seemed to want to come to Florida.' She hesitates. 'Why, Ellen? Why would you never come home? I don't understand why you never wanted to come home.'

She senses Ellen stiffening. The ease between them that had been such a relief a few moments ago is gone. There's a thickness in the atmosphere between them.

'Is it because of what happened to John?' she asks.

'Yes.' Ellen is tight-drawn again, the tension a wire from the depths of her stomach to her throat so that it is difficult to breathe. She is wondering suddenly if her mother knows what she knows, has known all the time. Why else would she ask that question?

But Nancy goes on: 'Honey, I know you thought the world of John. We all did.'

'I know you did. You worshipped the ground he walked on. That was the reason I was so sure that it was him who was your love child.' Her voice has an edge of frost in it once more. 'Why did you favour him, Mom?'

'I didn't favour him,' Nancy protested. 'I never favoured any one of you. You were all my children and I loved you all.'

'No, you favoured him. It was like he could do no wrong in your eyes.'

Nancy smiles faintly. 'Perhaps it seemed that way because he never did do much wrong. He was always an easy child. You could be wilful and stubborn, and Ritchie, well . . . things didn't come as easily to him as they did to John. We did our best, tried to help him catch up – Joe tried especially hard. But it didn't seem to help. John was gifted in so many ways and Ritchie wasn't, and in the long run there's not a whole lot you can do about that. He had such a chip on his shoulder where John was concerned. Still has, come to that.'

Nancy shifts in her seat, retying the sash of her kimono, which

517

has worked loose. 'John dying when he did . . . well, Ritchie just has that golden image to live up to and it's been hard on him. Which is a shame, because he's got so many good points. But everything he's tried to do, he's left feeling John would have done better. Take the business. Ritchie's done his level best, but times have changed; there's no room for small outfits like ours any more. It was one thing when we were operating out of a shack with just a couple of small aeroplanes. These days the big boys have taken away a lot of our lucrative contracts with freight and stuff. There ain't much mail any more now everybody does business on the internet, and we're left with casual jobs that don't guarantee much in the way of profit. And what there is goes on the overheads. It's no sure thing if John had been running it that he could have made it pay any better than Ritchie; in fact, I reckon he'd have cut his losses and sold out long before now. But that's not the way Ritchie sees it. He thinks he's failed again. Let down me and his dad both. He thinks I blame him for it and nothing I can say makes it any different. He reckons if John had been in charge we wouldn't be in trouble now. And there ain't nothing that's gonna change his mind.'

Ellen sighs. 'Maybe you're right. But he hasn't exactly covered himself with glory in any other area of his life either, has he? Three failed marriages can't be good for his self-esteem either.'

'He's made mistakes, it's true,' Nancy says regretfully.

'He's bound to feel that if John were still alive, that alone would be another avenue where he's failed and John would have succeeded.'

'You don't know that,' Nancy says.

'No, but I can hazard an educated guess. John wouldn't have three ex-wives bleeding him dry, I'd take bets on it. He'd be married to a nice girl, have two or three kids, all doing well, and a home of his own.'

'I don't think so,' Nancy says. Her tone is reflective, wistful almost.

'For sure he would.' Though she's lived in England for close on forty years, Ellen is already slipping back into the Americanisms that were her first language.

'Not a wife and children,' Nancy says.

Ellen's eyes narrow in a puzzled frown. Nancy doesn't sound like she's theorising; it's more as if she's stating facts.

'What do you mean, Mom?'

Nancy is silent for a long moment. Then she sighs, meets Ellen's eyes directly.

'The truth is, Ellen . . .' another pause, '. . . the truth is, John was gay.'

'*What?*' Ellen can scarcely believe her ears. '*John? Gay?*' She's speaking in italics. 'Mom, you've got that wrong.'

'No.'

'What the hell makes you think he was *gay*?'

'I don't think, Ellen. I know.'

'But . . . he had girlfriends. The girls used to flock around after him.'

'Yes, they did, didn't they?' Nancy smiles, a sad, wistful smile. 'He was pretty good at hiding it, I grant you that. I'm not surprised you didn't suspect. His father didn't either, thank God. It would have killed Joe if he had. The disappointment, the shame . . . It was a cause for shame back then. People didn't take the liberal view they do nowadays. Not that it would have made much difference to Joe, though, whether it was then or now. I don't think he'd ever have been able to come to terms with the fact that his son was a . . . well, you know the sort of term he'd have used. And it wouldn't be "gay" or even "homosexual". John knew that. He knew it would break his father's heart. That was one of the reasons he kept it a secret.'

A secret. More secrets. Is there no end to them where this family is concerned?

'I can't believe it,' Ellen says, though that is just her way of expressing her shock; she knows Nancy has no reason to lie. 'John . . . gay. When did you find this out?'

'Not until after he was dead, for sure. I'd suspected it for some time, I don't know why, a mother's intuition, I suppose.' She pauses, considering. 'Maybe you were right, Ellen. Maybe I did treat him a little differently from you and Ritchie. I guess I always knew somehow that he was different, special, somehow . . . oh, I'm not putting this very well. I think I knew that he needed special understanding, something that was quite outside my range of experience. For all his success at everything he did – and my goodness, he was successful, wasn't he? – I always kind of felt there was something troubling him. There was a vulnerability about him I couldn't fathom, couldn't reach. I can't explain it. But I think deep down I knew, even before he knew himself.

'He tried to deny it, you know, for a very long time. Tried to convince himself he didn't really feel the way he felt, wasn't the way he was. He had his girlfriends, tried to act with them in a way he thought was "normal". Couldn't really work out why it didn't seem right. And then he went to Vietnam.'

She pauses again, knotting her hands around the long-empty mug on the table in front of her, mustering her thoughts and emotions, mentally regrouping. This time Ellen does not interrupt. She waits, silent and patient.

'He met someone in Vietnam,' Nancy goes on at last. 'They . . . fell in love. And John realised for sure just what it was that was missing in his life. He'd been living a lie, trying to find what he was looking for with girls. He realised that all his deepest feelings were reserved for another man.'

'Oh God,' Ellen says. She is trembling; the bottom of her stomach seems to have dropped away. Her brother, John, the golden boy, not just satisfying his sexual urges with another man, but in love. For all that she has always believed herself to be broad-minded, liberal, absolutely not homophobic, she finds herself shocked to the core. To hear her mother talk so matter-of-factly about John being in love with another man strikes at some primeval, primitive taboo buried deep within her psyche, of which she is deeply ashamed.

'Vietnam was hell, you know that,' Nancy is continuing. 'It was hell for every man who fought there, and many of them have never been able to get over it. Even those who came home physically whole still bear the scars, emotionally and mentally. But it was a special kind of hell for John. You know the way most of the boys relieved the pressures of war – the number of American babies left behind is proof of it. They went off to the flesh-pots in Saigon, whoring and drinking. They paid for women in the towns where there were brothels, and they took them in the villages where there weren't. John didn't want that, but he didn't want to parade the difference in his sexual orientation either. He knew the kind of treatment he could expect from all those macho womanisers if they suspected the truth – the ridicule, the disgust. So he went along with it, though the torment of it was tearing him apart. And then . . . like I said, he fell in love. Damon Jameson, his name was.'

Ellen is shaking. She tries to compose herself. 'So what happened. Did they come out?'

Nancy shakes her head. 'I don't think so. Not in the way they would today. They were pretty discreet about it. But I guess some of the others had their suspicions. Especially afterwards, when they saw how hard John took it.'

'Took what?'

Nancy turns the mug again between her hands. 'He was killed, Damon Jameson. The Vietcong came over, strafing their base, and Damon was hit. He died in John's arms.'

She looks up, directly at Ellen. 'That was what finished John,' she says simply. 'That was the reason he couldn't bring himself to go back. He was deep in grief for Damon and he just couldn't face life without him. That and the homosexuality. For all that he believed he'd begun to come to terms with it, deep down he was still ashamed. And he knew the way he'd be treated, the scorn, the contempt. With Damon, he'd felt they could get through it together. Without him . . . well, the truth was John didn't think life was worth living. And I do think he was probably worn down by his experiences in that terrible war too.'

'Mom.' Ellen can scarcely breathe. 'What are you saying?'

'I'm telling you what happened all those years ago,' Nancy says simply. 'Some of it he told me himself that last leave, right here in this yard. Talking, long into the night, just like we're doing now. The rest . . . well, he wrote the rest down in the letter he left.'

'Letter?'

'Yeah. It's gone now. I destroyed it, right after I found it in his room and read it. I didn't want Joe seeing it, the truth would have killed him, and John didn't want his father to know either. The letter was addressed to me; it was for my eyes only. So I tore it up and burned it, though it broke my heart to do it, the last letter John would ever write to me. And I let Joe think what everyone thought. That the plane crash was an accident.'

'Oh my God.' Ellen thinks she is going to faint. The blood is hammering in her temples; everything seems to be going very far away. All these years she's blamed Ritchie for John's plane not being airworthy, even harboured the dark fear that it might have been no accident. Now . . . 'Mom?' Her voice is just a whisper, and Nancy's reply seems disembodied, echoing in the chasms of her mind, her heart.

'It was no accident, of course,' Nancy says. 'John was too good a pilot. He flew that plane straight into the sea on purpose, Ellen. He'd had enough. And he ended his life the best way he knew how. He knew what he was doing when he took off that day. And he sure as hell did it. John killed himself, Ellen. And now you know everything.'

Well, not quite everything, she adds silently. The doctor's diagnosis is still her secret. But that can wait. She couldn't load that onto Ellen as well. Not tonight.

Back in her room, Nancy sits quietly and thinks about it. She's not looking forward to the end, especially now she knows how she is going to die. The pain, well, she thinks she can cope with that. It's losing her dignity that worries her most. Being so weak she's totally dependent on others. If it hadn't been for that damned burglary, and Ritchie insisting she get checked over thoroughly, she might never have known. It would have crept up on her stealthily. But at least the knowledge has given her some sort of control. At least she can meet what is coming head on. And she will be able

523

to meet it knowing she's done what she should have done years ago. Told Ellen and Ritchie the truth.

A small reflective smile curves Nancy's mouth. She'd done right. She and Ellen have made their peace. She can die happy.

IV

Ritchie is already in the office at Varna Aviation when Monica arrives. She's a bit late, unusual for her, and also a bit hung over. She had a glass of wine too many last night, she thinks ruefully, but hell, it isn't often she lets her hair down, and she'd been having such a good time, dammit. Officer Vesty – Roy, she must get used to calling him Roy – took her to the new Italian place on Main Street, right next door to Annie Obern's gift shop. They had a good laugh, checking out Annie's twisted display rack, the one the tourist had driven his hire-car into, and that was even before they started on the bottle of Chianti Roy ordered. Annie had been fair mad enough to set off a forest fire, Roy said, and just to complicate things, the tourist had been Japanese. Roy had had one hell of a time sorting things out.

They ate a real fine meal and Monica had to drink most of the bottle of Chianti because Roy was driving and couldn't afford to take a chance on being over the limit, and it had seemed a real shame to waste good wine. And on top of that, she had a nightcap when Roy took her home and came in for a coffee. Maybe that was the reason she let him get real cosy, or maybe she would have anyway. She liked him a lot and she felt pretty damned comfortable with him now they'd gotten over their initial awkwardness. And neither of them had any ties, they were both free agents, and old enough to indulge in a bit of nooky if they felt like it. Which they had. She was paying for it this morning, though. But hell, it had been worth it!

'You're in early, Ritchie,' she says now cheerfully, oh so cheerfully, though her head is pounding.

'Yes, well, I've got to get down to the Windies, haven't I?'

'Oh yes, so you have.' Her mood darkens a little. 'Ritchie, this is gonna be the last time, right?'

'You know it is. Just gotta do the follow-on to Houston tomorrow, and that'll be it. I've told the boss we're pretty well done; that before you know it, Big Brother will be watching me.'

'And just as well too.' She's as sorry as Ritchie to see the end of Varna Aviation as a separate entity but relieved too. As long as Wings West keep to their end of the bargain, she and Ritchie will both have their jobs secured and no more worries. No need for these damned trips for Dexter Connelly. No chance.

Ritchie finishes filling in his pilot log, fetches himself a coffee from the machine.

'How are things at home?' Monica asks. 'Ellen and Nancy getting on OK?'

Ritchie snorts. 'There was a fair old ruckus last night.'

'Really?' Despite her hangover, Monica's natural curiosity is coming into play.

'Sure was.' But he doesn't elaborate. Doesn't want to go into details yet, if at all. Some things are kinda private, even if Monica is practically family. And it's shaken him a bit, he has to admit.

Who'd have thought it – Mom getting knocked up by some English guy when she was married to Dad? If it had been John who was illegitimate, as he'd always thought, he could understand it. These things happened, especially when there was a war on. But afterwards, when she was back in Florida, married to Dad, and John around . . . It didn't add up, and he didn't know that he wanted to think about it, much less talk about it to Monica.

He just couldn't figure Ellen, though. Once upon a time they'd been so close, but John's death had put an end to that. She'd blamed him, he knew and he'd understood that. Heck, he'd blamed himself, gone over and over the preparations he'd made that day, wondering if there had been something he'd missed, though he'd been so sure he'd done a thorough job. He'd hoped the years would have softened her attitude towards him but it hadn't. Not a bit of it. Well, there was nothing he could do about that. But what he really couldn't understand was why she was so prickly and volatile with Mom too. There was no reason for that that he knew. Maybe she got her funny ways from her father. He'd always thought it was having a different father that made John the golden boy, different too. But it seemed he'd been wrong. He and John came from the same gene pool.

Ritchie drains his coffee and gives a puzzled little shake of his head. Well, what d'you know? Perhaps he has it in him to be as good as John after all. He checks his watch.

'Monica, will you give Mary-Lyn a call for me later? She won't have surfaced yet. Tell her I'll see her tonight, OK?'

'OK,' Monica says. For once she doesn't look pained hearing him mention his ex-wife's name. He's glad about that. He'd thought Monica had a bit of a thing for him and felt a bit guilty that he couldn't reciprocate. She's a good girl, Monica. He likes her a lot, even if she does bawl him out sometimes. But he just doesn't fancy her. He knows her too damned well. And let's face it, her butt is too big.

Ritchie pulls his aviator specs down to cover his eyes, stuffs his pilot log into his flying bag and hooks it over his shoulder. Then he heads off out to do the final checks on the Beech Baron.

He's glad he's more or less through with Dexter Connelly. Quite apart from the chances he's taking, he doesn't trust the guy. Certainly not since the burglary at Mom's house. And he's not sure Connelly trusts him. That would explain why he's sending one of his side-kicks along with Ritchie to Houston tomorrow. No, Connelly is a dangerous man, and Ritchie wishes he hadn't been fool enough to get himself mixed up in dangerous business. And the worst of it is his mother has been dragged into it.

Thank the Lord it's nearly over. Just this one last trip down to the Windies, and one tomorrow to Houston and that will be it. Wings West will be taking control and they won't have any truck with Connelly.

Ritchie climbs into the Beech, straps himself in and starts the engine.

Ellen is still fast asleep when Bob gets up. He has a feeling she was up in the night; he woke once and found her side of the bed empty and guessed she was having trouble sleeping. Perhaps it was his snoring keeping her awake, he thought; the way she complained about it at home you'd think he was holding a rave, or whatever the kids called it these days, on his side of the bed. He wondered if she'd gone down to lie on the couch to escape it, toyed with the idea that maybe he should go down and tell her he'd take the couch instead. But maybe she'd just gone to the bathroom. He'd give her five minutes.

Five minutes later, though, and he'd nodded off again, and next time he came to she was back, curled up with her bum resting against his hip and breathing deeply, even snoring a little herself. He didn't know why she went on so about him snoring; he quite liked hearing her. He'd missed it since she insisted on having separate rooms, missed the warmth of her body beside him too, and the scent of her hair on the pillow. Ah well, *c'est la vie* . . .

He decides now not to waken her. She had a pretty traumatic time last evening and really upset herself. Let her sleep.

He goes downstairs. Sarah and Nancy are both up, Ritchie apparently has already left for work. Nancy looks tired, with dark circles under her eyes, and she's sitting at the table letting Sarah make breakfast.

He feels awkward for Ellen that she'd made such a scene last night. He understands she was upset, but all the same, she ought to have a bit more thought for her mother.

'Morning,' he says, trying to sound normal.

'Morning, Bob.' For all that she looks so tired, Nancy sounds pretty chirpy. 'Ellen still asleep?'

'Yes.'

'I'm not surprised. We had a pretty late session, she and I. Oh, it's OK,' she waves a hand as she sees his look of alarm, 'it was good. We straightened quite a few things out.'

'Oh, good.' He doesn't know what to say. But he's not going to pry, that much is for certain. Ellen will tell him all about it when she's good and ready.

'Are you ready for some breakfast, Dad?' Sarah asks, turning round from the cooker.

'What's on the menu?'

'How about eggs, sunny side up?'

'Sounds good to me.' He smiles to himself.

Sunny side up. He fervently hopes that goes for more than just the eggs.

Ellen comes to slowly. It's broad daylight, and she's alone in the bed. She checks the clock – almost ten. She can hardly believe it. When did she last sleep till nearly ten o'clock? But then, when did she last go to bed with dawn breaking? She sits up, and suddenly it's all there in her head, all the things Mom told her last night, and she lies down again, plumping the pillow behind her, trying to get a handle on it. She can't. It's just too much to take in all at once. She can't even really work out how she feels. There are so many emotions churning round inside her.

But one stronger than all the others. Guilt. It lies in her stomach like a heavy meal eaten too late at night. She wants to cringe and run and hide from it, so ashamed is she. All these years she has blamed Ritchie for John's death, and he hadn't had anything to do with it. She's cut herself off from her family because she was so sure of it and she was utterly, completely wrong. Ritchie wasn't to blame at all. John had killed himself. Because . . .

Her stomach gives a sickening lurch and she folds in on herself. *John, oh, John! So tortured and we never knew. So tortured you took your own life. So much for the golden boy, on whom everyone's high expectations rested.* Perhaps that had been part of the trouble: he'd known he couldn't live up to them. Oh, John, John . . .

Ellen pushes aside the covers, unable to bear them on her a moment longer, pads to the window, draws back the drapes. The sun at this time of day comes from the other side of the house, so it throws a huge shadow across the lawn, and the tree outside the window is just a mass of dark green, not the delicate tracery it will become later in the day. Ellen stares out, her heart, her whole being aching with her long-lost brother's pain and the terrible sense of inadequacy that comes from knowing he was hurting so much and she had done nothing to help him.

She can see him now in the shadow on the lawn, just as when she arrived two days ago he seemed to be in every corner of the house. She saw him in the back yard, fixing her bicycle, pumping up the tyres, greasing the chain. She saw him emerging from the bathroom, towel wrapped around his waist, fair hair darkened because it was still wet from the shower. She had heard him singing along to the rock 'n' roll music he had loved: Bill Haley, Little Richard, Elvis. Now she sees him mowing the grass, wearing a pair of scarlet running shorts and a black vest, the early sunlight turning the feathering of fair hairs on his arms and chest golden. Oh, John, John . . . suffering alone, and we never knew. Suffering so much . . . and we never for one moment guessed.

Secrets! Ellen bares her teeth suddenly in a grimace that is almost feral.

So many secrets. They've all been guilty of keeping them. Her mother. Her father. John. Herself. And where has it got them? Here, that's where. A family torn apart by secrets. Ritchie, it seems, is the only one who has none. All his faults are clearly on view, he's the only one who doesn't hide them away. Ironic, really. At least if you know someone's faults there are no shocks in store. You take them as they are or leave them. And the one she blamed most turned out to be the only one with no secrets at all.

How the hell could it have happened? Because of the way things used to be, she supposes. Everyone used to care so much about appearances. When moral standards were supposedly high no one dared be seen to slip beneath them. Her generation and the one before ridiculed the Victorians for their double standards, covering the legs of their pianos because they deemed them improper, whilst carrying on in private in the most debauched fashion. But they weren't so different. Human nature never changes, only attitudes to it. Today you could have as many children as you cared to as a single parent and no one turns a hair. Today you can be proud to be gay, adopt children and get married even. A generation ago it would have been unthinkable, a matter for shame.

And so in the name of respectability the secrets had piled up, compulsively kept, hidden from the light of day, to fester and give rise to suspicion that gnawed away at the edges of the mind, feeding on the lies and half-truths.

Footsteps on the stairs; the bedroom door opens softly.

'Ellen? Oh, you're awake then.'

Bob. She turns to him, sees a solid figure who has been and still is the constant in her life. No secrets between them. He knows her through and through for what she is, and miraculously still loves her. And she knows him. Over recent years, the very fact that she knows him so well has become a source of discontent: habits, responses, all so familiar, she has become almost contemptuous of them. Now she sees what a safe haven that familiarity really is. They may not always approve of what the other does, may not even like aspects of one another very much, but when the chips are down they will support one another to the hilt. That is the legacy of forty years of life together, the ups and the downs, the problems and the good times, all shared and worked through.

Perhaps that was how it was for Nancy and Joe. Almost certainly it was. Whatever the secrets they kept from the rest of their family it seemed there were none between them. What they had lacked in a great romantic beginning was compensated for by a willingness to work together so that love and mutual respect grew into that unity that Ellen remembers she always sensed between them.

'Are you OK, love?'

She looks at Bob, standing there in the doorway, concerned for her, and thinks that she has been very lucky. Maybe their grand passion is gone now, but they had it once. Unlike Nancy, whose grand passion was for a man who was destined never to be hers. She and Bob shared their glory days, and though the ardour has dimmed, it has transmuted into something of the utmost value. Something she does not think she could go on without. Something she is not at all sure she deserves.

'Yeah, I'm OK,' she says. 'A bit shell-shocked, but OK.'

And she smiles at him, a little wanly, but with determination. She's got a lot of making up to do to a lot of people. And she's going to start right now. The first day of the rest of her life.

V

It's around five p.m. when Ritchie gets back from his trip. He lands, ties the Beech down and heads back to the office. Monica is still there, but packing up ready to go home – early for her. She avoids asking him anything about his trip and he guesses she doesn't want to be involved any more than she has to be.

'Anything happen today that I should know about?' he asks her.

'There was a call about your Houston trip tomorrow. The note's on your desk.'

Ritchie is getting himself a cup of coffee. 'Can't you just tell me?'

'Something about your passenger won't be on board. And they want you to go a couple of hours later. Mid-morning instead of first thing. Like I say, it's on your desk.'

'OK.' Ritchie doesn't quite know what to make of that. Perhaps Dexter Connelly has decided to trust him alone after all. But he doesn't understand why the change in the timings and he's not entirely happy about it. He'd prefer to get this over and done with as early as possible. Then again, a later time might fit in well with his own personal plans; it will give him far more flexibility if he doesn't have to be up at the crack of dawn.

'Did you call Mary-Lyn for me?' he asks Monica.

'I tried. Two or three times. She wasn't answering, though. All I got was her messaging service.'

Ritchie grimaces. He hopes she's not up to her old tricks. He's working very hard at trying to patch up his marriage, and he really does want to see her tonight. Besides which, he surely doesn't fancy another evening spent listening to his family rowing and tearing one another apart.

'I did leave a message,' Monica says. 'She'll get back to you, I reckon, when she's good and ready.'

'Sure thing.'

Monica leaves, and Ritchie decides to try Mary-Lyn himself. He's luckier than Monica was; she answers more or less right away.

'I was thinking,' he says, 'maybe we could take a trip down to Miami, have ourselves a good time. And if we're enjoying it we could stay over. I don't need to be in work until mid-morning tomorrow.'

He's holding his breath, and to his delight Mary-Lyn agrees.

'We'll see how it goes, but that sounds good to me.'

Ritchie's smiling to himself as he locks up and leaves. Things really seem to be taking a turn for the better.

Monica and Roy are down by the Marina, sitting at a table outside one of the little bars, watching the boats come in and the sun set, a deep red, like a wash of fresh blood over the sea. They've enjoyed a good meal – snapper and fries – and Monica can't believe her luck. Two nights in a row she hasn't had to make herself dinner and eat it all alone. There's something a little bit odd about Roy tonight, though, but nothing she can put her finger on. It's just as if there's something on his mind that he's not saying. Yet. She hopes it's not that he's getting cold feet, that last night had been going too far, too fast for him. If he's trying to work up the courage to tell her he thinks they ought to cool it, she'll be gutted. It's just so damned good, being with a guy she really likes and who seems to like her.

'That boss of yours,' Roy says unexpectedly. 'Runs a pretty regular outfit, does he?'

All of a sudden her nerves are twanging. 'How d'you mean?'

Roy shifts a little awkwardly in his chair. 'He's not into something he shouldn't be, is he?'

'Ritchie?' She's real flustered now; her voice comes out too shrill. 'Of course not! What makes you ask something like that?'

Roy takes a long pull of his beer, clearly ill at ease. 'Just wondering . . .'

Monica's alarm tightens a notch, pulling strings in her stomach. This conversation is highly peculiar, especially given that Roy is a police officer, has been all his life. It's in his blood. Could it be that he's got his suspicions about what Ritchie is up to? Is that why he's suddenly come on so strong – because he wants to pump her? She can't believe she'd be so naïve as to be taken in by something like that, but hell, something just ain't right here.

'Ritchie's OK,' she says. 'He's got his little ways, but he's got a good heart.' As a character reference it's barely adequate, but it's the best she can do, knowing what she knows. She's not going to lie to Roy; it wouldn't be a good start.

Roy takes another pull of his beer, relaxing a little. 'That's OK, then.'

Monica thinks she should let it go at that, but she can't.

'Why d'you ask?'

'Oh . . . just something I heard that got me a mite worried.'

'Like what?'

There's a long silence. Roy is obviously struggling with his conscience. Then he says: 'Don't s'pose I should be telling you this, but we've had the DEA boys nosing round the last few days. Drugs Enforcement Agency, you know. Seems they've got it in their heads there's something going on round here that shouldn't be going on.' He pauses, she waits. 'Drug running,' he says.

Monica's heart seems to miss a beat, then start up again very rapid and uneven. All of a sudden she feels sick. 'Drug running?' she repeats, almost inaudibly.

'So it seems. A lot of moonshine, if you ask me. Can't see anybody running drugs into Varna myself. An' even if somebody is, it wouldn't be a respectable, well-run outfit like Varna Aviation. Nancy would never countenance anything like that going on.'

'No, she surely would not!' Monica says emphatically, glad to be able to voice at least one opinion with conviction.

Roy drains his glass. 'No, I reckon they're wasting their time watching Varna.' He levels his gaze with Monica's. 'This is just between ourselves, mind you. My job would be on the line if it got out what I've just told you. Me and my big mouth could cost me my badge.'

There's something in his eyes that's hard to read, but she has a feeling she knows what it is. Roy is warning her. He doesn't know for sure that Varna Aviation is running drugs, but he knows they're under suspicion and being watched. And he doesn't want her mixed up in it. He cares enough about her to put his job in jeopardy, disclosing information he knows darned well he shouldn't.

They sit in silence for a moment and then Roy says: 'Why don't you take the day off tomorrow? I've got a day off myself. Maybe we could take a run down to the Everglades, spot ourselves a few alligators.'

The change in direction doesn't fool Monica. The minute he says it, her head is spinning, her throat gone dry. Oh my God, something is going to happen tomorrow. Either at Varna or in Houston, maybe both.

'How about it then?' Roy presses her.

'Yeah,' she says faintly. 'Why not?'

'Great.' Roy's shoulders relax, he pushes back his chair, nods in the direction of her glass. 'Another drink?'

'If it's all the same to you, and seeing as we're making a day of it tomorrow, I think I could use an early night,' she says.

'Oh.' He looks a little nonplussed.

'We were pretty late last night. A girl's gotta catch up on her beauty sleep sometime.'

'OK, if you say so. Though you're looking pretty good to me.'

'Nice of you to say so.'

But all the pleasure has gone out of the evening. Monica is worried sick.

She has to do something, and she doesn't know what. She doesn't want to get Roy in trouble for spilling the beans on what is clearly a covert operation. But she can't let Ritchie walk into a trap either. He shouldn't have done what he's done, of course. He should never have got mixed up with this business. Hadn't she told him that? But he'd done it anyway, out of desperation. And now he wishes he hadn't. Hell, she's seen how relieved he's been that there's a way out of the mess he's gotten himself into, so relieved that he's resigned himself to the deal with Wings West. He's not a bad man,

539

just a damned foolish one. If he gets caught, he'll go to gaol for sure. He'll be finished. And Nancy . . . oh my God, if he goes to gaol, it'll kill Nancy.

Monica is pacing the floor, beside herself with worry and not knowing what the hell to do for the best. Really, aside from warning Ritchie, there's not a whole lot she can do. She can't go out to the airfield and get rid of the stuff herself, and if what Roy said is right there's a good chance the airfield is under surveillance and any unusual activity would be noticed. Much as she wants to save Ritchie's bacon there is no way she is going to implicate herself. She's fond of him, yes, protective even, but not so besotted she's going to be a stooge for him, especially when he knew darn well what he was doing was wrong, when she'd told him so herself.

Monica picks up the telephone, punches in the number of Ritchie's mobile. She'll warn him, without any mention of Roy. She'll warn him as best she can, and then it will be up to him.

But Ritchie isn't answering his phone. She can't even get his messaging service. And she can't try to see if she has any more luck with Mary-Lyn because she doesn't have her number. It's in the book at the airfield, but she's never had any reason before now to want to call Ritchie's ex-wife when she's at home. But if Ritchie's phone is switched off, then Mary-Lyn's most likely is too. They've gone out somewhere, no doubt, and don't want to be disturbed.

A thought occurs to her. Perhaps they're at home, the marital home they'd once shared, and where Mary-Lyn still lives. Monica doesn't have that number either, but Nancy surely will.

She picks up the phone again and dials Nancy's number. It rings for a long while and she is just about to give up and disconnect when Nancy herself answers. She sounds surprised to hear Monica's voice.

'We're all sitting outside by the pool. Have you been ringing long?'

'Not long,' Monica lies. 'I'm real sorry to disturb you, Nancy, but I'm trying to get hold of Ritchie. You wouldn't happen to know where he is, would you?'

'As a matter of fact, for once I do. He and Mary-Lyn have gone over to Miami. He told me not to expect him home tonight. In fact, I think he might go straight to the airfield in the morning. He's got a trip booked to Houston, he said.'

Monica's heart sinks. 'You don't happen to know where they're staying?'

'Sorry, no. Is it urgent, then? Anything I can help with?'

Monica is close to tears of desperation. 'No, but I really need to speak to him. If he calls . . .'

'I doubt he will.'

'But if he does . . . or if he comes home to change in the morning . . .' She brightens, grasping at straws. 'Surely he'll come home to change? His Houston trip isn't early . . . they changed the time. It's not until eleven thirty now. Will you get him to call me before he goes anywhere?'

She breaks off as a thought strikes her. She won't be reachable in the morning, or at least, she won't be alone. Roy is picking her up at nine so they can get well on their way down to the Everglades before it gets too hot. She can't talk about this in front of Roy. He mustn't know she's passed on his warning to Ritchie.

'Oh shit,' she says, 'that's no good.' She's thinking furiously. 'Will you give him a message for me?' It's not what she wants, but it's the best she can do.

'What kind of message?' Nancy sounds puzzled.

Good question. What kind of message.

'Tell him to call off the Houston trip. And tell him to leave the Beech right where it is. Not to go anywhere in it. Not to unlock it even. Just to leave it alone until I've had a chance to speak with him, and he's had a chance to contact Dexter Connelly.'

'Monica,' Nancy says, 'what in the world are you talking about?'

'He mustn't move the Beech. Not even go near it.'

'But why? And what has Dexter Connelly got to do with it?'

'Nancy, I can't tell you. Believe me, you don't wanna know. But if Ritchie tries to go anywhere in the Beech tomorrow, it's odds on he's gonna end up in gaol.'

'What?'

Monica is really flustered now; she's said far more than she meant to.

'Oh gee, Nancy, I'm sorry, but it's a real mess . . .'

'What is?'

'Nancy, I can't say. You'll have to ask Ritchie,' Monica says miserably.

'I'm asking you.' Nancy's voice is very firm suddenly, very authoritative. 'If Ritchie's mixed up with Dexter Connelly, I want to know about it. And you can tell me right here and now what it is or consider yourself fired.'

Monica grips the receiver, stares heavenward, her eyes wild. She's talked herself into a corner here, and there's no way out. She doesn't want to involve Nancy, doesn't want her worried. Nancy is an old woman. She shouldn't have this thrust upon her. But hell, it is her business, and Ritchie is her son. She has the right to know, and it's better that she hears it from Monica than getting the most terrible shock with the DEA knocking on her door, or even breaking it down. But oh lordy, how the hell is she going to begin?

'I'm waiting, Monica,' Nancy says severely.

Monica takes a deep breath and tells her.

For a long while there's silence at the other end of the phone. Then Nancy says wearily: 'How could he be so darned stupid?'

From long habit, Monica finds herself defending him.

'He thought the business was going under, Nancy. He was just so desperate to save it. He didn't want to let you down.'

'And he thinks running drugs isn't letting me down?'

'He just saw it as a way out, Nancy.'

Nancy snorts. 'That I can believe. But I'm surprised at you, Monica, being party to it.'

'I didn't condone it, Nancy, if that's what you think. But I couldn't stop him either. I know we were both relieved when you signed the deal with Wings West.'

'Much good that will do Ritchie now,' Nancy says.

'I'm real sorry, loading this on you, Nancy. I just didn't know what to do.'

'I'm glad you did. At least now I'm in the picture.'

Voices in the background, calling to Nancy, asking who is on the phone. What is keeping her?

'I'm just coming,' Nancy calls back, her tone not betraying anything of what she must be feeling. And to Monica: 'I have to go, Monica.'

'But what are we going to do?'

And Nancy, with all her old firmness and vigour, replies: 'You, Monica, are going to do and say nothing. Nothing at all. I'm only sorry my son involved you in this, and I'm grateful to you for telling me about it. Go to bed, get some sleep and do whatever it was you planned tomorrow.'

'But—'

'Monica,' Nancy says, 'just leave it to me.'

* * *

543

The house is sleeping when Nancy creeps silently out; no one hears her. The sky is rosy with dawn. She gets out her car and drives to the airfield.

There's a car she doesn't recognise parked up on the road outside, which worries her for a moment. Has the DEA got the airfield under twenty-four-hour surveillance? But as she passes she notices the man behind the wheel appears to be dozing and she breathes again. She can't help feeling a little sorry for him, though. If he is an officer of the law in an unmarked car who's fallen asleep on the job he's going to have to answer to his superiors over this. But it means she can get in unobserved, and she thanks her lucky stars for it.

She parks around the side of the offices of Varna Aviation, out of sight of the road, opens the door with her own key and goes in. A few minutes later she re-emerges with the keys to the Beech, struggles up onto the step and climbs in. She doesn't dare delay doing power checks in case the man in the car is a police officer and the sound of the engines being brought up to full power alerts him. She taxies to the runway, then turns the throttle to full, holding the Beech on the brakes while the power builds, squinting at the rev counter with enormous concentration because her eyes are not so good any more. But she can more or less tell from the engine note anyway. Though it's years now since she flew, there are some things you never forget.

OK – ready. She lets off the brakes and the Beech hurtles forward, gathering speed. She's watching the instrument panel again, waiting for the magic moment to . . . rotate. The nose lifts, the wheels are off the ground. She adjusts the angle of attack to a gentle climb, watching the grass around the runway fall away beneath her. And fills up with the most enormous sense of relief and exhilaration.

*   *   *

Nancy is enjoying this. Actually enjoying it. Yes, it's a horrendous physical effort, with her hands so stiff and useless, and the pain from them shooting fire through her wrists and up into her arms. Yes, there's an ache around her heart that it has come to this. That Ritchie could have been so darned irresponsible and stupid. But then, that's Ritchie all over. Trying so hard to get something right he just can't see that he's getting it all wrong. He's always been the same; judgement is not his strong suit. She only hopes that if she can wipe the slate clean and he can begin again, this time he'll have more sense. Perhaps Ellen will tell him about John, and knowing he wasn't after all the perfect son living the perfect charmed life might help Ritchie overcome his inferiority complex and make a go of things with Wings West, and Mary-Lyn too.

She only hopes he won't blame himself for what she plans to do. She's left a letter, explaining what the doctor had told her last week: that there's a cancer growing inside her and she's got six months left at most. That now she's set all the records straight she's decided to end it all swiftly, doing something she truly wants to do, rather than linger, in pain and dependent on others. She makes no mention of the illicit cargo of drugs aboard. She hopes Monica won't let on to Ritchie that she knew anything about them and the fact that the plane was going to get busted the moment Ritchie climbed into it. But just in case she does, Nancy has stressed that nobody is to feel bad about this, she's doing things her way. It's her choice, to make things easy on herself. And she adds how much she loves them all, and this way is better than a long goodbye.

And so it is. Perversely, she's almost glad she's been pushed into this. It is just so darned good to be in the left-hand seat of an aeroplane again, making gentle adjustments, banking a little and seeing the horizon tilt, raising the nose and feeling the response in the pit of her stomach. She turns towards the Gulf of Mexico, climbing to two thousand feet. High enough. She won't be going playing in the clouds today. She needs to do what she needs to do whilst the strength in her aching wrists holds out. And simply flying again is enough. No need to do aerobatics or fancy tricks. It's enough just to be up here one last time in the singing silence.

As she heads out towards the sea, flying straight and level, a sense of peace overcomes her, a feeling of satisfaction, of rightness, as if this was meant to be. It's better by far that it should be this way rather than slowly fading to a useless wreck of her former self. And she's ready. Even before that inescapable prognosis, she'd felt tired, as if she'd had enough. Death itself holds no terrors for her. The ones she has loved – Mac, Joe, John – have gone before her and are waiting for her. She's ready to join them. She's made her peace with Ellen, thank God. She's left all her affairs in order. And this one last thing she can do for Ritchie. There won't be a scrap of evidence against him, she'll make sure of that. And she'll achieve it by doing what her beloved John did.

Nancy's eyes, fixed on the horizon, go misty, and for a moment she is in total empathy with her long-lost son. The vista she is looking at now is the last vista he saw too. Only the time of day is different, the sky streaked pink, the bands of aquamarine sea beneath her a darker hue than the ones he would have flown over. Oh, John, dear John, did you feel as I do, the peace that comes after the torment of indecision? The utter acceptance that soon it will all be over?

She thinks then of Sarah, and takes a moment to feel the warmth of gratitude for everything Sarah has been to her, and to pray that she will find the happiness and contentment that have so far eluded her.

She thinks of Joe, dear Joe, who loved her so much that he was prepared to forgive her for all the hurt she caused him, and hopes that in the end she was able to give him the happiness he so richly deserved. Something softens inside her as she thinks of him. They had something very special; surviving the bad times formed the basis of a very close relationship, and as she once said, long ago, loving Mac didn't mean she didn't love Joe. She loved him very much, just in a different way. Mac was a distant dream; Joe became the reality, her husband of so many years, the father of her children. And they built up the business together. She thinks Joe, of all of them, would understand why she is doing this. For Ritchie and for the reputation of their other baby, Varna Aviation.

She thinks of Mac. Oh dear God, when has she not thought of Mac? He's beside her now, in the right-hand seat, face all planes and shadows above the collar of his flying jacket, looking at her, one eyebrow raised slightly.

'I suggest you watch your altimeter, Miss Kelly.'

'This plane smells like a French brothel.'

'Come to England with me, Nancy.'

'Do you love me, Mac?'

'You know I do.'

'Say it. Say it for me.'

'I love you, Nancy.'

She's way out over the Gulf of Mexico now. Way, way out.

It's time. Time to do what she has to do.

Nancy climbs another thousand feet, just to be sure. Then she lowers the nose and points it at the water. The yoke shudders, protesting, beneath her hands. Nancy summons all her failing strength to hold it forward. The water is rushing up at her, she's dizzy, dizzy. But determined. And content.

What a life she's had! Now, at the end, to be able to do this one last thing, is a blessing and a benediction.

And then, almost before she knows it, it is all over. The Beech hits the water, begins to disintegrate and is gone. There is nothing left now but the surge of the sea and the sky on the horizon silvering towards full dawn.

VI

'**A**re you sure about this, Mum?'

Sarah, driving, shifts her gaze from the road ahead momentarily to glance at Ellen in the passenger seat beside her. It's not far now to the turning to Monkshaven, the hamlet built along a cul-de-sac. Once they are on that road there's no place to turn that doesn't involve keeping straight on past Chris Mackenzie's cottage.

Ellen is a little pale, Sarah thinks, but she can see that her mouth is set in a determined line.

'Quite sure, Sarah. Let's just get it over with.'

It's three weeks now since they got home from Florida, and the first numbing shock at Nancy's death has transmuted into raw grief. Sarah can hardly bring herself to believe she will never see her beloved grandmother again; Ellen, devastated by the finality of it, is nevertheless truly grateful that she was there, and that she made her peace with her mother.

She only wishes, though, that Nancy could have shared with her the news that she was dying. It was the most terrible shock when

549

she discovered Nancy's note propped up on the kitchen counter and learned to her horror that her mother had left the house with the intention of taking her own life, and the reason she was doing it. Why, oh why, in their new-found closeness, hadn't she shared it with her? They'd have found a way to make Nancy's last months as comfortable as possible, allowed her to die with dignity. Ellen would have been more than willing to move here, to Florida, to look after her. It would have given her the chance to make up for the years of estrangement, and rediscover the relationship they had once shared. And yet in a way, she understands. It was Nancy all over to want to take control of her own fate; not to become a passive victim at the mercy of this cruel disease.

And then, right on top of those shocks came the others. First it was the police officers who came knocking on the door, making it quite clear it was not so much Nancy they were interested in, but a missing plane they had had under surveillance, and then Monica arriving, utterly distraught, with a garbled story that blew Ellen's mind. According to Monica, there were drugs on the plane that Nancy took, drugs that Ritchie was smuggling, and Monica phoned Nancy last night and warned her there was going to be a raid this morning.

'It's my goddam fault!' Monica had wept. 'She said to leave it with her, and I did. But I never guessed for a moment what she was going to do. If I'd known I'd never have told her what I knew, never!'

'Monica, she did it because she'd been diagnosed with terminal cancer,' Ellen said. 'She left a note. Here, you can see it.'

Monica was shaking her head. 'Maybe that's what she's saying. But I know Nancy. I know different. Oh, I knew in my gut something was awful wrong. I was on my way down to the Everglades with Roy and I just knew it. She did it to get rid of the evidence, that's what she did. If it had just been what she said, she wouldn't have taken the Beech. She'd have taken one of the Cessnas. Oh my God. Oh, Nancy.'

Shaken to the core, Ellen pressed her for all she knew, and began to realise that Nancy had indeed had another motive. She had no reason to disbelieve Monica and she knew that Nancy had been very quiet after she had taken a telephone call last night. Besides this, she had thought there was something strange about Ritchie when he'd got home from Miami and learned what had happened. He was distraught, yes, utterly grief-stricken, but there had been something else, something she couldn't quite put her finger on. 'The Beech,' he'd said. 'She took the goddam Beech.' She hadn't understood what he was getting at and she hadn't pressed him. She was too upset. She'd put it down to his peculiar way of reacting to the shock and their dreadful loss. Now she began to understand and her fury with Ritchie flared all over again; how could he have got mixed up with something like this? But at the same time she knew that if he realised the real reason his mother had done what she had done, it would utterly destroy him.

'For God's sake, Monica, don't tell Ritchie what you've just told me,' she said. 'If Mom did this for him, he mustn't know it. We've got to let him think it was just a coincidence that she took that Beech. It's what Mom wanted.'

And Monica agreed.

How ironic it was, Ellen thought, that all these years she had been blaming Ritchie for something that wasn't his fault, and now that she knew his culpability in her mother's death, she was protecting him. But as she said to Monica, it was what Nancy would have wanted. Nancy was no longer here; it was up to Ellen

551

to see that her wishes were carried out and Ritchie got his best chance of making a fresh start with Wings West, and making a go of it with Mary-Lyn.

They weren't easy, those last days in Florida, when tensions underlaid their grief and they waited for any news of wreckage. But there was none. The Beech, and Nancy with it, had disappeared without trace. Eventually Ellen, Bob and Sarah left for home, promising Ritchie they would come back in a month or so to help him sort out Nancy's things since to do it so soon after her death seemed disrespectful.

They brought a few items with them, though. Ellen chose some mementos that held special significance for her: the china rabbits from her bedroom (she left the rosette where it was, though), some photographs and a few pieces of her mother's jewellery. The wedding ring, which Nancy had had cut off when her fingers had become too swollen to wear it any longer, she gave to Sarah. Sarah packed the snapshots Nancy had shown her of her days in the ATA, the blue-bound journal and some earlier ones she discovered, exercise books that charted Nancy's younger years. And of course, the DFC.

They discussed at length what should be done with it. Sarah now knew, of course, the reason why Chris Mackenzie had been reluctant to accept it. He had known what she had not: that Ellen was Mac's daughter, and she was his granddaughter. But the fact remained, as Mac's son, Chris had equal rights to it, and it seemed Nancy had wanted him to have it.

In the aftermath of her revelations to Ellen the medal hadn't been mentioned, and in the absence of any fresh instructions as to its disposal, Sarah felt that it was only right to stick to her original wish that it should be returned to Mac's English family. And

Ellen agreed, though presumably, under the terms of Nancy's will, which, apart from a bequest to Sarah, left her entire estate to be divided equally between Ellen and Ritchie, she would be legally entitled to hold on to it herself. But she didn't feel that would be right. As it was, she was reduced to tears to discover that she and Ritchie were the main beneficiaries.

'All these years I never came to see her, hardly ever even talked to her on the telephone, and still she left me pretty well half of everything. Why would she do that?'

'Because you were still her daughter, Mum. And she loved you.'

'I don't deserve it. You're the one who should have it, Sarah. You're the one who was here for her . . .'

'And she remembered me. She's left me a good legacy. I didn't expect that, and I don't want anything else.'

'Well, you'll have it,' Ellen said, adamant. 'When it comes through, I shall give it to you.'

'You'll do no such thing. You can remember me in your will when the time comes. Though I hope that won't be for a very long time. In the meantime, spend some of it on yourself. Do whatever it is you've always wanted to, and not felt able to because it wasn't your money you were spending.'

'Your father has never stopped me having anything I wanted,' Ellen said, bridling in Bob's defence.

'No, but it's not the same thing at all,' Sarah said. 'This will be yours, absolutely, to do as you want with. That's what Grandma would have intended. And doing what she intended is the important thing now.'

Which brought them back to Mac's DFC.

'I know he originally meant it for you,' Sarah said, 'but I suppose he didn't know then that he would go on to have a son here in

England. I think the right thing to do would be to at least discuss it with Chris now we're in full possession of all the facts.'

So Sarah telephoned Chris and arranged to go to see him. She didn't go into details of what had happened over the telephone, simply said that Nancy had died.

'I'd like to come with you,' Ellen said.

Sarah was surprised. Ellen had been so against her trying to find Mac's English family. But everything had changed, of course. Chris Mackenzie wasn't just some stranger now. Well – he was a stranger, but he was also her brother.

'I think I should meet him,' Ellen said.

'Are you sure?'

'Sarah,' Ellen said with a touch of her old asperity, 'I think I am old enough to make up my own mind.'

Which is why they are on their way to see Chris Mackenzie now.

They've reached the turning into the cul-de-sac. A mile and a half or so and a couple of minutes and they'll be at Chris Mackenzie's cottage. And though she would never admit it, Sarah is every bit as nervous as her mother.

'There's somethin' I gotta ask you, Monica,' Roy says.

They've had a leisurely breakfast in Monica's yard, ham and eggs and good strong coffee, and not a Krispy Kreme Doughnut in sight. Roy stayed over last night, and Monica couldn't believe how good it had been, sharing her bed after all the years of sleeping in it alone, waking up to see Roy's close-cropped head on the pillow next to hers. She's feeling warm and content, but his words, and the serious way he's looking at her, make her stomach fall away and she thinks: oh God, he's going to ask whether it was me who blabbed to Ritchie and Nancy about the DEA investigating Varna Aviation.

Perhaps it's surprising she should leap to such a conclusion when it's more than three weeks now since Nancy flew the Beech and its cargo of drugs into the sea, and not a word has passed between them regarding it, apart from Roy saying right at the beginning: 'Darned shame about Nancy Costello.' But then, she thinks, it's pretty strange that's all he *did* say. It's like he's avoiding the subject, and she's pretty sure she knows why. It's worried her ever since. He was good enough to tell her in confidence about the planned drugs bust because he didn't want her around and involved when it happened, and she betrayed that confidence. He made it as clear as he could that his job could be on the line if she didn't keep it to herself, and she didn't. The whole damn investigation went pear-shaped because of her. And though she hasn't heard he's been called to account for his part in it, she's been worried sick he still might. They are bound to realise there's been a leak, and try to find out where it came from, and they sure as heck won't have to look far before they put two and two together and make four. Heck, he's made no secret of the fact that he's seeing her, and she works at Varna Aviation. She wouldn't set much store by their ability to detect crime if they couldn't work that one out.

But Roy hasn't even mentioned it. Until now.

'There's something I've gotta ask you, Monica.' He can't look at her as he says it. He's shifting in his chair, real uncomfortable, and she's uncomfortable too.

What the hell is he going to think of her, letting him down like that? It'll be the end for them, not a doubt of it. You can't have a police officer dating a lady who can't keep her big mouth shut if he happens to let slip something confidential. That's why he hasn't said anything before now, most likely. He knows it'll spell the end of what they had going. But now . . . well, things have taken a turn towards being more serious and he's gotta lay it on the line.

Did she, or didn't she? And if she did, well, curtains, Monica.

She feels sick, full up with despondency, already knowing just how sad she's gonna be when he walks out the door. How she'll miss him. All these years she's waited for someone just like him and now, just when it all seems to be within her grasp, she's gonna land up on her ass again. Alone. Monica the not-so-merry widow.

But there's no way she's gonna lie. He'd know, and in any case, it's not her way. She's gotta be straight with him. A relationship based on anything less just ain't worth its salt. And she's gonna make it easy on him too.

'You don't need to ask, Roy,' she says.

'I don't?' He looks a bit taken aback.

'No, you don't. I'll just tell you straight out. It was me tipped Nancy off about the DEA. And I reckon that's why she took the Beech and crashed it in the sea. So they'd have no evidence against Ritchie. I know I done wrong. I know you told me in confidence and I should've kept my big mouth shut. I know you could wind up in trouble because of it and I'm real sorry about that. But I couldn't let them bust Varna Aviation. Not after all the years I've worked there. And I knew it'd be the death of Nancy if their name was dragged through the mire and Ritchie went to gaol and—' She breaks off, realising the irony of what she's just said. 'Well, I guess it was the death of her anyway,' she says, drily, sadly. 'I never thought she'd do somethin' like that. I guess she thought it was the only way. Anyway, I know I let you down, and I'm real sorry.

And if you wanna call things off with me and save your career, if you still can, then I quite understand.'

Roy is staring at her. There's the faintest smile quirking the corner of his mouth and she can't understand why.

'Have you done?' he asks.

'Done what?'

'Done confessing. You think I didn't know it was you, Monica? What sort of a cop do you think I am?'

'A darned fine one. Which is why it'd be a crying shame if you lost your badge because of me.'

'I ain't gonna lose my badge.'

'No?'

'No. The powers that be know that Dexter Connelly is behind what's been going on, and they reckon the reason their operation went pear-shaped is that there's at least one crooked cop in Varna, and maybe more, in Connelly's pocket. Oh, they know he's behind this operation all right; they just wanna catch him. But somebody keeps tippin' him off. He's always one step ahead. Was this time too, I reckon. They changed the time of the trip to Houston at the last minute, didn't they?'

'Yes, they did,' Monica says, surprised he knows about that.

'And pulled out their man who was s'posed to have been going with Ritchie? They were going to leave him to carry the can, not a doubt of it. They're cute as a cartload of monkeys, Connelly and his pals. And having somebody in the know on their side makes sure they don't get caught. Don't you worry, honey, they ain't looking for anybody in touch with little folk like you. There's a full-scale investigation going on right now to find out who it is that's taking sweeteners from Connelly, an' a good thing too, if you ask me. I got no time for crooked cops.

When they find out who it is, heads'll roll, and not before time neither.'

'Oh.' Monica is speechless for a minute. Relieved, but speechless.

'An' I don't blame you for what you did, so don't think I do,' Roy goes on. 'I shouldn't have liked to see Nancy's good name dragged through the mire neither. I guessed when I told you you'd warn Ritchie off. Though I didn't know what he could do about it. I never expected Nancy would take things into her own hands like she did. An' I'm real sorry 'bout that.'

He stops, staring into space sadly. He had a lot of respect for Nancy Costello. Everybody in Varna did, and he didn't like to think of her at the bottom of the Gulf of Mexico.

'Well,' Monica says, recovering herself, 'I got you wrong then, Roy. But if you weren't gonna ask me about spilling the beans about the drugs raid, what were you gonna ask me?'

Roy looks awkward again suddenly, shifting in his chair. Then he looks directly at her. 'Truth is, Monica, I was gonna ask what you'd say if I was to ask you to marry me.'

Chris Mackenzie must have heard the car coming down the lane: he's in the doorway as Sarah pulls onto the hard standing beside the path. A pulse jumps in her throat. Oh my God, he is so fanciable! No rose petals in his hair this time, the roses around the door have more or less finished flowering, there's just the occasional flash of white amongst the thinning leaves. But the sight of him triggers the same tug of attraction in the pit of her stomach that she felt before.

Don't be so bloody stupid, Sarah. He's your uncle.

There's a dog at his heels, a golden retriever. It follows him to the gate and stands close to her legs, head alert, eyes soft and patient, tail at half-mast but waving gently. Sarah and Ellen get out of the car, walk around.

'Hi, you made it then.' He's smiling easily. Sarah envies him his composure, wishes her own stomach would stop tying itself in knots.

She half turns to Ellen. 'This is Ellen, my mother. Mum – Chris Mackenzie.'

Chris holds out his hand; after a moment's hesitation Ellen takes it. It seems an odd sort of greeting between brother and sister, Sarah thinks. But then, they are strangers.

'Nice to meet you, Ellen,' Chris says.

'Yes.' All her reserve is there in her voice, dry and cool.

'Well, come on in. Don't worry about Polly. She's very friendly.'

'I don't remember seeing a dog when I was here last,' Sarah says, anxious to try to relieve the awkwardness.

'No? I'd loaned her out, I expect. I often do on a Sunday. The boys next door like walking her and it saves me from doing it. They're away for the weekend, though, so today Polly's exercise is down to me.'

'Right.'

'We talked in the garden last time, didn't we? I'm not sure it's warm enough today. There's quite a cold wind.'

'Yes, there is.'

'We'll stay in here then.' 'Here' is a kitchen diner, which Sarah walked through on her last visit without really noticing much about it. Now she sees it is divided more or less in half, a cosy living space with a large pine table and chairs, a wood-burning stove, a TV and a sofa covered with an Aztec-patterned throw separated from the slate-tiled kitchen area by a granite-topped island. Pots and pans are suspended from a rack above it, a range-style cooker is set into a granite worktop, stainless-steel sink gleams beneath a mullioned window.

'We could go into the sitting room, but . . .'

'This is fine.'

'Sit down then. I'll make a cup of tea. The kettle has just boiled.'

Sarah and Ellen move to the table where the *Sunday Times* lies in an untidy heap. The *Culture* is on top, open to the biography reviews. Sarah's chair faces the wood-burning stove. There are photographs on the shelves surrounding it, but she can't see them clearly from this distance and she doesn't like to stare. Instead, she fishes the box containing Mac's DFC out of her bag and puts it on the table in front of her.

Chris comes back with mugs of tea, makes another trip to the kitchen, and returns with his own mug and a biscuit tin. Inside it is a packet of chocolate digestives, still in their wrapper. He sweeps aside the various sections of the *Sunday Times* and puts the tin in the centre of the table.

'There's a biscuit, if you'd like one.'

'Not for me, thank you,' Ellen says.

Sarah hides a smile. She doesn't think she's seen her mother eat a biscuit in years.

'Sarah?'

'Not for the moment, thanks.'

'Well, I will if you don't mind. I missed lunch walking Polly.'

At the mention of her name, or perhaps at the sound of the packet of biscuits being opened, Polly materialises from behind the dividing island, sits expectantly beside her master. He breaks off half the biscuit and gives it to her.

'Now go and lie down, Polly. I don't want you there drooling.'

The dog lingers, looking at him with liquid eyes. 'No more. Go and lie down, I said.'

Reluctantly the dog does as she is told, settling herself with nose laid between her paws on the hearth rug. But her eyes are still peeking up hopefully.

'So,' Chris says, looking from Sarah to Ellen and back again.

'I think Sarah told you on the telephone that we lost Nancy,' Ellen says.

Again Sarah cringes. *Lost Nancy.* Well, yes, that is pretty close to the truth, but Chris won't see it like that. He'll see it as a euphemism, and doctors don't use euphemisms for death, do they? It's kind of embarrassing.

'The plane she was flying crashed into the sea,' she says.

Chris's eyes narrow. 'She was flying?'

'Yes. She took a Beechcraft Baron from the field . . .'

'We didn't know what she was doing,' Ellen says defensively. 'If we had, we'd have stopped her, of course.'

'Well . . . yes. At her age . . . it's no wonder she had an accident.'

'It wasn't an accident,' Sarah says sharply. She is instantly aware of Ellen's warning glare, but she doesn't care. Nancy would have hated anyone to think she made a mistake or was incapable of flying an aeroplane. And she didn't, and she wasn't. She did exactly what she intended. She deserves credit for that. 'She died when she chose, doing what she loved best,' Sarah goes on.

Chris frowns. 'You mean . . . ?'

'She took her own life, yes,' Sarah says. 'And she did it . . .' *Just the way John did*, she was going to say. But realises this is going a step too far. John, she now knows, in no concern of Chris's. They don't have to tell him about John. '. . . the way she chose,' she finishes instead.

'Well, I'm very sorry,' Chris says. And then, reflectively: 'Nancy was a remarkable woman. It must have been a terrible shock for you.'

'It was. But at least we won't have to see her growing more frail, losing her faculties. And she'd just learned she was suffering from an inoperable cancer too.'

'I'm very sorry,' Chris says.

'So are we all. But in the end it was the way she wanted it.'

They are silent for a moment or two. Sensing that their attention has strayed, the dog stirs, eyes homing in longingly on the biscuits. Chris stays her with a firm gesture. 'Did you have a chance to talk to her?' he asks.

'Yes, we did.' Sarah looks at Ellen, a question in her glance. *Do you want to take over, Mum?*

Ellen does. 'I understand I'd got things wrong, Chris. I'd always been under the impression that John was your father's son. According to Nancy, I was mistaken. Instead, it seems, I am his daughter.'

Chris nods, satisfied. 'I'm glad she told you.'

'You know.'

'I've always known, yes. We didn't have any secrets in our family. It wasn't my father's way. But when Sarah came to see me and I realised she didn't know the truth . . . well, it put me in something of an awkward position. I didn't feel it was my place to enlighten her.'

'So.' Ellen laughs, a little shrilly, a little self-consciously. 'I suppose that makes you my brother.'

Chris looks almost equally embarrassed. 'I suppose in a manner of speaking, it does.'

'Which brings us to your father's DFC,' Sarah says. She's anxious

562

to get down to practicalities; the way Chris makes her feel is making her uncomfortable; she'd really rather not talk about their relationship. She slides the box towards her, opens the lid so that the silver cross flory catches the light, gleaming dully against its bed of deep blue velvet. 'We never did get round to asking Nancy who she would like to have it.'

'But I think it should be you,' Ellen says. 'Mac might have been my father, but I never knew him. You did, and I dare say when he sent it to Nancy to be passed on to their child, he didn't know that he was going to have a son. If he had known that, I think he would have wanted you to have it, Chris.'

'Hang on a minute . . .' Chris is looking a bit nonplussed.

'Please,' Ellen says. 'You are his son. It belongs with you.'

'Actually, no.' Chris is shaking his head. 'No, I'm not Mac's son.'

'But . . . you said . . .'

'I've always thought of him as my father. Always called him "Dad". And he was, as good as. I was only a baby when he and my mother married. My father was killed in a climbing accident – rock climbing, that is – before I was born. But Mac was not my biological father, so I'm afraid I'm not actually your brother, Ellen.'

'Oh!' For once, Ellen seems totally at a loss for words.

Sarah – well, Sarah's heart has given the most enormous leap. She hasn't quite taken it in yet, she only knows she suddenly feels incredibly light-hearted and light-headed too.

'My mother and father never had any other children,' Chris is going on. 'My mother suffered complications when I was born, as I understand it. So, as far as I am aware, Ellen, you are Mac's only child.'

'But . . .' Ellen is floundering, 'you looked on him as your father. I still think . . .' Clearly she is relating to the way she felt about Joe.

'No, I can't take it,' Chris says. 'He meant it for you.'

Ellen pulls the box towards her, staring down at the DFC. She touches it gently, reverently almost, lifts it so that it rests on her index and middle fingers. If Sarah didn't know her better, she might think there were tears in her eyes. Mum, crying? Never!

Then Ellen relinquishes the medal, returning it to its velvet cushion, and pushes it across the table towards Sarah.

'I think you should have it, Sarah. If that's all right with you, Chris.'

'Mum . . . no!'

'Yes. He was your grandfather, and you . . . well, we wouldn't be sitting here now, would we, if it wasn't for you? You've always been so close to Nancy. I think she'd like you to have it.'

'Mum . . .' Sarah is filling up now.

'I agree with your mother,' Chris says. 'You should have it, Sarah.' His gaze on her is warm, but for the moment whether he might feel about her as she feels about him is the furthest thing from her mind. 'You look like him too,' he adds with a smile.

'I do?' Sarah has always thought she took after Nancy.

'Just a bit, yes. I can see a likeness, definitely. Your eyes, the way you look when—' He breaks off, grinning.

'When . . . ?'

'Never mind. There's something there you've inherited from him. And I do think your mother is right. You should have his DFC.'

'It'll be yours one day anyway,' Ellen says.

'Oh, Mum, don't . . .'

'So you might as well have it now.'

Sarah swallows hard. 'Well, if that's what you both want.'

'It is.'

564

'Definitely.'

'Then in that case,' Sarah's fingers close over the box, 'in that case, I will. I'll cherish it, I promise. And thank you.'

They stay a while longer, but not too long. Ellen is anxious they shouldn't 'outstay our welcome', as she puts it. But this doesn't stop her from asking Chris questions to elicit as much information as she can about him and his family. Sarah cringes at her bluntness.

'Are you married, Chris?'

'Not any more. It didn't work out.'

'Is she from around here, your ex-wife?'

'No, from London. But she lives in Holland now. She married again, a biochemical engineer, who works for a company with their HQ in Amsterdam.'

'Do you have any children?'

'No, we don't. We never got around to it.'

'And do you plan on staying in Gloucestershire?'

'I certainly do. If there ever was a good place to put down roots, this is it.' He catches Sarah's eye, smiles. Sarah returns his smile, then turns quickly away, feeling her cheeks burning.

'Mum – how could you do that?' she asks Ellen when they're in the car again, driving away. 'How could you ask him so many personal questions?'

'Why not? And they weren't so personal. I'm sure he didn't mind.'

'Perhaps not. But . . . well, it's not as if he turned out to actually be your brother, after all.'

'Just as well, isn't it?' Ellen says archly. 'Considering that you've taken quite a fancy to him, and he's taken a fancy to you.'

'Mum!' Sarah's face isn't just burning now. It's flaming.

'Well, you have, haven't you?'

'Yes,' Sarah admits.

'And he seemed very keen to exchange telephone numbers.'

'That's just so we won't all lose touch again.'

'You think so, do you?' Ellen smiles. 'You really think it's *me* he wants to keep in touch with? I don't think so somehow.'

'Mum, you are incorrigible!'

'It really is time, Sarah, that you found a nice man and settled down.'

She's tingling now, just thinking about Chris. '*Mum! Stop it!*' But there's a fluttering excitement deep inside her, a sensation of standing on the edge of a precipice, and a crazy hope flaring that something very special is just around the corner and nothing is ever going to be the same again. A feeling, in spite of everything that has occurred, that is very like the beginnings of happiness. It's far too early, of course, to know whether anything is going to happen between them, but she has the strangest feeling that it will.

Did Nancy feel this way when she first met Mac? When she was upside down in a plane she'd turned over, looking at a man in a worn leather jacket and flying boots? Sarah likes to think she did.

The difference is that there were too many obstacles for Nancy and Mac. Too many other people to whom they owed allegiance. Theirs was a love that was not meant to be. But she and Chris . . . there's nothing to prevent them being together if they should decide that is what they want.

Sarah is suddenly filled with the longing to talk to Nancy, to tell her all about it. But does she need to? She has the strangest feeling that Nancy knows. That she's smiling that sweet smile of hers, pleased at the possibility that her granddaughter might be falling in love with Mac's stepson.

'Well, that's that chapter laid to rest,' Ellen says. Her thoughts have clearly moved on from what she hopes will be a budding romance for her unattached daughter.

'Yes.'

But another one is just beginning. She can feel it.

They'll make their mistakes, no doubt, but of one thing she is sure. There will be no secrets in this chapter. No deceptions. No lies. There is no need of them.

'Let's go home, Sarah.'

Sarah glances at Ellen and feels a warmth for her mother suffusing her. All this has somehow subtly shifted something in their relationship too. They've become more like equals. Sarah has seen the hurt that Ellen has borne through the years, and can sympathise. One thing for sure, she won't allow them to become estranged as Nancy and Ellen were.

'OK, Mum,' she says, turning onto the motorway. 'Let's go home.'

Now you can buy any of these other bestselling books by
Headline Review from your bookshop
or *direct from the publisher.*

FREE P&P AND UK DELIVERY
(Overseas and Ireland £3.50 per book)

The Pirate's Daughter	Margaret Cezair-Thompson	£7.99
The Island	Victoria Hislop	£7.99
The Sweet Life	Lynn York	£7.99
The Sisterhood	Emily Barr	£6.99
That Summer Affair	Sarah Challis	£6.99
The Vanishing Act of Esme Lennox	Maggie O'Farrell	£7.99
Bright Lights and Promises	Pauline McLynn	£6.99
Beautiful Strangers	Julie Highmore	£6.99
An Offer You Can't Refuse	Jill Mansell	£6.99
The Mathematics of Love	Emma Darwin	£7.99

TO ORDER SIMPLY CALL THIS NUMBER

01235 400 414

or visit our website: www.headline.co.uk

Prices and availability subject to change without notice.